PARADOX

BY DOUGLAS PRESTON

Dinosaurs in the Attic**
Cities of Gold
Talking to the Ground
The Royal Road
The Black Place
Jennie*
The Codex*
Tyrannosaur Canyon*
The Monster of Florence (with Mario Spezi)
Blasphemy*
Impact*
The Kraken Project*
The Lost City of the Monkey God
The Lost Tomb
Extinction*

BY DOUGLAS PRESTON AND LINCOLN CHILD

Relic*
Mount Dragon*
Reliquary*
Riptide
Thunderhead
The Ice Limit
The Cabinet of Curiosities
Still Life with Crows
Brimstone
Dance of Death
The Book of the Dead
The Wheel of Darkness
Cemetery Dance
Fever Dream
Cold Vengeance
Two Graves

White Fire
Blue Labyrinth
Crimson Shore
The Obsidian Chamber
City of Endless Night
Verses for the Dead
Crooked River
Bloodless
The Cabinet of Dr. Leng
Old Bones
The Scorpion's Tail
Diablo Mesa
Dead Mountain
Angel of Vengeance
Badlands
Pendergast: The Beginning

* Published by Tor Publishing Group
** Published by St. Martin's Press

PARADOX

DOUGLAS PRESTON
&
ALETHEIA PRESTON

TOR PUBLISHING GROUP
NEW YORK

PARADOX

Copyright © 2026 by Splendide Mendax, Inc.

Endpaper art by Adobe Stock

A Forge Book
Published by Tom Doherty Associates / Tor Publishing Group
120 Broadway
New York, NY 10271

www.torpublishinggroup.com

Forge® is a registered trademark of Macmillan Publishing Group, LLC.

EU Representative: Macmillan Publishers Ireland Ltd, 1st Floor, The Liffey Trust Centre, 117–126 Sheriff Street Upper, Dublin 1, D01 YC43

The Library of Congress Cataloging-in-Publication Data is available upon request.

ISBN 978-1-250-41390-1 (hardcover)
ISBN 978-1-250-44418-9 (international, sold outside the U.S., subject to rights availability)
ISBN 978-1-250-41391-8 (ebook)

Our books may be purchased in bulk for specialty retail/wholesale, literacy, corporate/premium, educational, and subscription box use. Please contact MacmillanSpecialMarkets@macmillan.com.

First U.S. Edition: 2026
First International Edition: 2026

Printed in the United States of America

10 9 8 7 6 5 4 3 2 1

TO MOM

Thanks for teaching me to be brave and to follow my dreams
—Aletheia Preston

We, all of us, are what happens when a primordial mixture of hydrogen and helium evolves for so long that it begins to ask where it came from.

—Jill Tarter

PARADOX

1

At four o'clock one dark morning in the Basilica of San Silvestro in Rome, Brother Padraig O'Halloran entered a side chapel and paused before a sealed glass cube to offer a prayer to the brown, waxy, misshapen object reposing on a bed of velvet within. His whispered words went on for several minutes, a susurrus of faith drifting through the great silence of the basilica.

When he was done, he opened his eyes and read, yet again, the label in Latin that identified the object in the box.

Caput
St. Joannis Baptistae
Praecursoris Domini

Brother Padraig, whose Latin was excellent, knew well the translation: "Head of St. John the Baptist, Forerunner of the Lord." This was one of the most sacred relics in all of Christendom, and every morning before Lauds, Brother Padraig would light a candle and enter the chapel to contemplate in prayer at the precious object.

More than anything, Brother Padraig cherished his role as a member of the Irish Pallottine Fathers of the Basilica, the religious order that served as caretakers of this holiest of objects. The relic was not, it must be admitted, the entire decapitated head of Saint John, but rather a model of his head made from wax, in which a large piece of the saint's actual skullcap had been imbedded. The wax model had suffered greatly over the centuries, softened and distorted by time, until it had taken on a strange, if not grotesque, appearance. Looks notwithstanding, its spiritual authority remained undiminished.

As every good Christian knows, Saint John the Baptist was the messenger of God sent ahead of Christ, the prophet who foretold of His coming—"He that cometh after me is mightier than I," Saint John proclaimed, "whose shoes I am not worthy to bear." It was Saint John who baptized Jesus in the River Jordan, and when Jesus emerged from the water, He received the revelation of God—"The heavens were opened unto Him, and He saw the Spirit of God descending like a dove, and lighting upon Him: And lo a voice from heaven, saying, This is my beloved Son, in whom I am well pleased."

That morning, as he often did, Brother Padraig contemplated the life and—particularly—the martyrdom of Saint John: how the woman Salome danced before Herod Antipas in his palace in Jerusalem; how Herod promised to grant her any wish; and how she had demanded the head of Saint John. And so the Forerunner of Christ was beheaded, and his head brought to Salome on a silver platter. The head was later taken from its resting place in Jerusalem to Constantinople. In 1204, Crusaders found it and carried it to France. In 1604, the back half of the skull of that holiest of relics was sent from France to Rome for the Basilica of San Silvestro, where it was incorporated into a wax model of the complete head.

When Brother Padraig first assumed his role with the Pallottine Fathers, the holy relic was absent from the Basilica. It had been taken from the church to be restored and stabilized. Brother Padraig well remembered that joyous day when the relic was returned to the chapel, to be placed in a climate-controlled glass cube that would preserve it for millennia to come. Every morning since, Brother Padraig had visited the chapel and offered a prayer to Saint John the Baptist, Forerunner of the Lord, by candlelight, as was proper.

On this particular morning, as he gazed at the holy object, eyes tracing the contours that he knew like the back of his own hand, he noticed something not quite right about it. He wasn't sure what it was, but the misshapen head didn't, somehow, seem the same. He approached closer and raised the candle, but the cube sat high on a golden plinth, and he couldn't get near enough to inspect it properly.

Brother Padraig cast about for something to climb on. The chapel had short wooden pews where the faithful could sit and pray. They were heavy, but Brother Padraig was strong, and he shifted one of them over to the base of the plinth and stood on it. Now he could look directly into the cube. Holding up the candle, he peered inside and immediately saw that something was indeed awry. The dome of the saint's actual skull had come loose from its wax bedding.

He squinted, peering closer. It had shifted, yes—but in addition, a square-centimeter piece of the skull was missing. Had it fallen out? Holding the candle this way and that, he examined the velvet cushion on which the head rested but could not see a fallen fragment. A more thorough inspection of the missing piece revealed that it did not look like a natural break—not at all. The edges were smooth. There was a light dusting of bone particulates on the red velvet cushion, as if the head had been cut with a small saw.

Brother Padraig suddenly felt faint. With great care not to fall, he climbed down from the bench and then sat upon it, trying to steady his mind and gain control of his breathing.

It was unthinkable, this desecration, this sacrilege, this despoilation of the holy relic, a crime scarcely to be comprehended: Someone had stolen a piece of the true skull of Saint John the Baptist.

2

Blood pounding behind her eyes, breath bursting from her chest, Frankie Cash dropped the rowing machine oar and jogged to the next station of her Orangetheory workout. She surveyed the web of straps and grips, trying to remember how the exercise was done. Sweat trickled into her eyes. Her brain was moving in slow motion.

Too late.

"Oh, Frankiiiie," sang the dreaded voice from behind her. "Don't *tell* me I see you resting right now, girl."

Cash turned in defeat. Her instructor, Max, hands on hips, head cocked to one side, evaluated her. The tiniest tank top stretched over his muscled chest, the words RAYS OUT GAYS OUT emblazoned across in green lettering.

"It goes like this." Max dropped down into a plank and stuck his feet in the straps. Without breaking a sweat, he scrunched his knees forward and up to the side, keeping his arms parallel and palms on the ground. "Pull, and twist. Pull, and twist," he repeated, and looked over at Cash from his position on the floor. "Easy."

He extracted himself in a single movement, stood up, and indicated with an open palm and dazzling smile that it was now her turn.

"Right . . ." Frankie said. "Pull, and twist." She wasn't so sure about the "easy" part. She awkwardly got down. Losing weight was pure torture, but she was damned if she wasn't going to stick with it. She'd already lost six pounds, and there was no way she was going to throw away the suffering that had required. As if on cue, a rivulet of sweat stung the corner of her eye. She flicked it off with determination, stuck her feet into the loops, and got ready to start the ordeal again, Max looking on.

The whistling ringtone of her cell playing the theme from *The Good, the Bad, and the Ugly* swelled into life from her pocket, barely heard over the pumping club music that filled the air.

"Don't answer that," said Max sternly. "You're *not* supposed to have that in here."

"I have to," said Cash, secretly relieved.

Max frowned as she disentangled herself from the apparatus and answered the call. "Cash here. Hold on." She turned to Max, covering the mouthpiece. "I'll take it outside."

As she left, he called out after her, "It better be a murder!"

She took a seat on a bench outside the front door. "Yeah?"

"Frankie," a familiar voice drawled, "if I didn't know you any better, I'd say you sound glad to hear from me."

Cash found herself smiling. "If only you knew," she said.

Sheriff James Colcord got right to business. "We got a homicide call. It's a weird one. An old guy dead in the Flat Tops Wilderness." He paused. "You know what that means."

"Neanders?" Cash sat up straight, alert now. In the first case they'd worked on together, Neanders—homicidal Neanderthals de-extincted by the Erebus Resort's crazy chief scientist, Marius Karman—had escaped from a laboratory and disappeared into the Flat Tops Wilderness. Cash knew it was just a matter of time before they'd resurface.

"Probably not, but there's a ritualistic aspect to it that's worth looking into. I'm on my way to the crime scene. Northwest of Burns. Remote. We have to hike in to the site. Will turn into a media shitstorm for sure. I've already called CBI to assist on this one—and asked for you. You heard from Holmes yet?"

"Nope," Cash answered. "But you better believe she'll be hearing from me. Shoot me the coordinates, will you?"

Her cell chimed immediately, and she loaded them and looked at the map. "It's on federal land. Do we even have jurisdiction?"

"Feds don't think it's connected to the Neanders and don't want it. You know how the US Attorneys' Office is—they spend more time trying to weasel out of cases than prosecuting them. Plus, the park rangers agree that CBI should have this one—they hate working with the feds. I'm not complaining. I just hope the FBI don't pull their usual and swoop in and take the case after we've done all the work."

"So you want CBI to take the lead?" Cash asked.

"Now, I wouldn't go *that* far."

"Are the remains in a structure or out in the open?"

"Inside a log cabin. Apparently, the victim was squatting illegally on federal land, but you're right—better safe than sorry. I've got a deputy writing the search warrant, which should be signed by Judge Greenberg by the time we get to the trailhead."

They set up a time to meet at the trailhead, and Cash ended the call, wondering why she hadn't heard from her boss, Blaisdell Holmes, the new director of the Colorado Bureau of Investigation. She hoped Holmes wasn't trying to give the case to someone else.

She had better get to the Lakewood CBI headquarters, and fast.

Cash took one of her famous "dunk and run" showers, barely letting the water run over her body long enough to rinse off the soap, taking care not to wet her hair. She threw on a pair of black slacks and a Milano blouse. Luckily, she had put on a pair of Ecco boots that morning, which she could hike in. A spray of dry shampoo fixed up her unwashed hair, and then she holstered her Baby Glock 9 and clipped her shield to her waist. The Baby Glock wasn't the standard weapon assigned to CBI agents, but she had asked for an exception; it fit so well in her hand. Throwing on a black suit jacket, she was out the door.

Cash squinted at the sun, which was barely peeking over the horizon as she took Kipling Street south toward CBI headquarters. She didn't have time for her usual post-workout cup of Café Bustelo instant espresso. She hoped Colcord would pick her up a coffee, but she was disinclined to give the old cowpoke the satisfaction of asking for one.

It was an eight-minute drive to the Lakewood headquarters, but it took Cash only five. Holmes's Mercedes CLS glinted at her from the near-empty parking lot of CBI headquarters as she screeched in. A Model Y Tesla she didn't recognize was parked a ways down—some other agent already in at six a.m., and she knew what that meant.

Holmes was giving away her case. She was sure of it now.

Half running, she threw open the doors of the CBI headquarters.

Slowing down to a brisk walk, she threaded her way through the drab hallways to Holmes's office. She found her there, door open, seated at her desk, with another agent standing with their back to Cash. Holmes, wearing her usual crisp black-and-white suit, stood up as Cash knocked once on the open door.

"Christ, Cash. Good morning. Everything all right?" Holmes asked.

Cash looked down at her blouse and realized she had buttoned it cockeyed in her haste. Feeling self-conscious, she smoothed down her hair and tried to ease her agitation.

"I heard about the new homicide in Eagle County . . ." She swallowed, took a deep breath. "I want it."

The individual Holmes was chatting with now turned, and Cash saw George Standish, an agent with barely two years on the job. His black hair was slicked back, a hopeful smile plastered on his pasty face. He smelled of baby oil, and Cash had to stop herself from wrinkling her nose. She wasn't a fan of his; he had always seemed to her the kind of person who brought polished apples to his teachers.

"Agent Cash." George Standish stuck out a bony hand. "Good to see you in so early."

Cash glanced at Standish, wondering if he was being sarcastic. She took his hand and realized it was clammy. She discreetly wiped her palm on her pants. Standish caught the movement. He shifted stiffly back toward Holmes.

"You're in early too," Cash said to him.

"I listen to the police band with my morning toast," Standish said defensively. "I heard the homicide reported and figured they might, ah, ask for CBI."

"Murder on toast. Nice," Holmes said dryly.

Cash still hadn't quite figured Holmes out. The new director had handled the media shit show after the Erebus disaster with surprising skill and a laconic sense of humor, while still maintaining a cool demeanor, somehow. But she was hard to read, a woman with depth.

Standish cleared his throat awkwardly and continued, "Yes, ma'am. As I was saying, I think this case would give me important experience in homicide. I've cleared my last cases. I've testified at several trials that resulted in successful convictions pursuant to my assistance of investigations. I'd like the chance, ma'am, to be AIC." He glanced at Cash out of the corner of his eye.

Cash watched him lace his fingers together to stop them from trembling. The guy was nervous. She had to give him credit—it took courage for a newish agent to request a case this big. She remembered not so long ago when she was in his position. But still: It wasn't good form for him to rush in like this, trying to scoop up a case that he knew very well should be hers. Colcord *had* requested her, after all.

"Plus, respectfully," he added, "I was here first."

Cash tried not to roll her eyes. What a crafty little upstart. "If I could interject," she said, "while I admire Agent Standish's initiative, I think this case might be a little complex as a *starter* case." Cash paused before deciding to play the Neander card. "I spoke with Sheriff Colcord, and he has reason to believe there's a ritualistic aspect to this homicide that might be connected to the Neanders."

Holmes did not look surprised to hear this. "I know the Neander investigation is of interest to you," she said, "but as you know, the FBI is handling that case now. If it's a Neander killing, we'll have to turn it over to them."

"That's exactly my point—we don't have nearly enough information to conclude—" George Standish began.

Cash cut him off. "Given my extensive experience both with the CBI and with the Erebus investigation, I think I'm better equipped to make that call. I have an established relationship with Sheriff Colcord. Furthermore, I was told he *requested* me for this case. If things were to go south, there would be less blowback if it could be shown you placed this case in the hands of an *experienced* agent." And she added, a little wickedly, "The press might, you know, have questions . . ." She let the sentence hang in the air. If this was a Neander killing, and it was shown Holmes knowingly gave the case to an agent with barely two years under his belt, it wouldn't look good.

Holmes raised her eyebrows. "The press might *have questions*? Oh my, wouldn't that be a shock."

Cash colored, realizing she had gone too far. Holmes wasn't as big of a media ass-kisser as her predecessor, McFaul, had been.

Holmes paused as if thinking. Finally, she said, "However, your other argument's persuasive. The case is yours."

"Thank you, ma'am."

Holmes regarded her coolly. "But make sure CBI takes the lead, and not Eagle County, okay? George, I've got another homicide for you to work on in the meantime."

Standish nodded stiffly. He didn't look too happy. Cash tried not to let it bug her—she was damned if she was going to let him guilt her into not taking this case.

"And you can assist Agent Cash in digital forensics, should that be necessary."

Standish was said to be a whiz with computers. Cash didn't see how the murder of a crazy old coot in the wilderness would need that skill, but you never knew. "Of course," she said, trying not to be cheered up too much by the pained smile fixed on Standish's face. "George will be a welcome asset to the investigation, if needed," with a slight emphasis on *if*.

Holmes nodded and consulted some notes. "Sheriff Colcord is en route. You'll have to hike in. Don't forget your sat phone, and if you see any sign of Neanders in the area, *anything* at all, get out of there and call for backup. We'll notify the FBI and get the National Guard out there if necessary. No messing around this time, got it?"

Cash nodded, biting her tongue. It had been Holmes's predecessor's reluctance to bring in the National Guard during the Erebus Resort disaster that had allowed the Neanders to steal explosives and blow up the labs. But Holmes knew that.

Holmes continued with a brief synopsis. "Victim is William Grooms, age seventy-five, living by himself—illegally, it seems—in the wilderness. A man named Paul Brooksfield found his body and reported it. He said something about the body having coins on the eyes, shrouded in white, wouldn't elaborate. Romanski's pulling together a CSI team, and the ME is also on his way."

"Thank you, ma'am," Cash said. She nodded at Standish as she went out the door, feeling satisfied that things had gone her way but a little worried that she'd made an enemy for life. Burns, Colorado, was about a three-hour drive, and it would take another couple of hours to hike the four miles to the cabin inside the Flat Tops.

Neander territory. Cash shivered at the thought.

3

Two hours and forty-five minutes later, Cash arrived at Forest Service Road 610, leading to the southern edge of the Flat Tops boundary. She was high in the mountains now, her GPS reporting over nine thousand feet of elevation. She eased her black CBI Tahoe into the forest road and slowed. It was a typical Colorado four-wheel-drive nightmare, the right side of the road gullied out with exposed rocks. But there was a strip of passable track on the left, which she edged along with care. She wondered how in the hell Romanski would get the crime scene van out here.

Tall firs rose like silent sentinels on either side, darkening the way. Cash gave an involuntary shiver, thankful for the sheet of glass between her and the surrounding forest.

Fifteen minutes later, she rounded a bend to see Colcord seated on the open bed of his truck. He was sporting his usual Stetson, boot-cut jeans, and a pair of muddy hiking boots. To her relief, two Starbucks cups rested next to him. He smiled and tipped his cowboy hat as she lurched up behind him and parked.

"Top of the morning, Cash." He eased off his truck and handed her a cup, throwing her an apologetic smile. "It's half empty. The other half is all over my front seat."

"No apologies necessary, as long as it comes with a curtsy."

He grinned and gave her an elaborate bow. "That satisfy you?"

She took a sip. The coffee was cold, but she was grateful for the caffeine. At the edge of the forest, everything was still and silent. Lofty fir trees closed ranks around them, trunks seeming to lean in toward her.

Two warring red squirrels flitted and chattered through the understory. Now that she was out of the Tahoe, the feeling of unease grew.

"Let's get going," she said, busily checking the GPS on her phone. Even out of cell range, the GPS worked, but she'd had to remember to download the maps ahead of time—or all she'd see would be a dot for her location on a blank screen.

A footpath followed a stream that gurgled on their left: Middle Fork Derby Creek, according to the GPS. The path itself was overgrown and faint, sometimes disappearing completely. Thankfully, after five minutes of hiking, they passed their first trail marker: a faded message informing them that they were entering the Flat Tops Wilderness, with Solitary Lake four miles distant.

"Well, at least there're some trail signs," Colcord said, negotiating his way over a fallen tree trunk. "Wouldn't want to get lost in Neander territory."

After the disaster at Erebus, the FBI had taken over the case from CBI and the sheriff's office. They had been going at it hammer and tongs now for eight months with no success: The Neanders seemed to have vanished. The popular consensus was that they'd moved northward in the Rockies, into Wyoming, or possibly even as far as Canada.

"Speaking of Neanders," he went on, "any news from your FBI pals? I heard a rumor the SAC is about to be fired."

"Normally, they don't tell us shit," said Cash. "But we did hear they're bringing in a new guy who's supposed to be a badass. CBI just got notice. His name is Makoto Ota. He's starting next month."

"You met him yet?"

"We liaise with him and his team on the twentieth. Seems he might be bringing CBI back into the case."

"About time," Colcord said. "Things are really getting out of hand. All these Neander admirers with their costumes and demonstrations— who would've believed it? And the 'Sapiens supremacists' who think the Neanders should be 're-extincted'?"

"It's the world we live in today," said Cash, shaking her head.

"God, I miss the old days—before the internet messed everything up. I used to hike into the Flat Tops as a kid, fishing in Trappers Lake. Some mighty fine native brown in there."

"You know the Flat Tops?" Cash was surprised.

"Just a part of it. It's a huge wilderness." Colcord paused to slap a mosquito on his neck. "So what's going on with the woolly elephants over in Erebus?"

"Mammoths," Cash said. "Being taken care of by wildlife biologists, along with the other megafauna. The valley's closed and being maintained by a nonprofit while the investors fight over ownership and liability."

"I'll never forget the size of those things."

They continued to hike in contemplative silence, the kind shared between old friends. The firs gave way to aspens, rustling in the wind. Despite the dappled sunlight, it was chilly, and she pulled her fleece around her.

As they crossed a meadow, it warmed slightly. Colcord stopped abruptly and pulled a pair of binocs out of his pack, motioning for her to stop.

"You see something?" Cash asked, mildly alarmed.

He peered into the trees. "Western tanager."

"We got a dead body up there and you're *bird*-watching?"

Colcord lowered the binocs, a grin stretching across his face. "I'd never let a stiff interfere with adding another bird to my life list."

"Life list?"

"A list birders keep of all the bird species they've seen in the wild during their lifetimes. I've got about"—Colcord paused, chin in the air to think—"six hundred and two."

Cash ducked to hide a smile. "All right, Mr. Audubon."

They continued onward, stepping around tufts of grass and low mountain brush. When her phone indicated they were about a half mile from the lake, they hit a steep set of switchbacks. By the time they reached the top, Cash was pleased with herself; the climb had been far easier than she'd expected, and she vowed to thank Max for kicking her ass during her workouts. Colcord, slower than Cash, was drenched and blowing hard when he joined her at the top, much to her satisfaction.

"You look as wet as a cold beer on a hot day," Cash said.

"Holy cow, that's some serious climbin'." He took off his cowboy hat and fanned himself. He paused to inspect her face. "Hey, Cash, without a hat, you're getting a little pink from this high-altitude sun—I got some sunscreen in my pack."

"I'm doing just fine," she said. "I need the vitamin D."

Colcord fixed the Stetson back on his head. "Gonna end up looking like a lobster, but hey, you're from Maine, right?" He gave a chuckle.

Cash swallowed her irritation at the dumb joke. They took a quick rest while Cash ran off to "water the trees."

When she rejoined Colcord, he looked concerned.

"Something moving over there," he said, indicating the edge of the forest.

Cash was immediately uneasy. She remembered how wily the Neanders had been. How well they had blended in with their surroundings. How goddamned *fast* they were.

"Let's keep going," Cash said, shielding her eyes against the sun. "I'll keep an eye out."

Walking quickly, with her hand on the butt of her gun, she followed the trail as it reentered the woods. The forest darkened as the sun hid behind a cloud, the wind making an eerie rustling through the firs. Suddenly, she heard it too: the crackle of a heavy step on twigs. They were being followed. Colcord unholstered his gun, and Cash did the same. Another step sounded behind her, and Cash whipped around, catching sight of a quick movement before it disappeared into shadows. She heard two more footfalls in quick succession, this time to her left.

"They've got us surrounded," Cash whispered. She could hear them rustling and weaving through the trees all around.

A creature leapt into the clearing, a flash of brown and cream. Cash froze, then lowered her firearm. It was an elk—a bull with a rack, who looked at her, unconcerned, in the manner of an animal that knows it's too big to be messed with, before ambling back into the shadows. A baby elk stumbled into the clearing too, its mother following, pausing to lick it absently on the head. More emerged, a dozen of them, paying no heed to the humans. The bull threw its head back, calling mournfully, before shaking big antlers and trotting onward.

"*They've got us surrounded,*" Colcord said, grinning and mimicking Cash's whisper.

"Shut *up*," Cash said.

They walked on through a dense forest at a clipped pace, making good time. After about half an hour or so, Cash checked her GPS and saw that they were almost at the lake.

Before she could update Colcord, he halted and pointed. "What the hell's that?"

A human skeleton made of welded angle iron and rebar stood to one side of the trail, grinning at them with teeth made from an old saw and gears for eyes. As she looked around, she could see more sculptures made of junk scattered through the forest: a horned monster erupting from a stack of tires; a hunchbacked figure draped in tattered black cloth with a cracked hockey mask for a face; a china doll perched in the hollow of a tree, mouth open, from which scuttled a black beetle; a set of wind chimes made out of rusted dip cans and old pipes hung from a bicycle wheel, now all tangled up.

"Looks like old Willy was an artist," said Colcord.

Cash squinted. It looked more like Grooms had raided a junkyard with a welding torch. Her eye alighted on the twisted shape of a rusted bear trap. She hoped this guy wasn't some doomsday prepper who had booby-trapped the place. She remembered a home raid once where Agent Manahan stepped through a string trap, and before they knew it, a board with spikes rammed his left arm. She picked her way through more carefully, eyes moving from object to object, alert for any signs of snares.

She paused as a glimmer of light caught her eye. Through the trees, she could see a log cabin and, beyond it, the shining expanse of Solitary Lake. The body was reported to be inside the cabin. She turned to Colcord, trying to keep her voice as casual as possible. "So, CBI's taking the lead on this one, right?"

Colcord frowned. "Hell no, Cash, I called CBI in for *assistance*, not to swoop in and take over. I don't know your new boss, but if she's anything like McFaul . . ." His voice trailed off.

"I'll be AIC on this case, not her. This is going to be a challenging crime scene—CBI should lead." She didn't add that Holmes ordered her to get the lead on the case. She suspected that would not go down well.

Colcord looked at her. "This is my county. I grew up here. I know the Flat Tops well."

"Whoa there, pardner. Don't play the 'I'm a local' card with me. I value your expertise—I didn't say I was kicking you off the case completely."

"*I* brought *you* in."

Cash took a deep breath. "The Flat Tops Wilderness spreads out over at least four counties. Last time I checked, you were the elected sheriff of only one. If for some reason the case spills over the line, we'd have to take over anyway."

Colcord shook his head. "Okay, okay. Fair enough. But if this goes south, it's on you. I'm the one who has to face the voters."

At that moment, a long, forlorn, sobbing wail echoed through the trees and died away.

"What the *hell* was that?" Cash said, her eyes darting around at the creeping shadows of the trees.

"Common loon. The lake is just through those trees."

4

The cabin became fully visible, perched on the edge of the lake, looking like it only needed a good shove to send it spilling into the water. It commanded a view across to Derby Peak, still covered with snowfields, and beyond it Flat Top Mountain itself.

"Solitary Lake," Cash said out loud. It certainly lived up to its name. Even more solitary now, with the Flat Tops almost devoid of backpackers and hikers out of fear of the Neanders.

The lake reflected the mountain as if in a mirror. Not too far out, a fish broke the surface, and the expanding ripples disturbed the image around it into a myriad of glittering points.

"Should've brought my fly rod," said Colcord.

"So you can fish while I do all the work?"

"Why do you think I let you take the lead?" Colcord winked at her, then began to scrape his mud-covered hiking boots against an unlucky stump.

Cash spied an enormous man sitting on a tire outside the cabin. He was large in a way that spoke of manual labor, wearing cowboy boots and a denim shirt with pearl snap buttons. He certainly didn't look as if he had been out here to hike. He sat in the shade of a blooming dogwood—a tree that must have been planted, since it was not native. He wasn't carrying anything but a water bottle, and Cash immediately wondered why he didn't have a backpack for such a strenuous hike. The man had an impressive red beard that took up half his face and chest. He lurched to his feet and held out a palm. Cash took it.

"Paul Brooksfield," the man said, giving Cash a formidable squeeze.

"Frankie Cash, agent in charge, Colorado Bureau of Investigation. This here is James Colcord, sheriff of Eagle County."

"Pleased to meet you, sir," Colcord said. "I wish it were under better circumstances."

Paul nodded curtly.

"Mr. Brooksfield, if you wouldn't mind moving over there to wait by that tree? We need to set up a perimeter. We'd like to talk to you after we've looked over the scene," Cash said.

Paul nodded, and as he seated himself farther away from the cabin, Cash and Colcord strung crime scene tape.

They finished, and Cash turned to Colcord. "What do you think? Do a walk-through or wait for Romanski?" Romanski was always a stickler for getting first looks with his team—but she was itching to get inside.

"I ain't waiting. We can legitimately tell Romanski we were securing the site." He unzipped his pack and pulled out a couple of sealed plastic packages. "Booties, hairnets, gloves."

"Damn, you've got everything. Must've been a Boy Scout," said Cash.

"Eagle Scout with twenty-one merit badges," Colcord said with a touch of pride.

They put on the protection and crossed the yard to a rickety porch, stepping over empty vodka bottles strewn about.

Guy must have really liked his vodka, Cash thought. "Wait," she said aloud, something catching her eye. "Look at this." She pointed to an upside-down bucket. There was a mark in the ground where it had previously lain. "And this." She gestured toward an old frying pan next to the porch steps. It too had been moved slightly, and recently, exposing some blades of grass that were yellow from lack of sun.

"Curious," Colcord said.

"You know," Cash said, "I get the feeling someone was looking for something among all this junk—but carefully. Wonder why? And for what?"

Colcord grunted. "Yeah. Interesting." There was a silence, broken by the whistling wind through the trees. "Well," he added, looking a little nervous himself, "we've got an appointment with a body. Are you ready, Agent Cash?"

5

As soon as Colcord stepped into the cabin, he was hit with a cloying smell, thick and chemical, that stuck in his nostrils. The smell was strangely familiar, but he couldn't quite place it.

"Stinks like a wet basement," Cash said, "with an old piece of cheese rotting in the corner."

"Creative take. Think the killers cleaned up?"

"Sure smells like it." Cash wrinkled her nose.

Colcord paused to survey the scene. The small room was filled to the brim with junk, but it did not look like it had been trashed in a search. Stacks of delinquent library books leaned like towers of Pisa. Broken furniture legs were heaped on top of an old mining cart, along with the skeletons of umbrellas. Stuff was everywhere.

They moved slowly into the center of the main room, floorboards creaking underfoot. There was what looked like a doorway to a small kitchen, blocked with a faded curtain. A cot stood in one corner, next to a woodstove. Colcord could feel the weight of silence in the cabin; the place gave him a bad vibe.

"I saw this in a home décor magazine once," Cash said. "Hoarder chic."

Colcord gave a reluctant chuckle, but his heart was beating hard in his chest. He paused to scan the book titles in a pile. *True Bigfoot Stories, Eyewitness Accounts of Killer Bigfoot Encounters, Hydrothermal and Placer Gold Deposits, Understanding Surveillance Technologies,* and *The Tao of Pooh.* He pointed to a copy of *The Fly-Fishing Guide to Colorado's Flat Tops Wilderness.* "Hey, I've got this one."

"Sounds like you two could have started a book club," Cash said. "And just a reminder, don't touch anything unless necessary, else you'll face the Wrath of Romanski."

"You see those wicked bear traps in the woods?" said Colcord. "We better be careful in case he booby-trapped the place."

"I'll keep an eye out," Cash said.

It was warmer in the cabin, stuffy almost. Colorful vodka bottles, some broken, lay about among rocks, pieces of metal, and scraps of paper with drawings of monsters and sketched maps. A workbench and stool took up one corner, surprisingly neat. Among the curling wood chips lay small carvings of wildlife—some of them quite beautiful. For an eccentric recluse, the guy was creative, Colcord had to admit. He spied a large basket of unpolished red and polychromatic jasper pushed under the workbench. Next to it stood a rack with a green canister of oxygen and a maroon bottle of acetylene, with attached hoses and regulators—a portable welding setup, evidently for the sculptures.

He went over and inspected the unmade cot. Peering under it, he noted various tins and a small cashbox. Someone had recently dragged it out from underneath, disturbing the dust, and then pushed it back in place. Could thieves have murdered Grooms for money? Colcord reached out to open it.

"I'd take a photo before you move it," said Cash.

"Lord almighty," Colcord said under his breath. He made a big show of snapping photos, then carefully slid the box out from under the bed. A large wolf spider, startled by the movement, scuttled across the floorboards, and it took Colcord an effort to keep from jumping back, knowing he'd never live it down with Cash.

The cashbox was unlocked. He unlatched and opened it.

"Whoo-boy," he said. Tucked in the corner were two rolls of what looked like hundred-dollar bills, held together with rubber bands. Several hefty nuggets of gold and a stack of Morgan silver dollars sat on top of a carefully folded piece of paper.

"Mind if I handle these, *Agent in Charge* Cash?" he asked.

Cash laughed. "Sure. Just take plenty of photos."

Colcord chuckled. His mother had been an unassertive woman who let his father take charge of the ranch animals and the alfalfa fields while she ran the house. Cash was the complete opposite: bossy, forceful, and irritating as all hell. It took some getting used to. But he couldn't help but feel a fondness for the woman. There wasn't a phony thing about her. She was Frankie Cash through and through and made no apologies for who she was. He supposed that's why he tolerated her—why he had requested her for this case. That and the fact she was maybe the best CBI agent he'd ever worked with. Hell, after surviving the Neanders together, she was like an old war buddy.

Colcord plucked out the nuggets with his gloved hands, took out the paper, and unfolded it. It was a meticulously hand-drawn schematic map of a mine complex, like a treasure map, with notations in red pencil and an X marking the spot. A blue symbol was scrawled at the mine entrance—a J rotated ninety degrees from the left. The letter-number combinations CH_4 and CO_2 were written underneath it.

"What's that?" Cash asked.

"The J—not sure. But CH_4 and CO_2 stand for methane and carbon dioxide. Looks like these are notations about gas hazards in a mine Grooms must have explored. Risky business, that." He took a few more photos of the map, then folded it and put it back into the box. Carefully removing one of the tins, Colcord opened it and exposed more rolls of hundred-dollar bills and chunks of ore: quartz threaded with wire gold. He peered under the cot, counting seven tins. If the other tins looked like this one, it was a hell of a lot of money.

Cash whistled. "Bold retirement plan," she said.

Colcord came to a realization. "If they were looking for something, it wasn't money." He put the items back where he had found them, careful not to disturb the dust.

The floorboards creaked under their collective weight as they made their way to the doorway into the kitchen. Colcord drew the curtain aside. There, on the table, lay Willy Grooms. At first glance, he looked to be peacefully sleeping. He was dressed in an old-fashioned nightgown, white, with a lace hem. His hands had been crossed over his chest like a corpse in a coffin . . . or a vampire. Silver dollars were pressed into the eyes, and the body appeared surprisingly clean. The skin was pale and rosy, even his weather-beaten face. There was no smell of decay—only that cloying chemical odor, as if the place had been scrubbed clean. Colcord did a double take.

The old man looked more alive than any dead body he had ever seen. Unnaturally so. He had to stop himself from checking for a pulse, telling himself Dr. Huizinga would do that when he arrived, and he didn't want to contaminate the body with his DNA.

"Poor Willy," Cash said.

"Take a look at that." Colcord pointed to a cut on the right side at the base of Grooms's neck, just above the collarbone, where a purplish bruise radiated around a small wound. "Was he stabbed in the neck?"

"Maybe," Cash said. "And look at that foot."

Colcord turned his attention to it. Both feet were bare; the right one was covered with blood. It had been crushed, all the angles wrong, the toes broken and the skin lacerated. The left foot was normal. What the hell could have done that?

Colcord turned his attention to Grooms's eyes. "Jesus, I think his eyes might be gone," he said, noting the sunken nature of the coins in the sockets.

"Just like what the Neanders used to do."

Colcord felt a rush of adrenaline, his body stiffening at memories he wished to forget. "You think it could have been them?"

"I hope to hell not. But I'll feel a lot better when the cavalry gets here. This place is giving me the creeps."

"I don't like it either. There's something about it . . ." Colcord couldn't quite figure out how to finish the thought. Damn, what *was* that smell? He shook his head again, bothered. All he knew is that he wanted to get the hell out of there, and as soon as possible.

6

Cash took a deep breath. Her Neander worries had largely abated. If they were around, they'd have killed Paul Brooksfield by now. With that off her mind, it was a relief to get back outside into the fresh air. She pulled off the booties, gloves, and hairnet. Brooksfield was pacing just outside of the perimeter, looking impatient.

Cash approached the man, Colcord in tow.

"Could we ask you some questions?" she queried.

Brooksfield nodded, crossing arms across his broad chest.

"Mind if I record?"

He shook his head.

Cash and Colcord took out their notebooks and she laid her cell down next to the man on a stump to record.

"Did you know the victim?" Cash asked.

Brooksfield let out a sigh. "Sort of. My wife, Margie, knew him better, used to visit him a lot. I sometimes kept her company hiking up here. I usually stayed outside. Margie said I made Willy nervous. I tried to stop her going up there, especially after that Neander business, but that woman's got a mind of her own. Stubborn."

"Do you live near here?"

"We have a ranch near Burns on Maple Road."

Cash eyed him closely. "What brought you up here today?"

Brooksfield sighed again, running a hand over his beard. "I was going to tell Willy to leave my wife alone. I felt like he'd been taking advantage of her good nature."

"Taking advantage of your wife? How so?"

"Margie likes to help people. She's a saint in a world of opportunists, but sometimes her generosity is a one-way ticket to being walked all over. She visited him regularly, delivering groceries and helping with all sorts of things. He's become a real burden on our family, so I came here to talk to him—man-to-man—ask him to ease off. And that's when I found him . . ."

"Why did Mr. Grooms need her help?"

"Well . . . Willy was a little . . . kooky. Had a fear of technology—Big Brother stuff. Moved out here to the mountains to get away from it. Said the government was spying on him through cell phones and computers. So, like I said, Margie would bring him food, keep an eye on him. He got his water from the lake, did some foraging and hunting, but not enough to live without help. Margie works for a financial firm as a CFP, that's *certified financial planner*, so she helped manage his money, file his taxes, that sort of thing."

"Grooms had money?" Cash asked.

"I guess he had some, but Margie doesn't talk about it. Said it was confidential."

"Did you know he kept money in the cabin?"

He shook his head. "No."

"Were there other reasons why you were concerned with Willy spending time with your wife?" Colcord asked.

"Well, he was a real nutjob. The guy was mentally ill—schizophrenia. Wasn't anything violent, but I worried that he was relying too heavily on Margie for support. We need her at the ranch. It's a lot of work running that place and taking care of our kids. Our daughter's got some serious medical issues too. I thought Willy was a bit of a leech."

"And how did the schizophrenia play out? What were the symptoms?" Colcord asked.

"Just a lot of delusions. He was convinced that there was a monster living in Keener Lake. Thought that snakes talked to him. He was always going on about UFOs—claims he saw one crash up there near Dome Peak. He said he could fly, and Margie had to stop him from jumping off the roof once to show her."

"So what was your plan when you got up here?" Cash asked.

Brooksfield's eyebrows drew together. "Hey, now. I didn't have anything to do with his death, if that's what you're implying. I came out here just to talk some sense into him—if any sense was to be had. Ask him to lay off Margie for a bit, maybe find someone else to help him out, so she could spend some more time with her family."

"And these, uh, sculptures"—Colcord gestured around—"are they his?"

"They sure are. Ugly things. Margie was convinced Willy had a talent for it. She even tried to get an art dealer out here once, but Willy chased the poor bugger off. Threw a vodka bottle at him." Paul scowled. "He was always shooting himself in the foot, despite Margie's best efforts at helping him."

Cash glanced around at the constructions of metal and junk. She couldn't imagine anyone wanting one of those monstrosities on their property.

"Although Willy did make some nice stuff too," Brooksfield added. "He would find jasper up by Flat Top Mountain, cut and polish it. He also carved little figurines out of wood and would paint them. That was another thing Margie did for him—delivered his carvings to a couple of local galleries downtown. More free labor from her."

"How long has Margie been coming up here?"

"Five years, maybe."

"And the last time she was here?" Cash asked.

Paul cocked his head to think. "Maybe four or five days ago, I suppose? Brought Willy some food."

"How did Willy and your wife meet?"

"Willy's son, Samuel, used to look after him, but he died of cancer. He was a member of Margie's church, and I think that's where she heard about Willy needing help."

"Is there anything else that you can think of that might be helpful?" Cash asked. "Like if Willy had any enemies, or any thoughts on who might have done this?"

He shook his head. "I don't think he had much contact with anybody in town or anywhere. But . . ."

"Yes?"

"This could be nothin'." Paul hesitated. "Willy's beard. It's gone. He'd been growing the thing for years, called it his 'mountain man beard.' Seems out of character he would shave it."

7

Detective Bart Romanski, head of the Crime Scene Unit at CBI, puffed his way up to the top of the trail, doubling over and gasping in the thin air as the cabin finally came into view. He had given up all semblance of pretending to be in shape about two miles back. He was skinny as a rail and always had been. Nothing to do except be proud of it. Plus, this was a tough hike. It was a good thing the body and evidence would be choppered out. Romanski's crime scene detectives followed behind him. The first CSA—a forensic specialist in trace chemistry, fibers, and miscellaneous evidence—was a new hire, a ball-capped redhead named Aisling Byrne, still too green and nervous to laugh at his jokes. She was accompanied by the crime scene photographer, Tyrone Harris, and a third CSA, a DNA specialist named Michael Reno.

As Romanski stopped to catch his breath, Harris bumped against Aisling behind him. "Whoops," he said, grinning.

Aisling giggled.

Waiting a beat, he joined them at the perimeter and dropped his pack with relief. "People, time to dress for the party." He pulled crime scene packages out of his pack and handed them out to the CSAs. They didn't need full monkey suits—apparently, the scene wasn't a bloodbath. Disappointing. Romanski loved a bit of gore.

Romanski scowled as he saw Cash step out of the cabin with the sheriff and duck under the yellow tape to join them. He liked the gal, but she was always barging into his damn crime scenes. Her face, tinged with freckles, was sunburned, auburn hair pulled back in a bun.

Colcord ambled after her with his usual swagger, blue eyes hidden in the shade of a cowboy hat.

"Cash," Romanski said, "may I ask what you were doing in my crime scene?"

"Don't worry—all we did was eat some sandwiches as we walked around, dropping crumbs and touching everything." Cash grinned and gave Romanski her hand. "Damn, you're all sweaty."

"And you're red," Romanski said. "Didn't have a hat?"

"No, I didn't have a goddamned hat." Cash frowned. Her eyes flickered to Colcord and back to Romanski. "Is it bad?"

"Like a ripe tomato."

Colcord coughed, hiding a smile behind his fist.

As they spoke, Dr. Chris Huizinga, CBI's chief medical examiner, glided up the hill with his technician Saanvi Gupta. Romanski noted that Huizinga, not a blond hair out of place on his aggravatingly handsome head, had barely broken a sweat.

Huizinga laid his pack on the ground, adjusting black-rimmed glasses perched on an elegant nose. He turned to Cash and plucked a squeeze bottle of Coppertone out of his breast pocket. "Agent Cash, you're rather red. You want some sun cream?"

Colcord chuckled loudly.

"If it'll shut everyone up, then fine." Cash snatched the squeeze bottle and began to smear her face.

"Not to interrupt whatever this is about," Huizinga said, "but can we get to the briefing?"

Cash got to summarizing the victim, background, murder scene, and basic facts. When she finished, Harris, following protocol, disappeared into the cabin to photograph while the rest waited. Around twenty minutes later, he reappeared, looking a little jumpy.

"All right, follow me," he said.

Romanski and Huizinga ducked under the tape, followed by the two CSAs.

Harris led them on the path he had delineated through the crime scene, Romanski picking his way among weird constructions and miscellaneous junk. He paused to admire a fish sculpture, with scales of colored glass held together with soldered foil. It was incredible what people threw away these days. The sculptures he had seen on his way here had been remarkably original works of art. Without electricity, Grooms must have used an acetylene and oxy setup. He wondered if the man had lugged all this stuff out here. A lot of the sculptures had been made from old mining equipment that he must have found abandoned in the area.

Romanski stepped around Aisling, who had knelt and was collecting trace evidence with tweezers. Reno followed him into the kitchen, DNA swab kit in hand.

There Willy Grooms lay on the slab of a kitchen table, body bathed in the dappled sunlight reflecting off the water, looking disturbingly peaceful and almost alive.

Romanski took a whiff of air. There was a peculiar smell that he couldn't quite place.

He and his team remained in the doorway while Huizinga went over to the body. He circled it like a predator, crouching low and sniffing like a dog.

"Jesus, why don't you buy the guy a drink first?" Romanski said.

Huizinga ignored him. They had been working together ever since Eagle County had replaced the coroner system with trained medical examiners from CBI. The new ME system was a huge improvement over an elected, and usually ignorant, coroner. Huizinga was both an MD and forensic pathologist, a fact he loved mentioning in a faux self-deprecating manner. He definitely knew what he was doing, but he could be a pompous ass and had no tact, was terrible at expressing sympathy to the families of victims. He also had a strange sense of humor.

Romanski watched as the ME checked for a pulse and respiration. "Definitely dead," he said as if it wasn't obvious. Or maybe he was attempting a joke. "The deceased looks to be in exceedingly fresh condition. I won't be able to tell the exact time of death until a thorough autopsy." He lifted one of Willy's arms and dropped it with a sickening thud back on the table. He examined the wrists and ankles, pausing to examine the bloody right foot. He then poked one of Willy's cheeks, nose as close as possible to the dead body without actually touching it. "He's unusually pink, plump, and firm."

"You sure he's dead? You wouldn't want to pull another Angelo Hays," Romanski said.

Huizinga raised an eyebrow in silent query.

"You know, Angelo Hays? Buried alive in the 1930s?"

"Well, he certainly won't be alive after the autopsy I'll be performing."

Typical Huizinga humor, Romanski thought.

Resuming his inspection, Huizinga nudged his glasses farther up the bridge of his nose with one gloved finger. "I note," he said, "that the victim was shaved postmortem. There are razor nicks that did not bleed. They must have cleaned up the hair and taken it with them. How odd."

Reno now appeared, surgical mask covering up his big handlebar mustache, swabbing samples around the body.

"It looks like the eyes might be missing," Romanski said. "Can you, ah, lift the coins to check?"

Huizinga lifted a silver dollar with his gloved fingers. "Yes, this one is indeed gone." He gently lowered the coin back in place.

"And the foot?" Romanski asked. "You see that?"

"Indeed I do," said Huizinga. "We shall certainly be looking at that with a CAT scan back in the lab."

Romanski rubbed his hands together. This crime scene was getting interesting. The curiously bloodless wounds—aside from the foot—the missing eyes, the posed and dressed corpse, and the postmortem shaving. It had the markings of a serial killer, and a demented one at that. He couldn't wait to get this stuff back to the lab and start putting the puzzle together.

"Think this could have been the Neanders?" Cash asked from the doorway, arms crossed.

"Very unlikely," said Huizinga. "The modus operandi is too different. I hesitate to draw conclusions until I perform an autopsy. But . . ." Instead of finishing the thought, he grasped the hem of the lace garment Willy was dressed in, drawing it up to expose the old man's naked body.

Romanski winced. "I did *not* need the full monty."

Huizinga ignored Romanski and leaned in and sniffed at two strange holes, one above, and the other to the right of Willy's belly button.

"Any idea of cause of death?" Cash asked.

Huizinga didn't answer right away. He took out a magnifying loupe and examined two odd lacerations at the base of the corpse's neck and the two marks near the belly button. Then he straightened up and tucked away the loupe and looked around, an odd expression on his face. "This corpse has been embalmed," he said.

Romanski stared. Of course—*that's* why the smell had been familiar: It was formalin.

"You can see," Huizinga went on, "these two incisions in the neck. One is to the carotid artery, where the embalming fluid was pumped in, and the other to the jugular vein, where the drain tube carried the blood out."

Romanski peered more closely, fascinated.

"Now I would direct your attention to the hemorrhaging and ecchymosis evident around those incisions, as well as the petechiae here, around the umbilicus, where a trocar was used to pump out the cavity fluid and replace it with preservative."

Huizinga now had everyone's undivided attention.

"This indicates the victim was alive when this commenced. If he were conscious—and I believe he was, due to abrasions on the wrists that suggest restraint—it must have been terrifying. *And* painful." He paused. "What I believe we are dealing with here is murder . . . by embalmment."

8

Colcord turned onto Maple Road, which zigzagged down a hillside and crossed the Colorado River on a pretty red bridge. Beyond the bridge, he stopped at the flashing lights of a train crossing, watching in his rearview mirror as a plume of telltale dust signified Cash's black Tahoe was still behind him. The arm came down, and a yellow train rumbled by on tracks that ran along the river.

The train passed, and Colcord continued on, bumping over a dilapidated cattle guard and past a barbed wire fence held up by aging posts. A sign announced that he was entering the Brooksfield Ranch—the *B* backward with a crude butterfly, painted by a child. A long-horned steer skull hung askew on a post next to the sign. The ranch house sat atop a hill overlooking the Colorado River and a large pasture sprawled along a hillside dotted with beef cattle. Their ears perked in unison, heads swiveling as he drove by, before returning their attention to the hayfield. The sun was lowering in the sky—it was late afternoon now. It had been a long day and he was exhausted.

After parking, Colcord slid out of the driver's seat and was immediately greeted with a wriggling red heeler who tried its best to melt into the front of his shins.

"Good boy," Colcord murmured, crouching to run the dog's pointed ears through his thumb and forefinger. As he petted the eager animal, he regarded the property. The main house was an austere log home with green shingles, surrounded by porches and grasslands. A white fence enclosed a handful of grazing horses, and Colcord admired a particularly gorgeous perlino quarter horse. It huffed when it saw him, pawing the ground, before cantering to the other side of its enclosure. The familiar musty smell of manure and the sight of a big rooster strutting about brought back memories of Colcord's childhood: mucking stalls, roping, and dodging their rooster, Claws, to collect eggs from the coop. He chuckled to himself, remembering how his mother had shrieked one day when Claws had tried to spur her. Claws had been conspicuously absent from the coop the next day, and that evening, his mother had served a delicious meal of coq au vin. Nobody said anything, but they ate with gusto and complimented the chef on the fine meal—and were glad of the quiet nights that followed.

He stood from his ministrations on the heeler, brushing himself free of dog hair as Cash pulled up and stepped out of the Tahoe. The heeler barked excitedly, zooming figure eights around them as they approached the front door. Cash knocked, and a woman answered almost immediately. She had red-rimmed eyes as if she had been crying.

"Paul with ya?" she asked in a strained voice. She was wearing a pair of jeans, and cornrows were tied out of her face with a silken scarf, her dark skin glowing in the afternoon sun. A child peeked out from behind her boots.

"We've got a head start on him," Cash said. "Some of our crime scene folks wanted to ask him questions. He's being taken care of, ma'am, not to worry."

She held out a hand. "Margie Brooksfield."

The woman shook Cash's and Colcord's hands in firm, successive shakes. Colcord noticed her forearms flexed with roped muscle—she was surprisingly strong. "I want to start by saying if Paul is a person of interest, I have no desire to speak with you without a lawyer present."

"He's not a suspect," Cash responded. "We're just looking to get some background, that's all. May we come in?"

Brooksfield's knotted expression eased, and she stepped aside, the child moving so that she continued to be hidden by Brooksfield's boots.

"The little peeper here is Lolly." Margie hauled the kid up on one of her hips. The little girl buried her face in Margie's shoulder. Margie took a seat on a leather couch parked in front of a stone fireplace, moving the girl onto her knee, and gestured for them to join her. Colcord noticed a cross hung above the fireplace, and a picture of Jesus and another of the Virgin of Guadalupe adorned the walls.

Colcord chuckled, sinking into a leather chair. "She's darned cute. How many you got?"

"Heck if I know. Paul's the one who keeps track," Margie joked, laughing an infectious, tinkling laugh that flashed a gold molar. "Five total. Lolly, who's six, then Susanna, twelve, the twins Waldo and Emerson, fifteen, and Adam, eighteen."

"How many cattle you got?" Colcord nodded toward the door.

"Sixty head. Black Angus. Five thousand acres total."

"That's a lot of land per head, especially seeing as the pasture looks to be high quality. Happy critters, huh?"

"It's excellent land, been in Paul's family for over a hundred years. I married into it. But it's hard to keep it profitable when you're a small outfit."

"How many workers you got?"

"Just Paul, our boys, myself, and a couple of ranch hands. I also supplement the beef income with some honey and goat cheese that we sell to Denver urbanites. That, and I make a living as a certified financial planner, managing money for some clients."

"So you raise bees and goats too?" Colcord was impressed.

"Sure do."

Cash cleared her throat and gave Colcord a look that said, *Hurry up already.*

"Right," said Colcord.

Cash said, "Mrs. Brooksfield, we have a few questions, and we'd like to record. Okay with you?"

"Sure," Margie replied, crossing her legs. She began to fidget and stroke Lolly's head.

Cash took out her cell phone and set it to record, putting it in front of Brooksfield. She also took out her notebook and pen.

Colcord watched as Brooksfield released Lolly, who scampered off to another room. He couldn't help but like the woman; she reminded him of his mother: a sensitive but no-nonsense straight shooter and talker.

"Did you know Willy Grooms?" Cash asked.

"He was a dear friend." Margie's eyes grew moist. She hiccupped and untied the scarf from around her head, dabbing at her nose. "I visited him on a regular basis. Brought him groceries, sometimes cooked him a

meal and read him the Gospel. Harmless ol' coot. I can't believe someone would do something like that to him."

"And you continued to visit him even after the Neander thing? Not
worried about that?"

"Not really. I heard they're gone, moved up the Rockies toward Canada."

This seemed to be one of the common views in Colorado, at least. Cash
scribbled some notes down. "When did you first meet Willy?"

"Samuel, his son, used to keep an eye on him, but he passed. He was
a member of our church. When I realized that nobody was seeing after
Willy, I felt it was my responsibility as a good neighbor and Christian to
check on him. Found him lying on the floor covered in his own . . . well,
I'll leave that part out. Skin and bones. Mumbling about lake monsters
and snakes. He was so skinny, I could circle his wrist with my thumb
and pointer touching. When I saw the state of him, I knew the Lord was
giving me a task."

"Was Willy ever threatening or violent?"

"Oh, no, never. But he had all these eccentric ideas—that a monster
was living in Keener Lake, that he was the queen of England's grandson,
and that he could fly. The first time I went up there, he talked about how
he saw a flying saucer crash up somewhere around Dome Peak. I thought
maybe it was a meteor or something, but Paul hiked all around there
with our sons and he saw nothing."

"When were you last up there?"

"I couldn't rightly tell you," Margie said, shifting uncomfortably. "I'd
have to look at my calendar."

"Did you know Paul was going out there to speak to Willy today?"

"No. He had no business doing that."

"Paul didn't like Willy much, did he?" Cash asked.

Colcord carefully watched Brooksfield for a reaction.

Margie's broad shoulders stiffened. "My husband had nothing to do
with his death, and I won't hear anything to the contrary."

"Just asking a question," said Cash.

Margie eyed her warily but continued speaking. "Well, you're right. I
knew Paul felt I was spending too much time up there. That I was getting
too involved. This ranch is a lot of work, and it's been a tough year. We've

had some medical issues, and then, of course, he was worried about the Neanders. And on top of that, we have to worry about trespassers. Hikers like to cut across our land, spooking the horses. Paul gets all incensed about that."

"I understand Willy had money?"

"Yes, he did. He was finding gold—he showed me a nugget the size of a baby's fist once. There are a lot of abandoned mines in the Flat Tops. When his son was alive and selling his gold for him, he built up quite a sum in his bank account."

"How much?"

Margie shook her head. "I'm sorry, I can't tell you that—client confidentiality."

Colcord now asked a question. "Do you know of anyone else ever visiting Willy?"

"Sure. Our priest, Timothy Moore, at Saint Mary's. I took Father Moore up there, and he baptized old Willy, to save his soul. I don't know of anyone else visiting him, and I'm sure he would have told me. Although . . ." Margie hesitated.

"Anything you can think of would help us," Cash encouraged.

"Willy sometimes used my sat phone to send texts and calls to someone. Wouldn't tell me what it was about or who he was contacting, was always secretive."

"Hang on. Didn't Willy have a fear of technology?" Colcord interjected.

"Well, yes—he did. But when I asked him, he said it was worth the risk."

"Can we take a look at those texts and calls?" Cash asked.

Margie visibly tensed, indenting the arm of the sofa with her fingers. "Certainly not. I don't feel comfortable letting the police go through my phone. Plus, I don't want to violate Willy's privacy. Even if he's dead."

Cash balked at the sudden change of temperature in the conversation, exchanging a glance with Colcord. No matter—this was something better looked into with a warrant.

The sound of a horse nickering floated through the window, with someone shouting. Brooksfield's brow furrowed at the gravelly sound of an approaching car.

Paul came ambling in the front door, and Margie jumped up to embrace him. Even though she was fairly tall, the top of her head hardly reached Paul's chest.

"You all right? Must have been horrible finding him like that," Cash heard Margie whisper to Paul.

Paul grunted in assent, stroking the back of her head fondly, before gently moving past her so he could address Cash and Colcord.

"Do you need anything else from us?" Paul asked. "It's been a long day, and we're both tired."

"Just a couple of questions for you," said Cash. "Margie mentioned a problem with hikers sometimes trespassing on your land. Has that happened recently?"

"Yes—four of them passed through not that long ago."

"When did you see them?"

"About a week, or maybe more."

"Can you think back, please, and be more specific? The date could be important."

After a moment, he said, "Nine days. I'm sure of it, because it was the same day that Adam—that's my son—got bucked off and took a spill."

"Can you show us where?" Cash asked.

Paul nodded.

"I'm going to check on the bees," Margie said, trotting out the front door.

Paul motioned for them to follow him out the back door. They left the covered porch and rounded a paddock recently seeded with grass.

"This paddock isn't being used right now," Paul explained, picking his way around some old cow patties. "We use rotational grazing. Rests our grass and distributes the cow shit best. But these back pastures are harder to monitor, since they're behind the hill."

At the far of the paddock, a line of pines started beyond the fence. Paul pointed to the trees.

"This is where I last saw them. All four duded up in fancy Gore-Tex camo. I bet they never hunted a day in their lives. Denver yuppies who think they can just hike through private land." He glowered. "I've got a loaded shotgun here. One of these days, I'm gonna give 'em a scare."

"You're sure there were four?"

"I just got a glimpse of them from afar—could've been more."

"Packs?"

"Yeah. They were loaded down."

Colcord turned his eyes to the ground. Beyond the fence, along the verge of the pines, was a layer of soft moss, and in it, he could see some indented footprints. He motioned for Cash, pointing them out. She nodded.

"Thank you, Mr. Brooksfield. You've been very helpful, and I appreciate you answering our questions. Mind if we look around some more?" Cash asked.

Paul assented, and they said their goodbyes. His big frame ambled back over the pasture over the hill toward the house.

Colcord had spent months in mountainous terrain in northern Iraq, desert landscapes like Anbar, and in the dense urban streets of Baghdad and Fallujah early in the Iraq War. He had learned to track with sensors and other surveillance tech as well as without. Despite his experience, when he knelt to inspect the moss to see if anyone had passed through, it took a couple of minutes of searching before he could find any sign of travelers. The hikers seemed to have been careful, and nine days was a long time for tracks to be preserved. Luckily, it hadn't rained. Finally, he found more faint tracks across a boggy patch of moss at the tree line. Four individuals, going into the wilderness. No return tracks visible. Colcord snapped a few pictures with his cell phone.

"I'm gonna follow these tracks." Colcord straightened, looking for the next sign. "Only step where I'm stepping, Cash."

It took him awhile, but around twenty feet farther into the woods, he spied it: a crushed fern. He took another photo. Around thirty more feet into the forest, Colcord found a patch of marsh grass that bowed in the opposite direction as the other blades. Upon closer inspection, he realized that it had been flattened and then, curiously, it seemed like someone had attempted to restraighten the grass manually. He was sure of it now: Whoever had been through here was covering their tracks. After a few minutes more of searching, Colcord found a pine cone that had been scuffed from the forest floor.

A quarter mile in, they reached an old barbed wire fence that was evidently the property line. Searching along it, Colcord located the place where the wires had been pulled apart to climb through, and then re-adjusted to give the impression that nobody had passed. He saw more signs of displaced needles and forest litter on the ground on either side. After climbing through the fence, they continued on.

Whoever had come through here had been extremely careful in placing their feet. There were almost no clear footprints, something difficult to achieve in this swampy terrain. He had to admit, he was impressed.

"Camo," Cash said. "Is that usual outside of hunting season?"

"Everyone wears camo these days," said Colcord. "It's become a fashion statement." He took out a compass and took a bearing. "It appears as if their trail is heading straight for Solitary Lake."

Cash swatted at mosquitoes that were now swarming around them in clouds. "I'm getting eaten alive here."

"Whoa, take a look at this." He spied half a clear footprint in a pocket of fine sand. Colcord knelt. "Fresh lugs, new boot." He took some photos, marked the location on his GPS, and straightened. He walked along farther, hunched over and peering at the ground, looking for a sign, but try as he might, he couldn't pick up the trail again. "We need to get Romanski out here."

"Nice work, Indiana Jones."

"Fortune and glory, kid." Colcord grinned.

Bitten and muddy, Colcord and Cash made their way through the back pastures toward the driveway once more. Colcord tried to make sense of what he had seen. Four individuals wearing camo, hiking toward Solitary Lake, covering their tracks, carrying big packs. This wasn't just some lone killer. But why this elaborate effort to torture and murder an old man living in the mountains—if not for his money—and then *embalm* him? Colcord couldn't make sense of it.

A high-pitched whinny interrupted his ponderings as he walked by the front pasture. He watched as a teenage kid with cornrows tried to control an Appaloosa colt. The horse reared above the boy, who shouted, pulling on the lead, raising the other arm instinctually. That was certainly the wrong move, and the horse—wide-eyed and frothing—squealed again as it came down hard, jerking the rope out of the boy's hands and galloping toward the fence, the lead flapping after it—straight at Colcord.

Spotting a rope coiled around a fence post, Colcord sprinted toward it. The horse launched over the fence. Colcord breathed hard, concentrating. He would only get one throw before the colt was out of range. Coils in his left hand, tail and loop in his right, Colcord swung and tossed the rope as he had so many times on his own ranch as a kid. He was rusty and thought for a second the loop would slide off the side of the colt's nose, but it landed square around the Appaloosa's neck and tightened. The colt reared again, dropped back down, and, feeling the rope around its neck, finally stopped, blowing hard through its nostrils.

"Darn, I'm sorry, mister." The boy vaulted himself over the fence, kicking up dust. "Fritz doesn't usually get boogered like this. That was some nice roping there."

Cash jogged up. "Wow, everything okay?"

Colcord cautiously approached and laid his hand on Fritz's neck, noticing the horse was shaking and slick with sweat. "He's not just spooked, he's terrified."

"They've all been skittish for a while, for some reason. My name's Adam, sir." Adam held out a hand politely.

"Colcord. What's the cause of it, do you think?"

Adam shrugged, then shaded his eyes to look across to the mountains. "I don't know. Wolves, maybe. They released some around here last year."

Colcord looked around, noticing the other horses were shifting about nervously. Something was making these horses restless, and he could feel it too—the same sense of malignancy he had gotten at the cabin.

9

Cash surveyed the church. It was a spartan building in whitewashed stone with a modest spire and cruciform ground plan, the neat façade flanked by two spruce trees. It stood at the top of the main street on a high point overlooking the town of Burns. A bust of Christ looking down with a kindly expression, His two fingers raised, occupied a niche above the entrance. Feeling its eyes upon her, she climbed the steps and heaved open double doors to the vestibule. She was immediately immersed in a cool stillness. The smell of incense mixed with stone wafted through the air.

Colcord followed her, removing his hat to reveal his receding fringe of blond hair.

Rows of oak pews stretched on either side, ending in an altar framed by several carved wood statuettes of robed saints in various poses of piety. Cash shifted uncomfortably from one foot to the other, taking in the grand pillars that rose on either side, feeling a bit like a little girl again attending Mass. An old, familiar feeling of anxiety began to steal over her, which she quickly pushed down.

"You all right?" Colcord asked, clapping a palm on her back, seeming to sense her unease.

"I'm good. Let's get this over with."

Cash strode down the center aisle. The church appeared empty, the trappings of what had possibly been a wedding adorning various pews. A lone priest wearing black robes materialized from behind the altar, a candlesnuffer in one hand. He was a mousy man with brown hair and a prodigious mole lodged to the right of a button nose. Bushy brows shaded eyes the color of cement. As he got closer, she realized the top of his head barely reached her chest. Despite his stature, he spoke in a polished voice that carried far.

"Good afternoon, Sheriff. Welcome to Saint Mary's Church. My name is Father Moore. How can I assist you today?"

Father Moore held out a hand to Colcord, who shook it and introduced himself.

The priest did not offer a handshake to Cash, and she stepped forward to introduce herself as well. "I'm Agent Cash with the Colorado Bureau of Investigation," she said, perhaps louder than she intended.

He turned to her with eyebrows raised in query.

"We'd like to ask you some questions about Willy Grooms."

"Has Mr. Grooms gotten himself into some trouble?" Father Moore turned back to Colcord and spoke to him as if he was the one who had made the request.

The church doors opened behind them, and a woman clicked into the vestibule and took a seat in one of the pews.

"Is there a place we can speak that's more private?" Colcord asked.

"Certainly, Sheriff." Father Moore led them around the altar and past the supplicating eyes of the statuettes. Cash recognized them as Saint Matthew, Saint Christopher, and a third she could not place.

Father Moore noticed her looking at the statue. "Saint Neot," he said, "my favorite saint. I had him added when I assumed my duties here. An ascetic, a wise man, and the patron of fish. Said to have stood four feet tall. There are many formidable men in history that were of short stature, you know."

"Right, of course," Cash said.

The tiny priest ducked through a nondescript door tucked into the wall, Colcord stooping to follow suit. Cash slipped through the miniscule door, wondering if it had also been added specially for Father Moore.

They passed through a sacristy and entered a spare office. A small photograph of the pope holding the papal ferrule aloft hung behind Father Moore's desk, the only decoration in the room. Cash seated herself across from Father Moore. Colcord set his hat on the desk and propped himself against the back wall.

"Mr. Moore—" she began.

"*Father* Moore, if you would. I did not go through seminary formation to be called 'mister.'" The priest folded his hands together and pursed his lips, his eyes shifting between Cash and Colcord, as if confused why Colcord was not conducting the interview.

Cash forced a strained smile. "Pardon. *Father* Moore. I have some sad news. Willy Grooms has passed away. The CBI and the sheriff's office are investigating his death as a homicide."

Father Moore's forehead knotted deeply. "Homicide? Good heavens. That is regrettable news, indeed. May eternal rest be granted unto him." He made the sign of the cross.

Cash ignored Father Moore's rather mawkish reaction. "I'd like to open by mentioning that this interview is completely voluntary. Do you mind if I record?"

Father Moore shook his head. Cash hit Record and placed her cell phone on the desk between them.

"How long have you known Mr. Grooms?" Cash asked.

"I met him three years ago, and only once," he began, speaking in an oddly sonorous and precise voice. "His son, Samuel, was a parishioner and rarely spoke of his father. Mr. Grooms suffered from severe mental illness and did not know Christ until Margie Brooksfield brought him to the light. He did not have the power to know God due to his mental state. *Invincible ignorance*, we call it—ignorant of God, but still able to achieve salvation. While he was not able to attend church on account of his disability, I was able to help him gain eternal salvation by baptizing him in Solitary Lake. It was the only time I met him."

"Did Grooms ask to be baptized?"

"Not in so many words," Father Moore responded. "But he was clearly aware of his original sin and responding in signs of humble gladness because of Christ."

"You mean, Mr. Grooms wasn't lucid enough to consent to the baptism at the time?"

Father Moore's gray eyes gazed at her almost too steadily. "In his

Confessions, Saint Augustine affirmed that mentally incapacitated peo-ple should be baptized. As a priest, it was my duty to ensure that he was able to enter heaven."

"No offense intended; I'm just trying to get a better understanding of Grooms's mental state. So, you hiked out to Solitary Lake about three years ago?"

"Yes."

"With Mrs. Brooksfield?"

"Yes. She brought me up there."

"Anything in the cabin that seemed unusual or out of place?"

"Plenty. You'll have to narrow it down."

"Discounting the sculptures, I mean. We're trying to establish if something was taken."

"It was full of junk as far as I could tell," Father Moore said. He checked an imaginary watch on his wrist.

"Do you know how Mr. Grooms made a living?"

"I haven't the slightest idea."

"What is your relationship with Margie Brooksfield?"

"Margie is an angel. A truly devout and devoted mother and wife."

Cash took a moment to consult her notes. "Mother and wife. Any-thing else?" As she said it, she realized there was a note of irritation in her voice, which she tried to cover up with a smile. She wouldn't allow this man to get under her skin.

"Being a good mother and wife should be enough for any woman in this world," he said.

She thought she saw his gaze drift to her bare ring finger. She fum-bled with her notepad, looking for the next question.

The priest turned to Colcord. "I'm sure, as sheriff, you know just how crime can be traced back to the home. The breakdown of the family."

Cash cast a rather pointed glance in Colcord's direction, and Colcord shifted awkwardly. He didn't respond, looking a little bit like a man caught between a rock and a hard place.

"Father Moore, if we could stay on subject here?" Cash said. She took a deep breath, trying to even out her voice. "How long have you known Margie Brooksfield? Is she a member of your congregation?"

Father Moore's eyes drifted once more to Cash's face, but he never quite met her own gaze. His eyes seemed to be fixed above, on her forehead.

"I've known Margie all her life, and her parents before that. Most of the good people of Burns are Catholics." He paused. "Are you Catholic, Agent Cash?"

She felt like she was being goaded—or was that perhaps her overly sensitive feelings about the church? She could never be sure, her thoughts were so complicated. "That's irrelevant," Cash said, trying to keep her voice neutral. "We're investigating a homicide, and if you don't mind, our role is to ask the questions, not yours."

The ends of Father Moore's mouth curved upward in a knowing smile, and he leaned back in his chair.

Cash tried to ease her breathing, feeling a little hot under her collar. "Was Grooms ever married?" she asked.

"I know very little about Mr. Grooms. I understand the son took care of his father until his passing. He was a *good Catholic.*" He spoke the last sentence rather pointedly.

"How was their relationship?"

"I honestly don't know. I think Samuel was embarrassed of his father, given his alcoholism and mental illness. Samuel never married, had no children."

"How large is your parish?"

"Out of the three hundred and fifty-three residents of Burns, Colorado, about two hundred and ninety attend Mass on Sundays."

Cash tried to put on a friendly smile. "Wow, that's impressive. I imagine you must know a great deal about the people in your parish."

"Yes." Father Moore preened. "Did you know that Burns has one of the lowest crime rates in the state? Which I would like to believe can be attributed to my guidance and that of Christ."

"Since you know so many people in town, are there any you might like to bring to our attention?" Cash asked. "Maybe someone who might have wished ill of Willy Grooms?"

Father Moore frowned, revealing lines characteristic of someone who scowled often. "I don't know."

Cash did her best not to return his scowl. This priest was going to drive her crazy. "We're just asking for a little help here solving a murder. As a priest, maybe you heard something, know something, that would be relevant."

Father Moore turned to Colcord. "I sincerely hope Agent Cash is not suggesting I violate the sanctity of the confessional."

Cash's fists whitened around her clipboard. "Father Moore, since I'm the one asking the questions, I'd appreciate you directing your answers to me."

"Of course. It's just that I'm not used to being interrogated by a . . . *policewoman*."

"If you need help processing that a woman's in charge, I can draw you a picture," said Cash.

Father Moore's penetrating voice spoke over her. "And I take issue with being asked to tattle on my parishioners by someone who doesn't seem to be familiar with the Catholic faith and the sanctity of the confessional."

Cash spoke, her voice shaking with emotion. "I *was* an obedient Catholic until I heard what our priest was doing to boys in the sacristy."

Father Moore's jaw tightened, and he responded stiffly, "It's not surprising someone with your disposition chose law enforcement. I imagine the badge offers a certain sense of usefulness when marriage is not an option."

Cash surged to her feet. "You sexist prick!" she snapped, immediately wishing she could take it back.

"Christ," Colcord muttered behind her.

Father Moore met Cash's stare not with fury but with eyes glittering with triumph. He rose stiffly, brushing his robes off with open palms, then gestured grandly to the door. "This interview is now concluded. I can assure you, the proper authorities will hear of this offensive comment."

"Father Moore," Colcord said hastily, "we're just trying to gather the facts with no intention of giving offense—"

"I ask that you both leave immediately."

Colcord grasped Cash's shoulder and steered her through the little doorway. She brushed him off, strode down the aisle, and shoved open the double doors to the outside. He jogged after her, a concerned look on his face.

"Cash . . . I love ya, but what the hell was that?"

"I know, I know." She squeezed her eyes shut in frustration. She couldn't believe she had let that insufferable jerk get under her skin. Her standing with CBI was already shaky. This unprofessional outburst could very well get her taken from AIC in the case, maybe off it entirely.

10

Forensic pathologist Chris Huizinga silently contemplated the body of William Barstow Grooms, the dressing gown having been removed and sent off to the lab for further examination. It always helped Huizinga to take a couple of moments of quiet before each procedure. To connect with the victim. To pay his respects. To stand witness to the timeworn lines of each individual that came before him—the wrinkles and furrows that had been grooved into them by a lifetime of hopes and sorrows, pleasure and pain—not to mention the perpetual pull of gravity. Each feature held clues to what kind of life they had lived. To memorialize these particulars before cutting into them, taking them apart, and destroying them forever. He was always curious how each person chose to present themselves, from acrylic nails, to facelifts, to carefully curated muscles from years at the gym. Even after they had been stripped of their clothing, their belongings, their personality—and their very lives—each cadaver told a different tale. Huizinga silently dipped his head in honor of the shriveled body that lay on a stainless steel table under the bright lights of the forensic pathology lab at CBI.

Grooms was wiry and fit, the body excessively clean, evidently done postmortem. Even so, he had visible cavities, a deeply lined face, and rough hands pointing to a lifetime of physical labor. But he also had deep smile lines of a life well lived. He might have been crazy, but he had been happy. Huizinga felt sadness for the man work its way through his heart. He pushed it aside as he prepared himself for the upcoming autopsy. The body was now ready for external examination and, then, the Y incision.

His assistant stood by, quietly, waiting for a signal from Huizinga that the show was about to begin. She was a new hire, a tall young woman with long black hair now gathered under a scrub bouffant cap and a nervous expression on her face. This wouldn't be her first autopsy, Huizinga knew, although it was her first at CBI. It wasn't going to be a particularly challenging one, at least from the point of view of decomposition or mutilation. Huizinga had been introduced to her, but the name was complicated and he'd forgotten it, as he so often did. He was terrible with names—maybe it was why others seemed to find him difficult or distracted. But he never forgot a face, and he knew he'd remember Grooms's expression until the day he died. It was so peaceful, almost beatific. And yet he could see, as plain as day, that the man had been horribly tortured, his foot cut and crushed by some implement, the bones fractured. He'd done some research the night before on possible torture instruments, and it seemed that what had been used on Grooms might have been a device known as the "Spanish boot," employed by the Inquisition to elicit confessions of apostasy. It was a boot made out of iron that could be tightened in such a way as to compress the foot, while also driving spikes into the soles—cutting and crushing at the same time. In addition to that horror, he had confirmed that the embalming fluid had been started while the heart was still pumping blood. That would have caused death as soon as the formalin, injected into the carotid artery, reached the brain—within seconds. But it must have been a terrifying and painful few seconds.

He turned to the assistant. "Ms.—? I'm so sorry. I'm bad with names."

"It's Zubriski," she said, "Ellen Zubriski." She then patiently spelled it out, making Huizinga feel a bit like a dolt.

"Ms. Zubriski, thank you." He wondered what to say to put her at ease. She appeared rather tightly wound. He knew he could also be a bit stiff and formal at times, and he often seemed to make people nervous. "I have a weird last name too," he said, "and I've had a lot of practice spelling it out. So I can appreciate the difficulty of your last name as well."

"Yes, Dr. Huizinga," Zubriski said formally.

Huizinga, realizing once again he might have said the wrong thing, cleared his throat and pulled up his mask. "Please start the recording."

"Yes, Doctor." She turned on the video camera, tested it, and nodded to him that it was working.

Huizinga went through the preliminaries, identifying the body, himself, the assistant, date and time, and the rest. Then he did a slow walk around of the body, commenting on the general appearance. He directed particular attention to the insertion and drainage points in the neck, through which embalming had been done. He hadn't performed an autopsy on an embalmed corpse since medical school, but it presented no particular challenge. Why the body had been embalmed was outside of his purview. In his comments as a pathologist, he rarely speculated, only observed. But he couldn't turn off the conjecture meter in his brain, and it was running riot with this strange corpse.

Now he did a closer inspection of the externals with a headband magnifier. As he went over the body, inch by inch, he described what he saw, in particular swelling on the internal and external hemorrhaging around the insertion and draining sites at the base of the neck. The wounds around the umbilicus, where a trocar had been inserted to drain and inject preservative in the abdominal cavity, did not show hemorrhaging, which meant the victim's heart had stopped beating by that point.

He next minutely described the external injuries to the misshapen and lacerated foot.

"Ms. Zubriski, please make a note to order up a CT scan of the left foot."

"Yes, Doctor."

Zubriski, at his request, then took a number of macrophotos.

His examination now circled around to the face. The eyes had been removed while the victim was alive, scooped out with something—Huizinga suspected a spoon. Ms. Zubriski appeared to be a little shaken by this, but she was covering it up well. Dr. Huizinga supposed he would have been shaken too when he was a newish MD.

He opened the subject's mouth and right away noted superficial lacerations to the oral cavity and residues of a starchy substance on the carious teeth.

"Ms. Zubriski, could you please take some samples of that?" he said, fixing a retractor holding the mouth open.

She was ready with the tweezers and evidence tubes, and plucked out a few sodden crumbs, placing them in.

"It appears the victim was consuming some sort of starchy substance when he died," Huizinga noted.

"Yes, Doctor."

Finally, closing the mouth, he said, "Ms. Zubriski, would you take a look at the face and give me your impressions?"

Zubriski, also wearing a headband magnifier, leaned over and examined the face for some time. "Doctor, it seems to me the expression on the face was fashioned postmortem. And the corpse was shaved postmortem as well."

Huizinga nodded. "My thoughts exactly. It's the sort of professional manipulation you might see in a funeral home, preparing a body for viewing."

"I would agree."

He wondered if at least one of the killers hadn't been a mortuary scientist, given that the body had been worked on with such assurance and skill. That speculation would go into his report. Beyond that, he wondered why the killers had gone to the trouble of not only embalming the body but also arranging the face. Was it to send some kind of message? Was it a sign of respect? But how could you show respect to someone you'd just tortured to death?

"Now for the Y incision," he said. "Ms. Zubriski, could you please roll over the instrument table?"

The assistant fetched it with smooth professionalism. She handed him the correct scalpel, without his having to ask for it. He made the incision, clean and deep, then peeled back the skin and tissue until the chest flap lay over the face. Using a Stryker saw, he made two cuts on either side of the rib cage, dissected the tissue behind it, then pulled it open to expose the organs.

He worked quickly and easily, describing out loud every step of the process. Zubriski proved to be a most able assistant, handing him the correct tools, taking samples, and following his instructions with skill and precision. She was good—very good—and it made Huizinga a little embarrassed that he'd forgotten her name. His previous pathology assistant had not exactly been stellar. He hoped they could keep her.

Huizinga quickly detached the larynx and esophagus, severing arteries and ligaments. With a series of quick cuts, he separated the attachments of the organ set to the spinal cord, bladder, and rectum—freeing it from its cage in the body.

"Ready to remove the organ set?" he asked.

Zubriski moved to the opposite side as Huizinga and slipped her hands beneath the organ package.

"On three," he said.

In a moment, the complete organ set was lifted out and placed on a secondary gurney for further dissection.

Huizinga now began cutting free the individual organs—heart, lungs, liver, and so forth—examining and describing them, weighing them, and taking tissue samples. Of these, the stomach was usually the most important, as it contained the victim's last meal, if any. It could also be useful in calculating the time of death, although the embalming of the corpse would greatly complicate that determination. Maybe, he thought, the embalming had been done for exactly that purpose: to make it difficult to determine the time of death.

"Scalpel," he said.

One was produced. He inserted it into the top of the stomach and made a clean incision, using retractors to expose the interior. A strong gagging smell of wine greeted his nostrils, and the incision revealed a mass that looked like it might be bread. It had not begun to digest, turning instead into an irregular lump of starch sodden with red wine.

Moving a magnifier over the mass, he could see some indications of structure—crackers, it looked like. A whole bunch of them: thin, hard, undigested crackers, barely chewed, and some swallowed practically whole. It looked like the poor guy had eaten an entire box of saltines or soda water crackers and chased them with a lot of red wine.

"Interesting last meal," murmured Huizinga. "Let's get some samples."

Zubriski used the tweezers to pry a piece off the mass and place it in an evidence tube, and collected the liquid with swabs and a suction dropper. She took her time doing it, and then lingered, bent over the stomach, making a close examination.

"Do you see anything of note?" Huizinga asked.

"Maybe," she said. "May I make a suggestion?"

"Of course."

"I see evidence of more starchy material extruding from the lower esophageal sphincter, there. I might suggest an incision opening the esophagus and pharynx."

Huizinga turned his attention to the bottom of the esophagus and could see what she meant: more residue was coming out.

"Good idea," he said, trying not to be annoyed that she'd noticed something he hadn't. He made a clean longitudinal slice of the lower esophagus and placed a retractor to keep it open, peering inside. "More crackers," said Huizinga. "Looks like he died in the process of eating and swallowing."

"May I, Doctor?"

He stepped back, and Zubriski moved in to take a close look, her magnifier almost touching the incision. After a while, she straightened up. "Those aren't crackers, Doctor."

"How can you tell?" Huizinga was taken aback and tried to tamp down the small annoyance this contradictory comment provoked.

His faint displeasure must have showed on his face, because the look on hers crystallized into a stubbornness that surprised him. "Forgive the personal question, Doctor, but . . . are you Catholic?"

He was taken aback at the question. "Um, no. Atheist, if you must know." He was immediately sorry he'd been provoked into revealing that and said sternly, "I hardly think the question is relevant."

And now Zubriski bestowed a rather knowing smile on him. "Well, I *am* Catholic, and it *is* relevant. They aren't crackers, they're Communion wafers—the Sacred Host that the priest gives you during the Eucharist. You can just make out the remains of the cross stamped on that one—do you see?—and this one just shows the faintest outline of the Lamb of Christ impressed into the wafer. I'm sure that's what they are—I, um, see them every week."

Huizinga stared, looking closely under the bright lights, turning his head to get a raking view. He was so astonished he couldn't immediately find the words to respond.

"And the wine, Doctor," went on Zubriski. "Also taken as part of Communion."

"What . . . do you make of it?" asked Huizinga, struggling to process the idea.

"It appears," said Zubriski, her voice flat, "that the victim, while being tortured, was eating Communion wafers and drinking sacramental wine."

11

Brother Niall Armagh of the Pallottine Order in the Basilica of San Silvestro in Rome had never been in the Camera dei Gobbi, the Chamber of the Hunchbacks, deep in the bowels of the Vatican. The chamber had been given that curious name because of the dramatic frescoes on the western wall of the room, painted by Fra Angelico in 1448, which feature a panoramic view of the tortures of hell. The centerpiece is a hideous scene depicting several hunchbacked figures, wailing and contorting as they are consumed by fire. The room, according to Vatican legend, had been built as a private retreat on the orders of Pope Nicholas V, to be a place where he could contemplate in private the horrors of hell.

In looking at the frescoes, Brother Armagh thought that Fra Angelico had done a fine job depicting those terrors, and he felt his own flesh creep at the sight of such despair, agony, and torment. He made an effort to avert his eyes.

He had been escorted to the Camera dei Gobbi by an *ispettore*, an inspector, in the Corpo della Gendarmeria dello Stato della Città del Vaticano—Vatican City's police force. He had some idea of what this was about, and he was apprehensive, which he concealed with a calm, pious expression.

The inspector indicated where he was to sit—in one of the elaborate wooden chairs lining the back wall of the room, the carved arms polished by centuries of use. The inspector took a seat next to him, and they sat in silence, waiting in the dark, empty chamber, lit only by the fire from a bank of candles. The close air was fragrant with the scent of smoke, wax, and stone.

Finally, the door creaked open and in entered a man Brother Niall recognized as none other than Cardinal Collini. It was all he could do to remain still as the tall cardinal strode in, his scarlet cassock sweeping behind him, dressed in full liturgical regalia, with biretta, fascia, and ferraiolo, the heavy pontifical cross swinging from his neck. Collini was not your typical stooped and decaying prelate—he was a powerful man with a handsome face who radiated stern, spiritual charisma. He was followed by three men in the uniform of the Corpo della Gendarmeria, one being the chief inspector himself, Commissario Leo Manicaldi.

Cardinal Collini took a seat at the head of the room, opposite Brother Armagh, while the three policemen took seats behind him.

A long silence ensued as Collini arranged his cassock, adjusting his cross and ferraiolo, then raising his eyes to Armagh, contemplating him with a severe gaze. He finally began to speak in Italian, his unexpectedly quiet voice almost a whisper. Father Armagh understood him—all the Irish Pallottine brothers in the basilica were fluent. It was a necessity in order to work with their Italian associates in the church.

"Brother Armagh," the cardinal began, "it's my understanding that you came to us not from Ireland but from Chicago?"

"Yes, Your Eminence."

"So you are familiar with America?"

"I spent nine years there, after graduating from the Pallottine College in Thurles."

"And in Chicago, you were a law enforcement chaplain, is that not correct?"

"Yes, Your Eminence. I served as chaplain for the Federal Bureau of Prisons, mostly at the MCC in Chicago. I counseled prisoners on their spiritual needs, and I worked closely with the FBI and other law enforcement as well as prison correctional officers."

"So you are familiar with American law enforcement, and you have much experience dealing with law enforcement and investigative personnel?"

"Yes, very much so, Your Eminence."

"You are no doubt familiar with the dishonor your order, the Pallottine

Fathers, have cast upon themselves in allowing one of the holiest relics in Christendom to be desecrated?"

Brother Armagh swallowed. The Italians had always looked down on the Irish fathers, and the desecration of the relic only seemed to confirm their skeptical view. "I am deeply sorry for it. We all are."

"Very well. But we are not here to discuss the security failures that led to it. We're here because His Holiness has charged me to oversee the return of the relic. And that is why I called for you, Brother Armagh."

Armagh nodded, his heart accelerating. The pope himself was involved.

Cardinal Collini now picked up the briefcase, placed it in his lap, and opened it. He removed a piece of paper.

"What we will now discuss is of the utmost confidentiality."

"Understood, Your Eminence."

"When Brother Padraig brought our attention to the desecration of the relic, we reviewed the security footage and quickly spotted the thief. The man had hidden in the church after closing, emerged at midnight, and disabled the alarm system most cleverly. He then broke the seal of the cube, lifted it, and used a small tool to remove a piece of the relic and placed it in a sealed tube. Afterward, he hid himself. When the church was opened in the morning, he mingled with a group of tourists and then left."

He paused dramatically. "He was hooded, his face obscured. Through extensive investigation, we were eventually able to identify him." He turned to the chief inspector sitting next to him. "Commissario, will you please review the file for us."

The chief inspector removed a file from his own briefcase, opened it, and began to speak in that monotonic style favored by the police. Brother Armagh listened intently, trying to memorize every word. He wished he'd thought to bring notepad and paper.

"The individual's name is Javier Castillo, an American, and a resident of San Francisco. Until recently, he was a professor of exobiology at San Francisco State University, a position from which he was dismissed.

"Castillo has no criminal record. He appears, at least on the surface, to be a respectable citizen."

He turned the page in his file and continued, "He flew to Rome on

May 9, vandalized the relic the night of May 10, and flew back to San Francisco on May 11. Castillo seems to have worked with an accomplice. While in Rome, before the crime, he made contact with a Portuguese man we've identified as Joachim da Silva—who appears to have supplied him with the specialized tools needed to disable the alarms and open the sealed cube containing the relic." He paused. "Unfortunately, two weeks after the theft, Joachim da Silva disappeared before we could get to him, and he has yet to resurface."

Now the commissario halted and looked directly at Brother Armagh, who dropped his eyes at the severe gaze. Then the commissario resumed.

"We do not know Castillo's motive for this crime and are investigating several possibilities. The most likely hypothesis relates to the fact that there are three other claimants to having relics purporting to be the head of Saint John the Baptist. This has long been an area of controversy: a debate over which relic is the true one."

He looked up again. "That is all, thank you."

Now the cardinal spoke again. "Brother Armagh, do you have any questions so far?"

Armagh tried to think. He had a million questions, but none seemed appropriate to ask at that time. "Not yet, Your Eminence."

"Very well. I have conferred with the pope about this matter. He does not want a scandal or publicity. He does not want the Vatican police to bring the matter to the Italian authorities, Interpol, or the Americans. He would like to keep it quiet—for now. That, Brother Armagh, is where you come in."

Armagh gave a slight bow of the head.

"You will travel to San Francisco and meet privately with Mr. Javier Castillo—and ask for the relic back."

A silence fell as Armagh absorbed this surprise.

"His Holiness would like this to be accomplished quietly and with dignity. If Mr. Castillo will not cooperate, then we will escalate. His Holiness is concerned that if Mr. Castillo learns he's under a criminal investigation, he might destroy the relic to cover his tracks. We would like to give him the opportunity to make things right, with no charges filed. That is where we need your help."

"Yes, Your Eminence. But . . . what if he no longer has it?"

"We haven't seen any evidence of it being passed along to a third party. But if he doesn't have it in his possession, you will *andrà a braccio* and induce him to cooperate in its retrieval. Commissario Manicaldi here will brief you on the details of your assignment in the Biblioteca Cardinalium later this evening. All the arrangements for your mission have been made—flights, hotel, car, ample funds. You will go as yourself, Brother Armagh, and you will leave tomorrow morning. You will appeal to Mr. Castillo's sense of fairness and his conscience, if he has one. You might also make clear to him the consequences of not cooperating—that he will be extradited to Italy and face trial here. We have security footage and additional evidence—everything we need to convict. He will face many years in prison. That, of course, is a last resort."

The cardinal leaned forward, a scowl on his handsome face. "This is an opportunity for you, Brother Armagh, to redeem your order from the dishonor that has fallen upon it."

"Thank you, Your Eminence. I greatly appreciate this opportunity." Even though his face remained calm, inside, Brother Armagh was reeling. This was not a simple assignment, and there was no telling what this Castillo was really like, why he'd done what he did, or how he would react to being approached. The burden of redeeming Brother Armagh's beloved order of Irish Pallottines was now on his shoulders. He couldn't help but think a success could lead to his becoming Rector . . . or failure to his disgrace and his departure from Rome to some backwater posting.

Cardinal Collini rose, and now a smile broke out on his face for the first time, dramatically transforming it from chiseled severity to radiant blessedness. He went to Brother Armagh and clasped his hand in both of his, pressing it warmly. "Brother Armagh," he said kindly, "I feel assured you will succeed at this important assignment. I know His Holiness shares my confidence in you. You know how to get along with Americans, how to interact with criminals and law enforcement alike. Handle this as you see right—we will not micromanage."

He turned to leave, his cassock sweeping the ground, and the three policemen with him rose as well and followed. As Brother Armagh turned to the inspector who had escorted him, his eye fell once again on the gaggle of burning hunchbacks with their twisted, screaming faces, illuminated in the flickering candlelight—and he shuddered.

12

Detective Bart Romanski crumpled an empty can of sugar-free Red Bull and tossed it into the hallway trash can before keying himself back into the CBI trace evidence room. Most of the room was dark, except for a corner with fluorescent lights where he and a technician, Michael Reno, had been laboring away, analyzing the remainder of the Grooms evidence. They had been working for sixteen hours straight now, and Romanski was hoping to get through the rest before dawn. It was nine o'clock at night, but he didn't mind; he worked best at night.

"Energizer Bunny recharged?" Reno asked.

Reno was Romanski's favorite technician to work with. He cut quite a figure with his handlebar mustache and rolled-up sleeves revealing a forearm tattoo of Homer Simpson eating a doughnut. What hair was missing on Reno's head was sticking out in tufts from the V-neck of his shirt. Before gowning up in lab gear, hairnet, and face mask, he looked more like a biker than a scientist. But Romanski loved the guy. He was a competent technician who kept things lively with a wiseass sense of humor, and he was the only one out of the bunch who regularly volunteered to stay late. Plus, they had survived escaping the Erebus disaster together. Trauma bonding, Romanski thought. He gave an involuntary shiver.

"Recharged. Ready to rumble?" Romanski grinned, pulling on a fresh pair of nitrile gloves.

"All set to go," Reno said.

Romanski measured out the different reagents that Reno would need to pipette into the reaction vials for the PCR run, handing them to Reno one by one, who hunched over the tray of tubes with his pipette, tongue sticking out in concentration.

"This Communion wafer shit is crazy, isn't it?" Reno said. "Can't believe the dude was eating Jesus bread when he died."

"Yeah," said Romanski. "I went down a rabbit hole on Communion wafers yesterday. Did you know that a long time ago, only bakers, parishes, and convents sanctioned by the church could make Communion wafers? And there was this whole sacred ritual that went into making them, even sprinkling the dough with holy water and using special ovens."

"All for a tasteless piece of cardboard."

"No kidding. But now they're manufactured by big companies."

Reno grunted in assent, continuing his work with the chemicals. The DNA recovered at the crime scene had been in the form of pin-sized drops of blood, and Romanski had opted for a PCR analysis, instead of a RFLP DNA analysis, which was more reliable in court but required a larger sample size. He watched as Reno pipetted the PCR buffer, deoxynucleotide mix, *Taq* DNA polymerase, and other reagents for the test into the reaction tubes, which would be centrifuged and then go through about thirty rounds in a thermal cycler, amplifying the DNA millions of times to an easily detectable level. The entire process would take about two to three hours. Romanski looked at his watch. If they pushed it, he could be out of there by two a.m.

Romanski dialed Cash's number, half expecting her to ignore his call because of the late hour. Instead, she answered the phone after half a ring, sounding alert.

"When can I drop by?" she asked.

Romanski was a bit taken aback, then reminded himself this was Cash. She always threw herself into her cases. "Well, we should have DNA results by twelve thirty, if you don't mind staying up late."

"Gotcha. I'll be there."

"Cool. Come join the party," Romanski said, and hung up. He sat down to finish typing up the forensic report on the other fluids they had collected.

"I hope you know I'll be out of here as soon as this hits the cycler," Reno said as he slid the test tubes into different sides of the centrifuge.

"Make sure to balance those out," Romanski said out of habit, almost forgetting Reno was one of his most experienced technicians, "one on each opposite end of the centrifuge. Use water if you've got an odd number."

"Dude, what's with the back-seat driving?" Reno closed the centrifuge and set the timed cycle. "Speaking of, how is that new girl Aisling doing?"

"She's pretty good. She attended CU Denver's forensic science program—same school I did—so I know she's got the smarts. I worry she's getting a little too distracted with Tyrone, though."

"I've noticed. Think they're—?" Reno made an obscene gesture with his hands and whistled.

Romanski laughed. "Not my business."

Reno retrieved the solutions from the centrifuge and began programming the thermal cycler.

"Can you handle the rest of this if I bounce now?"

"Absolutely. Thanks for staying late, Reno, as always." Romanski clapped a hand on Reno's shoulder. "Say . . ." Romanski paused, wondering if he should even ask, but decided it was better to check in than to sweep it under the rug. "How are you doing?"

Reno had taken a month off from work after the Erebus disaster, but after his first week back, he'd suffered a massive anxiety attack, leaving him a hyperventilating mess crouched in the corner of the lab. After a second and longer break, he had returned to work and now appeared to be doing better—so Romanski hoped.

Reno busied himself cleaning up his station. "My psychiatrist says I have PTSD, but what can you do? One step at a time." He began wiping down the area near the weighing station. "Do you ever dream about the Neanders?"

"No," Romanski lied. "You?"

Reno hesitated. "Yeah. I dream that I'm trapped down in the mines, lost, and no matter where I turn, it's a never-ending tunnel of darkness and stone, and I can hear them in the pitch blackness behind me." Reno shivered. "It always ends the same way. I'm choking on acrid smoke and those creepy, high, breathy voices get louder and louder before they grab me and tear me apart."

Romanski frequently woke up screaming too, his husband shaking him awake from the same nightmare: that he was tied up at the Neander altar, about to be burned, human heads on spikes around him. But no way was he ever going to tell anyone at work about that. Never.

Reno said, "The FBI seems to have dropped the ball. And then all these crazy pro-and anti-Neander protestors? Holy fuck, the world's gone mad."

"They're getting a new special agent in charge," said Romanski. "And they're gonna bring CBI back in, they say."

"No thank you. I don't want back in."

"I'm not sure we have a choice," Romanski said, feeling jumpy in the dark lab.

"Sure you don't want me to stay, boss?" Reno asked, pausing from unbuttoning his lab coat.

"Naw, Cash'll be here soon," Romanski said. "Get out of here before you grow fangs and start hissing at sunlight."

Reno brought the right unbuttoned side of his lab coat across half of his face like a cape. "*There are bad dreams for those that sleep unwisely,*" he intoned in a fake Hungarian accent.

Romanski gave a chuckle.

Reno gathered his belongings and paused, silhouetted in the doorway from the hallway light. "Hey, Romanski, thanks for checking in on me. You're a decent boss . . . and also a friend."

Romanski watched the door close behind Reno, leaving him in the silence of his lab. He fiddled with his Bluetooth speaker, and soon Etta James's crooning broke the stillness. Feeling a little better, he resumed typing his report.

About an hour later, the thermal cycling was complete. Romanski pipetted the samples into individual wells of the gel box and ran the gel with electrophoresis—the electric current would move the DNA molecules through the gel, allowing the bands of DNA to be seen under a UV light. That process would take an additional hour.

To pass the time, Romanski took out a sketchbook and began drawing his next sculpture. In a junkyard, he had found a pair of rusted boilers, some condensers, warped springs, a crate of angle iron, and a large box of gears. He had previously decided to make a giant head out of it. But seeing Willy Grooms's creations had given him inspiration to make something different, something creepy. Maybe a winged creature—with bones of angle iron and torn cloth for wings. He began to draw in confident strokes as the electrophoresis worked the DNA through the gel in the background.

Another hour passed, and the gel was done—the DNA had been mapped. Where that would lead, who it might connect to, would come later. Just as Romanski was finishing up, he heard Cash's light knock on the door window, causing him to jump. He let her in, noticing she looked different from her usual getup, having donned sweatpants and a wrinkled Red Sox T-shirt. Dark circles ringed her eyes, auburn hair uncombed. She didn't look good. Probably working too hard, Romanski thought.

"Burning the midnight oil as usual?" she said, putting on a disposable lab coat, hairnet, gloves, and a mask. She sat at one of the center tables as Romanski collected and stacked the reports.

"You're also up past your bedtime," Romanski remarked.

She ignored his quip and gestured at the reports. "Can you summarize those for me—and mind if I record? I need to play it back for Colcord tomorrow."

"Go ahead."

She placed her cell phone on the table and pulled out her notebook.

"I'll make it quick, 'cause it's late," said Romanski. "I'll start with fingerprints. We found a bunch of latents, mostly Willy's and Margie Brooksfield's. A few old latents from Samuel Grooms, Willy's son. He has a short rap sheet for drunk and disorderly and a DUI in his twenties, which is where we got the hit from the database.

"There were glove smears in the kitchen, bedroom, and living room," Romanski continued. "Whoever killed Willy Grooms was wearing gloves. There was a thorough cleanup. Serology kit showed there was a wipe-down using bleach, peroxide, and two professional crime-scene-cleaning enzyme solutions. Spotless. These folks were professional and organized." Romanski paused for dramatic effect; one of his favorite parts of the job was presenting his findings. "But we managed to get three partial prints with a plastic casting kit outside the cabin and four latent prints in one corner of the victim's bedroom. The floor of the cabin appeared to have also been cleaned thoroughly, but they missed the spot where we found the latents. Footprints showed us there were at least three individuals of varying shoe sizes walking around the cabin wearing identical, almost-new hiking boots, and two of those individuals' footprints were also found inside the cabin. They matched the prints we collected at the Brooksfield Ranch."

Cash whistled. "Nice work. I needed some good news about the case today."

"Why? What's wrong?" Romanski asked.

"I called a priest a sexist prick."

Romanski leaned back in his chair and cackled. "Get out! Really? That's awesome." His face grew more serious as he saw that Cash wasn't sharing his mirth. "Does Holmes know?"

"She will."

"You're gonna get spanked."

"Yeah, yeah. Soak it up while you can. He deserved it, but still." Cash rubbed her temples. "All right, what else?"

Romanski pulled up a picture on his laptop and slid it over so Cash could see. "Bloodstains and patterns in the kitchen indicate Grooms was tortured on the table. Traces of formaldehyde, glutaraldehyde, methanol, and other solvents were found around the table, indicating that Grooms was probably also killed in the same place, through embalmment, as Dr. Huizinga noted in his initial examination. Objects had been carefully moved and replaced. Vegetation had been flattened. The area had been thoroughly and carefully searched—inside and out."

Cash leaned forward with anticipation. "DNA swabs show anything?"

"We swabbed literally everything, as usual. Found a couple of hairs with roots attached. Hair DNA indicated it was elk, beaver, Willy Grooms himself, Margie Brooksfield, and another hit on Samuel Grooms. Found some deer bones in the cabin too. Nothing else."

"Interesting. Grooms must have been a hunter."

"Trace tox on what little blood Grooms had left showed some blood alcohol content—but BAC scores after death can be unreliable, as fermentation could have produced a higher BAC score, and the addition of methanol to the circulatory system really screwed that up. Nothing else was found outside of those embalming chemicals. Electrophoresis analysis of spilled liquid in the kitchen showed that it was red wine with elevated levels of sucrose."

Cash gave him a quizzical look.

"Sweet wine, like what you get at Communion," Romanski elaborated. "We also analyzed the stomach contents, which showed that Grooms had eaten about two pounds of Communion wafers. But here's something crazy." He paused dramatically. "Judging by the progress of digestion, he had been fed wafers and wine for approximately three days before he died."

"Jesus. That's a hell of a lot of wafers and booze."

Romanski nodded. "Like Dr. Huizinga noted, Grooms was killed by the injection of embalming fluids. The embalming messes up everything, but it appears that Grooms's time of death was about five to six days before we arrived on-site. We managed to find a couple of wafers mostly intact," Romanski clicked to the next photo. A circular, partially degraded wafer flicked onto the screen. He zoomed in. "See that?"

"It's Baby Jesus."

"Exactly. A nice little piece of art stamped into it. The other ones were stamped with lambs and crosses, but this is one that drew my attention."

Cash leaned in to take a closer look. "The Communion wafers I've seen don't usually look this elaborate. But that," she added, "was a long time ago."

"The other night, I did a deep dive to figure out where the Baby Jesus wafers were sourced. Did you know about two-thirds of all Communion wafers come from the Cavanagh Company, a big factory out of Rhode Island? It was the Cavanagh Company that sourced the wafers with the cross and lamb on them that we found inside Grooms's stomach, which isn't helpful, since almost all churches buy from them. However, this Baby Jesus wafer was *not* sourced by the Cavanagh Company." Romanski held a suspenseful silence.

Cash rubbed her eyes. "Okay, get to the point: Who sells them?"

"It's a convent in the town of Penne, Italy. Convento di Santa Chiara Offredusio—"

"*Offreduccio*," Cash said, correcting Romanski's mangled Italian, "one of the followers of Francis of Assisi. You sure about this?"

"Positive. They are the only ones who use this particular stamp for their wafers."

"So someone brought them over from Italy."

"Something like that."

"Wow. Romanski, this is really good work. We can start looking for people arriving in Colorado with Italian passports, add that to our APB on four hikers decked out in camo."

Romanski beamed. "No problem, Cash. You know me, I'm a problem-solver. Now for the foot."

"Oh yeah."

Romanski clicked and pulled up several pictures of Grooms's foot. "Pretty gruesome. You'll hear this from Dr. Huizinga later, but we're pretty sure a Spanish boot was used to torture Grooms."

"What the hell is a Spanish boot?"

"It's a boot made of iron—a torture instrument from the Inquisition—that was placed on a foot and screwed in, which slowly compressed the foot while also driving spikes into his soles. It was only used on one foot—that's why one of his feet is fucked up and the other is fine."

"Holy shit," Cash said.

"The holiest of shits." Romanski grinned.

Cash rolled her eyes in response.

"Anyways," Romanski continued, "blood-spatter patterns and pooling in eye sockets tell us that poor old Grooms also had his eyes scooped out antemortem—and after the boot was used on him. His vocal cords were also swollen . . . which indicates that he was screaming, a lot, during his last hours—or days—alive. His wrists were tied, and he pulled so hard on his bindings that he suffered torn ligaments."

"That's awful," Cash said.

"Yeah, it's all really macabre. I saved the best for last. . . . There were superficial lacerations to Grooms's oral cavity. Dr. Huizinga asked me to look into torture implements based on these marks." With a flourish of pride, Romanski clicked to the next slide. "A speculum oris—specifically, a Maunder's screw gag—was used to force Grooms's mouth open."

"Oh my God." The blood drained from Cash's face as she came to a gruesome realization. "To force-feed him the host and wine."

"Exactly. While he was dying, they were stuffing him like a Thanksgiving turkey."

13

Cash stepped into Colcord's office. She liked the smell of it, of old leather and books, and the atmosphere was more like a study than an office. It was the complete opposite of her own. A large bookshelf covered one wall, lined with Jonah Hex and Lone Ranger graphic novels, a complete shelf of Louis L'Amour hardbacks, along with books on fishing and hiking. An old bridle hung on one wall, above a bronze sculpture of a cowboy on a bucking horse. Several pictures were hung neatly on another wall, and as Cash stepped closer, she realized one was a photo of a young Colcord with a full head of hair, looking handsome and fit, laughing as he slung an arm across the shoulder of a burly man in a cowhide vest. A modest barn stood behind them, a field of purple-and-green alfalfa beyond that.

"Just hung that one. Me at twenty and my dad," Colcord explained, shuffling a huge sheaf of papers that cluttered his desk. "He was a real cowboy. Earned his stripes through a lifetime of calluses, rope burns, and dusty Justins."

"Wow, you look like you could have been on the cover of a magazine. What happened?"

Colcord looked at her with a half smile. "The stress of working with you aged me beyond my years."

"Sorry, I didn't mean it that way," Cash said, with a laugh.

Colcord gestured for Cash to sit in the empty leather chair across the table from him. "Want some coffee?"

Cash nodded, and Colcord busied himself peeling open a new jar of instant Bustelo.

"I didn't know you liked Bustelo," Cash said.

"I don't. Stuff's awful."

Cash wondered why he had a new jar in his office if he didn't like it. "Well, thanks . . . I guess."

Colcord settled down across from her, with an espresso for himself pulled from a fancy machine in one corner.

"Got an update about the wafers. Followed up with that convent in the town of Penne, Italy. Convento di Santa Chiara Offreduccio."

"Yeah?"

"Apparently, they make wafers specially for priests conducting the conservative Tridentine Mass, but they only sell within Italy. Our killers, or their supplier, must have brought them into the US themselves. They were pretty cagey about their clients, but they claim that none were sold to Americans."

"So basically a dead end," Colcord replied.

"Not totally. We now know the murderers might not be American or at least were in Italy at some point."

"What's the Tridentine Mass?" Colcord asked.

"A Mass that the traditionalist Catholics want to resurrect. I looked it up. Very formal and all in Latin—not like modern-day Mass. Now let's see what you got," Cash said.

Colcord slapped down a file and opened it. On top was a standard search warrant for a cell phone and another for a sat phone, followed by documents with rows of phone numbers on them. He laid a black satellite phone next to them.

"I had a deputy go out and collect Margie's Iridium sat phone through a warrant. The parameters of the warrant allow us to search outgoing and incoming calls and texts during her visits to Willy Grooms's cabin. I plugged in the GPS location data and narrowed down the scope of our search to these ninety-eight days that she visited the cabin, which occurred over the course of several years. That's the warrant we served on BlueCosmo, the company that provides sat service for Iridium, and got back these call records and text messages on those dates as well—so we can cross-reference in case she's deleted anything. So . . . what we need to do now is run these numbers through TLO and Accurint. And here's a stack of her text messages to read through." Colcord paused. "And last but not least, I brought pecan buns from the Ore House for sustenance." He whisked a box of pastries from under his desk and opened it, shoving it under her nose.

Cash eyed them: flaky, gooey, buttery. Colcord's café—the Ore House—was legendary when it came to pastries—all family recipes. "You're killing me, Colcord."

"A cheat day won't hurt."

"Damn you," she said, and picked one up. It was still warm. She bit into it with her eyes closed, savoring the sweet mix of nuts and sugar. It was a hell of a lot better than the kale and granola she had been living on these past couple of months.

They began their work, Cash sifting through the printed stacks of text messages and running the numbers through the TLO and Accurint databases on her clunky CBI-issued laptop. Colcord did the same using his iPad. There were 106 pages of texts, and they started with the recent ones, working backward. Most of the texts were between Margie Brooksfield and her husband, talking about domestic matters and the medical problems of one of their children. Cash learned more about Paul Brooksfield's ongoing back rash than she had ever wanted to know.

After a couple of minutes had passed, Colcord interrupted the silence. "I think I've found something." He slid over a number that he had circled in pen. The number repeated on the last seven days Margie had visited Willy Grooms before his death. The calls ranged from one hour to two hours long.

"That last call was around the same time the torture of Grooms started."

"You don't think she was involved, do you?" Cash asked.

"I don't think anything—yet. But the timing doesn't look good."

"So who does the number belong to?"

"A Javier Castillo, out of San Francisco. I think I found his LinkedIn page." Colcord turned his iPad to face Cash.

A handsome man with curly black hair, a trimmed beard, and ears that stuck out a little too far smiled from his LinkedIn profile picture. Underneath was a tagline that said, "Open to work."

Colcord slid the iPad back in front of him. "His last employment was as professor of exobiology at San Francisco State University."

"What's *exobiology*?" asked Cash.

"According to this, it's a branch of science that explores the possibility of life on other planets and a bunch of related subjects."

Cash's brows drew together in concentration as she typed something else into her computer. Her eyes skimmed the results. "Looks like Castillo was recently sacked from San Francisco State University."

"What for?"

Cash began reading from the screen, "'After an investigation, Javier Castillo, tenured professor of exobiology, has been terminated with cause by San Francisco State University. According to the provost, James Dalton, accusations of professional malfeasance against Castillo were levied after an investigation into his research revealed "negligence" and "scientific fraud." In a report made public by the university, Mr. Dalton wrote that investigators from the university looked into allegations that Castillo doctored videos of purported UAP sightings. In a statement to *San Francisco Unmasked*, Mr. Dalton said that as a result, San Francisco State University had retracted four scientific papers authored by Castillo and had called into question the validity of other papers of which Castillo was the principal author. Repeated attempts to reach Castillo were unsuccessful. However, in a letter to a journal that retracted one of his studies, Castillo denied the allegations, saying he had been the victim of fraud himself, of accepting as authentic videos that had been doctored by others. In a response to his termination, Castillo stated that the university had denied him due process and that he had been subjected to "a witch hunt to undermine exobiology as a multidisciplinary and respected scientific discipline."'"

"And look," said Colcord. "He runs a blog. I'm emailing you the link."

Cash clicked into it and started reading. "There's some weird shit in here," she said. "Listen to this: 'The question is not whether extraterrestrial intelligent life-forms have made contact with planet Earth. We know that to be a fact. The question is: What are they doing here? *What is their plan?* To assume they are benign and well meaning is, in my view, a dangerous and unwarranted assumption.'"

Colcord chuckled. "Sounds like a nutjob."

"Or eccentric. I mean, who knows, maybe there's something to it."

"Don't start with me on this alien stuff." Shaking his head, Colcord opened his desk drawer to fish out his cell phone.

Cash spied a flash of blue and purple ribbons. Her eyes widened. "Are those medals?"

Colcord shut the drawer with a thud. "It's nothing."

"That isn't nothing. What are they for?"

Colcord shifted uncomfortably, saying nothing.

"Let me see."

Colcord hesitated before opening the drawer and pulling out two loose medals, tossing them down on the pile of papers.

Cash immediately recognized one—a Purple Heart. The other one, a bronze cross with an eagle and scroll, she didn't recognize. "Holy shit, Colcord. You got a Purple Heart! You were wounded?"

"Yeah."

"What happened?"

Colcord looked out the window, strips of sunlight from the window shade playing across his face. "A fire."

Cash hesitated. She didn't want to pry, but this was a side of Colcord she had no idea existed. "And the other medal? What's that?"

"Distinguished Service Cross." Colcord—face unreadable—swept up the medals and shoved them back in the drawer among a pile of rubber bands, paper clips, and other junk.

Cash wondered why she hadn't heard about this in the news when Colcord had run for sheriff. That was the kind of thing most people running for office would trumpet.

"Don't wanna talk about it?" she asked.

"No. Let's get back to this guy Castillo. I think we should call him."

"When?"

"Now."

"Hell, why not?"

Colcord dialed the number and put the phone on speaker and to record, and set it in the center of the table.

A man answered after a couple of rings. He had a light, educated voice: different from the picture Cash had painted in her head.

"Javi Castillo. How may I be of service?"

"Mr. Castillo—this is Sheriff James Colcord of Eagle County, Colorado, and Agent Cash, Colorado Bureau of Investigation. We're investigating a murder, and I'd like to ask you a few questions."

After a pause, "Murder of whom?"

"Willy Grooms."

"*What?* Willy Grooms is dead?" There was a pause, and then he began to speak in a stream of breathless, broken sentences. "Oh my God—I can't believe this. Who killed him? Do you have any leads? Is anyone in custody yet? How?"

"He was killed in his cabin up in the Flat Tops Wilderness. I'll start with asking a general question: Is there anything you can tell us that might assist with the investigation?"

They could hear Castillo breathing hard on the line.

"How do I know you're who you say you are?" He spoke in a hoarse, frightened whisper. Suddenly, a *click*, and the line went dead.

Cash shot Colcord a glance, eyebrows raised. "That went well," she said.

"Absolute loony. He and Grooms were birds of a feather, I bet—two conspiracy theorists."

"He sounded terrified. Might be worth pulling him in for questioning."

"From California? Good luck getting the warrant."

"One of us could fly out there to interview him. I mean, the last phone calls Grooms made were to him—and they were long."

"Yeah, yakking about all the UFOs they've seen." Colcord rolled his pointer finger in a circular gesture near his temple.

"Still . . ." Cash trailed off. "It's a valid lead." She didn't have to believe in UFOs to see the value in interviewing a possible witness. Colcord could sometimes be unimaginative.

Colcord drummed large fingers on the table and scowled. "I agree we need to talk to the guy. But if you want my two cents, I bet Castillo's a red herring. We need to stay focused. We've got a whole bunch of local leads to follow up with. The media is all over us as it is, and if they catch wind we're talking to a UFO crackpot, they might paint us to look like idiots. Did you see that piece in the *Eagle County News*? Front page and everything. Grooms believing he could fly and talking to animals—all sorts of nonsense. It's not a good look for our investigation."

Cash had seen it. She had expected media coverage, but it was getting a little out of hand for it being so early in the case. Colcord was right, this could turn into a shitstorm. Another Erebus. Every reason to follow the leads they had. However . . . "We need to interview him now, Colcord. The last five phone calls Grooms made on Margie's satellite phone were to him."

"All I'm saying is, we've got a ton of local leads to follow up on before chasing down someone in San Francisco."

"It's my call. I'm going."

Colcord leaned back in his chair and laced his fingers behind his head. "Okay then. But bring me back a tinfoil hat or two—will ya?" He shot her a grin.

Cash, annoyed, stood up and began to clear the table of crumpled serviettes and coffee cups and shove them into the empty pastry box. She rammed the box into the garbage in the corner, grabbed her coat from the back of the chair, and left.

14

By the time Cash reached the inner sanctum of the Battery Club in San Francisco, she was irked and, truth be told, intimidated. This was exactly the kind of exclusive club whose pretentious existence irritated her, and as soon as she was inside, she realized she had dressed wrongly, looking frumpy and out of place in her muddy sneakers, black jeans, and a collared shirt she had spilled a spot of coffee on earlier in the day. The excessively neutral looks she got from the doorkeepers—as if they were struggling to hide their disdain—further annoyed her.

She had wanted to meet in a coffee shop, but Castillo had insisted on meeting her at "his club." He explained it was "for security purposes," because the club had strict no-photo and no-video policies in place, and there was a record of everyone who was signed in. As if a UFO crankologist had to worry about being overheard spilling world-shattering secrets.

A uniformed club attendant directed her to the billiards room. The room was a busy space with two beige-colored pool tables, unconventional art, and loud wallpaper. Crimson benches that appeared as if they were made from fluffy tiramisu biscuits rimmed the space and made up a sitting area. There was only one person there, a man shooting pool by himself: Castillo. She had seen pictures of him online, and now she paused in the doorway to take his measure in person. He was a lanky man, mid-thirties, trimmed beard, a black turtleneck, skinny pants, and pointed black shoes. The one imperfect note was his radar ears.

And his pool game. Cash could see he was bad at it—really bad. She could've beaten him with one hand tied behind her back. But his movements were smooth and full of confidence, even if he was missing every single shot he tried to make. He finally looked up from the shot he was lining up—she could see he was going to hit it wrong—and gave her a big smile, his immaculate white teeth gleaming in the light. Putting down the cue, he strode over, hand extended.

"Javi Castillo," he said. "So good to meet you, Agent Cash."

Cash wasn't used to this warm a greeting from an interviewee, especially one who had hung up on her, and it threw her off-balance. "Thank you, Mr. Castillo. We appreciate your cooperation," she said, more formally than she intended.

"Please call me Javi," he said.

She didn't reciprocate the offer, and there was a brief silence.

"Shall we sit?" She gestured toward the seating area.

"I have a better spot, one that's a little more . . . secure." Javi beckoned Cash to follow, and limped up some stairs to a higher floor. Cash followed, a little in awe at how big the club was. Only a handful of people milled about, and most of them appeared to work there.

"Doesn't usually get busy during the day," Castillo said, "but there's a nice out-of-the-way room where we can talk. Here's the Musto Bar." He gestured grandly around them as they entered yet another extravagant room. "Everything you see was designed by Ken Fulk."

She didn't know who Ken Fulk was and couldn't care less. Passing to the back of the bar, they entered a lounge area with a pink piano sitting in the corner. The walls were painted swaths of dark forest green and black. A rather handsome guy who looked barely in his thirties, wearing a funky shirt with martini glasses and sporting a man-bun, greeted Castillo by name, nodding at him over a glass he was polishing.

"Hey, Jared, my man," Castillo said, and grinned in response.

They approached a bookcase in the far wall. Castillo rubbed the head of the bust of Woodrow Wilson set into the bookcase, and a panel swung inward to reveal a hidden room with two couches and musical instruments affixed to the walls.

"The Green Room," Castillo explained. "Fun, right? Nobody comes in here during the day. I like to hold meetings in here. It's quiet."

Cash settled into one of the couches and placed her cell on the little table between them. "Mind if I record?"

"As long as it's kept confidential."

"We keep a tight lid on all evidence and interviews," said Cash.

"Very well, you may record, but you might get scolded by the staff if they notice." He crossed his legs, in so doing revealing that he had a prosthetic lower leg, gleaming in titanium and steel. She quickly covered up her surprise.

"So," he continued, "I was terribly shocked to hear about Willy Grooms. What a sweet old man. What can you tell me about the murder?"

"He was found in his cabin in the Flat Tops five days ago. I'm afraid I can't share most of the details, as they're still confidential, but it appears . . ." She hesitated, wondering how much she should share with him. "He may have been tortured." She looked closely for the reaction.

Castillo appeared confounded. "Tortured? By whom?"

"That's what we're trying to find out, Mr. Castillo."

"How?"

"That's confidential, for now."

Castillo ran fingers through his hair in distress.

She could see that Castillo made an effort to pull himself together. If this was an act, Cash thought, it was a damned good one.

He crossed and uncrossed his legs several times and then said, "Tortured? Hell, I need a drink. And you?"

"I could use a cup of coffee. Instant coffee, if they have it. Cream and sugar."

Castillo crossed the room and pushed a button in the wall to open the panel, and disappeared for thirty seconds to speak to the bartender. Cash shifted on the uncomfortably soft couch as she waited, and busied herself, studying the chandelier made out of lollipops that hung from the ceiling. Curious decoration for a social club, she thought. Castillo quickly reappeared, explaining he had ordered himself a vodka martini and her a coffee.

Cash went through the preliminaries and then asked, "What was your relationship to Mr. Grooms?"

"If you've done any background research on me, you'll know that I have a PhD in exobiology, from UC Berkeley, and I am one of the world's foremost researchers on UAPs. I founded an organization that has amassed an encyclopedia of UAP activity—video, witness reports, you name it—that is second to none."

"UAPs?" Cash pretended not to know the acronym, despite her prior research.

"Unidentified anomalous phenomena. Formerly known as UFOs. As you know, there's a great deal of controversy on the subject—"

"How did you meet Grooms?" Cash tried to keep the conversation focused.

"I never did actually meet him. I heard rumors that this old guy in the mountains claimed to have seen a UAP crash. I spoke to him on the phone several times, and he sounded legitimate."

"The reason for my visit to you, Mr. Castillo, is that the last calls Mr. Grooms made from a satellite phone were to you. Can you tell me what those calls were about?"

"I certainly can. Again, this is confidential?"

"You have my assurance." Of course, she could assure no such thing if it became evidence necessary for trial, but no point in discouraging a witness unnecessarily.

Cash paused as the waiter arrived with her coffee and Castillo's vodka martini. Castillo made sure the panel was closed again before continuing.

"Mr. Grooms is—was—a very important witness. A rare witness to UAP activity."

"Meaning?"

"Like I said, he claimed to have witnessed a UAP crash. In the wilderness where he lived. As the world's foremost UAP researcher, I naturally wanted to know more about it. That is the reason for our many phone calls. I was trying to organize an expedition into the Flat Tops—which Mr. Grooms said he would lead to the site of the crash."

"Okay," said Cash. Her heart was sinking—were the phone calls really only about UFOs? "And you're aware that Mr. Grooms was diagnosed with schizophrenia?"

At this, Castillo leaned back. "I'm well aware of that. Schizophrenics are just as capable of witnessing a UAP crash as anyone else."

"But much better at seeing things that aren't there." Cash sipped her coffee—not Bustelo but not bad. This club was perhaps growing on her.

"That's always a possibility. Agent Cash, I am a skeptic. Don't mistake me for one of those UAP nutjobs. I spoke many times to Mr. Grooms. I am absolutely convinced he witnessed the real thing."

"And how do you know that?"

"Details. Nuances. My previous in-depth research. Trust me, I can smell a phony UAP story a mile away. What Mr. Grooms witnessed lines up with so much of my research—things he couldn't possibly know. He saw the real thing—I promise you."

Cash nodded. "Okay. What else did you discuss in those calls?"

"He liked to talk about his gold mining and his sculptures, that sort of thing. Oh, and the monster in a lake. There's your schizophrenia at work. I've no interest in those things—only the UAP crash."

"So you never met Mr. Grooms in person?"

"No. I was hoping to." Castillo shook his head again, looking down at his lap. "I can't believe he's gone. What a shock."

"Did Grooms have any enemies that you know of? Someone who might wish him harm?"

At this, Castillo fell silent.

Cash waited as the silence stretched on. Finally, she spoke. "If you know anything relevant to the homicide, now would be the time to tell me."

"May I ask you a question?"

"Go ahead."

"Was the cabin searched by the killer?"

"It was."

"Carefully and thoroughly." He said it more as a statement than a question, seemingly deep in thought.

"Yes."

"Ah. Well, that confirms my initial suspicions."

"Which are?"

"Well, I hesitate to share with you my thoughts in this area."

"Why?"

"Because you won't believe it."

"Try me."

Castillo took a deep breath. "Okay. Here's what Grooms told me. He saw the UAP crash—"

"When was this?"

"Ten years ago, plus or minus. He was a little vague."

Cash nodded.

"He immediately went up to the site of the crash . . . and found something."

"What did he find?"

"An alien artifact. And he took it. Later, he said, the aliens cleaned up the crash site so you'd never know anything had happened there." Another silence.

"So . . ." Cash said slowly, stopping an exasperated breath. "An alien artifact. See any proof of this artifact?"

Castillo shifted uncomfortably, seeming to note Cash's cynicism. "No."

"What was it?"

"He wouldn't say."

"Did Grooms often make things up, or claim something existed when it didn't?"

Castillo leaned back, irritation playing across his face. "Well . . . I'm not going to lie to you. Yes, he did. But this felt different. Usually, his delusions were scattered and nonsensical. When he spoke about this, it was a coherent story, and the details fit with other UAP observations I've seen throughout the years."

Cash rubbed at her temples with pointer fingers. Jesus, this was all too much bullshit to sort through. "So . . . if Grooms had the alien artifact, is it possible that others might have wanted to get their hands on it—and kill him for it?"

"That's a possibility. But I think it's a lot more likely that the aliens themselves would want it back and come after him." Again, Castillo hesitated and then said, in a rush, "I think that's exactly what happened."

Cash stared at Castillo. She could already hear Colcord's cynical laugh when he heard the outcome of her trip. "Killed by aliens," she said, deadpan.

"I knew you wouldn't believe it."

"And this was what you talked about on those phone calls? Grooms told you all this—about seeing the crash, finding the artifact, and so forth?"

"Yes."

"And nothing else? No discussion of money, disputes, personal conflicts, anything of that sort?"

"Only chitchat about searching the mines for gold, finding jasper, making sculptures. His hobbies, basically."

"No discussion of who else might have contacted him about wanting that artifact?"

"No."

"Did you ever discuss his friend Margie Brooksfield?"

"He mentioned her from time to time. Nice lady. Brought him food. She arranged to have him baptized. I spoke to her once on the phone when she was visiting Willy."

"What for?"

"Ah, no reason. Wanted to meet one of Willy's friends, I suppose."

"How did he feel about being baptized?"

"He said he'd recently had a strange religious experience and he figured it was worth hedging his bets."

"What kind of religious experience?"

Castillo shrugged. "No idea. Nothing that made sense, I'm sure. As you know, the guy was schizo."

"Anything about how Brooksfield handled his finances, managed his money?"

"Nothing about that."

"Did you know she handled his finances?"

"I . . . didn't know that."

"No idea who might have killed him—besides aliens? I know it's not as exciting, but we have solid evidence that humans were responsible." She wasn't going to tell him about the embalming and the Spanish boot. The investigation was keeping that information strictly confidential for the time being.

He looked at her steadily. "I don't know about your evidence. As far as I know, he was a harmless old coot who didn't have an enemy in the world—at least, a human one."

Cash shook her head, reached over, turned off her cell phone recorder, shut her notebook, and stood up. And Castillo looked so normal—proof that you never could tell with these conspiracy theorists. "Thank you, Mr. Castillo, I appreciate you meeting with me and sharing your thoughts." She hesitated and took out her card, giving it to him, but not without misgivings. "If you have any further thoughts on *humans* who might have wished him harm, will you please let me know?"

15

Cash had met Colcord on one end of Main Street in Burns that morning, with the idea of making a quick canvass through the tiny town to see if anyone knew Grooms or remembered any strangers passing through nine days earlier. A June rain shower hit just as they arrived, busting out a flurry of raincoats and bobbing umbrellas. The two of them had wound their way down the street, making pit stops to interview a florist, a cheese shop owner, and a wine bar proprietor. All had said pretty much the same thing: They knew or had heard of Grooms, thought he was harmless and mentally ill, and had no idea why someone would want him killed. While there had been the usual backpackers and hikers stopping or passing through—many fewer since the Neander disaster— nobody had seen anything out of the ordinary in terms of equipment or demeanor. No recollection of four backpackers in camo.

Cash and Colcord now stood, shivering and dejected, in front of their last stop: the gas station at the end of Main Street.

Cash eyed the shabby station, which looked empty. "Should we call it a day?" She flicked away a lock of brown hair stuck to her cheek from the rain. She was wet, cold, and feeling especially irritable.

"But, Cash," Colcord said in a teasing voice, "we haven't got a lead yet on the intergalactic murderers."

"You shut your face," Cash said. "You know I had to check those phone calls out."

A drop of water dripped from the tip of Cash's nose, and she wiped it away with her sleeve.

"You know what the problem is?" he asked.

"What?"

"You left your tinfoil hat back in the office."

"Fuck off," Cash responded, but the side of her mouth twitched upward into an involuntary smile. Colcord had been razzing her ever since hearing about her interview with Castillo. "Let's get this over with."

They stepped inside. Cash unzipped her raincoat and shook it on the straw entrance mat that said *Live, Laugh, Leave.* A woman with bleached-blond hair and black roots was seated behind the cash register. Her thumbs moved across her phone with lightning speed to the sound of musical pings and beeps—playing some game, Cash supposed.

"Good afternoon," Cash said. "Sorry to interrupt."

"What do you want?" the woman said in a smoke-cured voice, without looking up from her phone.

"Do you have a moment for a few questions?"

The woman sighed heavily and put down her phone. She stared at Cash with open hostility, but her demeanor changed completely when her eyes fell on Colcord in his uniform.

"Well, good afternoon, Sheriff," she said, her voice higher-pitched now and more feminine.

"Afternoon, miss."

The lady smiled coquettishly at the last word. She shifted herself forward, bringing her arms together in front of her so that her breasts were almost falling out of her low-cut blouse. "What can I do for you?"

"We're investigating the murder of Willy Grooms."

Now the woman was really interested. "Of course. Anything I can do to help. Just terrible, what happened to that old man up in the mountains, right? My name is Sassy. Short for Sassafras. Have you found who did it?"

"We're still investigating. May I have your last name?"

"Newton." The woman's eyes glittered. "I heard the killers dressed him up as an angel. Is that true?"

"I'm afraid we can't talk about the details."

Cash placed her phone on the counter to record.

"How long you been in Burns?" she asked Colcord, her eyelashes fluttering.

"A couple of days," Colcord said briskly. "Now, ah, Ms. Newton—did you know Mr. Grooms?"

"I only heard of him, never met him. I'm very busy these days. I'm an entrepreneur, you see." Sassy leaned forward even farther in her chair toward Colcord, her breasts clinging to fabric for dear life.

Cash tried to keep her eyes on Sassy's face.

"I only work here part-time," she went on, making a disparaging gesture at the surroundings. "I run my own business. Maquillage."

Cash did not know what that was and was disinclined to ask. "Were you working here Wednesday or Thursday, June 4 or 5?" she asked.

The woman thought for a moment. "Yes, I was. Both days."

"Did you happen to see four or more people, wearing camo, passing through town around that date? Perhaps with an unusual amount of equipment?"

Sassy cocked her head to one side to think. "I haven't seen anyone new at all, except for you two, of course. What kinda equipment?"

"Something possibly in backpacks, duffel bags, boxes, carrying cases," Colcord replied.

"Nothing like that. I'm sorry, Sheriff. I wish I could help you." Her voice deepened as she leaned toward Colcord. "Say, it's quitting time for me—you ever been to the Wet Whistle? They serve a killer margarita."

Cash glanced over at Colcord with an amused look. She was gratified to see Colcord shifting uncomfortably and blushing furiously. He spoke faster. "Nothing out of the norm, then, at all this past week or so?"

"Well . . . there was one thing. I was taking an important business call out back. I saw something in the mountains."

"Something in the mountains?"

"Lights up by Dome Peak. Probably someone's campfire."

"How long were the lights visible?"

"A while. Just some flickering. Off and on."

"When was this exactly?"

"Right when my shift was over—ten o'clock."

"And the date?"

She twisted her lips to one side in thought. "Maybe around that time you mentioned, first week in June. Don't remember exactly."

"Would you be willing to check your cell phone history and give us an exact time?"

"Sure thing." She fiddled with her phone. "Okay, it was June 5, at ten thirty."

"That's helpful. Anything else?"

"Not that I recollect."

"Okay, thanks for your help. Have a good evening." He turned as Cash grabbed her phone and they walked toward the door.

"Oh, Sheriff?" Sassy called out.

Colcord paused in the doorway, not turning around.

"I'll be at the Wet Whistle at eight—just sayin'."

"Thank you," said Colcord, hastening his pace.

Out on the wet street, walking back toward their vehicle, Cash imitated Sassy in an undertone, "Oh, She*rrrifff!*"

"Please."

"But She*rrrifff,* you aren't going to *wet* your *whistle* with me at the Whistle?"

"Can it, Cash."

She gave a low laugh. "Lights up by Dome Peak? What do you think?"

"That's nowhere near Willy's cabin," Colcord said grumpily.

"Maybe we should get a list of people who applied for wilderness camping permits up there during that time period," Cash said.

"I don't think the killers would have been stupid enough to get permits."

"No shit. But the permit holders might have seen something."

Colcord grunted. "Okay, not a bad idea." He turned suddenly—out of nowhere, the fuzzy head of a microphone was thrust into their faces. A contralto voice rang out. "Our viewers want to know: Are the Neanders back and killing again?"

They both halted as the person who had just ambushed them—a reporter—blocked their way forward.

Behind the reporter, a man crab-walked with a television camera plastered with *KBFR,* the logo of a local television station, on his shoulder.

Shit, thought Cash, *we're on camera.*

"Do you mind?" Colcord asked.

"Robin Twen, KBFR Investigative Beat. Can we have a moment of your time?"

The press had been instrumental in screwing up the Erebus investigation, and Cash was none too keen on repeating the experience here in Burns. At any hint of the Neanders, they seemed to froth at their collective mouths. At the same time, it was never a good idea to snub the press, and people did have a right to know.

Cash regarded Twen. The reporter was in their mid-twenties, wearing black dress pants, suspenders, and a pastel-blue bow tie. She—or he, Cash wasn't sure—was tall and skinny, wearing tinted lip gloss and sporting an inky pixie cut that stuck out every which way in spikes.

Cash coolly stepped forward to the mic. "The Neander case has been taken over by the FBI," she said. "We're no longer heading that investigation."

"You must be Frankie Cash," said the reporter, "of the Colorado Bureau of Investigation. I'm Robin Twen. They/them. Pleased to meet you."

"I'm sorry?"

"My pronouns."

"Oh . . . right, of course." Cash shifted. "I use *she* and *her*. Sheriff Colcord here is *he* and *him*."

She glanced at the sheriff, who looked bewildered. Cash had to stop herself from rolling her eyes at his confusion. The old cowpoke had been living in Colorado long enough to know about this pronoun stuff—he needed to get it together.

Twen continued, "I understand the murder of Willy Grooms had certain bizarre ritualistic aspects to it. Could you elaborate?"

Cash needed to cut this interview short. "Unfortunately, there isn't any information we can disclose at this point."

"The folks in Burns and the surrounding area are looking for reassurance," said Twen. "What can you tell us about the state of the investigation? Are there any suspects? Are people *safe*?"

Colcord interjected quickly, Twen swinging the mic over to him, "Although there are no suspects at this time, we're following up a number of leads and making good progress. We believe this to be an isolated incident and that there's no danger to the general public."

Twen swung the mic back to Cash. "I understand, Agent Cash, that CBI took charge of the investigation and that you're pursuing a possible UFO angle?"

Jesus Christ, Cash thought, *how does Twen know that?* "CBI is in charge," she said, "but there's absolutely no 'UFO angle.'"

"It is also my understanding that you interviewed Father Timothy Moore, the local priest at Saint Mary's. How do you respond to his allegation that you were aggressive in your questioning and disparaged his Catholic faith?"

Cash took a step backward, feeling really ambushed now. "I did no such thing. He was being uncooperative."

"He also claims you called him an obscenity that I cannot repeat on air. What do you have to say to these allegations?"

Cash's mouth dropped open, and all she could do was stammer.

Colcord hastily stepped in front, putting himself between her, and the cameraman and Twen. "I can assure you, it was a routine and respectful questioning according to long-established procedures. Naturally, we're sorry Father Moore feels there was a misunderstanding, but nothing improper occurred."

"Are you sure, Sheriff? According to Father Moore, Agent Cash specifically said—"

"I'm so sorry," Colcord interrupted, "but we've got urgent matters to attend to. I can assure you that the situation with Father Moore was a misunderstanding, nothing more."

He ushered Cash away and toward his patrol vehicle. Twen didn't follow.

"What the hell, Cash?" he said as he slid into the driver's seat and slammed the door. "Calling him *uncooperative* on camera? Not to mention your stammering—you look all sorts of guilty."

Cash thumped down in the passenger seat, breathing hard. "Just lay off a second and let me think, all right? Damn it to hell." She banged the side of the car door with a fist in frustration.

"She seems to know a whole lot more than—"

"*They*, Colcord. Don't you know about pronouns yet?"

"For chrissake. All right. *They* are no dumb reporter, and they already know a whole lot more about the investigation than they should. And you, Cash—*you* botched that question."

"I was ambushed," Cash said weakly.

"This is gonna be on the evening news," Colcord said, rubbing his temples. "We need to be prepared for fallout."

16

"Mr. Drewe is here," said the assistant, peeking into Cash's office at CBI.

"Give me a minute," Cash said. An assistant in her office had gone through the tedious process of contacting all the hikers who had pulled wilderness permits for the Flat Tops. There weren't many—ever since the Neander business the Flat Tops had been mostly deserted. The assistant had passed on to her a few names of possible interest, and she had called them this morning. There had only been one that she was interested in talking to.

He was now waiting outside her office, a hiker named Robert Drewe, and he seemed to have solid and potentially important information to give her related to the case.

She hit the intercom. "Ready for Mr. Drewe," she said.

The hiker came in, looking nervous. Cash invited him to sit. Drewe had pulled a permit to backpack into Edge Lake and camp for four days—around the area known as Meachem. He had told the initial CBI interviewer that he had seen lights in the same approximate location and time as the woman, Sassafras Newton, from the gas station.

Fortunately, Drewe was from Denver, and she'd persuaded him to come in for an interview. Here he was, adjusting and readjusting himself in the chair, sweat breaking on his brow, looking so nervous that you might think he was guilty of something. But Cash figured he was probably just one of those people uncomfortable with law enforcement, or maybe just awkward. She could respect that.

"Mr. Drewe, thanks for coming in," she said. "Can we get you anything? Coffee? Water?"

"No thanks."

He was small and nearly bald, despite his age, which couldn't be more than twenty-five. What little hair he had hung down his back in a long, limp ponytail. He had a wispy bit of blond hair underneath his lower lip—what did you call that?—a soul patch. A sharp runny nose, skinny physique, and a tense air rounded out the picture of a most uncomfortable young man.

"Mind if I record?" she asked.

"Do you have to?"

"I don't have to, but it would make my job a lot easier."

"All right."

She laid her cell phone down and turned it on and went through the usual preliminaries of name, date, time, and permission.

"Mr. Drewe, could you please tell me in your own words the details of your trip into the Flat Tops?"

He began speaking very fast. "I hiked in on June 5. I had a four-day permit to camp at Edge Lake, so I was there from June 5 to 9."

"Where did you hike in from?"

"The trailhead at Sweetwater Road."

"How long a hike is it?"

"It's twenty-three miles into Edge Lake."

"Wow—you hiked twenty-three miles in a day?"

"Well, yeah. I got an early start."

This guy was more adventurous than he looked. "Did you see anybody on the trail?"

"Not really. There's almost nobody in the Flat Tops these days, on account of the Neanders."

"So you weren't concerned about the Neanders?"

"Not at all. In fact, it's a good thing—emptied out the place, turned it back into a true wilderness."

"Okay. So you arrived at Edge Lake. What time?"

"Let's see." He thought for a moment. "I got there around sunset—I guess that would be around eight thirty. I never carry a watch."

"And then?"

"Set up camp, made dinner, ate, then settled by the fire reading a book. When it was completely dark, I saw lights on the slopes of Dome Peak—that's a small mountain at the far eastern end of Flat Top."

"What time was that?"

"I'm not sure, but it was maybe an hour or two after sunset, so I guess around ten or ten thirty."

"What kind of lights?"

"Bright lights. Not flashlights. Way too bright. It seemed weird to me. I mean, nobody's in the Flat Tops these days. And up there on those slopes, there's no place to camp. And the lights were moving around."

"How many?"

"Maybe four or five?"

"For how long?"

"It's hard to say. Two hours?"

Cash now reached down and pulled out a USGS topographical map, 1:24,000 scale, which she unrolled and placed in front of Drewe on the table, weighing down the corners. "Can you mark where you were camped and where you saw the lights?"

Drewe bent over the maps and quickly made a mark at the shores of Edge Lake. Then, after some thought, he drew a large circle on the western slope of Dome Peak. "They were moving around inside that circle, more or less."

"That's half a mile in diameter."

"It was night and I couldn't really see the outline of the mountain. And they were moving a lot."

"In what way?"

"They were moving back and forth. Lights blinking on and off, on account of all the trees, I guess."

Cash felt a tingle of excitement. "And you're sure of the date? June 5?"

"I'm sure because it was my first night at the lake."

"And they went from ten to when, around midnight?"

"I'm just guessing, but yes, I'd say around midnight."

"Did you see the lights any night after that?"

"No. And I looked. It was kind of freaky."

Cash thought for a moment. "Did the lights ever cease moving and, say, come together in one spot?"

At this, Drewe's face brightened. "Yes, now that you mention it, they did. At one point, they sort of bunched up before they spread out again."

"And then around midnight, what happened?"

"They came together again, and then they all blinked off."

"You seem to have been watching rather closely," said Cash. This guy was a good witness.

"There wasn't much else to do. I'd stopped reading because I wanted to save my batteries. It seemed pretty strange to me, to be up on that mountainside at night walking around."

"You sure you didn't see anyone in your four days up there? Anyone at the lake or coming back on the trail?"

He cocked his head to the side. "Like I said, nobody's out there on account of the Neanders."

Cash collected the map and rolled it up. "Anything else you think we should know?"

He shook his head, hesitated. "Can I ask a question?"

"Of course."

"Did . . . the Neanders do it?"

"You mean, murder Willy Grooms?" She shook her head. "No. He was killed by regular old *Homo sapiens*."

"Really?" Drewe, to her surprise, looked disappointed. "You think they're still in the Flat Tops, or do you think they went north like everyone says?"

"The FBI's taken over the investigation," she said, "so I'm not up on the latest."

"I hope," he said, almost to himself, "that they never catch them."

Cash was startled. "And why do you say that?"

At this Drewe flushed. "There's something . . . I don't know, *thrilling* in having real live Neanderthals living in the Colorado Rockies. I mean, we drove them to extinction once, but now we've brought them back to life. It's sort of like . . . *atonement*."

Cash said nothing—but she wondered how many others thought that way.

17

It had been years since Brother Armagh had been to the American West Coast. During his prison ministry in Chicago, he had been to San Francisco several times, and he was shocked by the change that seemed to have taken place since his last visit. Back then, the city was lively, vibrant, full of bustle, with people on the streets, buskers playing music, restaurants overflowing, pop-up art markets in vacant lots. Today, there were some big, new, shiny buildings to be sure, but they seemed empty and forlorn. The city had a postapocalyptic air to it, as if most of the population had disappeared in some disaster—all except the poor and forsaken homeless, who had started spreading from the Tenderloin into other neighborhoods.

He called the driver the Vatican had set up for him—a silent mouse of a man—and slipped into the back of the car to the address he had for Javier Castillo. He had contemplated at length what would be the best way to approach the man—whether to call him ahead of time or just show up. The Vatican had provided him a file on Castillo, which contained details about the man's life, including his cell phone number and email address. In the end, Armagh had opted to show up unannounced. Calling ahead would allow Castillo to prepare a response or, worse, vanish. He was a criminal, after all. Better to surprise and corner him unprepared.

As he stood below the building, he felt a twinge of misgiving. The file said Castillo was well-off—family money, supposedly—but this was more than just money. The man lived in a beautiful glass low-rise condo in the Marina District, with unobstructed views of the Golden Gate Bridge and the boats in the bay. Armagh could only imagine how much it cost—millions, to be sure. This Javier Castillo was no common thief or dysfunctional obsessive. A man with this kind of lifestyle had risked a great deal to steal that relic, and he must have had an important reason to do so. But what could that reason be? Either way, it was highly unlikely Castillo would give the relic back to him without pressure being brought to bear, and as he looked up at the gorgeous low-rise, Armagh felt the answer was to come down on Castillo like a ton of bricks and threaten him with criminal prosecution. A fellow like this had so much to lose. Appealing to his better nature would be useless. Putting the *literal* fear of God in him was the way to go.

Brother Armagh now approached the building at a brisk walk, and as he neared the door, it was whisked open by a doorman in a blue uniform with red piping, who greeted him with fake geniality. Armagh entered a lobby of chrome and marble. There, at the far end, a second uniformed gentleman sat behind a counter.

The person glanced up from his phone, an expression of surprise on his face as he saw that Armagh was a monk.

"Good afternoon, Father," he said.

"Good afternoon, sir," said Armagh. "And a lovely afternoon it 'tis." He laid the Irish accent on thick—that always seemed to impress Americans.

"Yes, Father, a beautiful day. How can I help you?"

"I am here to visit Mr. Javier Castillo," said Armagh. "In apartment 5C."

"I'm sorry," said the man. "But Mr. Castillo is out of town. Did you have an appointment?"

"No, I'm just an old friend," Armagh lied, feeling guilty but not overly so. It was exciting, playing the role of an investigator. "I found myself unexpectedly in town and thought I'd drop in. Where has he gone, if I may ask, and when is he expected back?"

At this, the man looked uneasy. "I'm sorry, Father, but we have strict rules about giving out any information about our tenants."

Armagh brought forth a smile. "Not even to his old friend and priest?"

"I'm sorry, it's the rules."

Armagh could see that the man was not going to be shaken. "Ah well, I'll have to catch up with him another time."

As he turned to leave, the man said, "I can take your name and let him know you stopped by when he returns."

Giving out his name would not be a good idea. "Not necessary, sir. I'll just give him a call later."

He crossed the lobby, and the man in the uniform opened the door. He found himself on the sidewalk in front of the building, wondering what to do now. Castillo had been fired from his position at the university, so he would get no help there. He ran some sort of UFO organization, but it was rather secretive and the Vatican had not been able to dig up any contacts there. Castillo belonged to a fancy club, but Armagh suspected he'd run into the same brick wall of privacy.

He decided to stroll around the block and get himself a cup of coffee while he pondered the problem. As he turned the corner of North Point and Divisadero, he saw, God bless, an elegant little espresso shop. He strolled to it and went inside. The place was empty, except for a brawny man with a big beard and lumberjack shirt behind the bar, who looked like he should have been on the American frontier chopping wood instead of manning a fancy espresso machine.

"Good afternoon to you, sir," Armagh said cheerfully, again laying on the Irish brogue.

"Afternoon. What can I get you?" the man asked.

"A triple shot of espresso, if you don't mind, *ristretto e forte*."

"Coming right up."

Armagh pretended to peruse the pastries in a case. "I wonder, sir," he said, "if you know a dear old friend of mine who lives around the corner, by the name of Javier Castillo?"

"Javi? Sure. He comes here every morning." There was a sound like the blasting of air from the espresso machine and a rumbling vibration that shook the entire shop, and then a cup of espresso with a lovely thick head of crema was set down in front of him. Just as Brother Armagh liked it.

"But not this morning," said Armagh, "as I understand he's away."

"Yeah. He said he'd be gone a week."

Armagh leaned forward earnestly, gripping the edge of the counter.

"It is of utmost importance that I get in touch with him. You see, a member of our congregation—his godmother—is extremely ill. So ill that, frankly, I'm not sure she'll last the week. They had a falling-out, years ago, but I know he would want to be there . . . for her passing."

The man stroked his beard. "Well, I'm not sure *exactly* where he went off to. He used a sort of vulgar expression that I wouldn't want to repeat to a man of the cloth."

"Come now. A priest like me has heard everything and more. What was the expression?"

"He said he was heading out to Kabumfuck, Colorado—sorry, Father, but you asked. . . ."

"Colorado, is it? Did he say *why* he went there?"

"He said something about helping the police with a murder investigation. Some guy in the mountains."

Now Armagh was taken aback. "A murder investigation! Good heavens."

"I know, kinda crazy."

Armagh downed the heel of the espresso. "Thank you," he said, and hurried out. He paused at the corner, pulled out his cell, and looked up "murder, mountain, Colorado." At the top of the results was a high-profile case in a town called Burns. Staring at the dot on the map, he thought, *Kabumfuck, indeed,* and wondered how he was going to get there and track down his quarry.

18

Cash felt elated. They had found a promising lead and none too soon. It had been Colcord's idea to request a search warrant for Margie's actual cell phone—not just the satellite phone—and to Cash's surprise, they had gotten one. Perhaps Judge Greenberg had been in a good mood that day.

And there they hit on something striking: a string of confirmation texts of wire transfers into Margie's bank account from an account ending in 4598—in Willy Grooms's name. It didn't look good—to Cash, it smelled of fraud or embezzlement. Of course, it wasn't good to jump to conclusions, but with that evidence in hand, they'd been able to get a further warrant to access Brooksfield's bank accounts.

Now, on a gorgeous June day, the air smelling of honeysuckle, Cash and Colcord found themselves outside a squat redbrick building covered in ivy, with a sign spelling out MOUNTAINVIEW BANK. Mountainview Bank was the only bank in Burns, a local business without other branches.

Cash clutched the warrant that would give them access to Margaret Brooksfield's financial records and steeled herself before going inside. That damn reporter, Twen, had been on the evening news talking about the Grooms murder, clearly with information from an inside source, and gave the killer a sensational name: the Shrouder. And then the priest, Father Moore, appeared, piously recounting to Twen the story of how Cash had insulted the church and asked him to "tattle" on his parishioners. Did she really intend, he said, for him to break the seal of the confessional? And the policewoman had called him a vulgar word, which he delicately declined to state. Cash had been waiting for a shoe to drop from her boss, Holmes. There'd been only silence. She didn't know if that was good or bad.

They entered the bank. Cash approached a pretty teller behind an old-fashioned mahogany counter along the far wall. The redhead dropped a stack of twenties into a bill counter, waited for it to run, and then typed something into her computer before addressing them with a grand smile plastered on her face. Perfectly coiffed waves of hair bounced around her face as she spoke.

"Good morning. Welcome to Mountainview Bank—where your banking dreams come true! How can I be your banking superhero to-day?"

"Good morning"—Cash tried not to cringe at the corny greeting as she read the girl's name tag—"Stacy. We're here with a warrant to collect financial records relating to a client of yours." She laid the warrant out on the counter.

Stacy did not bother to look at the warrant. Instead, she began to recite from rote memory, the smile still plastered on her face. "Unfortunately, it's Mountainview Bank's policy, in accordance with federal law, to maintain the confidentiality of a customer's financial information. Please submit a request for records, in writing, through our website. Thank you, and have a nice day!"

"In accordance with federal law," said Cash evenly, "the bank must respond to this warrant now. Could we please speak to someone in charge?"

Stacy paused, looking confused, as if she hadn't expected resistance. "I'll be right back." She disappeared into a back room. After a couple of minutes, she returned, trailed by a squat woman with shoulder-length brown hair and a lumpy nose like cottage cheese rolled into a ball.

"Good morning, Sheriff Colcord and Agent Cash," the woman spoke in a nasally but commanding voice, "my name is Agnes Huntsman. I'm the president of Mountainview Bank. What can I do for you?"

"We are serving a warrant to obtain the banking and financial records of Margaret Brooksfield."

"May I see some ID?" Huntsman said. She was dressed in a pink paisley blouse, a pair of hobbit feet looking as if they would explode out of the vintage Mary Jane shoes she had buckled herself into. A string of pearls encircled her neck, and a beige skirt reached her knees. She looked like someone's formidable grandmother—down to the air of authority she projected.

Cash fished for her identification on a lanyard around her neck, and Colcord furnished his badge. Huntsman perused them with tight lips. "Unfortunately, it's Mountainview Bank's policy, in accordance with federal law, to maintain the confidentiality of a customer's financial information. You'll need to submit a request for records, in writing, through our website."

It was almost a word-for-word repetition of what Stacy had told them.

"Ms. Huntsman." Cash raised her voice just enough to allow it to carry across the room. "I am an agent with the Colorado Bureau of Investigation, and this is the sheriff of Eagle County. Now: Are you telling us you do not intend to comply with this signed warrant?"

Everyone in the bank was now listening—it was so quiet you could hear a pin drop. The fake smile on Huntsman's face vanished. Her eyes flicked around, a brief scowl marring her face. "Follow me, please."

Cash and Colcord followed the woman into a spacious back office.

"Sit." Huntsman gestured to a pair of austere chairs.

Cash remained standing, holding out the warrant.

Huntsman grabbed it, put on a pair of spectacles, and examined it for a long moment. "I'll be right back," she said, scurrying from the room.

She returned with a burly man with bushy eyebrows, the warrant clutched in his hand and held inches from his face. "General counsel Monson Benedetto," he said to them as introduction, without looking up from his examination of the warrant.

Cash noted the expensive suit and a heavy gold Rolex on his wrist. A high-priced lawyer for a small bank like this? Something weird was going on here.

Now finally he looked up. "As much as we'd like to assist law enforcement, I'm afraid to say this warrant is not valid. Rule 41 of the Colorado Criminal Code states that the affidavit section of the warrant must establish probable cause that grounds for issuance of the warrant exists. All you have here in this affidavit is . . . wire transfers from a murder victim's account into the Brooksfield account. Is wiring money now a crime, Agent Cash?"

"It certainly is a crime if there are implications of financial fraud in connection with a murder. Plus, a warrant is a warrant, Mr. Benedetto, as I'm sure you know well. The judge has approved it. You are *required* to comply." Cash knew that the basis for the warrant was a little shaky, but damn it all, it had been signed by a judge. It wasn't legal to refuse a warrant—it was up to the attorneys to get the evidence excluded at trial if the warrant was found to have been improperly granted.

Benedetto went on, in a tired, gravelly voice, "There's not enough detail here in the probable cause section of the affidavit for this to stand up in court. I would hate to place Mountainview Bank in a position of liability if we allow a search of one of our esteemed clients' records. I fear you also may have run afoul here of the Right to Financial Privacy Act, which requires you to provide bank customers notice and the right to challenge requests for their financial records. Have you notified Mrs. Brooksfield of your intention to peruse her financial records and given her a chance to respond?"

Cash felt a welling of irritation at this legalistic obstructionism, but it was soon overtaken by another idea: The bank was really pulling out all the stops here. Why? She leaned forward. Luckily, she was well versed in this area of the law. "The Right to Financial Privacy Act applies to federal, not state, requests for financial records. Furthermore, I am not going to argue the validity of a warrant that has been signed and granted by an appointed judge of this state. You are welcome to contest the validity of the warrant in court."

"I am merely attempting to comply with the law. Section 11–105–110 of the Colorado Revised Statutes provides a safe harbor for disclosing financial records of a customer *only* if the request is initiated by a *legitimate* governmental authority. Who's to say you are who you say you are?"

"We've already furnished Ms. Huntsman with our identification."

"Those could be fake." Benedetto crossed his arms.

Cash had had enough of this. "Either you comply with the warrant now, or I will have you both arrested and cuffed for obstruction of justice. Wouldn't that make for a lovely parade through the bank in front of all your loyal customers and employees?"

"You wouldn't dare," Huntsman said, removing her spectacles and staring Cash in the face.

Cash said nothing—she merely slipped out her cell phone as if to make a call.

Huntsman shot from her chair with surprising agility for her age. "I'll get the records." Benedetto followed her out, stepping heavily.

Cash now settled down into one of the wooden chairs to wait. She could hear a muffled but animated discussion in the next room.

"Hot damn," Colcord said, casually sitting next to her. "Nicely done, Counselor." He winked at Cash. "I wonder why they're giving us so much trouble today."

After a good twenty minutes, Huntsman came back with a stack of documents in her arms. She thumped them down unceremoniously in front of Cash.

Cash frowned. "We'd prefer to have electronic copies."

Huntsman crossed her arms. "The warrant did not specify how the records were to be furnished."

Cash said nothing. Next time, she'd make sure the warrant was more specific. "The sheriff and I are going to look through these right now, just to make sure everything is here in good order. Is there an empty office we could use?"

Huntsman's lips thinned. "You can use this office."

They began to go through the documents while Huntsman brooded in a corner chair, the scowl back on her face. It quickly became clear that large deposits had been transferred from Grooms's account into Margie Brooksfield's. Very large—over $2.5 million, at least. And suddenly, Cash could now understand why Mountainview Bank had been so obstructive of the warrant—all the transactions were suspiciously just under the reportable limit of $10,000. They flowed from Grooms's account to Brooksfield's, and thence to an account in the name of a nonprofit organization named Paradox. Paradox . . . what a curious name.

"Ms. Huntsman," Cash said, "was Mountainview Bank trying to avoid filing currency transaction reports with all these transfers?" Judging by the paling in Huntsman's face, Cash realized she was on the right track. "This two point five million—Brooksfield must be one of your top clients. I bet she threatened to take her business elsewhere if you filed CRTs—am I right?

While not filing CRTs might be technically legal, I'm pretty sure a judge could see these transfers as an attempt to evade currency transaction laws."

Again, Huntsman did not respond. Cash wondered just how many clients Mountainview Bank was doing this for.

Cash put the papers back in the according file and snapped shut the elastic band. "Thank you, Ms. Huntsman. I'm sure you will be hearing from us again."

Outside, Colcord turned to her. "Jesus, you were a barracuda in there. How'd you know all that legal stuff about banking and financial transactions?"

"My first case at CBI was about money laundering."

"So you think this is money laundering?"

"It could be money laundering, could be tax evasion, fraud, embezzlement . . . but somehow, I think it's deeper than that. What was Margie Brooksfield up to? And what the hell is Paradox?"

19

Sitting in a camp chair on the shores of Solitary Lake, looking out over the mirrorlike water to Derby Peak and its glittering snowfields, Deputy Maureen Clausen was pissed. Even though the sheriff had assured her he had picked her name out of a hat, she wondered if maybe she'd done something to pull this shit assignment guarding the crime scene. She was bored out of her mind, there was no cell service, and she'd forgotten to bring a book.

As if that were not enough, the sky was now growing dark. The usual summer afternoon thunderhead buildup had started. It looked like she would be hiking down in the rain, on a slippery trail. She glanced at her watch. Two o'clock. Two more hours up here and she was done for the week. Tomorrow, some other poor slob that the sheriff had supposedly drawn from a hat would take the rotation, and she would be back to her normal routine.

There was a distant rumble of thunder, and the air seemed to get thicker in a way that presaged a storm. As the creeping shadow of bad weather fell across the lake, the surface turned the color of dull steel. A rising wind set the fir trees swaying and creaking. This whole place gave her the creeps—not just from the bizarre murder that had taken place there but also from the general atmosphere of loneliness, solitude, and abandonment. Those crazy sculptures didn't help, especially the oversized one that looked like a human skeleton. As if the threat of Neanders wasn't enough, that guy Grooms had to make the woods even creepier with his weird art.

Something about the wind moaning in the trees, the advancing darkness, and the thunder started to make her uneasy. She dismissed the feeling as silliness—who would possibly come up to the cabin? Surely the killers had no reason to return. There was hardly any point to her being there—she hadn't seen anyone all day. No curious hikers, no rubberneckers, and certainly no threatening people. The rumors added to her unease, even if most of them were absurd—that a coven of devil worshipers had established a camp in the wilderness and were murdering people as part of some satanic ritual, or it was a Manson-like gang of preppers stockpiling weapons in the area.

Another rumble of thunder, this time closer. Son of a bitch, she would definitely be hiking down in the rain. She picked up the chair and turned to carry it up to the cabin before the sky opened up, when she thought she saw a movement in the fir trees. Elk? She'd seen a small herd near the lake, beyond where the canoes were pulled up. She put down the chair and squinted into the dim forest.

She saw it again—a movement—and it was no elk. It was a person. *Inside* the crime scene perimeter. She swore under her breath.

Whoever it was appeared to be a man and had evidently not seen her. She quickly ducked behind a tree, removed her sidearm, and took a few deep breaths. Who the hell could it be, coming up here, ignoring the police cordon, and sneaking around like that? A dumb kid? Or worse, the murderer revisiting the scene? Peering from behind the tree, she could see his dark shape moving through the tree trunks, then stopping and bending over one of the junk sculptures. He began to pull it apart, giving it a few blows with a hammer, searching it—and then toppling it over and scouring the ground underneath.

The figure moved on to another sculpture and did the same thing, probing through the pile of junk, prying off pieces, whacking it with a hammer, making a lot of noise, and then shoving it over in what looked like frustration.

Clausen wondered if he was armed. He seemed erratic and maybe dangerous.

Looking around, she quickly came up with a plan. Taking a deep breath, she crouched and scurried from the tree to behind the cabin. The man didn't see her—he was too engrossed with searching the junk sculptures, looking for something and pissed off because he wasn't finding it.

She snuck around the back of the cabin and peered around the corner, gun drawn.

He was gone.

She clutched her gun tightly with sudden alarm. Where had he gone? Had he seen her?

Then she heard heavy footfalls on the wooden porch at the front of the cabin and heard the door creak open.

He'd gone in the house. Crouching low, she backed up and took a position below a window. She could hear him banging around inside, moving furniture, tossing things. There was the sound of breaking glass. Fuck, he was really doing a number on the crime scene—her boss would have her ass if she didn't stop this right away. She slowly raised up to peer over the sill. She was confronted with the silhouette of a tall man, searching the place and really trashing it. She watched as he knocked over a pile of books, sorted through them, opening each one and holding it by the spine, shaking it out and tossing it aside. That done, he lurched across the room and pulled the cot away from the wall, exposing some tin boxes. He reached down and opened one, rummaged around—and then tossed it aside. It was empty. What the hell was he looking for? She tried to determine if he was armed. He didn't appear to have a gun, but you never knew what people had tucked out of sight somewhere.

Clausen was scared, but she had no choice. She ducked back down from the window and ran at a crouch along the rear of the house, rounded the corner, came up the side and around, and set foot on the creaky porch.

The wood groaned loudly, as she'd feared. There was a sudden silence from inside; the man must have heard it too. She waited next to the door, gun drawn—it was now or never. She took a deep breath and said, loudly, "Deputy Clausen, Eagle County Sheriff's Office. You are under arrest for trespassing and vandalizing a crime scene! Come out with your hands up!"

Silence.

Still crouching by the door, she said, "I'm armed! Don't do anything stupid! Come out with your hands raised."

More silence.

What to do now? Suddenly, she heard a massive crash of glass.

Clausen raced around to the back of the house, just in time to see the figure making a mad dash toward the forest. The maniac had jumped through the fucking *window.*

"Stop!" she called out.

He kept going, fast.

She raised her weapon. "Stop and raise your hands!" she screamed. He continued running. She lowered the gun, furious and frustrated, as the rules of engagement did not allow her to shoot a fleeing man in the back.

Suddenly, the man tripped, careening face-first into the mud with a yell of pain. She ran up to him with her gun pointed at the ground, ready for anything. To her relief, he raised himself to a seated position and thrust his hands in the air.

"Stand up!"

The man complied, struggling to his feet and panting.

She walked toward him, keeping the Glock aimed at the middle of his back. Coming up behind, she hooked her foot behind his, as she'd learned in the academy, and with her Glock in her right hand, used her left to pat him down. What the hell was this on his lower leg? "What's that? A knife?"

"A prosthesis. Difficult to run with, as you can see."

She stepped back. "Turn around slowly."

He did as she said, and she clipped cuffs around his wrists. She was surprised to see the man's well groomed, good-looking, mild-mannered face, with blue eyes and curly black hair. She also noticed his expensive hiking gear—covered in mud now, but it was easy to see that it had cost him a pretty penny. This guy didn't look like a criminal at all.

"Um, can you lower the weapon?" he said. "It's making me nervous."

Ignoring him, she fished into his pocket, withdrew his wallet, opened it, and removed a driver's license—California, in the name of Javier Castillo.

She Mirandized him—and then began walking him back up the hill toward the cabin. "You realize you were trespassing on a crime scene? Tampering with evidence? Other charges come to mind as well—interfering with a police officer, resisting arrest, fleeing—mister, you're in deep shit. What the hell were you doing?"

The man replied, in a calm voice, "I decline to answer questions without my attorney present."

"Oh, so you're one of those assholes. What were you looking for?"

"You have my answer."

"Okay, Javier, smart-ass."

"Call me Javi," he said pleasantly.

At this point, a scattering of heavy drops began to fall, and there was a close peal of thunder as they approached the cabin again, keeping outside of the line of tape this time. She paused and took a moment to get herself under control, take a deep breath, get her heart rate down—and not let herself be provoked. This shitty day had turned even shittier, somehow. But maybe—just maybe—this could be the big break in the case they were waiting for.

"Okay, *Javi*. Here's what we're going to do. You're going to walk in front of me. We're going to hike back down to the trailhead, where we're going to be picked up by my partner, and we're going to take you in. Do you understand?"

"But it's raining."

"Looks like you're gonna get wet. At least it's washing the mud off yah. Now get your ass moving down the trail."

20

Sheriff Colcord, mightily ticked off, looked at the man sitting on the bench in the holding cell—the idiot his deputy Clausen had brought down from Solitary Lake. This jackass had tried to run from his deputy, scared her half to death, and vandalized the crime scene—the paperwork alone was going to be a nightmare. Fortunately, she was one of his best and had handled it well.

This was the same guy Cash had gone to see in San Francisco. The nutjob who claimed Grooms had been murdered by aliens. Colcord had thought it was funny when Cash had unearthed the alien-murder conspiracy, returning a little peevish. It wasn't so funny now.

Colcord looked him over. He was dressed in expensive hiking clothes. A well-formed guy, trim, polished—if a bit damp and slightly muddy—who toted a fancy prosthetic leg. Here was a guy who should have known not to mess up a crime scene and then try to flee from an armed deputy. And now he was trying to lawyer up. Wasn't it a *shame* his attorney from San Francisco was on vacation in Tulum. Instead of waiting two nights in jail, Castillo had agreed to be questioned in the presence of a local defense attorney.

Colcord unlocked the cell door and swung it open. "Mr. Castillo?"

The man rose.

"Your attorney is here and is waiting for you in the interrogation room. Would you come with me, please?"

Colcord walked down the bare corridor, Castillo shuffling behind him, and they entered a spartan room with a table and a handful of metal chairs.

Cash was also waiting there, and she rose as they came in. She looked annoyed as all hell. "Well, well, Mr. Castillo," she said. "We meet again."

"I'm your attorney," a man said, wiping the palm of his hand on his wrinkled pants and sticking it out to shake Castillo's. "Mort Randall. Would you like to confer with me before the questioning?"

Colcord was amused at the look of disdain that gathered on Castillo's face as he laid eyes on his attorney for the first time. Randall was known for his sartorial ineptitude, his big suits flapping about him like loose sails, his ties too long, and his comb-over plastered across his pate with excessive tonic. He looked more like a used car salesman than a lawyer. It was a good day for the cops when Randall was sitting on the other side of the table.

"Not necessary to confer, Mr. Randall," said Castillo. "I'm pleading the Fifth across the board. Not answering any questions."

"Have a seat," said Colcord, pointing to a metal chair.

Castillo sat down grudgingly, and Randall took a seat next to him. Randall was sweating profusely, nervously picking at a frayed string on his jacket sleeve. Castillo wrinkled his nose and edged away so he was seated as far as possible on the edge of the metal chair.

Colcord pulled out a card on which he had jotted some questions, and they started the video recorder. This wacky guy had flown in from San Francisco and gone straight to the crime scene. According to Deputy Clausen, he had messed it up too. Why? What the hell was he doing up there?

"Now, Mr. Castillo," Colcord began, "you're looking at a long list of possible charges: evidence tampering, disturbing a crime scene, interfering with a peace officer, resisting arrest, and vandalism, among others. Whether or not you cooperate with us will be reported to the DA's office when they make charging decisions. Do you understand?"

He waited for an answer, but Castillo said nothing.

"So we'd like to ask you, first—why'd you come here all the way from San Francisco?"

Castillo leaned forward in his chair and laced his fingers in front of him. "I plead the Fifth."

"What were you doing up at Solitary Lake?"

"Fifth."

Colcord let out a sigh. "Really? I don't think the DA is going to be happy when they hear you refused to answer any questions."

"He pleads the Fifth," said Randall unnecessarily. Colcord could see Castillo's jaw working in irritation at the sound of Randall's voice.

"You were looking for something. What was it?" Colcord asked.

"I'm not answering that."

"For chrissake, are you really gonna pull this on us? We're trying to solve the brutal murder of your apparent friend. You seem to know something about it. Why were you vandalizing those sculptures?"

"Fifth."

Colcord turned to Cash. "You want to ask anything?"

"Sure." She turned to Castillo. "In our previous interview, you said that Mr. Grooms had seen a UFO crash, gone up to the site, and found something up there. Is that what you were looking for?"

"He pleads the Fifth," said Randall again.

Cash stared at Castillo. "If you don't cooperate, Sheriff Colcord here is going to return you to your cell and your chance to clear your name will be gone. He's gonna keep you overnight, and tomorrow, there will be a bail hearing, with Mr. Randall here representing you. Sheriff, what kind of bail are you gonna recommend for Mr. Castillo here?"

"At least a quarter million," Colcord said. For a crime like this, even if he requested bail that high, he likely wouldn't get it. But Castillo didn't know that.

"Ouch. You got that kind of money? You can get a bail bond, but the fee is ten percent—twenty-five grand. Ouch again. And if you can't raise bail, you're gonna stay right here in Eagle. When the charges are filed, there will be stories in the newspapers. Even if you post bail, you'll have to come back here again for the preliminary hearing—maybe even a grand jury proceeding. Are we gonna need to convene a grand jury on this one, Sheriff?"

"Felonies committed on public land. Certainly a grand jury will need to be convened."

Colcord could see Castillo inspecting Randall warily from the corner of his eye. Randall dabbed at his wet forehead with his sleeve. Castillo grimaced.

"Grand juries take a lot of time, Mr. Castillo. What's the hourly rate of your attorney in San Francisco? Unless, of course, you choose to be represented by the very capable Mr. Randall here. You're gonna be tied up for months, maybe years. Lawyers are so expensive these days! That club you belong to—what are the membership fees?"

Castillo raised his hand. "All right, all right! For chrissake, I'll answer your fucking questions!"

"What were you looking for at Solitary Lake?"

"I was looking for the alien artifact that Grooms claimed to have found."

"And what *is* this artifact?" Cash asked.

"Grooms wouldn't tell me."

"Was it important?"

"He . . . wouldn't tell me."

Colcord began shaking his head. This whole thing was ridiculous. He couldn't help but feel a little resentful that Cash, against his advice, had gone to San Francisco to talk to this nutjob. He told himself that she couldn't have known the maniac would follow her here, all the way to Burns, and then tear apart their crime scene . . . Still. This was a whole lot messier now.

"You told me," Cash said, "that the aliens had killed him and taken it. So why were you still looking for it if the aliens had it?"

Colcord shot her a look. Why was Cash playing into Castillo's alien narrative?

"I was hoping maybe the aliens hadn't found it after all. Grooms said it was well hidden."

"Did he tell you where he'd hidden it?"

"No."

"If you didn't know what the object was, how was it important?"

"Any alien artifact would be important. Earth-shattering. It would be proof that we're being visited by intelligent beings from another galactic civilization. It would be the greatest scientific discovery ever made."

Colcord let out a long, audible sigh. They needed to get rid of this guy, not try to make sense of his ramblings. He couldn't have this guy wandering around, causing trouble.

Cash glared at Colcord and forged on. "Why were you breaking apart and knocking down those sculptures?" she asked.

"I thought the alien object might have been incorporated into one of them. You know, disguised."

"But you didn't find it."

"No."

Colcord cleared his throat and spoke. "Mr. Castillo, let me get this right: You came all this way, flying from San Francisco to Denver, renting a car, and hiking up to the cabin in hopes you might find some alien object Grooms claimed he found in the wreckage of a UFO many years ago. You busted up some junk sculptures looking for it before you were apprehended by one of my deputies. Have I got your story right?"

"More or less."

"And you also think aliens murdered Grooms. Correct?"

"Correct."

Colcord glanced again at Cash, raising his eyebrows. He had had enough of this. This entire line of questioning was a waste of police resources and time. He just needed to get rid of Castillo. Get him out of Colorado. The man probably wasn't a threat to society—at least when he wasn't wrecking crime scenes—and prosecuting him would just occupy space on a judge's busy docket. Space that was needed to prosecute real criminals. "Mr. Castillo, you are wasting our time."

Castillo shifted in his chair, face unreadable.

"We can forget all about this," said Colcord, "and decline to forward charges to the DA's office if you'll just go back to San Francisco and leave our investigation alone. How about that?"

Castillo didn't respond immediately. Randall said quickly, "I advise you to accept the offer, Mr. Castillo."

"Shut up, Randall," Castillo said.

Randall's face morphed into a mask of anger mixed with embarrassment.

Colcord sighed, holding up his fingers. "Choice one: Felony charges, bail, grand jury proceedings, hearings, trial, conviction, appeals, big-time legal fees. Choice two: Drive your rental car straight to the airport, get on a plane, and get the hell out of Colorado."

There was a long silence. Castillo finally said, "All right. Fine. I'll go back to San Francisco. Do I . . . have to sign anything?"

"Nope. Just leave." Colcord turned to Cash. He could see she was irritated with him—but to hell with it; it had needed to be done. "Any objections?"

Cash drilled him with her eyes but did not respond.

"Very good." Colcord turned to a deputy. "Please escort Mr. Castillo out—and do him the courtesy of driving him back to the location of his rental vehicle."

"Yes, Sheriff."

Cash waited until they had left before clenching her fists in frustration and approaching Colcord, who had gotten up and was busy making some coffee. "So that's it? Just give him the bum's rush out of town? That guy was lying. He knows more than he's letting on."

"Maybe so, Cash," he said, "but like I said from the beginning, he's crazy. Aliens? Aliens don't torture people with Spanish Inquisition contraptions. Aliens don't feed their victims holy wafers and wine. Aliens don't embalm people. We already know that four actual real human beings dressed in camo went up there and killed him. Their footprints were all over the crime scene."

"Right, but there's another possibility—that Grooms was killed by some alien conspiracy theorists looking for that artifact he supposedly found."

"That's a stretch."

"No, it isn't. There's a whole movement out there of people and organizations investigating UFOs and extraterrestrial contact, and some are very serious and have deep pockets. I did some digging into the foundation he runs—Paradox. The one that Margie was transferring money to. It's a legitimate, registered 501(c)(3) nonprofit with a board and an endowment, all aboveboard. Castillo's the chair. These aren't just a bunch of nutjobs. And the guy wrecked our crime scene. You're gonna let him get away with that?"

"The scene was processed. Sure, we could have charged him, but to what end? And yeah, I hear you about the alien conspiracy angle, but we know where Castillo is and can always question him again."

Cash shook her head.

Colcord gave her a conciliatory smile—she was a good agent, but sometimes she got sidetracked. "Cash, I respect your judgment. I appreciate your leadership in this case. I promise you, if something additional turns up to implicate him, we can always drag him back here and charge him."

He busied himself with his espresso machine again, trying to hide his vexation. Cash's insistence on following these dead ends was going to put them in the hot seat—he just knew it.

21

Blaisdell Holmes pulled up a news report as she waited for Frankie Cash to arrive in her office. She wanted to make sure she had all the details of this fuckup at her fingertips when she reprimanded the agent. She had let a day pass, to help her cool down and think through how best to deal with the situation.

The television news report popped up onto her computer screen. The reporter was walking down the sidewalk of a small mountain town, passing by shops and a lone movie theater. "There's usually not a lot going on in the sleepy town of Burns, Colorado," they began in the matter-of-fact voice that reporters used. "Located along a remote stretch of the Colorado River, the town boasts a nonexistent crime rate—until recently. The grisly murder of a man named Willy Grooms has deeply shocked the community. Grooms, seventy-five years old, was found dead in an unauthorized cabin on Solitary Lake in the Flat Tops Wilderness. A source close to the investigation indicated that the body was shrouded in white and there were signs of torture. The Colorado Bureau of Investigation has taken the lead in investigating what has become known as the Shrouder murder, led by Agent in Charge Frankie Cash. She is being assisted by the sheriff of Eagle County, James Colcord. Investigators claim they are following up on leads and have 'persons of interest,' but won't say more—and there are apparently no actual suspects at this time. But that isn't the only problem with the investigation." The reporter stopped in front of a church, giving a flourish of their hand toward the mountains rising behind them. The camera zoomed in dramatically on the reporter's pale face. "Agent Cash has been accused of aggressively questioning and making highly offensive comments to a beloved local priest, Father Timothy Moore." A scene change occurred, and then the reporter was in a church, now sitting next to a diminutive man on a bench in front of an altar. The priest had his hands clasped piously in his lap. There was an arrogant air about him that Holmes found off-putting.

"Father Moore, tell us what happened with Agent Cash." The reporter held the microphone close to his face.

"Of course. Agent Cash visited my parish—the Church of Saint Mary's—on June 16. She had some questions about one of my parishioners, Mr. William Grooms, and I was happy to cooperate. What should have been a simple interview turned into an aggressive interrogation. Not only did Agent Cash suggest that I should report on the activities of my parishioners—outside of the sanctity of the confessional—but she also needlessly disparaged the Catholic Church regarding recent controversies and called me an, *ahem*, an obscene and offensive expletive, which I naturally decline to repeat."

The scene changed back to the reporter walking alone on the main street of Burns. "We managed to get in touch with Agent Cash, who had *this* to say about the incident with Father Moore."

The camera skipped to a bedraggled-looking Cash, standing in front of a gas station in the rain. She had the wide-eyed look of a wet dog being scolded for shaking.

"He was being uncooperative," Cash said into the mic.

Holmes winced.

"He also claims you called him an obscenity that I cannot repeat on air. What do you have to say to these allegations?"

Cash merely stammered something unintelligible.

Holmes closed her eyes as if willing it to go away. What the hell had Cash been thinking?

The reporter's voice continued as the camera panned across a picture of a squat building, which Holmes recognized as the Portland, Maine, CID office. "This isn't the first concerning incident involving this law enforcement officer. Agent Cash has a history of aggressive and allegedly discriminatory behavior. Sources indicate that ten years ago, Agent Cash was terminated from the Portland, Maine, CID for behavior termed as 'racist' by some reports, when she fired a Taser at a homeless French Canadian man, resulting in his death.

"Furthermore, Agent Cash's investigation seems to be going 'off planet.' I have confirmed that a UFO expert named Javi Castillo was allegedly questioned by Agent Cash as part of the investigation. Mr. Castillo had previously been fired from his position as professor of exobiology at San Francisco State University. Mr. Castillo has claimed that aliens were responsible for Mr. Grooms's murder. With all these problems surrounding the investigation, the question remains: Is the Colorado Bureau of Investigation handling the investigation of the Shrouder murder in a competent manner?"

The reporter continued to speak, now in front of a green screen. "In other news, the controversial Neander search headed by the FBI remains at a standstill. The Neanders appear to have vanished. Sources close to the KBFR Investigative Beat report that the special agent in charge of that investigation, Roger McBride, is being replaced by AIC Makoto Ota, a decorated agent with over twelve years of experience and known for a firm hand. Will the FBI finally make headway, or will the Neanders continue to roam about the Rockies unchecked?"

Finally, the camera panned back to the reporter. "Robin Twen, reporting for KBFR Investigative Beat."

Robin Twen . . . a new reporter on the scene. Twen was making the CBI look like a bunch of blustering idiots. Furthermore, how in the hell had Twen known about Castillo, the UFO angle, and the torture of Grooms? *Shrouder murder.* Ridiculous name. Twen had a source somewhere—she hoped it was in the sheriff's office, notorious for leaking, and not CBI. She was pretty certain it wasn't Cash. Nevertheless, Holmes needed to respond firmly to Cash's mishandling of the public relations side of the investigation.

First came a dressing-down. Holmes had to admit Cash was a good agent: competent and smart. But she had her drawbacks. She could be a pain in the ass, hotheaded, and she talked too damn much. This thing with the priest was a perfect example. If she nipped this in the bud now—showed Cash that Director Blaisdell Holmes was not going to tolerate any outbursts or wildly inappropriate comments—then Cash might think twice before opening her mouth.

Second, Holmes needed Cash to prepare a statement for her to present during a presser. She had thought about making the statement herself but figured it would be more effective coming straight from the AIC. Make her stand up and be accountable. Holmes smiled at the thought. Having four kids of her own had taught her that. Most CBI agents were like kids; if you forced them to clean up their own messes, they were less likely to reoffend.

Third, she needed to make sure Sheriff Colcord made his own appearance at the presser. The public would be reassured by his good-old-boy presence and see that Cash was not the only one on the case. Colcord had a calming drawl that would look good next to Cash and help cancel out that clusterfuck of a news report.

As if on cue, a rap sounded through her office door. Blaisdell closed out of the news report, straightened her beige pantsuit, and sat up. She pretended to busy herself typing something on her computer. She decided she would be pissed, but not too pissed.

Cash poked her head through the door crack, looking apprehensive. "You wanted to see me, ma'am?"

"Yes. Thank you for coming. Please sit." Holmes gestured at the chair in front of her desk. She kept typing for several minutes, letting Cash sweat a little.

Holmes finally pushed her keyboard to the side and folded her hands in front of her. "About that news report night before last, Agent Cash."

"Right . . . the one with Robin Twen. I just wanted to say—"

"Agent Cash, let me start with a question." Holmes raised her voice—but only a little. "Is it true you called the priest a 'prick'?"

Cash colored. "Um, yes. A sexist prick, to be precise."

Holmes stopped herself from asking what had triggered the comment—that was irrelevant. She took a deep breath. "Good God. This is truly unacceptable deportment from a CBI agent in my bureau. I expect my agents to behave with civility and professionalism. From my understanding, Father Moore is an important person in Burns. You grossly mishandled what should have been a respectful interrogation by allowing yourself to be provoked. I expected you to be smarter than that. And that's not the worst of it." She paused, studying Cash for a reaction. The agent was tense, as well she should be. Holmes continued, "Father Moore has filed a formal complaint that I'm required to refer to Internal Affairs. Notwithstanding that, it *appears* you have a history of overly aggressive behavior from your time in Portland, Maine. I have a copy of the CID file with the Taser incident."

Cash sat like a statue, a hint of anger playing across her face. A little anger was good. Get the blood boiling, make her feel like Holmes was doing her a favor—make her grateful to be here.

Holmes continued, her voice softening. "Of course, we knew about the Maine thing when we hired you. I went back into our files and did a little reading up on the incident on my own. Off the record, I realize that the Portland CID might have overreacted. The incident report in your file did not show culpability on your part, in my opinion. Honestly, I was confused about this charge of racism—I didn't know white French Canadians were, ah, considered a protected category, but then I've never been to Maine. And I'm not one to pass judgment on something that occurred under someone else's direction. The real problem was *how* you responded. You didn't help yourself with unfortunate and inflammatory comments to the press and public. And now this. But I'm giving you a second chance. Or maybe we'll call it a third one, after the Erebus disaster. In the meantime, I've put a written caution in your file."

She slid a copy over to Cash, who took it and without looking at it folded it into a pocket.

"I'm not taking you off the Grooms case for now. But I have to tell you that continuing as AIC hinges on the conclusion of the IA investigation. 'Sexist prick'—what on *earth* were you thinking?"

"I wasn't."

Holmes slapped the file shut and pushed it aside. "On another note, the DA's office is getting more involved, and I've heard they might be assigning the case to a new prosecutor. Her name is Nova Euclid. I want to make sure you cooperate fully and give them everything they need."

"Of course."

"Did you have anything to add, Agent Cash?"

"No, ma'am."

Smart woman, Holmes thought. Cash might just learn how to hold her tongue.

"We're holding a presser on the Grooms case in two days' time. I expect a draft of your statement by tomorrow afternoon. And I hope you make some more progress in the case."

Cash seemed surprised. "You want me to give a statement?"

"I do. Show yourself as the steady AIC I know you can be. I'll help you draft it. You need to work on your media skills. One of the attributes of a good agent is being able to handle these pesky reporters—don't you agree?"

"Yes, ma'am," Cash said.

"Don't let my magnanimity fool you, Cash. After Erebus, this is your second warning—clear?"

Cash nodded. "I won't let you down, ma'am."

Before Cash could leave, a short rap resounded. Romanski peeked his head through the door crack, a big grin on his face, waggling a manila envelope. He didn't seem to notice the somberness of their meeting.

"Mind if I interrupt? I have something both of you might be interested in."

"Not at all," Holmes responded.

Romanski slipped through the door the rest of the way, dropping the envelope on Holmes's desk. "We've been cataloging all the documents from Willy's cabin—and we found this. You're gonna love it."

Holmes snatched it, unclasped it, and pulled it out. She glanced at it and then stared, her eyes widening.

22

Paul Brooksfield admired his wife from the driver's seat of their GMC Sierra truck. Her cornrows were tied up in a silk scarf. She was just as beautiful as the day she'd sashayed through the bar door in low-cut jeans and that sparkly backless top. Toward the end of that night, her increasingly drunk blond friend had finally ended up sprawled on the floor. Margie—stubborn even back then—had tried to haul the blond out by herself rather than ask for help. Paul remembered how she had struggled until he rushed to her aid. But she had laughed too, always finding the humor in life—a great tinkling laugh that echoed across the bar.

As she saw him staring, she smiled back at him.

"Whatcha lookin' at, handsome?" She winked a big brown eye. Hook, line, and sinker. Even after all these years, she could flip his heart over.

He tried to smile, his hands tightening on the steering wheel as they pulled into the Eagle County Sheriff's Office lot.

"You ready for this?" he asked.

"If we can survive the ire of Grandma Brooksfield, we can make it through anything."

Paul grimaced at the thought of his mother, Jolene, who had written him out of the will when he brought Margie home. Sullying the family line, she had implied many a time—but never said outright. The ranch, at least, had been in a trust that she couldn't mess with, but it came with no money, and they'd been struggling ever since.

"Margie . . ." Paul reached for her hands. "Are we sure about our story? They're gonna have questions."

"What do you mean, *story*? This is the truth." Margie pulled her hands away and didn't meet his eyes, staring instead out of the dusty windshield at the glass office building shimmering in the sun.

Paul felt uneasy. There was something she wasn't telling him—he could just feel it.

Paul parked and got out of the truck and Margie followed. He could sense the heat radiating from the pavement, inhaling the tarry scent of it. A blistering day.

Their attorney, Belen Caldas, was just getting out of her car. Paul greeted her with a handshake. She was wearing a crisp black suit, sunglasses, and incommodious-looking stilettos. A halo of black hair poofed about her face in ringlets. Despite her elegant appearance, she was said to be a bulldog, which was why Paul had hired her. He hoped she would live up to her reputation—and expense.

Caldas removed her sunglasses and swiped at her forehead with her palm. "Jesus, it's hot here. This is really in the middle of bum-fuck nowhere, huh?"

"Our mountains," said Paul, "are a lot taller and prettier than your Denver glass-and-steel towers." He tried to cover up his racing heart with a joking attitude. He had never been involved with the police before.

"I prefer glass and steel," said Caldas, shrugging. "Even my plants are plastic." She turned to Margie. "All right, remember what we practiced." As they approached the building, she slipped her shades into her pants pocket. "Keep your mouth shut, let me take the lead, and keep your answers absolutely short and to the point. Got it?"

"Yes, ma'am."

"Do they think Margie's a suspect?" Paul asked.

"We have to assume she is—even if she isn't."

Paul watched as Margie began to fuss with her cornrows like she did when she was nervous. It was absurd that anyone would think she might have had anything to do with Grooms's death.

They entered the drab interior of the sheriff's building and were led into an interrogation room. Four chairs squatted around a metal table, and a clunky out-of-date video camera was tucked into a corner where the ceiling met the wall. Margie and Caldas sat side by side. Paul, who was not being questioned, was allowed to be present, seated in a chair against the wall. The room smelled faintly of piss, and he wondered how many low-life murderers, rapists, and drunks had been hauled through these doors. Caldas would set this straight, that was for sure.

Sheriff James Colcord and CBI Agent Cash strode in, closing the door behind them, and situated themselves at the table on the opposite side to them.

"Good morning," Agent Cash said.

Caldas stared at Cash with a jaw like stone. "It will be a better one once we get my innocent client out of here. I want to be clear: We are here voluntarily to set the record straight, not because we believe this investigation into my client has any merit whatsoever. Everyone around this table knows you're chasing shadows, Agent Cash."

"We're just here to ask some questions," Cash responded mildly, not provoked in the slightest. "Mind if I record?"

"You may," Caldas said.

Cash placed her phone in the center of the table and hit Record.

Caldas began speaking right after she hit Record. "Agent Cash, I would like to ask: Are any white suspects being interviewed, or is Margie Brooksfield—the only African American in the town of Burns—the lone suspect you are pursuing?"

If Cash was rattled, she didn't show it. "I am not familiar with the demographics of Burns—"

"There are only three hundred and fifty-three residents," Caldas interrupted. "It's not difficult to confirm—"

Cash continued to speak over Caldas's interruption and then leaned forward toward Margie. "Mrs. Brooksfield, I want to thank you for coming in today. I know it's scary, but you're doing the right thing by helping us solve the murder of Willy Grooms. Can you spell and state your name for the record?"

Margie did so.

"Has Willy Grooms ever spoken to you about a man named Javier Castillo?" Cash asked.

"No, ma'am," Margie responded. "Never heard of him."

"So, if I remember correctly, you work as a financial adviser?"

"A certified financial planner."

"And your bank is"—Cash shuffled through some papers, then leaned back in her chair—"Mountainview Bank?"

Cash threw a leg over her thigh, casual-like. Caldas had warned them about this, Paul thought. The police will pretend to be your friends; don't be fooled, she had said.

"Yes."

"And to your knowledge, that was Willy Grooms's bank as well?"

"Correct."

"And you were advising him on his finances?"

"Yes."

"Do you enjoy your work?"

"I love it. Get to make my own schedule, which is nice," Margie said.

"Well, you can't beat that. I wish I had flexible hours." Cash laughed and scooched her chair closer to Margie. "Say, I've been rude in not offering you something. Coffee? Tea? Water?"

"Oh yeah, tea would be nice. With milk and sugar."

Cash flapped her hand at Colcord, who obediently got up and left the room.

"From my understanding, you're a pretty intelligent woman, in terms of financial stuff—right?"

"I hope so," Margie said. The fussing with her hair had stopped, and she was looking more relaxed. Caldas, on the other hand, appeared tense. Paul had an uneasy feeling about this that he couldn't shake. Margie was too trusting, always had been.

"Agent Cash, if you could give yourself and my client a little more distance, please," Caldas said.

Cash shrugged and moved back a little, but was still seated next to the edge of the table. Colcord came back in and placed a steaming cup of tea in front of Margie. There was a chocolate chip cookie on a small side plate as well.

"Thanks," Margie said, and settled into her seat more comfortably as she began to dig into the cookie. Paul wanted to tell her that she was getting too relaxed, but he'd been told not to say anything.

"You know I've been investigating this case from the beginning." Cash leaned back in her chair again, tapping a pen against her leg. "Since you're so good with this financial stuff, if someone wanted to defraud Willy out of money, what do you think we should be looking for?"

"Well, I'm not sure."

"We're not here to deal with hypotheticals, Agent Cash," Caldas interjected sharply. Her arms were crossed now, hands gripping her forearms and crinkling her suit.

"No, no, it's okay," Margie said, taking a sip of her tea. "I really don't know, Agent Cash."

"You can call me Frankie."

"All right, Frankie."

"Thing is, Margie, we have Willy's financial records from Mountainview Bank. Do you think there's going to be anything suspicious that we find?"

"More hypotheticals. My client declines to answer."

Paul glanced nervously at Caldas, who was scowling now. He had a feeling this wasn't going as well as they had hoped. He could see Cash's charm working on Margie in real time.

"No problem, no problem," Cash continued in the same conversational manner. "Thing is, CBI has a financial crimes department, and they're pretty good. They're going to be looking through Willy's records to see what's going on. If it came back that there were some large transfers of money, let's say, how would you explain it?"

"I don't know—it depends on if something did show up—I don't know."

Margie was stammering. Paul shifted nervously in his seat. He was very worried now, but Caldas had told him under no circumstances was he to speak or interfere.

"You see, our financial crimes division is also taking a look at your financial records. So if your records were, say, to show something similar to what Willy's records showed us—how would you explain that?"

"Again, it depends on what shows up." Margie put the tea down a little too hard; it splashed over the side onto the table. She crossed her arms.

"Think there could be anything suspicious about those kinds of transactions?" Cash asked.

Margie didn't say anything. The fussing with her hair had begun again. Paul looked at Caldas, wondering if she was going to stop this. Caldas was staring hard at Margie, but didn't intervene. Maybe this was part of her strategy.

"What would your explanation be, though?"

"I have no clue. I don't even know what to look for."

"But you work as a certified financial planner, right? That's part of your job, right?"

Caldas interrupted then. "This is bordering on harassment."

"Apologies, Margie. I hope you didn't feel harassed." Cash scooched her chair a little farther back with a friendly smile. "Willy's mental state wasn't so good, was it?"

"No. He really struggled with his mental health."

"He probably wouldn't notice if something was off about his financial records, right?"

"Yes, and that's why I was helping him. He wanted to keep everything confidential. He made me promise."

"What did he want to keep confidential?"

Colcord leaned forward now. He was on Margie's left; Cash was on her right. She looked a little like a trapped animal from where Paul was seated. Paul's hands were clutched on the edges of the metal chair. He wanted to launch himself from the chair, to stop this interrogation. But he remembered what Caldas had said: *Don't interfere.*

Colcord spoke, his voice low. "There are some things that just need to be cleared up here. I think you're a very good lady—"

"I try, I try—" Margie laughed, but it was forced.

"A God-fearing woman who's dedicated to the church. And you know sometimes everybody has a breaking point and makes bad decisions. . . . Well. Some of these records that we've been looking at, I think . . ." Colcord sighed, looking troubled. "I think you're aware of why we're here."

"Maybe. I don't know."

"I think you know what we're talking about," Colcord repeated.

"Get to your point, Sheriff. She's not a mind reader," Caldas snapped.

"Sure." Cash slid a sheaf of paper over to Margie. Paul recognized it as the bank statements showing the outflow of cash to Paradox. Caldas had prepared them for this. Margie and Caldas read it in turn.

Caldas threw the paper back on the table. "We know all about these transactions. Tell *Agent* Cash about what these transactions are." A slight emphasis on the *agent* part, as if to remind Margie that these were officers of the law.

"I made a promise to Willy not to talk about these."

"Willy's gone," said Colcord. "And we need to know."

"They're . . ." Margie collected herself. Paul hoped she remembered what they had practiced over their Zoom calls. "They're donations I was making on behalf of Willy Grooms. There was an organization that he was supporting. . . . It's called Paradox. He never told me what the organization was, or what the money was for. But he promised it was for a worthwhile cause. He asked me to make these donations on his behalf. The reason I transferred the money into my account and then out again was because Willy asked me to do it that way. He was a little paranoid— but he's my client, so I did what he asked me to do."

"And are there any written records of these requests?" Colcord asked.

"Well, no. . . . We talked about it in person. But it's not like I was keeping all the money; I was transferring it back out to Paradox."

"The Brooksfield Ranch," Cash said, "was struggling recently, isn't that right?"

"We have our ups and downs, like any business."

Cash pulled a few more papers from the stack in front of her and slid them across, tapping a forefinger on some lines. "Looks like you had some heavy medical expenses too—your daughter—Lolly, I believe?—has Turner syndrome. Looks like you went into the red here, isn't that right?"

"The insurance . . . wouldn't pay," Margie said. "She had to have heart surgery, and they wouldn't pay."

"I don't see what this has to do with anything," Caldas said.

"They're just questions." Colcord nodded at Cash to continue.

"Looks like you were late on some payments but then used part of the transfer from Willy Grooms's account to pay off those bills, right? See this sum here?"

"Well, yes. Willy paid me for my services. I transferred what he instructed over to Paradox, retaining the remuneration we both agreed upon for my services."

"Do you have invoices for those services?"

"No, like I said. We handled all these transactions verbally, in person. Willy didn't want anything put down in writing. But I have a list of payments."

"But no records. You agree that as a certified financial planner, it's pretty important to keep records, right?" Cash raised her eyebrows.

"Don't answer that," Caldas said.

"When you do the math, looks like you retained the sum of $220,000 with those last transfers. Is that what you agreed on with Willy?"

"The insurance company wouldn't pay."

"But did Willy *agree* on that sum?"

"I . . . borrowed the money. I was going to pay it back."

"You borrowed the money. Without Willy's knowledge?"

Margie said nothing. Paul stared at her, confused. *Borrowed the money?* That wasn't what she'd told him. They had gone through an awful time with the insurance company and in the end never got reimbursed. They said the surgery was "elective."

"I was going to pay it back . . . ," she said.

"So you borrowed the money from Willy, without his knowledge."

Margie didn't speak.

"We also found this." Cash slid over the document Romanski had found in the cabin.

Paul craned his neck to see what it was. Margie took it up and began to read it. Her hand began to tremble.

Cash continued, "Margie, I know this is tearing you up because you're a good person. I know you wouldn't normally do something like this. I think you were just pushed to the brink. The ranch was struggling. You weren't just broke, you were almost bankrupt. You had medical bills. You and your kids didn't deserve that; nobody does. Willy didn't need the money, right? He didn't have bills to pay. That's why you took almost a quarter million dollars. And then there's *that*."

"Hang on a second—" Caldas snatched the paper from Margie and began to read it. "You can't *ambush* my client with new evidence during questioning."

"We sent it to your email this morning," Colcord said mildly.

Cash ignored her, continuing, "You couldn't take it anymore. That's why I'm giving you this chance. People are going to look at this and

say, 'You know what? She made a mistake, but she owned up to it.'"
She paused. "Or are you going to be the person who comes in here and
doesn't tell the whole truth—and people are going to say, 'Well, she's not
as good a person as we thought she was'?"

Margie shrank back, looking panicked. "I—"

"Don't answer that," Caldas interjected quickly, holding the paper
up. "Where did you get this?"

Cash continued in the same forceful voice, "Here's your opportunity
to explain, Margie. We're talking at least a few million dollars. That's a
lot of money. It would do a lot of good for your kids and pay off the medical bills. I can understand the pressure you were under." Cash leaned in,
stabbing her finger at the paper. "That's Willy's last will and testament,
and guess who's getting all his money. You. There are a few million still
in his bank account. *Did you kill Willy Grooms for this inheritance?*"

"I—I had no idea—I've never seen that—he never said—"

"You had no idea? But, Margie, look here, *look* at the signature of the
person who *witnessed* this document—you. *You signed this!* And now
you're telling us you've never seen it, had no idea?"

Margie stood up abruptly, sending her chair tumbling.

"This interview is terminated," said Caldas in a fury. "This is an ambush. You'll be lucky if any of that makes it into court."

Margie was already on her way out of the room. Paul jumped up and
followed her out into the hall, where she had come to a halt, head in her
hands, sobbing. "He never told me . . . ," she sobbed. "I never knew . . .
He had me witness and sign all kinds of nonsense. . . . I was just trying
to help."

Caldas came out, her face dark. She was angry. She took Margie's arm
roughly. "Let's go. Now," she said, and began to steer her down the hall.
Paul, in a panic, followed, and then as they were about to exit the double
doors, he glanced back. Cash and Colcord had come out of the room and
were standing in the hall, both with triumphant, almost giddy looks on
their faces, which frightened Paul almost more than anything that had
happened in the room.

23

Tyler Hill sat on a flat rock at the edge of McMillan Lake, knees tucked under his arms. The hot sun throbbed on his shoulders as water dripped down from his recent swim. Lacey Flowers lay on her back next to him. An open copy of *The Grapes of Wrath* obscured her face from the harsh sun. The thump of house music emanated from a Bluetooth speaker nearby.

Tyler's friend and college roommate, Walter Towles, sat on the far end of the rock, sucking on a vape and puffing smoke rings that dissipated into the air. Walter was a muscly guy, a gym rat with eyes set deep into his skull and a broad head with a military cut of black hair.

"Hey, Lacey, you want some?" Tyler held out a can of beer beaded with water.

He watched Lacey's toned stomach and the curve of her breasts as she removed the book from her face, shading her eyes with the other hand, and sat up in one lithe movement. She squinted at the beer's label.

"Oh, gross. No. Where are those canned Cabernets?"

Tyler shook his head. "We forgot them in the car."

"Well, I guess I'll have some, then." She grabbed the can and took a swig, and handed it back. She rolled onto her stomach close to him, the sunscreen sticking their arms together, not unpleasantly.

Walter began to rap along to his music, filming himself with his iPhone and throwing up gang signs for the camera. Tyler had to stop himself from rolling his eyes. Trust fund Walter was the furthest thing anyone could be from gangster.

"Wanna jump in again?" Lacey asked, moving her head to kiss his shoulder. He breathed in the scent of her cherry shampoo and the sweetness of her sunscreen, and turned her chin to kiss her more fully, running his other hand across the toned muscles in her thigh.

"Definitely." Tyler stood, limbering his arms above his head, and regarded the lake.

He had been taking girls here since he was fifteen. The routine was perfected now. Two days at the lake, then take her to that fancy restaurant Egg and Bone, and then back to his place. He regarded Lacey, a bead of sweat trickling down the curve between her breasts. He liked Lacey maybe even enough to take her out on his motorcycle.

He scooped her up in both arms. She shrieked as he hollered and heaved her into the lake. She surfaced, laughing, and pushed the sheet of hair from her face.

"Tylerrrr!" she said. "It's cooold!"

He ululated and dove in. He opened his eyes, looking up at Lacey's kicking legs near the surface. He could see for miles down here. Fish flittered about where the water got darker below. He watched as a particularly big fish—a cutthroat trout, he was pretty sure—flicked its tail toward some reeds near the shore and nipped at something white and sluglike, circling around and diving at it again in that plucking manner that fish had. The sluglike thing was poking from a black shape tucked in the reeds near the shoreline. It looked out of place.

He breached the surface of the lake, gasping from the cold, and whipped his hair out of his eyes.

"Tyler, you all right?" Lacey called, seated again from her position on the rock.

"Yeah!" he shouted back. "I think I found something!"

He dove again, eyes open, seeing the blurry white thing in the reeds once more, and frog-stroked over to it. The trout was still picking away at it, clouds of silt kicking up. As he got closer, he realized it wasn't a slug at all. He couldn't quite make it out in the murky water he'd stirred up, but it was fat, like an elongated golf ball, poking from a suitcase. The white thing was extruding from a gap where the two zippers had come apart.

Tyler surfaced, realizing it was shallow enough to stand. The water was up to his chest, and the suitcase was by his feet. He reached down, blindly grasping, and snagged its handle. It was heavy. Putting his face in the water, he opened his eyes to see what he was doing. Maybe he should unzip it. He wiggled the zipper to open the suitcase. It partially unzipped, and the sluglike object became dislodged and floated lazily sideways—with a glint of gold. He grabbed it and stuck it in his pocket to investigate later, keeping the other hand fastened on the zipper. He grimaced, took a deep breath, and then tucked his face back into the water to resume working at the zipper. Slowly, it inched open. Small pieces of debris floated upward and into his face from the widening crack, obscuring his vision. The zipper was caught on something inside the bag. He gave it one more enormous yank, and the zipper came free in a jolt. He felt something squishy float out and bump softly against his shins. He waved at the specks of white debris, trying to make out what it was.

Suddenly, a face emerged from the silt, floating up toward him—a grotesque visage, fat eyes extruding like golf balls, lips blue and sucked in, forehead tight and glossy like a water balloon about to explode, skin mottled with lilac, one ear hanging by a thread, filaments of flesh waving.

Tyler jerked his head out of the water with a scream and thrashed about, trying to get away even as he could feel several more soft things floating out of the suitcase, bumping his legs as they trundled up to the surface. He made a mad scramble for the shoreline, clawed fiercely through the reeds of the bank, falling into the mud and scrabbling his way back up.

Hearing his screams, Lacey came running, a panicked look on her face.

Out of the water, he turned, gasping and watching in horror as the suitcase's contents gently surfaced, like a nightmarish game of bobbing for apples.

"Oh my God, oh my God, Tyler! Are you okay?" Lacey cried, not yet seeing what he saw.

Walter jogged after her in bare feet, laughing. "Holy shit, dude. You sound like a dying pig." He then halted as they both saw what was now floating on the surface.

Walter pulled out his phone and began to record. Lacey began to shriek.

Tyler reached into his bathing suit pocket with a shaking hand, fingers closing around the thing he'd retrieved. He drew it out and opened his palm. A bloated finger, violet in color, wearing a gold band.

Lacey continued to scream as Walter now swung his phone from the collection of body parts to focus in on the finger in Tyler's frozen hand—which he dropped with a yelp.

"Holy shit . . . holy shit . . . holy shit," Walter kept murmuring as he once again turned his camera toward the dismembered body parts drifting to shore.

24

Colcord was late getting to McMillan Lake, having driven all the way from Eagle and then hiking up a mile-long trail. He arrived, huffing for air, embarrassed at how out of shape he was and thinking he really needed to restart his military calisthenics training.

She had gotten there an hour ahead of him and was waiting. When he came up beside her, she was standing with crossed arms, a fierce scowl on her face, flushed and sweaty in the heat of the day. She looked pissed. Really pissed.

"Fucking vultures," she said, gesturing. Catching his breath, Colcord was astonished to see a crowd had gathered behind the crime scene tape, extending well into the trees, dozens of gawkers milling about, many with their cell phones out taking videos. There were a bunch of reporters there too. He spied Robin Twen wearing a pair of black velvet corduroys and a collared shirt, standing a distance back and speaking briskly into the microphone, a cameraman and soundman recording.

"What the *hell* is this?" he said, staring at the seething crowd. He could hardly believe it. "How did they find out so quickly?"

"Some college kid took a video of the body," said Cash. "It's all over social media."

"Jesus. All right, let's take a look," Colcord said.

Cash made a motion for him to follow, and he hurried after her. They had to plunge into the crowd to get past it, shoving and pushing. The press of people was formidable, and some of them seemed to be protesting and waving placards. Colcord felt claustrophobic. The smell of sweat and the frantic pushing of hands and limbs filled him with apprehension—it felt like the restless crowd was about to explode into violence.

"Get back, get back!" he shouted, trying to bull his way through. The usual deference his sheriff's badge and uniform seemed to award him was lost on these people. He continued forcing his way forward, using his elbows to jab and carve an opening. But a sudden surge of people caused him to stumble backward, and he lost Cash ahead of him in the crush. This was unbelievable.

"Out of the way!" he said. "Law enforcement!" He again pushed forward, jostling a man with long hair who was punching a sign into the air, his face distorted with fury. He was chanting some slogan, but in the general hubbub, Colcord couldn't make out what it was. He could see what was on the sign, however—a caricature of a Neanderthal, with beetling brows and a sloping forehead, giant nose, and small chin. The profile was slashed through with a red bar, and above were words scrawled in black marker: SHOOT THE BRUTES!

What the hell? They were anti-Neander protestors, it seemed, wearing blue armbands with what Colcord now realized was an anti-Neanderthal symbol, a few carrying signs that said RE-EXTINCT THE FREAKS and NEANDER KILL ZONE.

"Re-extinct the freaks! Re-extinct the freaks!"

This was nuts. They found a chopped-up body in a suitcase—it had nothing whatsoever to do with Neanders. But lately, it seemed that even public events like concerts in Colorado were attracting anti-Neander protesters. Colcord caught sight of Cash, and he grabbed her arm. Together, they stumbled into the perimeter and ducked underneath the tape.

"We need more deputies up here," Colcord panted, getting on his radio to call in.

"No shit," said Cash.

Colcord made the call and re-hooked the radio to his belt. "What a bunch of assholes!"

Cash shook her head. "God knows. So far, they're staying behind the tape, but if it breaks, we might be looking at a stampede. And the messing up of our crime scene."

"You see those signs?" Colcord said, pointing to the gaggle of protesters wearing blue armbands. They had just forced their way through. "What are they doing here?"

"They seem to think the Neanders did this," Cash said.

They hurried through the trees to the plastic privacy tent set back from the shore. The tent was askew, appearing as if it had been hurriedly set up. Tyrone, from CBI forensics, greeted them in a shaky voice as they entered, along with Michael Reno, his bald pate resplendent in the sun filtering through the entryway. Four sodden suitcases sat side by side on a tarp laid on the ground. One was open, containing a bluish hand and forearm and a mangled foot and calf, nestled among rocks, evidently put in there for weight. A musty smell of wet leaves and the sweet beginnings of rot filled the air. Aisling, all suited up, was crouched, taking samples. Romanski was perched nearby on a steel folding chair, supervising the scene and taking notes on an iPad, his brows drawn together in concentration.

"Got started without ya. Hope you don't mind," Romanski said. "I didn't want these out in the open longer than needed. Those ink slingers are taking pictures of everything. People are going crazy out there."

"How many bodies?" Colcord asked, looking at all the body parts.

"Just one," Romanski said. "I'm pretty sure."

A cell phone rang among the CSAs working on the crime scene.

"Hey! Silence that shit," Cash snapped. "We got enough noise around here." She swung around to Colcord. "When are your deputies gonna get here?"

She was in a foul mood, Colcord thought—and no wonder. "An hour, at least. Coming in by chopper fast as they can."

"Shit," said Cash.

Romanski hopped down from the steel folding chair. "You folks wanna hear my exciting summary of how the body was dismembered?"

"I guess," Colcord grimaced.

"I'll have a toolmark specialist check it out, but at first glance, it appears there are marks on the bone consistent with a saw. From a naked-eye perspective, the kerf is wider, which generally means a reciprocating blade was used rather than a handsaw—"

"Kerf?" Cash interrupted. "English, please."

"Kerf—the width of the cut. There are breakaway spurs where the bone was sawed through almost completely and then forcefully broken the rest of the way by whoever was performing the work. An individual or individuals of some strength performed this dismemberment. There were a couple of false starts—you can see incomplete saw marks on several of the bones where the saw was initially placed before a full cutting motion was made. Once we have a chance to look at these false starts under a microscope, it should provide information as to the tooth pattern and size of the saw. Cut marks on the cartilage will be difficult to analyze, since it's bloated and warped from sitting in the lake. And . . ." He hesitated. "Take a look at that mangled foot." He pointed to the open suitcase.

"I see it," Colcord said.

"Looks like what they did to Willy's foot. Put a Spanish boot on this guy."

"Christ. Cause of death?"

"Not sure yet," Romanski responded. "Need to lay out all the body parts to do that, and that's Huizinga's job."

Colcord could hear the chanting of the crowd getting louder.

"If that crowd breaks through the perimeter," said Romanski, "we're gonna have a lot more than social media posts to deal with."

"I don't suppose you have an ID on the body yet?" Colcord asked.

Cash sighed heavily, looking tired. "Yep," she said, "unless it's a crazy coincidence."

"What do you mean?"

Cash gestured to Aisling. "Open that one again for us, please."

Aisling crouched over one of the suitcases and carefully raised the lid. Inside was what looked like half a rib cage and a pile of intestines. Nestled up against the slimy coils, Colcord could see the gleam of a prosthetic leg.

25

Cash stepped into the Santa Fe Plaza and angled across it toward her destination. It was brutally hot, and she was sweating despite having donned a sleeveless shirt and light pair of cotton pants tucked into rubber boots. Her hair was up with untidy strands sticking to her face. Sweat pooled in the small of her back, and she could feel the beginning tingles of sunburn across her nose and cheeks. The smell of melted cheese and chile wafted across the plaza, making her mouth water. She was hungry—but also late. No time to stop.

She made her way to the adobe façade of the hotel La Fonda, pausing just inside the door in appreciation of the sudden cold rush of air-conditioning. Thank God. She threaded her way through the colorful interior and to the lobby.

"Lumpkins Ballroom? For the UFO convention?" She leaned up against the concierge desk.

The man eyed her with disapproval and finally said, "You mean *UAP* convention? Down the hall to the left."

Cash made a note to herself not to use the UFO acronym.

She had decided to take a quick flight from Denver to Santa Fe—just for the day—to find out more about Castillo, his *UAP* activities, and who might have wanted him dead. According to Reddit, this convention—Truth in the Skies—was one of the more important UAP conferences held in the United States. Castillo had attended as a speaker and panelist the past two years, and according to phone calls and emails found on his cell, he was planning to attend this year as well. She was hoping she could find some attendees who knew him—and she never turned down the opportunity to dig into some New Mexico green chile while in Santa Fe. Her empty stomach rumbled at the thought.

She headed toward the ballroom, perusing the occasional shop window displaying wood carvings and chunky New Mexican jewelry. She passed a blue-haired woman wearing a T-shirt printed with a picture of a flying saucer and stenciled with the words I BELIEVE, DO YOU?

"Convention pass?" said a messy-haired young person manning a desk at the ballroom entry.

Cash pulled out the day pass she'd picked up at the registration desk, and he nodded her in.

She entered the ballroom, keeping her law enforcement badge and lanyard hidden underneath her jacket. The ballroom featured several grand chandeliers and booths lined strategically across a garish red, yellow, and green carpet. The room was crowded, laughter and conversation filling the space.

Cash stopped in front of a booth run by a man with brilliant blue eyes encased in wrinkles. Strands of sandy hair had been swept across his scalp in an unsuccessful attempt to hide his age-spotted scalp. He handed her a pamphlet, which Cash stuffed into her pocket without a second glance. His booth displayed several black-and-white aerial photographs of a circular scar on the land and surrounded by trees lying flat on the ground in a radiating pattern.

"What's this?" Cash said, pretending to be interested.

The man's eyes lit up at the opportunity to speak to a visitor. "The Tunguska event. You've heard of it, of course?"

"A little," Cash lied.

He began gesturing with liver-spotted hands at the various photos that had been pinned to corkboard across his booth. "Occurred on June 30, 1908, near the Tunguska River in Siberia. Two thousand square kilometers of forest flattened with no explanation. A blinding blue light was seen in the sky, shock waves sent people tumbling hundreds of kilometers away, and windows were shattered. The force was more powerful than an atomic bomb. NASA claims it was an asteroid that exploded in the skies over Siberia. But of course"—the old man raised his chin—"we know the truth."

"Aliens?" Cash tried to keep the sarcasm from her voice. She needed these people on her side if she was going to find anything out about Castillo.

"Of course," the man said, not seeming to notice. "A spaceship that landed on Earth. It's the only explanation that makes sense. There was no physical evidence of an asteroid. No crater. A Russian expedition claims to have recovered unusual metal fragments from the impact site. There have been other Tunguska-type impacts as early as AD 1178. I analyze these facts in my book, *Earthfall of Unidentified Aerial Phenomena*."

He handed her a copy from a stack on one of the tables. She flipped it over. A much-younger version of the man in front of her smiled at her from the back cover. She took note of his name: Earl Wield.

"How long you had a booth here at Truth in the Skies, Earl?"

"Around five years, but been coming for fifteen."

"How much for a copy?" She waggled *Earthfall of Unidentified Aerial Phenomena* in the air.

Wield grinned excitedly. "Twelve dollars, miss."

Cash fished a twenty out of her wallet and handed it to Wield. "Keep the change, but mostly for addressing me as *miss*." She smiled. "Listen— maybe you can help me. There's a UAP scholar I was hoping to meet. Javier Castillo. He spoke here last year. Do you know him?"

"Sure." Wield rubbed his chin. "Lots of people know Javi."

"What did he talk about last time?"

"The Pentagon cover-up. Smart guy. We spoke at length about the Tunguska event. He runs a nonprofit that was investigating UAP touchdowns around the world. Wanted to know more about my work."

"What was the nonprofit called?"

"Paradox." The man chuckled. "Cool name."

Cash remembered Castillo telling her he ran a nonprofit investigating UAPs. Paradox was the same organization Margie Brooksfield had been transferring money to. But Brooksfield had denied knowing Castillo, denied having any idea who Grooms was calling on her sat phone. Had she been lying? Could Brooksfield and Castillo have conspired to defraud Grooms out of his money? The possibilities swirled in her mind.

"Um, why is it called Paradox?"

"It's short for *Fermi* paradox, of course."

"Fermi paradox?"

He looked at her a little oddly. "You don't know about that?"

Cash internally winced. She was looking more and more out of place here. "Can you refresh my memory?"

"It goes back to a famous incident in 1950, in the secret city of Los Alamos. Four physicists, including Enrico Fermi, were walking to lunch. The conversation turned to flying saucers and aliens before drifting on to other subjects. Halfway through lunch, Fermi suddenly blurted out, 'Where is everybody?' and then he scribbled a bunch of equations on the probability of advanced civilizations in the Milky Way capable of space travel. The numbers showed that the galaxy should be teeming with aliens and that we ought to have been visited many times. That became known as the Fermi paradox—the paradox being that we seem to be alone. The mystery of the *silentium universi*, the silence of the universe."

"Interesting. Did Javi mention any specific UAP touchdowns he was looking into?"

"Not that I can recall. But he's good friends with Lyla Castleton, who runs the forbidden archaeology booth. She might know more. Why you wanna know?"

"Interested in learning more about UAP touchdowns." Cash kept it short and simple. It was the truth, after all. "Where can I find the forbidden archaeology booth?"

Wield pointed across the ballroom. "Booth closest to the stage. Can't miss her. Bleached blond and loud. But smart as an octopus—high brain-to-body ratio—she's got an Ivy League PhD."

Cash nodded, thanked the man, and snaked her way through the booths toward the stage. She heard Castleton before she saw her. A clarion voice echoed through the room, and as Cash approached, she saw that an excited group of people were clustered around the booth.

Castleton was one of the tiniest women she had ever seen, with an enormous head that looked out of proportion to her body, like a bobble-head one stuck on the dash of a car. She sported a helmet of bleached-blond hair that made her head look even bigger than it was, and she was wearing a bright green collared shirt and dark slacks. She was mid-speech when Cash approached.

"—and our consciousness expands a little more and we're floating on a blue-and-green pebble in space and not the only ones here."

It was clear what the excitement was all about. Castleton's booth contained an intricate construction of colored paper cut and folded into 3D structures of sci-fi-looking cars and cities. The impressive features of the booth were made even more compelling by Castleton herself, who was a masterful speaker full of energy and inflection.

Before approaching, Cash waited until the woman had finished her presentation and the crowd had dispersed a little. She considered for a second continuing to pretend to be a civilian, but decided against it. She took out her lanyard and let it dangle for a moment.

"Lyla Castleton, my name is Agent Frankie Cash."

Castleton considered her. "You're investigating Javi's death."

"Yes."

Castleton motioned to a young girl to take over the booth and stepped away. "I need a drink." Cash recognized her change in demeanor as grief. "Let's check out the Fiesta Lounge."

They made their way back to the front of the hotel to a nondescript bar next to the lobby, and Castleton plopped tiredly into the seat.

"Mind if I record?" Cash asked.

"Yes. I do. No recording," Castleton said, with a finality that warned Cash not to push the issue. She leaned forward, eyes bright with moisture. "I saw the video of his body. Those horrible kids. Saw his head floating in the lake—" She choked up, looking at a point past Cash's left shoulder. "Do you know what it's like to have *that* be your last memory of a person you cared about?"

"I'm sorry, Lyla. I really am. What can you tell me about him?"

Castleton dabbed at her eyes with a bar napkin. "Shot of Hornitos tequila," she said to the bartender. She downed the shot as soon as it was placed in front of her and then ordered another one on the rocks. She sipped this one now, deep in thought. Cash made no move to rush her.

"Coauthored a paper with me. A genius, Castillo was. Always thinking outside the box. He could also be a flake, unfortunately. Stopped answering his phone and email halfway through the study, and I ended up having to complete the paper by myself." Castleton took a sip of the tequila. "Found out later he'd rushed off halfway around the world in pursuit of some Laotian guy in the jungle claiming an abduction. He was a good person, despite his faults."

"May I ask how he lost his leg?"

"That's a story. About three years ago, he was trekking out to a UAP crash site in Portugal in the Serra da Estrela mountain range. Waded into a river to get a picture of a water vole on his iPhone, cut his leg. Sepsis did the rest. UAP-ology had taken his career and his leg, he used to say. The man was obsessed."

"What can you tell me about his organization, Paradox?" Cash asked.

"That was his baby. A nonprofit investigating UAP evidence."

"That's it?"

Instead of answering the question, Castleton asked, "You think his involvement with Paradox has something to do with his death?"

"Maybe. Who else was involved with Paradox besides Castillo?"

Castleton's mouth turned downward in a frown. "Castillo claimed he ran it. He was board chair. But . . . there were rumors."

"What kind of rumors?"

"That some European big shot was the firepower behind it all."

"What's his name? And where in Europe?"

"I don't know."

"Why the secrecy? Was there some kind of other purpose to Paradox besides UAP research?"

"I don't know." Castleton's eyes shifted away from Cash's gaze. "I hope you find whoever did this."

"Did he have any enemies? Anyone who might want him dead?"

"I don't think so. Everyone liked him."

"Back to this European guy. Can you tell me anything about him? Any other rumors about him?"

Castleton shook her head. "I don't even know if he exists." She stood up, brushing invisible crumbs from her pants. "Gotta get back to the booth."

Cash could tell she was done answering questions. She watched her disappear from the bar. She paid the bill and returned to the convention, which was winding down for the day. She asked around. Everyone knew about Paradox—it seemed to be a respected and legitimate nonprofit—but nobody seemed to know anything about a cryptic European recluse or what his connection was to Paradox.

26

"Sheriff, there's a priest here to see you," came the voice over the intercom of Colcord's office. "He won't say what it's about."

Colcord sighed. Ever since that damn video of the Castillo body had bounced around the world, the sheriff's office in Eagle had seen a steady stream of overimaginative witnesses, psychics, amateur detectives, and other cranks—all coming out of the woodwork. The major social media platforms had taken the video down, but it had been too late—like the contents of Pandora's box, it could never be put back. Incredible to think that forty million people had passed around a video of bloated, dismembered body parts floating in a lake, with a girl screaming in the background. Many had reposted it with music and supposedly funny commentary. What the hell was wrong with the world?

"Priest?" he asked crossly.

"Um, Irish, I think."

"And he won't say what it's about?"

"Only that it has to do with the Castillo case."

A priest. His first impulse was to send him away, but he already had one priest raising hell and certainly didn't need another. "Send him in."

A moment later, he came in. Colcord was surprised—although the man was dressed in the usual clerical garb and collar, he was a big, awkward, genial redhead with freckles.

He stuck out his hand. "Brother Niall Armagh, of the Pallottine Fathers."

Colcord shook his hand. "Sheriff Colcord. Please, have a seat."

The father, or brother—Colcord wasn't sure what the difference was— took a seat. There was something appealing and disarming about the man in his awkwardness and earnest demeanor. His Irish accent was faint and slightly overlaid with what sounded like a Chicago drawl.

"Now, ah, Brother Armagh, what can we do for you?"

"I have information that I believe might be relevant to the Castillo murder."

"Please go on."

The priest hesitated. "Before I speak, I need to ask you to keep this strictly confidential."

At this, Colcord gave an audible sigh. "Brother Armagh, we'll keep it confidential for now. But if it somehow is relevant to the murder, we can't promise confidentiality if it goes to trial."

After a hesitation, Armagh said, "Very well. I'm a brother of the Irish Pallottines in Rome, in the Basilica of San Silvestro. One of our responsibilities is looking after an important Christian relic, the head of Saint John the Baptist."

Colcord began to feel a little uneasy. "I'm not sure I quite understand. Not being Catholic, you see."

"Of course. Saint John, the Forerunner of Christ, was beheaded. Our basilica in Rome has a holy relic from his body—the parietal bone of his skull, to be precise. It is mounted on a head modeled in wax and kept in a chapel in a sealed, atmospherically controlled glass box."

"I see." Colcord shifted in his seat, thinking this all sounded quite ridiculous.

"Two months ago, that relic was vandalized. An individual broke into the sealed container, interfered with it, and removed a piece of bone. We captured the entire episode on video. Rather than alerting the Italian police, the Vatican looked into the case quietly. They quickly identified the individual—an American."

He paused. Colcord waited for him to continue.

"I was asked by the Vatican—actually, on direct orders of the Holy Father—to come to America and quietly retrieve the object. The goal here is simply to get it back, not involve the police."

This was getting crazier by the minute. Colcord wondered if this man really was a priest—or just some nut in a dog collar. "Just a moment," Colcord said. "You're saying you were sent here by the *pope*?"

"That's correct." The man laughed disarmingly. "I know, it sounds dubious. Just hear me out, please."

Colcord suppressed the urge to eject the man outright. "I'm listening." He made a point of looking at his watch.

"Well, that's just it. I flew to San Francisco and went to his residence. He wasn't there, and after asking around, I learned he had traveled to Colorado. As I was about to board my flight, I heard a news report about a rather gruesome video circulating on the internet—and that's how I learned the man I was seeking had been murdered. His name is—was— Javier Castillo."

Colcord rose: It was time to terminate this absurdity, this man who claimed the pope had sent him on a secret mission. This case was just one rabbit hole after another. "I appreciate you bringing this to my attention. We'll add it to the case files. Thank you."

But Armagh didn't move. Instead, he reached into his cassock and removed an envelope, from which he took a folded piece of paper and laid it on the desk in front of Colcord. "I realize that everything I've said probably sounds made-up. This is a copy of a letter signed by His Holiness, authorizing my mission. If you call that number, you can confirm everything I've told you."

Colcord glanced at the letter. It had a conglomerate of stamps and seals and gold embossing, with a big flourish that purported to be the pope's signature. It looked like something Armagh could have created with colored paper and some candle wax. What a joke. "We're very busy here. Thank you for your information. I'll see you to the door."

Armagh rose. "I have some security footage of the crime on my phone I can show you."

"I'm sorry," said Colcord. "I don't have time right now to look at a video."

"Well then, I'll leave the letter with you, Sheriff. At the bottom is the private phone number of a cardinal in the Holy See who can confirm my mission. Please call it any time of the day or night. *Please.* And my cell number is written below it so you can get in touch with me."

"Thank you, Father," said Colcord, barely hiding his vexation now. He had a lot of work to do.

The man got up and left. With a huge sigh of annoyance, Colcord snatched up the letter and looked at it more closely. Impressive job, realistic and fancy, stamped and embossed, written in Italian and English. The cardinal's number was there—an overseas number.

He tossed it aside to be filed away and forgotten with the growing mass of other bullshit evidence.

He went back to what he had been doing before the phony priest came in—checking security camera footage from stores in downtown Burns the night the four hikers had trekked through the Brooksfield Ranch. A lot of the footage had been taped over by the time they contacted the various businesses, but it was taking an inordinate amount of time to get through the footage they did recover. The more recent footage from the day Javi was murdered hadn't given them anything either. He was almost certain he was wasting his time.

After an hour, his eye strayed to the letter. He stretched, taking a break from hunching over the computer. Could it really be from the pope? Totally crazy. But . . . he needed a break from the monotony of this task anyway. He pulled the letter back in front of him. It was a photocopy, but the copy itself had been embossed and stamped and fancied up. Of course it was phony. He pursed his lips, then, after a long moment, pressed the button on his intercom. "Maggie, could you please call this overseas number and put me through?" He read her out the number.

Ten minutes later, Colcord dialed the cell phone of Brother Armagh, who answered immediately. Colcord asked him to return to his office in one hour sharp. Then he called Cash. He knew she was in Burns, a fifty-minute drive away.

"You gotta get here right now," he said. "We've got what I think might be a major break in the Castillo murder."

27

Brother Armagh had spent the time waiting for the call from the sheriff looking up parishes and priests in the area. The little town of Burns had an interesting church, Saint Mary's. And Burns, he learned, had been founded by miners from Silesia who had been brought over to Colorado in the 1880s during the silver rush. As a result, the little town was still almost entirely Catholic, and the congregation of Saint Mary's was active and lively, run by an energetic priest named Timothy Moore. Intrigued, Brother Armagh decided to make a courtesy call on Father Moore as soon as he could.

Meanwhile, he had a sheriff and some police officers to talk to. He returned to the sheriff's office at the appointed time and was ushered into a conference room.

"Father Armagh," said Colcord, far more warmly than before, "thank you for coming back. I do apologize for, well, not taking you as seriously as I should have. This is a high-profile case, and we've been deluged with unreliable witnesses."

"Quite understandable. I'm glad it worked out. And it's Brother Armagh—I'm not an ordained priest."

"Oh, I see. I'd like to introduce you to Agent Frances Cash of the Colorado Bureau of Investigation. She's in charge of the investigation."

"Thank you," said Agent Cash, standing up and giving his hand a good firm shake. She looked like a no-nonsense woman, obviously capable, perhaps even formidable. "Brother Armagh," she said, "the sheriff explained in brief your mission here. I want to assure you we're here to help you and the church recover the relic that Mr. Castillo seems to have stolen and to solve his murder. To do that most effectively, would you be willing to answer some questions?"

"Of course."

"May we tape the conversation?" She held out her cell phone.

Armagh hesitated. "The Holy Father," he said, "was hoping to avoid publicity and a potential scandal."

"And so are we," said Cash. "Most definitely." She put the cell phone away and took out a notepad and pencil. "Better?"

"Thank you."

"We'll do everything in our power to keep this confidential," the woman said. "But there could be a connection between the Castillo homicide and this theft. So any information you can give us will benefit us both—you in recovering the relic and us in solving the case."

Armagh nodded.

After going through some preliminaries, the woman asked, "Can you please tell us about the theft, when it took place, how it was done, and how you identified Mr. Castillo as the thief?"

"Gladly. Our order of the Irish Pallottines serves the Basilica of San Silvestro in Rome, and we are custodians of its relics. We have a long history there, going back centuries."

Cash nodded.

He held up his phone with a wry smile. "Ready for that security footage now?"

"Yes."

Armagh showed it to them, while filling them in about the details of the crime.

"Tell me," said Cash when the video ended. "How was he able to bypass the alarm system?"

"The fellow had an accomplice, a man named Silva, who knew exactly what to do and supplied him with specialized equipment. He had a device that he plugged into the same circuit that serviced the alarm on the relic, tripping the circuit breakers. Unfortunately, the alarm wasn't set up to go off during a power failure."

"No backup battery?"

"No. I'm afraid, Agent Cash, that we weren't as sophisticated as we should have been. Anyway, he then went into the chapel, stood on a bench, used a handheld cutting tool to open the seam around its base and lift it. With another fitting on the same power tool, he cut out a piece of the skull and put it in a glass tube, sealing it. He then carefully fixed up the relic and replaced the cube on top, trying to make it look undisturbed."

"When you say 'carefully,'" Cash asked, "did it seem he was trying to cover up evidence of the disturbance?"

"Definitely so. I've seen the videotape, and he was clearly trying to make everything look as it did before, hoping the theft wouldn't be noticed."

"But it *was* noticed."

"Thanks to one of our eagle-eyed brothers, who prayed to the relic every morning."

"So how did Castillo exit the church with his relic?"

"He went back into hiding, and as soon as the church opened that morning, he mingled with the visitors and walked out."

"And the accomplice, Silva?"

"He vanished completely. We tried to find him—and believe me, the Vatican knows how to find people."

"How did you identify Castillo and track him down?"

"Rome is blanketed in CCTV cameras these days. We were able to trace him from the church to his pensione and back. In Italy, you have to show a passport to check into a hotel. It was forged. But by tracing his movements from the pensione to the airport, we were able to establish his real identity, because he flew in on a real passport in his real name."

"And you think Castillo still has, or rather had, the relic?"

"We do. While we can't know for sure, from all we can tell, he didn't pass it along to anyone."

Now Cash leaned on her elbows and gave him a searching look. "Do you or the church have any idea of his motive?"

Armagh spread his hands. "At first, we thought it might have something to do with a dispute about the authenticity of the relic. There are four churches that claim to have relics of Saint John, and perhaps this was an attempt to prove our relic was bogus, or the opposite."

"And how would they prove that?"

"By scientifically dating it, for example, to see if it really was two thousand years old. Or testing the bone to see if it was human. But then I found out that Javier Castillo was Jewish. That seemed to rule out an internal Catholic dispute or conspiracy."

"Castillo was Jewish?"

"Yes. At least, that's what the Vatican investigation established."

At this, Cash made a note. "Any other theories?"

"All I have are guesses."

"So tell us, Brother, how did you become involved?"

"The Holy Father was consulted, and he wished to avoid publicity by sending someone to track down Mr. Castillo and see if he could be persuaded to give back the relic. I was that person, because I'd worked for years in prison ministries in Chicago. So I flew to San Francisco, I learned he had come to Colorado, I followed him out here—and then, of course, I found he'd been murdered."

"How were you planning to persuade him?" Cash asked.

"I was going to threaten him with criminal prosecution."

"You weren't going to appeal to his better nature?"

At this, Brother Armagh chuckled. "During my years in Chicago, I quickly discovered that appealing to someone's 'better nature' rarely works. I was going to take a strong line with Castillo. He was a wealthy man with a great deal to lose."

"Up to threatening him with actual violence?"

"Agent Cash! Of course not. We are a peaceable, pious, and pacifist order. I resent the implication."

"Apologies," said the woman, not sounding apologetic at all.

After a short silence, the sheriff, who had been silent, cleared his throat. "Brother Armagh, I have a few questions."

"Yes, Sheriff?"

"Is it possible the killing might have been in retaliation for the theft and desecration of the relic?"

"I greatly doubt it. Nobody knows about the theft beyond a small circle in Rome—the Pallottine Brothers, the Holy Father, Cardinal Collini, a few others. There are no murderers in our midst, I can assure you. And once again, I must protest the implication that any of us would be involved in murder."

"I'm sorry, Brother, but it's our job to ask offensive questions."

"I realize that, Sheriff, but to think that one of us is a murderer . . . Impossible."

"Having worked in a prison ministry," said the sheriff mildly, "perhaps you've learned that anyone might be capable of murder, given the right circumstances?"

At this, Armagh colored. The sheriff, of course, was right. "I see your point."

The sheriff looked at Cash. "Any more questions?"

"Not at the moment."

"I have a question for you, if I may," said Armagh. "I would love to know if you have any leads as to where the relic might be."

"Not yet," said the sheriff, "but we're on it. We're liaising with the San Francisco police and are getting a warrant to search his apartment. We've searched his luggage and hotel room here, with no success. Of course, it may be those who murdered him took it. Or that he did, in fact, deliver it to someone else. We've been trying to piece together his movements before his death."

"You will let me know your progress?"

"Absolutely, Brother. You will certainly be kept abreast of our investigation."

Cash spoke. "How long do you plan to stay?"

"I'll not be returning home until I have the missing piece in my possession," he said firmly. "If it takes the rest of my life."

28

Nova Euclid pulled up her assignments on her Karpel legal case-management software and scrolled through some of the new ones. Five new greenies—the nickname deputy district attorneys had for unfiled cases because of the green paper they used—had popped up in the last twenty-four hours. She grimaced. Her caseload was getting longer by the minute. She paused, briefly, on an unfiled case entitled *People v. Brooksfield*, which was marked with an exclamation point to signify importance. She grinned, feeling her heart quickening in pace. Could this be the case she thought it was?

She quickly scrolled through the case's files, which included a recording of an interrogation, a couple of police reports, completed lab work that had been forwarded to their office, a recording of a 911 call, and some other miscellaneous items. It was definitely the Willy Grooms murder, and now it had been assigned to her. The Colorado Bureau of Investigation was involved, and so was the sheriff's office. Suggested charges that were forwarded from CBI: two counts of first-degree murder after deliberation, four counts of money laundering, two counts of embezzlement, one count of forgery.

Euclid noticed with distaste that defense counsel was Belen Caldas, an aggressive and expensive defense attorney. Caldas had recently mopped the floor with Lukas Otto during a felony theft trial, despite the fact that Otto was a seasoned prosecutor with over thirty trials under his belt. She would have her work cut out for her, that was for sure.

Euclid pulled up the case notes. Among them was a request to visit the district attorney, Udoka Adewale, before filing. *People v. Brooksfield* was the highest-profile case currently being assigned out. After two years of working as a deputy district attorney in the homicide unit, this would be her biggest one yet. A real beaut. A career-maker.

Euclid closed her laptop and disconnected it from the monitor before hurrying down the hallway of the Fifth Judicial District Attorney's Office, dodging gaggles of penguin-suited prosecutors on their way to their morning hearings. She paused in front of the DA's mahogany door, distinct from the hollow-core wood doors to other offices that lined the spartan hallways. She rapped politely and heard the muffled invitation through the thick wood.

Euclid angled open the door, shutting it quietly behind her, and stood to attention in front of Adewale's executive desk—also mahogany—which was the size of a pool table. Adewale held up a finger to signify to Euclid she was finishing up something on her computer. Euclid rarely had the occasion to come in here, and she was curious. The room smelled pleasantly of lavender and coconut. An extravagant standing lamp depicting hanging wisterias cast an orange-blue glow. A row of legal books were stratified along the wall behind Adewale's desk. A copy of *Crime and Punishment* sat on the corner of the desk closest to the door, which looked like it had been placed there for show instead of reading, next to a family photo.

"You're here about the Brooksfield case," Adewale stated, rather than asked, sliding out from her seat and holding an elegant hand out for Euclid to shake.

She was a tall and thin woman, with a crop of tight black curls and skin so dark it was almost ebony. Simple gold jewelry encircled her neck and wrists. The woman was formidable—and intimidating. Euclid swallowed the frog in her throat and stepped forward with false confidence to shake Adewale's hand.

"Yes, ma'am," she said, "This is the one that's all over the news?"

"That would be a correct assumption." Adewale spoke unpretentiously, but with intention. "There is some unfortunate footage of the second victim that has gone viral on social media. I need someone who can handle the press with tact and care. Naturally, I thought of you. I was pleased with the way you handled the Scalzi case last year."

Euclid smiled, trying not to get giddy from the compliment. Adewale's praise was rare, and when she gave a compliment, she meant it. "Thank you, ma'am."

"This will be a vertical prosecution case. Meaning that you will be the only prosecutor involved from start to finish. Of course, I'll assign one of the newer DAs to help with trial prep later on. I want you to start getting involved in the case now. We aren't ready to file charges against the suspect, Margaret Brooksfield, yet." She tapped the file on her desk with a long polished fingernail. "We need more evidence. Caldas is too good of a lawyer, and we can't let Brooksfield wriggle out if we bring them too early. I've hired a PI to make sure she doesn't flee the country. Philip Ross—I think you've used him before. Make sure to let him know you've been assigned the case and to keep you apprised of any updates, no matter how small."

"How solid is the evidence against Brooksfield?"

"We have DNA evidence of her on scene. Suspicious transfers of two-point-five million dollars of Grooms's money to an account of a nonprofit organization called Paradox. She's admitted to embezzling two hundred and twenty thousand dollars from those transfers. Not only that, but she's the sole beneficiary of his estate, which it turns out is worth millions. She claimed to know nothing about that, despite the fact that she witnessed and signed the will—and admits that it's her signature."

"Solid motives there."

"Yes. And there are some religious aspects to the first homicide with the wafers and Communion wine—Brooksfield is deeply religious. We have evidence of her presence at the cabin during the general time period when the torture and homicide were committed."

"Is there any direct physical evidence connecting her to either crime?"

"Not yet, and that's a concern. Investigators are working on it. We're pretty sure she knows more than she's admitted so far. We also know at least three other individuals were involved in the murder. Our strategy is to put pressure on her to turn state's evidence and plead. Maybe we won't even have to file charges."

Euclid felt a little uneasy about the approach, but it was pretty standard, and after all, the defendant had already admitted embezzlement. While the evidence for murder was circumstantial, Brooksfield was no innocent.

"What are our talking points for the press?"

"I'm sure you know this, but it doesn't hurt to have a reminder: Ethical rules of conduct prevent prosecutors from making public statements that would prejudice the proceedings or rile the public. This is a big one, so I'll handle the pressers, which you'll also attend. There's one this Wednesday at eleven a.m. If you get ambushed, our sound bite is, *We are working closely with the sheriff's office to efficiently resolve the case and cannot comment at this time on an active investigation.* Don't mention CBI. There's some bad press going around about CBI Agent Cash, and I want to distance ourselves from it where possible."

Adewale turned to look at Euclid with fierce green eyes. "Not that this is an issue, but I want you looking smart, clean, and lively every day. This case will be a lot of work, and we can't have you leaving the office looking like you slept on your desk—even if you did."

Euclid laughed. "Got it."

"Lastly, case files don't leave the office. I've heard through the grapevine there might be a leak."

"Definitely won't have to worry about that with me."

Adewale nodded. "Margie Brooksfield was not working alone. The torture, the subsequent embalmment—this screams conspiracy and that she was almost certainly an accessory. We need the people she's working with, and for that, we need to put maximum pressure on her. More evidence is essential. When we strike, we want to charge as many counts as possible to encourage the defense to bargain them away."

"Agreed."

"I'm counting on you, Nova. This is your first big one. If you crush it, there could be a promotion for you on the horizon."

Euclid said her goodbyes and left Adewale's office. This was her moment, and she would be damned if she would let it pass her by. Belen Caldas was going down.

29

Cash watched as Blaisdell Holmes folded her hands together and leaned forward across the elongated conference table, pinched brow marring her normally smooth features. Huizinga and Romanski were there—along with George Standish. He caught her eye and gave her a two-fingered salute across the table, which immediately annoyed her. She pondered for a moment how unfair it was for her to be so judgmental of the guy. But then again . . . why would a grown man use baby oil in his hair?

"I've called this meeting to review the facts. The DA's office is now involved and it's become a vertical prosecution case, so the sheriff's office and CBI will be working closely with them. Given the media attention this case is getting, DA Udoka Adewale will be heading all pressers. She's being assisted by Deputy DA Euclid. I might add, the media drumbeat, that unfortunate video, and a perceived lack of progress by law enforcement has caused a backlash of adverse publicity."

A young woman seated near Holmes—presumably Euclid—nodded at the introduction. Adewale was seated next to her. Cash examined the two women. Euclid looked young, but she had the collected manner of someone older. Bright green eyes were shadowed by strikingly dark eyebrows, and a slight dusting of freckles was scattered across her cheeks. The DA, Adewale, was an alarmingly thin woman with high cheekbones and an imperious air about her. Cash had heard she was supposed to be good. She wondered about Euclid's experience—she looked fresh out of law school.

Cash never liked these meetings in the DA's office. Like most government buildings, the room smelled musty, the once-white walls a faint yellow, the halls permeated with the scent of old coffee. At least the conference table was new, a shining expanse of oak.

Holmes continued, "I cannot impress upon all of you the importance of your media training at this sensitive time. The country is looking at us. The assumption should be made that everything we say or do in public will be recorded. With social media, anything can be spliced, edited, and taken out of context—therefore any statements we make to the media will be brief and to the point. Longer statements will be left to DA Adewale."

Colcord shot Cash a pointed look, which she did not appreciate. She glared back at him.

"Furthermore"—Holmes gave a sigh—"I'd like to note that there appears to be a press leak, possibly in the sheriff's office or CBI. This case will be proceeding on a need-to-know basis. Do not talk about it with anyone outside this room unless absolutely necessary. And when you do, keep a record of everyone you've spoken with and the details of the conversation. The Brooksfields' defense attorney, Caldas, has informed me that someone leaked Margie Brooksfield's name to the press. There is currently an encampment of reporters and protesters on public land outside of her client's ranch. This is not a good look, people—and it's also a safety issue. Sheriff Colcord has been forced to dispatch deputies out there to maintain the peace. Another point on the media—and I can't even believe I even have to say this: no talk about aliens."

A cascade of laughs ran around the table. Holmes did not join in, offering the room only a faintly ironic smile as she gazed coolly at each of them in turn. "The alien narrative is already out there, and if it takes flight, we'll be the laughingstock of the entire country. Any questions about aliens by the press or public should be immediately dismissed as ridiculous—and it should be stressed that *we are not pursuing that angle*. I'm turning this over now to CBI's chief medical examiner, Dr. Huizinga, who'll be presenting the autopsy results of the Castillo homicide."

Huizinga stood to the electric whir of a projector screen sliding down from the ceiling against the far wall. He clicked through some slides briefly reviewing the Grooms murder, then he started in on the Castillo case.

A close-up of a bloated bluish foot appeared on the screen, painting the onlookers with a sickly cerulean glow. The foot and shin were misshapen, as if made of molded putty. He clicked, and a CAT scan of the foot took up half the screen. Cash was no doctor, but she could tell by looking at the scan that the bones in Castillo's foot had been broken in multiple places, essentially crushed.

"This is Castillo's left foot. The base of the tibia and fibula, along with the talus, navicular, calcaneus, cuneiforms, and all five metatarsals are fractured. This is exactly what we saw in Grooms's foot, and it leads me to the conclusion that the same device, an iron-cased torture instrument for the leg and foot called a *Spanish boot*, was used on Castillo as it was on Grooms.

"However, there was also a second torture instrument used. Trace evidence of iron oxide indicates that there was a metal band secured around the victim's throat. Perimortem bruising indicates it was there for an extended period of time. Cause of death was the severance of Castillo's spinal cord. A circular hole consistent with a large screw was bored through the back of the victim's neck and through his spinal cord. Detective Romanski looked into what could have caused these injuries, and he discovered that an instrument called the *garrote vil* was likely the murder weapon. The use of seventeenth-century torture instruments here would be consistent with the modus operandi of the Grooms murder."

Dr. Huizinga clicked through to the next slide, and an ancient-looking wooden chair with a metal band looped toward the top—approximately where the neck would be if one was sitting there—popped up. A wicked-looking metal spike jutted from the back of the chair at the same height as the loop. Underneath was the text: *Garrote vil., Exposición Inquisición en el Palacio de los Olvidados de Granada.*

"This is obviously not the actual garrote vil used, just a picture so you can get the idea. You screw from the other side, and the spike goes into the neck like this—" Huizinga bent to grasp the back of Romanski's neck, made turning motions with his hand along with squishing sound effects from his mouth.

"Easy there, Doc," said Romanski, with a nervous laugh.

"All right, Dr. Huizinga. No need for the theatrics. We get the point," Holmes said. "I'll state the obvious: That chair is a large device, and that implies the killers have a safe house or base of operations somewhere nearby. This is a route of investigation we're now pursuing. Continue to the next slide."

"Yes, please do," Romanski said, rubbing the back of his neck. He cast a rueful smile at Cash behind Huizinga's back.

Huizinga went on, "The body was disarticulated postmortem—here's a diagram."

Cash stared at a schematic of a human body, spread-eagled, with black lines indicating where cuts occurred.

"The limbs were separated at these various articulations through use of a blade to cut through harder bone and cartilage. Efficiently done. The body parts were placed in four identical black nylon suitcases along with large stones and sunk in the bottom of McMillan Lake. I understand forensics is attempting to trace the origin of the suitcases, so far without success. One of the suitcases was found by college students—you've all seen the video, I assume. The other three were found by the diving team in various deep parts of the lake.

"Based on Reh's forensic immersion tables, degree of maceration and putrefaction, bacterial load and osmolarity of the water, temperature, and degree of bloating, all indicate the submergence occurred not long after death. The interval of submergence was no less than eight and no more than thirty-six hours.

"Dissection of the stomach found no evidence of Communion wine or wafers. The body was also not embalmed. DNA, trace evidence, and other investigative methods are ongoing by Detective Romanski and his team but have not as yet turned up any of use."

Cash shot a quizzical look at Colcord. Why had the body not been embalmed, but the other was?

Huizinga made a small, awkward nod to Adewale and sat abruptly to signify he was finished.

"Thank you, Doctor." Holmes stood now, clasping her hands behind her back, and began pacing slowly at the front of the room as she spoke. "Based on what Dr. Huizinga has presented, that means Castillo was murdered in late June. Getting back to the Grooms homicide," she said, "our main suspect so far is Margaret Brooksfield, 'Margie,' whom we believe is an accessory. She benefited from his death as the only heir to his estate worth several million dollars. Furthermore, she'd embezzled almost a quarter of a million from him in the preceding several years to pay medical bills. She was in the vicinity of the cabin around the time it has been estimated the torture of Grooms began. There was movement of funds from his account through hers to an offshore entity called Paradox, and from there, it disappeared into a network of shell companies to disguise ownership—which looks a lot like money laundering. Castillo was the founder of Paradox and served as the chair of its board, and it seems he pretty much ran the show. What's also clear is Brooksfield did not act alone, judging from footprints, witness observations, and the elaborate, ritualistic nature of the murder. There's a lot to untangle here, and unfortunately, we do not believe we have enough evidence yet to arrest her." Holmes turned, gesturing at George Standish. "We're bringing in Agent Standish to assist with this part of the investigation, as he is a specialist in digital forensics at CBI."

Cash kept a carefully neutral face as she digested this news.

"Adding to the complication, it appears Castillo is a suspect in the theft of an important Christian relic from a church in Rome—a piece of the cranium alleged to be from Saint John the Baptist. I've included more information on that in your reports. How this connects with the two homicides, if at all, is unknown at this time."

She looked around. "That's it. Are there any questions?"

After a moment, the deputy DA, Euclid, spoke. "There's a lot of circumstantial evidence here, but what we lack is some actual physical evidence or eyewitness testimony connecting Brooksfield with either murder. A major question is: Why would Brooksfield participate in the ritualistic aspects of the killing if her motive was just money and to cover up embezzlement? The MO suggests something else must have been going on."

Holmes smiled for the first time at Euclid. "Excellent question, Ms. Euclid. And that 'something else' is what I'm tasking all of us here with finding out."

The DA, Adewale, spoke for the first time. Her voice was clear and commanding, and she had a quiet confidence about her that impressed Cash. The table immediately hushed. "Regarding eyewitness testimony, there's an important point that just came to my attention that even my deputy doesn't know about," she said. "I assigned a PI, Philip Ross, to tail Brooksfield to ensure she does not flee the state. He reached out to me this morning, just before this meeting, and informed me of a fact of significant importance to the case. It appears that Javier Castillo visited the Brooksfield Ranch on the morning of the day before his death for approximately two hours. He got into a visible shouting match with Margie Brooksfield that day. Ross couldn't make out exactly what they were arguing about, but he described Brooksfield as angry. Paul Brooksfield, the husband, ended up chasing Castillo away with a gun."

Cash raised her head in surprise. This was big. "We interviewed her with her lawyer present the very next day, and she made no mention of seeing Mr. Castillo. In fact, she vehemently *denied* knowing him." She had felt sympathy for Brooksfield, especially after learning about her daughter's illness and their crushing medical debt—even though she had admitted to embezzlement. She had not struck Cash, however, as a likely accessory to murder. But this new bit of news made her wonder.

"Interesting, indeed," Adewale said.

Colcord leaned forward, arms crossed, blue eyes sparkling with intensity. "Ms. Euclid called for eyewitness testimony. Now, it seems, we have it. Brooksfield saw Castillo the day before he was murdered. She had a serious conflict with him and then lied about it. The victim was, furthermore, threatened with a gun." He looked around the room. "I propose that we now have enough evidence to bring her in."

30

Euclid raised her arms as a young deputy with curly blond hair—couldn't have been more than twenty-four years old—slipped a heavy bulletproof vest over her head. He was handsome, sporting a crooked nose that looked like it had once been broken.

"Is this really necessary?" Euclid chuckled nervously.

"Better to not want it and have it than need it and not have it." He smiled at her reassuringly, squeezing her arm. "You're gonna do great."

He handed her a ballistic helmet, and Euclid clipped it under her chin, feeling a little like a toddler in oversized clothing as it slipped down over her forehead. Now outfitted, she took a seat in a plush office chair in the corner of the Eagle County Sheriff's Office.

A team had been assembled at the behest of District Attorney Adewale to execute the arrest of Margie Brooksfield. It was four thirty in the morning and still dark, the eastern sky just edging into a shade of dark gray that signaled approaching daybreak.

The request for Margie to turn herself in, made to her attorney, Caldas, had been ignored. Euclid could guess why: Caldas wanted a scene of her client's arrest that would make a big splash in the news. It would be a way to take control of the narrative, but even more so to create a spectacle with many opportunities for law enforcement to make missteps that could then be used in court. The goal was, therefore, to effectuate an uneventful and smooth arrest. The team had been carefully picked and was comprised of the primary arrest officer—Sheriff Colcord—along with Agent Cash, six backup officers, a media-coordinating officer, and a weapons specialist. Paul Brooksfield was a gun owner, after all, and who knew how he would react.

Adewale had asked Euclid to accompany the arrest team. It was unusual for the vertical prosecutor to be present for a routine arrest, but this was a high-profile case, and there was some media value in it. There were also complexities surrounding the Brooksfield arrest that might require immediate legal advice, as well as a "supervisor" for evidence collection. Caldas was known for getting her clients off on technicalities, and everything had to be perfect. Everything. That's where Euclid came in.

Her lips thinned in determination. She felt adrift in unfamiliar waters here. But with the promise of a promotion on the horizon, and with her natural instincts making her want to kick Belen Caldas's butt in the courtroom, she knew her attendance would give her an edge.

"All right, quiet down a sec!" Director Holmes shouted above the hubbub. A hush fell over the room. "As you all know, this is a tricky arrest. Our private investigator said there are reporters and protestors camped outside of the Brooksfield Ranch. Where's our media coordinator?"

A pale woman with a beautiful face and a black bob raised a hand. "Josephine Smith, Director."

"Good. I'm sure Sheriff Colcord has gotten you up to speed. You're going to be debriefing the press and public while the arrest occurs. Keep them distracted. Coordinate a path with our deputies through the crowd that we can bring Margie Brooksfield through. It's early, so hopefully there won't be that many camped outside the place. Weapons Specialist Orlov, can you say a few words?" Holmes peered over the sea of tactical helmets. A burly arm was raised. A bear-like man with a hooked nose stepped forward. He towered over the rest of the officers.

"Boris Orlov, ma'am." He craned his neck around to address the room. "Our main priority should be ensuring a peaceful arrest, and compliance from Mr. and Mrs. Brooksfield. Sheriff Colcord and I have debriefed the deputies on how to use our specialized breaching equipment and gone over risk mitigation. I've also impressed the importance of only using weapons like bean bag rounds and Tasers to maintain control and safety. We certainly hope it will not come to that. I've gone over with the deputies what to do if Paul Brooksfield arms himself and resists."

"Good, good. Now the prosecutor?" She looked around.

Euclid stood, clearing her throat nervously. "Here, ma'am."

"Officer Cassian Wiley is your point person. Stick by him."

The attractive blond deputy with the crooked nose nodded somberly at her.

"If any of you have any legal questions," Holmes continued, "ask Deputy DA Euclid here. These include questions on what and where you're allowed and not allowed to search. Questions on escalation of force. Anything of a legal nature at all. And, Ms. Euclid," Holmes said, "if you see any behavior that falls into the gray or red area of the law, please make yourself known. We can't have Caldas bringing anything into court over what happens today."

"Yes, ma'am."

"Let's move out."

Pretty soon, Euclid was sandwiched between Officer Wiley and a female deputy in the back of an SUV, bumping down a remote Colorado road. Agent Cash was driving. Euclid eyed her curiously. Muscles rippled under her shirt as she manipulated the steering wheel. She seemed capable, and Euclid felt a little safer in her car.

But when they arrived outside the Brooksfield Ranch, Euclid was dismayed to see several tents set up on federal land outside. Some had been pitched in the road itself, blocking the gate. Press vans had pulled off the road, idling like sharks waiting to close in for the kill. As they grew closer, she could see signs and placards had been scrawled and staked next to the tents. She strained her eyes to make out what they said, and a flash of headlights on them revealed the words. JUSTICE FOR JAVI, KILL THE FREAKS!, BACK TO EXTINCTION!, NEANDERS: A GOVERNMENT PROJECT, SAPIENS SUPREMACY, and RE-EXTINCT THE FREAKS! Other signs were less aggressive, some of them bearing crosses. IT'S A CRIME TO BE A GOOD CHRISTIAN, they said. Others still said, MARGIE BURN IN HELL, LOCK HER UP, and AREA 51.

"What's all this?" Euclid asked, confused.

"We got crazies," said Agent Cash from the driver's seat, "who think the Neanders are responsible and that Margie Brooksfield is a government plant. We got members of her church protesting. We got people demanding her arrest. And then we got people—" Agent Cash paused to inspect the signs. "Well, I don't know what the hell *they're* protesting."

"Did we know they had blocked the road? Is there another entrance?"

"No," Officer Wiley responded, a troubled expression on his face. "This isn't good, but we'll clear them out."

The train of SUVs slowed to a halt in front of the gate. Sheriff Colcord vaulted out of the front car with several deputies to approach the four tents pitched in the road. Agent Cash followed. It was still dark, and lights began to switch on in the tents, shadows stirring inside. A reporter holding a microphone, followed by a cameraperson, sidled up to one of the SUVs in front of them, shouting questions through the tinted windows. Pretty soon, another reporter was at Euclid's window, shining a flashlight inside. Euclid squinted and shielded her eyes, ignoring him.

"After I leave, make sure that door's locked," Wiley said.

"Where are you going?" Euclid asked, alarmed.

"To help them clear a path. You stay put, doors locked, windows up. Won't need you until we get to the house anyways. I'll be back."

Officer Wiley and the female deputy disappeared from the vehicle, leaving Euclid alone. She watched as they gently shooed the cameraperson away. Angry cries erupted across the dirt road. Euclid couldn't see well through the tinted windows—but well enough to see several men and women were exiting the tents with metal baseball bats, shouting. Some of the deputies had now pulled up the tent stakes and were dragging them off the road, even with people inside. The commotion worsened. Josephine Smith was trying to move the television crews back from the road, as they were shooting the enfolding events.

"Get back!" Cash shouted.

More people poured out of the tents, some picking up signs, others with bats, shouting anti-government slogans. Euclid could see many of them wore blue armbands with Neander profiles crossed out. The dark fury on their faces surprised her—they were beyond angry. Orlov's huge silhouette stepped from one of the cars, wielding a Taser and shouting for them to stand back, temporarily halting their advance. But the crowd was seething, and Euclid could see the beginnings of actual violence.

An especially angry teenager with a pinched brow and a blue bandanna wrapped around his lower face approached her SUV, shouting and holding a bat aloft. He jabbed the bat into a side window, shattering it. Before Euclid could react, he'd reached in, unlocked the door, and pulled it open. She scrambled over to the driver's side and seized the door to pull it closed, but the kid managed to thrust the baseball bat into the doorjamb. He yanked it open.

"Well, lookie-loo here," he said, crawling into the vehicle. "Got myself a government piggy all by herself."

"Get the hell away from me!" Euclid yelled, looking around for Wiley. Where was he? She pressed her back to the passenger door, fingers clawing behind her for the handle to get out the other side. The guy grabbed her foot, and she felt herself pulled toward him. Finally, her fingers snagged the handle just enough to click the door open. She jerked her foot away and went spilling into the dirt of the road. She leapt to her feet, taking off running. Glancing back, she saw the masked teenager coming out the other side of the SUV and start after her.

Everything was in chaos. Shouts and yells reverberated around her. Dust was rising, adding to the bedlam. Euclid couldn't believe how fast everything had happened.

"Come back here, you little bitch!" She heard the voice behind her again as he caught up to her, his hand grasping the backstrap of her bulletproof vest. He jerked her back. She swung around and hit him in the face. Crying out in surprise, he released her and dropped the bat, giving her time to turn and run again. A bang echoed to her left, and another, and acrid smoke suddenly filled the air, an unfamiliar, pungent stench attacking Euclid's nose and lungs and blinding her. She staggered, coughing, her eyes, nose, throat on fire. Jesus Christ, someone had deployed tear gas. Had it been police or protesters?

Suddenly, a palm fell on her shoulder. She whipped around. A terrifying black mask emerged from the smoke like some demented plague doctor. She tried to scream but couldn't. She was choking and could hardly see to move. She stumbled back.

"It's Officer Wiley," the familiar voice said. "I've been looking everywhere for you."

She felt something slip over her head and face, and suddenly, she could breathe again. It was a gas mask. She took deep, gulping breaths, hacking. Her entire face was wet with tears and snot. Another bang, and more gas hissed into the air. She could hear crying, coughing, and screams from the fog. The smoke was everywhere. Euclid could barely see through her tears. Her assailant seemed to have disappeared.

Euclid felt faint and stumbled against Officer Wiley. He scooped her up with ease. One arm looped under her knees, the other supporting her back. Her cheek bumped softly against a muscled shoulder as he strode toward an idling SUV.

"I never should have left you alone. I'm sorry," Wiley said.

He opened the door and placed her behind the passenger seat. Someone had swept the seats free of broken glass.

Next to her was a handcuffed woman in a gas mask who could only be Margie Brooksfield. Euclid could just make out the terrified expression through the mask.

"We got Brooksfield," Wiley said. "Gave herself up voluntarily to try to stop the situation from escalating. Let's get the hell out of here."

Cash was in the driver's seat, and Officer Wiley sat next to her. The CBI agent revved the engine and peeled off down the road, emerging from the clouds of dust and tear gas at speed. Euclid glanced back at the Armageddon they had left behind, the press rushing this way and that, smoke drifting in the air. She was horrified to see an SUV upside down and on fire—a fire that was now spreading through the dry grass and licking up the ranch fence. She could hear sirens wailing in the distance.

Euclid pulled off the gas mask. "What . . . happened?" she panted, raising her arm to wipe snot and tears off her face.

Wiley grabbed her arm to stop her. "Don't—your shirt's still covered in tear gas." He handed her a towel from the front, and she took it gratefully, cleaning herself up.

"Oh my God," she said. "Who deployed the tear gas?"

"They tried to flip Sheriff Colcord's police cruiser and set it on fire with two deputies inside," Cash said. "They barely got out on time. That's when we deployed the tear gas. Several of them attacked our people with bats. An absolute shit show."

"Jesus." Euclid laid her head back on the seat, ears ringing. This had been a catastrophe. Her eyes stung, and her throat was swollen and on fire. She could barely swallow. Belen Caldas would have plenty to work with, that was for sure. Euclid couldn't even begin to imagine how she was going to explain this to the judge. What a mess. She just hoped nobody had been killed.

31

Detective Bart Romanski rapped on the door of Dr. Hitch Baker. The door was ajar, and it eased open at his touch. The doctor was expecting him, but Romanski still felt intrusive as he stepped inside. A ding resounded in the house as his feet crossed the threshold.

"Bart, you can't just *let yourself into other people's houses*," his husband, Nick Wu, exclaimed from behind him.

"Dr. Baker told me to. Said he'd be gardening out back."

Nick tentatively stepped halfway through the door after him, and Romanski grabbed his hand and pulled him the rest of the way in. The door's mechanism dinged again, which Romanski hoped alerted the historian to their presence.

"Calm down. You're always an anxious mess, babe," Romanski said with a wink, squeezing his arm. Normally, Bart would not have brought his husband along on semiofficial CBI business, but Nick had begged and pleaded to have a tour of what he called the "Jack the Ripper museum." He had always had a gruesome imagination.

Nick crossed his arms, and a faint smile appeared on his lips. "Got to keep you out of trouble."

Dr. Baker entered the house through a back door, brushing at the dirt caking the front of his bib overalls. He was a plump fellow, with a congenial air about him that put Romanski at ease. His cheeks were ruddy and his nose was threaded with a web of veins that spoke of drink. He waddled forward with a grin emerging from the center of a bushy white beard.

"Hello, hello!" the man said in a jolly tone of voice. He held out a filthy hand for Romanski to shake.

Romanski stared at it, hesitating.

Nick strode past him to shake the doctor's hand. "Nick Wu. This is my husband, Bart. Thank you for seeing us today."

"Of course, of course. *When you learn, teach; when you get, give,*" Dr. Baker intoned, and raised his eyebrows at Romanski expectantly.

He stared blankly back.

"Dr. Maya Angelou," said Nick.

Romanski was suddenly grateful he had brought his husband along.

"Excellent!" Dr. Baker said as if praising a student. "So," he continued, eyes glinting with interest and sliding to each of them in turn, "you'd like to know more about the Spanish Inquisition and its devices, eh? A fraught subject. Makes a man wonder what for? Curse of being an academic, ever curious—some might call it *snoopy*."

Romanski hesitated. The fact that a Spanish boot had been used to torture the victims hadn't been released to the public. "It's just part of an investigation we're doing, looking into a few things."

"A few things . . . Very well then, *don't* tell me why you're interested. I understand. You are here to see my, shall we say, cabinet of curiosities. Are you familiar with the concept?"

Romanski shook his head.

"There are many books depicting such cabinets. The book *Origins of Museums* is a fascinating historical account of sixteenth-and seventeenth-century cabinets. Then there is *The Cabinet of Curiosities*, a fictional version. A thriller." Dr. Baker turned his nose up slightly. "I don't usually read them, plagued with cheap thrills and tropes, and that trash book is no exception."

"Right." Romanski cleared his throat, not caring to hear more about thriller writers or history books. "Could we see your, ah, cabinet?"

"Follow me."

They threaded their way through the home. It was a rambling, endless old place.

Baker unlocked a door in the back. "Many of these objects are quite valuable," he explained.

They stepped through the threshold.

Romanski looked around, feeling like he was being transported back to the Middle Ages. An orange glow from the early-morning light lit up a bizarre collection of artifacts, relics, bijoux, and odd-looking antiquities. A medieval book of hours stood open on a pedestal in a glass case, and Romanski paused to admire the vibrant hues, gilding, and sweeping strokes of ink that decorated its pages. A full-sized suit of armor stood at attention in the corner. A marble bust was engulfed in a tapestry next to it.

Dr. Baker led them through the room and down a hall lined with books, past a bookcase housing old pottery shards, and into a dustier section of the house.

"Ah, here's something you might like." He stopped in front of an old scroll framed on the wall. It depicted a mechanical woman covered in spikes, stalking down a cobblestone street while peasants cowered in fear. "The Apega of Nabis. A machine the king of Sparta made in the image of his wife, which patrolled the streets of the city to extort money from citizens. If they refused, it would hug the victim, impaling them with spikes. Marvelous, isn't it? I believe this to be one of the earliest depictions of a robot—excluding of course the mechanical bird powered by steam proposed by Archytas of Tarentum in the fourth century BC."

"How romantic," Nick murmured. He slid his arm through Bart's and propelled him forward.

"Charming, I'm sure," said Romanski.

"And here, the infamous thumbscrew." Dr. Baker opened one of the glass cases that lined the walls, pulling out a curious metal contraption. He smiled, holding it aloft with excitement. "The thumbs would go there and would be compressed by a metal bar through twisting this screw. The bones in the fingers would be crushed. One of the most common torture devices used during the Spanish Inquisition—and very effective. Agonizingly painful. Could be used on the toes too."

Nick raised his eyebrows in interest over Dr. Baker's shoulder. "Cool."

Romanski inwardly grimaced, sorry he'd let himself be talked into bringing Nick, who seemed to be enjoying himself a little too much.

Nick peered into a particularly lavish case housing an enormous emerald necklace next to a strange, A-shaped metal frame contraption.

"Ah, I see you've discovered one of the more obscure devices invented during the reign of King Henry VIII." Baker scuttled across the room and placed a loving hand on the device resting on its velvet pillow. "The head of the victim is strapped in here at the top of the A point, the hands here, and legs here. The frame folds and compresses the body until the victim bleeds from the nose and ears. Would you like to try it out? Without folding it, naturally." He directed this question at Nick.

"Well—"

"We don't have time," Romanski interjected quickly.

"Are you sure? It's not every day you get to see a Spanish tickler in person. I sometimes bring these devices on my LARPing trips—that stands for *live-action role-playing*—to make the experience more authentic. LARPers love it. Almost as if you personally were awaiting trial in some dark catacomb, knowing you would be found guilty no matter what you told your captors."

Romanski said, "Actually, Dr. Baker, I'd like to see the garrote now, if you don't mind."

"Ah yes. We mustn't get sidetracked, of course." Baker, looking crestfallen, led the way even farther to the rear of the house.

"*Spanish tickler*," Nick leaned over to hiss in Romanski's ear, winking.

They were led farther back, the neglect of this wing of the house becoming more evident.

"Here is what you're searching for. The garrote vil." Dr. Baker grasped the edge of a white sheet and flicked it off its resting place like a bullfighter. A cloud of dust billowed through the air, and a smell of mildew overwhelmed Nick's cologne.

Underneath was something that looked almost like a simple wooden chair. An iron ring, large enough to support one's neck, was nailed into the post, with smaller rings for the hands and feet. A large crank was attached to the larger iron neck ring. This particular version of the garrote was lacking the spike that Romanski had seen on websites online. He wondered how it worked. He didn't have to wait long to find out.

"This is a Spanish garrote vil actually used by the Inquisition. The seat constrains the condemned person, and the executioner tightens this crank here and suffocates the victim. This type of execution lasted until 1978, when Spain abolished the death penalty."

"The ones I've seen online have a spike."

Dr. Baker's lips thinned. "The ones with spikes are called Catalan garrotes, used as late as 1940. They incorporate a spike directed at the spinal cord to quicken the breaking of the victim's neck. The Philippines was captured by the United States after the Spanish-American War in 1898. The Catalan garrote continued to be used there to execute prisoners until 1902, when the US finally put a stop to it. Frightening how long it took to eradicate such a vicious practice."

"How many of these things still exist?"

"Impossible to know. As you can see, they are fairly simple to make, and I couldn't tell you how many are in museums and private collections around the world."

"What about a Spanish boot and a Maundy gag? You have those in the collection?"

A troubled look now marred Dr. Baker's happy demeanor. "Are you working on a case where these were actually used?"

Romanski didn't answer, and Dr. Baker shook his head. "I don't— those two are rather uncommon. It's one thing to read about the depravity of the Inquisition in history books. But to think of someone inflicting this level of pain on an innocent human being today, if that's why you're indeed inquiring . . . Good heavens!"

Romanski nodded, images of the crushed and mangled foot of Castillo, dismembered and bobbing in waters of a mountain lake, flashing across his mind's eye. "A terrible thing indeed, Doctor."

32

Colcord looked around Javier Castillo's low-rise apartment in San Francisco, not without curiosity. It was graced with a stunning view of the Golden Gate Bridge through the glass wall that stretched across one side of the living room. He imagined it would be a perfect place to see the Fourth of July fireworks that would be happening that very night at nine thirty p.m. They'd twisted some arms to get the search done ASAP, as the pressure on the case had almost reached the breaking point. Too bad they couldn't stay. The furniture was mostly mid-century modern, the floor spread with abstract rugs, with an inlaid miniature piano squatting in one corner.

The San Francisco Police Department was currently going through the Castillo place, wreaking havoc. The objective was to look for records and documents relating to Paradox or Margie Brooksfield, as well as anything that might be related to the homicide. The missing relic was not specified on the search warrant. Apparently, Javi Castillo's next of kin had been uncooperative in consenting to the search, forcing them to obtain a warrant, and the cops were pissed about that and slinging shit everywhere. Not to mention angry that they were having to work on the Fourth of July instead of hoisting beers at a barbecue. Patagonia jackets and elegant suits were strewn across the bedroom floor. Titles like *How to Win Friends and Influence People* and *The Multifamily Millionaire* were being pulled from bookshelves, opened and shaken, then tossed onto the carpeting.

Now they were going through a collection of meteorites in a glass case, fumbling around, and flipping over a bunch of framed photos of flying saucers on the wall. One fell to the floor and broke, the cops walking over the glass, crunching it into the rug.

"You gonna say something?" Cash asked in a low voice. She must have seen the troubled expression on his face.

Colcord attempted to smooth his features. "Nah, not my department."

She gestured her chin toward the man in charge, a big gut-swinging detective who was currently texting something in the corner. "He doesn't seem to be overseeing."

"Let's not annoy the locals," Colcord said. "It's Independence Day, after all."

Cash crossed her arms. "I'm gonna check out the kitchen before they trash it."

"I'll do the office." Colcord moseyed through the barking SFPD officers. Technically, they weren't supposed to get ahead of the local search, but he doubted they'd give a damn or even notice. Most of them were trying to get out of there as fast as possible.

The office was a small room, with a desk tucked against one wall. A dead pothos vine snaked across a side table, reaching for the window. A stack of papers was piled on one corner of the desk, and Colcord began shuffling through them. A scholarly article entitled "The Cosmic Evolution of Biogenic Amine" caught his eye, and he skimmed through it—quickly realizing he didn't understand a damned thing. He took a picture just in case. There were some blown-up photos of pages from an illuminated medieval manuscript showing a scholar holding a roundish, purple-tinged sphere, or possibly an almost round egg, a trancelike expression on his face, with rays of bloodred light radiating from his head. While it didn't seem pertinent, it was so odd he took a picture anyway.

He was about to look through the papers piled everywhere on the desk, but then paused. He had the distinct feeling that the papers—and indeed everything on the cluttered desk—had been moved, examined, and put back. As he peered closer, he could see the faintest outline of dust where a piece of paper had once rested, then replaced slightly off-center. He looked around the room and the feeling grew: Someone had searched the room, a few weeks ago by the look of it, and taken great care to leave no trace.

He turned his attention to the papers that were piled under the desk, taking several photos, because who knew how long it would take the SFPD to get him the evidence they'd collected? They were mostly receipts, tax documents, and bank statements—but suddenly, there it was, nestled between two tax returns: a torn piece of paper with eleven handwritten numbers separated by spaces. He immediately recognized it as a SWIFT code—a unique identifier for banks and financial institutions to facilitate international money transfers. He took more pictures.

He heard Cash behind him. "Check this out," she said. She was wearing nitrile gloves, holding up a key chain with an odd-looking key on it, enameled with the blue capital *B* and a stamped number.

"What's that?" Colcord asked.

"I remember this blue *B* logo. It's to the club Castillo belonged to. The Battery Club."

"And?"

"I found it hidden in the freezer between two steaks. Weird place to hide a key."

"Could have accidentally put it there."

"I don't think so. This place, in case you hadn't noticed, was recently searched."

"Yeah, I saw that."

"Castillo was way too clever to leave the relic in his apartment. What better place than to hide it in a locker at a high-security, members-only club?"

"There's just a wee problem here, Cash: We don't have a warrant for the club."

"We'll talk our way in."

"Yeah right."

She slipped the key into her pocket and threw him a wink. "Watch and learn."

Now the cops filed into the kitchen and began opening cabinets, hauling out dishes, pots, and pans. Cash and Colcord went back into the living room to get away from the noise.

"I found something too, by the way," he said, taking out his phone and showing her the picture. "It's a SWIFT code."

"Good one," Cash said. "Maybe that'll help trace the Paradox transfers."

33

Cash pulled the rental car into the drop-off zone for the Battery Club and turned to Colcord. "You coming in?"

He gave a sigh. "What's your plan? This joint looks pretty uptight."

"Trust me, Colcord. I'll get in."

"Someone better stay with the car," he said with a weak smile. "Otherwise, we'll get towed."

"Good point." She got out, leaned in the open window. "Back in five."

"I'll believe it when I see it."

As she strode up to the glass doors, Cash was thankful she was in uniform. The club was open for the holiday and busy. Taking out her badge, she passed through the heavy doors and went up to reception, laying it on the counter. "Happy Fourth," she said to the man behind the glass.

"And to you too, ma'am. What can I do for you?"

She fished in her pocket and removed the key. "Is this one of yours?"

He looked at it. "Sure is. Gym locker. Someone lose it?"

"No. It belonged to one of your members. Javier Castillo. You know him?"

"Not offhand."

"He was just murdered in Colorado. I'm a special agent with the Colorado Bureau of Investigation in charge of the homicide case, and I'd like to take a quick look into his locker. No warrant—just hoping for voluntary cooperation."

The young man looked troubled. "I'll have to take this to management. I'm sorry. I don't mean to be obstructive, but I'm pretty sure they'll say you'll need to get a warrant."

Cash gave him a relaxed smile. "A warrant's only necessary if access isn't voluntarily granted. You, sir, actually have the legal power to let me in. Five minutes is all I need."

"I'm sorry. I can't let you in without a warrant."

"Did you see the video?"

"Video?"

"The guy who was dismembered and tossed into a mountain lake in Colorado? All those body parts floating up to the surface, that kid screaming?"

She saw recognition dawning on the man's face.

"That's the murder I'm investigating. Javi Castillo. You didn't know he was a member of your club?"

A chill silence greeted this news.

"Getting a warrant, just so you know, might create unwanted publicity."

"Publicity?"

"A warrant's a public record, and this is a high-profile murder. A lot of cops will show up, and some reporter will inevitably get wind of it. Think about it: The murder and dismemberment of a member of one of San Francisco's most exclusive clubs, body parts floating in a lake, video gone viral around the world—hell yeah, we're talking big-time publicity. The last thing the Battery Club would want to do is insist on a warrant, trust me. Now, if you'll direct me to the gym, I'll be in and out in five."

After a long pause, the man said, "Basement level; elevator's down the hall to the left. But, ma'am—it's in the *men's* locker room."

"No problem. I've seen plenty of dicks before."

Five minutes later, Cash was sliding into the seat next to Colcord. Without a word, she slipped a stoppered glass vial from her pocket and held it out to him in the palm of her hand. He took it and squinted at the tiny brown square half the size of a pinkie nail. "Jesus, Cash, how'd you manage that?"

"Charmed my way in, went down into the men's locker room, opened the locker, and there it was, tucked into a sock."

"So what are you gonna do with it?" Colcord asked.

"The warrant called for anything that might be related to the homicide, which sure seems to be the case here. I'm keeping it and logging it in."

"To give back to the priest?"

"No. As official evidence."

Colcord frowned. "I'm not sure your boss is going to approve of holding it as evidence."

He handed it back, and she put it in her pocket. "It's my case, not hers. And every time you've told me to ignore Castillo," she said, "it's bitten us in the ass. I'll be shocked if there isn't some connection to be made here."

"Cash, just stop a moment and think: What evidentiary value could you possibly extract from a two-thousand-year-old holy relic—which, by the way, the pope himself wants back?"

"And he'll *get* it back, but not before I've analyzed it. With all the media crap I'm getting about Maine, the last thing I need is you against me too. It's my call, Colcord—*end of discussion*."

34

Cash tried to breathe through her mouth as Standish inclined backward in his chair, a grin plastered across his face, a fat file containing his Paradox results in front of him. They were in her office at CBI—a spartan room Cash rarely saw because she was so frequently on the road. Her entire office now smelled of baby oil.

"So, how's the case going?" Standish said it in a way that implied, or so it seemed to her, that he thought the case wasn't going well at all.

"It's going just fine," Cash said defensively. It was not, in fact, going just fine. Her business from Maine was all over the news. And despite all their efforts, the media was making hay with the idea that CBI and the sheriff's office might be investigating aliens as murder suspects. There was a leak somewhere in the investigation. The witness she had visited in San Francisco, which the press was now saying she had "brought back" to Colorado, had turned up murdered. Plus, it felt like Colcord was now second-guessing every decision she made.

But as she looked at Standish swinging in his chair, she felt she had not been fair to him. He was, basically, a gigantic nerd. He got on her nerves, but nobody said he wasn't a good agent. Even though she was annoyed that Holmes had put him on the case, his digital forensic skills were in fact needed. For better or worse, she was going to be working with him going forward.

"Just fine . . . okay." Standish kept on with the infuriating smile, swinging back and forth in the chair like a goddamned marionette.

Cash took a deep breath. "Look, Standish, I think we got off on the wrong foot," she said, with a tight smile.

Standish stopped swinging, his expression changing to neutral as he leaned forward with folded arms. He raised his eyebrows. "Really?"

"Yeah. I realize that it probably didn't feel good to have me swoop in and take this case from you."

Standish shrugged, but the tightness of his shoulders gave him away. "You've got seniority—I get it."

"No, really. I'm sorry. I don't usually do that—but this case means a lot to me, you know? I thought it might be a Neander case, and I wanted it. I just wanted to clear the air—and let you know I appreciate you helping out now."

Standish smiled then—a genuine smile. "Thanks, Cash. I appreciate you saying that."

"Good, well, let's move on from that." Cash let out a breath. She hated apologizing, but she felt guilty about her letting Standish get under her skin like that. It wasn't professional. "What have you got for me so far on Paradox?"

Standish patted the file and flipped it open. "First of all, Paradox may be a 501(c)(3), on paper, but it is nothing more than a front. Period. The money goes in and then out. I traced the money through a chain of shell companies in different jurisdictions. It was time-consuming, but I finally tracked down the discretionary trust behind Paradox."

"What's that?" asked Cash.

"A company can be owned by a trust, with the beneficiaries being the actual owners. The trust allows them to remain anonymous. This would have taken some pretty expensive lawyering to set up. The takeaway is, these people *really* didn't want to be found. That's why they chose countries known for their limited regulations and strong privacy laws to run their shell companies through."

As Standish spoke, Cash got a feeling that he admired these people.

"I initially went the legal route and requested a subpoena for the trustees' records, the trust deed, the name of the beneficiaries through the bank accounts used by Paradox to receive and transfer funds from Brooksfield, but we simply did not have enough evidence for the judge to grant it. Paradox's lawyers did make one mistake, though, which I caught. Can't pull one over on me so easily." Standish paused, a self-congratulatory expression on his face. "The trust owns a property in Italy—an apartment in Florence—and under the Fifth Anti–Money Laundering Directive, Italy maintains a beneficial ownership registry for trusts that own real estate. It's not technically fully open to the public, but there are some laws allowing individuals with a legitimate interest in preventing money laundering to access it—so long as they justify the request. It took some persuading, but I charmed my way in. I do, after all, speak Italian." Standish smiled proudly.

Cash was surprised by this. "Italy. That seems to be a common thread here. What did they say? Who's the owner?" She tried to keep impatience from creeping into her voice. Standish may be a pain in the ass, but damn, this was good stuff. She imagined he could find all her missing socks from the laundry if she put him to the test.

"Javi Castillo is just the front man to the public. 'Board chairman'—except there is no board. The real owner and controller is Krikor Khachatryan, an Armenian citizen—he's a total ghost, no digital trail anywhere. That's your guy."

35

Nova Euclid leaned forward in her chair, the email from Belen Caldas maximized so that it took up her entire monitor. It had just come in this morning.

"For crying out loud!" she exclaimed to herself, eyes skimming the text.

"What's wrong, gorgeous?" Wiley's husky voice emanated from the piled red velvet comforter on her California king bed.

Officer Wiley, Euclid chided herself for using the title in her own thoughts. She should be calling him *Cassian*, not *Officer*. Not after they had been so . . . familiar. She supposed it wasn't entirely appropriate what they were doing, but it's not like anyone would find out. And even if they did—well, she wouldn't be the first DA to fuck an officer assigned to one of their cases. Who was she to break tradition?

"It's the Brooksfield case. Caldas is screwing with me." Euclid blew out air in frustration, flipping away one of the brown curls that had fallen across her vision.

Caldas had filed not one, not two, but *four* motions with the court. She had probably recruited a team of first-year associates to stay up all night with her to write them. Euclid clicked open the first one, a motion to dismiss the case for due process violations during Margie Brooksfield's arrest. She hissed through her teeth. It was strongly worded. This was not good, not good at all. If the case got dismissed on her watch, she would be totally screwed.

Wiley padded up behind her, pulling a curtain of hair aside to kiss the nape of her neck.

"Cassian," Euclid griped, but she was grinning, "give me like five minutes."

"Your wish is my command." Wiley began to massage her shoulders, and Euclid leaned her head back against his bare, hard stomach. He was wearing nothing but a pair of white boxer briefs. The last thing she wanted to be doing was working right now.

"Okay, really. I can't concentrate with you standing there."

"You can't?" Wiley leaned down, giving her a devilish smile. She admired the handsome contours of his jaw before leaning forward to peck his lips.

"Go play with Walt—he's lonely," she said, referencing her rescued pet raccoon, Walt Whitman Euclid. Named after her favorite poet.

"Where is that little bugger anyways?"

"Likes to hide between the bookcase and wall."

Euclid listened to the sound of tussling as Wiley manhandled the fluff ball. Raccoons were technically not legal to own in Colorado unless you were a licensed wildlife rehabilitator, a hobby that Euclid had engaged in while in law school. She used to have a lot more animals housed on the expansive acreage that her parents had left her but had slowly donated them to other rehab centers as she became more and more engrossed in law. Walt was the last mammal standing. She loved Walt, would never be able to part with him.

She clicked back to the other tab open on her computer to finish reading a news article. Across the front page of *The New York Times* was a picture of Margie Brooksfield—wide-eyed and terrified—being escorted past the burning Brooksfield Ranch sign in between two deputies wearing gas masks, who had their hands firmly secured on her shoulders. An absolute catastrophe. The headline was even worse: CHAOS ERUPTS AS BROOKSFIELD ARREST SPARKS FIRE, TEAR GAS, AND BROKEN BONES.

Adewale had planned a presser that Euclid was supposed to attend this morning, and she wondered how she was going to do that with these motions hanging over her head.

Grabbing her cell, she dialed her boss.

Adewale answered on the first ring.

"She filed *four* motions this morning," Euclid said, without waiting for her greeting.

"Figures. The presser's been canceled anyways. Too much media craziness. The press are going nuts, and the public is feeding off of it like wolves."

"Thank God. Gotta write the oppositions. On a scale from one to ten, how bad is the Brooksfield situation now?"

"Let's just say I canceled my meeting with the governor over budget allocations today."

"Fuck." Euclid winced at the slip. She had forgotten that she was speaking to *the* district attorney, not some coworker. "Uh, pardon my French."

"No, *fuck* is right." The curse sounded forced and against the grain of Adewale's usual refined speech.

Another email dinged in from Caldas, and Euclid clicked it open immediately. "Oh, wow. She's also filed a motion for change of venue. She's claiming the pretrial publicity prejudices Margie Brooksfield negatively in Eagle County." She winced as something made out of glass broke behind her. She shot Wiley and Walt a glare with her hand cupped over the mouthpiece.

Sorry, Wiley mouthed.

"We cannot allow her to change venue." Adewale's voice was emphatic. "Under no circumstances. This is our case. We have to show them that despite the . . . *difficult* arrest, we are on the right side of the law here. I don't want some other DA taking credit for our hard work."

Euclid wondered what hard work Adewale was talking about but bit her tongue. Adewale wanted this case—probably because of the prestige it awarded her office if they won it—and Euclid would keep it in Eagle County for her.

"Got it. I'll make sure that doesn't happen." Euclid paused, wondering if she should bring it up, then decided to anyway. "Do you think we, uh, jumped the gun on arresting Brooksfield?"

A silence on the line, where Euclid imagined Adewale was giving the mouthpiece of her cell phone a frosty glare. And then, slowly, "No. Do *you* think we did?"

Euclid balked at the sudden change in temperature in the conversation.

"Certainly not," Euclid lied. The case felt rushed—she had a vague feeling they were missing something big. But Adewale wasn't having it, and Euclid wouldn't be any help if she was taken off the case.

"Let's leave it at that, Nova. Keep me updated."

"Yes, ma'am."

A dial tone sounded.

"Five minutes is up," Wiley called from the bed.

"You're goddamned right it is." Euclid stood and stretched, then untied the cinch of her silk robe and let it fall to the floor. The motions could wait.

36

Brother Armagh parked his rental car in the church lot, climbed out, and looked around with curiosity. Saint Mary's was a pretty little church of whitewashed stone, set against a backdrop of mountains still patchy with snow. Evergreen trees climbed the slopes above town, perfuming the air with a piney scent. Armagh breathed deeply of the high mountain air. This was a lovely place, he thought, to worship God and His creation.

Armagh had tried to get in touch with Father Moore, the parish priest, but apparently, the good father did not have a cell phone—that, while inconvenient, Armagh couldn't help but approve of. While waiting in Eagle for developments in the Castillo murder case, aside from his usual church attendance, he had found time hanging heavy on his hands and decided to call on some of the far-flung parish priests in the area. Burns had especially interested him.

He took another breath and climbed the steps to the church's doors, which stood wide open and welcoming. As he went inside, he appreciated the shift into the natural coolness of a stone church. He paused in the aisle, looking around. The sanctuary was empty. It was a simple church, no fancy embellishments, frescoes, or decorations beyond some stained glass depictions of the Stations of the Cross. This was very much to Brother Armagh's taste. He often found the ornate Baroque embellishments of the churches in Rome to be tiresome and not in keeping with the simplicity of belief that he valued, not to mention the vow of poverty he had taken when he became a monk.

He made his way down the aisle and spied the door to the sacristy.

He advanced to it, raised his hand, and gave it a timid couple of raps. He heard a rustle, and the door opened to reveal a most impressive figure—a monk in black Benedictine robes, well over six feet tall, a powerful figure of a man with a craggy face that looked not unlike that American president, Abraham Lincoln, only without the beard.

"Father Moore?" Armagh ventured, surprised that the priest also appeared to be a member of the Order of Saint Benedict.

"Ah, I'm sorry, no," the monk said, his face breaking into a broad smile. "No, no. I am Brother Gregory. Welcome!" He extended an enormous hand, and Armagh enthusiastically took it—surprised at its gentleness in enveloping his own.

"Brother Gregory, how good to meet you. I'm Brother Armagh, Niall Armagh, of the Pallottine Brothers in Rome."

"Ah, from Rome! Please come in," said the monk. "What a wonderful surprise."

Armagh followed him into the sacristy, another room of divine spareness. They passed through it to a small office in the back. The monk offered Armagh a chair and took one of his own, seating his powerful figure with grace, deftly arranging his robes as he did so.

"Brother Niall," asked the monk, "are you a friend of Father Moore's?"

Armagh was pleased by the warm reception and curious about what a Benedictine monk might be doing in such an out-of-the-way place. "I was in the area and thought I'd pay a social call. I don't know him, but when I travel, I like to visit my fellow religious, and I couldn't help but be curious when I heard about Burns and the little church here. I couldn't get hold of Father Moore by phone, so I thought I'd take a chance and drop in."

"Ah yes. I'm here on a visit to Father Moore myself. He kindly puts up visiting religious in the presbytery next to the church. Modest but comfortable accommodations." The big monk shifted in his chair, which creaked under his great frame. "It's unfortunate that Father Moore is not here. So, what brings you to our side of the Atlantic? Vacation?"

Armagh had been ordered not to reveal, even to a fellow religious, the purpose of his mission except where necessary. As a result, he was well prepared for the question and answered it smoothly.

"As I'm sure you can tell from my accent, I'm Irish, as all the Pallottine brothers are. And yes, I am here on a wee vacation, visiting family and taking a breath of fresh mountain air."

"Wonderful!" said the monk. "Family, you say? Here in Burns?"

"No, in Eagle." He redirected the conversation. "And you, Brother Gregory—what is a Benedictine doing out here? Is there a monastery in these parts?"

"There is indeed—Saint Benedict's of Aspen. We're a small community in a scenic mountain valley northwest of Aspen, in the heart of skiing country. Sadly, there are few of us left to carry on the Cistercian tradition, and I'm afraid the monastery is slated to close. We just can't keep up with the expenses."

"I'm terribly sad to hear of it. Where will you go?"

"Most of us are heading to Christ in the Desert, in New Mexico. It's a beautiful monastery, but I have to admit, I will miss the skiing!"

"Do you ski?" Armagh asked.

"I do. And I must say, in all modesty, I cut quite a figure on the mountain, shredding fresh powder in my black robes." He tipped back, laughing a deep, sonorous laugh. "There are many ways to bring people to God, and I find skiing to be one of them. When people ask me, 'Why do you ski?' I say, 'I'm skiing for God! Because everything we do, we do for God.'"

"How very true." A skiing monk. It was certainly unusual, but Brother Armagh thought, *Why not?* The Order of Saint Benedict was known for mixing with the world more than other orders. You could save a soul as well on the mountain as at the altar.

"And I've had some interesting conversations on ski lifts," the monk continued. "Being cloistered to contemplate the love of our Heavenly Father is fine, but getting out in the world, uplifting the poor, tending the sick, and doing good works is better."

"I couldn't agree more," said Armagh approvingly. "I spent nine years in a prison ministry in Chicago."

The monk paused and looked at him with even greater interest. "I'm so glad to hear it. That's exactly what I mean. Sometimes I feel the church focuses to its detriment on censuring and judging people over issues like homosexuality and abortion, when what truly concerned Jesus was greed and poverty."

Armagh was considerably surprised by this statement, which meshed with his own, rarely expressed private thoughts. "I have often felt that way myself, Brother Gregory," he said. "Are all the brothers of Aspen so liberally minded?"

"We are, and we find ourselves rather on the outs these days with some of our more conservative brethren, such as my dear friend Father Moore. He's a bit old-fashioned and limited in his views—and he has that rather odd collection, but he is a man of God with a good heart."

"I'm glad to hear it."

The monk leaned forward. "The Pallottine brothers . . . Now aren't you the order in the Basilica of San Silvestro?"

"Indeed we are."

"Ah, how interesting! It's been so long since I last visited Rome."

"It's the beating heart of our faith. I hope you get the chance."

"I hope so too," he said. "Say, isn't San Silvestro where the most holy relic of Saint John the Baptist can be found?"

"Indeed so." Armagh was suddenly watchful. He wondered if, somehow, word of his mission might have gotten around. It seemed impossible, especially in an out-of-the-way place like this. But to his relief, the skiing monk continued on, unaware of the vandalism. "I've sometimes thought we Catholics overdo the relic thing. It's not so different from worshiping a graven image."

Armagh felt slightly offended at this. "People need objects of faith. Holy relics inspire them—and remind them of those who've suffered for the sake of our Lord."

"You make a good point, Brother," said the monk, slapping his knees. He rose. "I'm afraid I have to get back to Aspen for Compline." He once again enveloped Armagh's hand in the warmth of his own. "It's been lovely speaking to you, Brother Niall."

Armagh said his goodbyes and left the church. As Brother Armagh was driving back down the road from Burns, surrounded by snowy mountains, he thought about the monk flying down the slopes, robes flapping, *skiing* for God. It was a most appealing image.

37

Euclid stood as the clicking stride of Belen Caldas's stilettos echoed down the courthouse hallway. She had been waiting outside of courtroom 4B in the hopes of resolving some of these motions outside of court. Or getting inside Caldas's head. Whichever worked best.

Caldas swiped off her sunglasses as she approached.

"You must be the poor sucker Adewale assigned the Brooksfield case. Nova, was it?"

Euclid held out a hand for Caldas to shake. "Nova Euclid."

Caldas gave her hand a pump. "Let me guess"—Caldas began polishing her sunglasses with a satin neck scarf—"you're gonna ask me to drop some of these motions?"

Euclid practiced her best contemptuous smile. "Well, you've been ignoring my emails. I think we can both agree that the motion to suppress evidence is brought on extremely questionable grounds. Judge Horton is easily annoyed by frivolous motions. I would urge you to reconsider making some of the arguments you brought up—at least for the sake of your client. I'm sure there's an agreement we can come to."

"I've appeared in front of Judge Horton more times than you've appeared for trial, Ms. Euclid. When did you pass the bar? Last year?"

Euclid tried not to bristle. She had moved up fast in the DA's office, and digs at her age were fairly commonplace. "I know the judge would prefer if we work this out between us," she said. "The motion for change of venue is *also* unsound. There's been little publicity denigrating your client, certainly not enough to warrant a change of venue—"

"Let me save you the trouble," Caldas interrupted. "I am not going to be dropping any of these motions. That absolute shit show of an arrest was not only embarrassing for the Eagle County DA's office but it was terrifying for my client. Not to mention she is injured because of it. I have body-worn camera footage to prove it."

"If you had informed your client about our request to surrender herself, the arrest would *not* have been necessary. You put her at risk—"

"I'm sorry that this is your first high-profile case, because it will certainly be your last after I'm done with you."

Caldas stalked past her and into the courtroom. Euclid gritted her teeth. She had heard that Caldas was unfriendly, but it was another thing to experience it. She also understood that most of it was for show and not personal. She followed her inside. Within moments, Judge Horton arrived in a flurry of black robes.

"Counsel." His eyes landed on Euclid. "Ah, Ms. Euclid. Glad to see you in my courtroom again."

From the corner of Euclid's eye, she watched with satisfaction as Caldas tensed.

"Thank you, Judge. Glad to be here."

Judge Horton called the court to session. Behind them, Margie Brooksfield—accompanied by her husband, Paul—filed in. Margie took her place beside Caldas, Paul taking a seat in the gallery. Margie looked gaunt and fidgety, her eyes dark. A smattering of press and the public had been allowed in the courtroom, taking up most of the seats.

"So we are hearing"—Judge Horton whistled between his teeth— "*five* motions today. I will hear argument for the motion for discovery of law enforcement conduct now. Ms. Caldas?"

Caldas stood and clasped her hands behind her back.

Euclid's fingers tightened around her briefcase as she noticed Adewale slide into the back of the courtroom. If she performed badly during this hearing, it could impact her career. Or if she lost the change of venue motion, the case would be ripped from their hands and given to another county. Adewale didn't play when it came to high-profile cases.

Caldas began her argument. She looked comfortable and assured in the courtroom, using small hand gestures as she spoke.

"Your Honor, the arrest of my client was a complete and utter disaster, and we need to determine if a violation of her rights occurred. She is suffering from a persistent cough, a swollen throat, and blurry vision as a result of being *tear-gassed* by the arresting officers. The gate to her ranch burned down as a result of this arrest. It is essential that the defense be given the information requested in our motion, including Internal Affairs files, disciplinary records of officers involved, and time to investigate whether there are undocumented incidents of aggressive or unprofessional behavior by those officers during prior arrests."

Caldas rapped the defense table as she spoke the last part, the sharp noise reverberating around the courtroom. Euclid could see she was a pro at acting pissed. The performance appeared to be working. Judge Horton nodded as if in agreement with her.

"That is very concerning indeed. I've watched the body-worn camera footage, and it is shocking, to say the least. Ms. Euclid, your response?"

Shit, Euclid thought. This wasn't starting well. She had originally planned to argue this was an inappropriate request that was overbroad, and that personnel records were confidential—who knew what bullshit Caldas could rustle up and try to throw her way—but her gut was now telling her not to make that argument. It was a risk, and the police department wouldn't be happy with this at all, but she knew Judge Horton. She had to trust herself and build credibility with the court so she could win her other motions.

She steeled herself. "Your Honor, I am willing to withdraw my opposition to this motion, as long as we limit the scope of the request only to the officer who deployed the tear gas and the ones involved with physical contact with the protesters. Asking for records on every single officer involved is overbroad." She turned and shot Caldas her best friendly smile. "If Ms. Caldas will work with me on this."

Judge Horton raised his eyebrows in approval.

Caldas scowled. "Absolutely not."

"Ms. Caldas, I am inclined to grant your motion for discovery of police conduct but with the scope limited as Ms. Euclid suggested here. Ms. Euclid is being *very* generous with her offer, and I suggest you take it."

Like Euclid had hoped, Judge Horton was souring slightly at Caldas's aggressive demeanor. Being an overly zealous advocate worked in most courtrooms, but not this one. To Caldas's credit, she seemed to sense the change of Judge Horton's demeanor.

"Very well, but if we cannot agree on the scope, I would ask that the court revisit this issue," Caldas said, suddenly warm again, but the tightness of her jaw gave away her true feelings.

Judge Horton nodded. "Let's move on. After reading your pleadings, I am inclined to deny the motion for a gag order." He shot Caldas a somber look. "You may make an argument, Ms. Caldas, if you'd like."

The last sentence was tinged with warning. Caldas's non-collaborative approach had irritated him. Euclid pretended to stack papers to the side of the table, turning her body in order to see Adewale's reaction. She could see her mouth turned up slightly at the edges in the faintest of smiles from where she watched in the back of the courtroom. If Euclid won the change-of-venue motion, she would be in the green. *Better* than in the green.

"Your Honor," Caldas said, "as is documented in the exhibits I submitted, the press is frothing at the mouth with this case. The viral video taken of Castillo's dismembered remains have been shared everywhere. The pretrial publicity for this case is off the charts and will greatly prejudice Margie Brooksfield if the gag order is not granted."

Judge Horton's brows drew together.

"But—" Caldas added hastily. "I defer to the court's decision."

"Thank you. I am denying the motion for the gag order. Lastly, I will be delaying the motion for dismissal for violation of due process until discovery is done."

Caldas took a deep breath. "Very well, Your Honor. I submit to the court's decision on those motions. However, I would like to be heard on the motion for change of venue."

Euclid tensed. This was the key point: They *had* to keep the case in Eagle County. She watched as Adewale leaned forward, intently watching the proceeding.

"You may proceed with your argument, Ms. Caldas."

"Your Honor, Eagle County is not an appropriate venue for my client. For one, the local media has *completely* railroaded Mrs. Brooksfield. If you would take a look at exhibit A—"

Caldas pulled up a photograph of protesters outside of the Brooksfield

Ranch holding up signs that said LOCK HER UP and FRAUDSTER. Euclid's mouth pulled down in a frown as she read BITCH JEZEBEL with a picture of Mrs. Brooksfield that looked like it had been pulled from her Linke-dIn profile.

"It will be impossible to ensure an impartial jury pool if selected from Eagle County." Caldas clicked to the next slide, which was an exhibit of the front-page story from the *Eagle County News*. A sensationalized headline, MARGIE BROOKSFIELD: MURDERESS AND FRAUDSTER OR GOOD CATHOLIC? was splashed across the top, accompanied by an unflattering black-and-white photo of Brooksfield in handcuffs exiting a black SUV.

"The media coverage is inflammatory and widespread and *certainly* would prejudice my client. Just take a look at this photo—is the media trying to portray an innocent person here? Furthermore, there is a leak from either CBI or the sheriff's office that released my client's name as a suspect even *before* her arrest. The incompetence and mismanagement by Agent Cash and Sheriff Colcord is overwhelming."

Caldas continued, pulling up the various news stories that had run about Margie Brooksfield on the pull-down screen to show the court. The exhibits painted a narrative that was sometimes inaccurate and sometimes provocative. Sensationalistic and shocking headlines meant to grab attention rather than report facts flashed across the screen. Caldas pulled one up that was clearly from the *National Enquirer*.

At that point, Euclid realized Caldas had made a serious misstep. "Excuse me, Your Honor, but it looks like this exhibit has cropped out the name of the newspaper it comes from."

Caldas scrolled up to reveal the *National Enquirer* banner.

"I hardly need point out," Euclid said, "that the *National Enquirer* is not a local Eagle County source."

Judge Horton's lips thinned in disapproval. "Noted," he said.

Nevertheless, Caldas forged ahead, showing a parade of more news stories featuring Brooksfield before ending her argument.

"Defense counsel has made its point," said the judge. "Ms. Euclid, your counterargument?"

"Thank you." Euclid swallowed, standing. She could feel Adewale's eyes on her, and she needed a win after the disastrous arrest.

"Your Honor, the defense has the burden to prove three elements.

One, that the publicity is widespread. I think we can all agree that the publicity is, indeed, widespread."

Caldas raised her eyebrows in surprise from her seat at the defense table and leaned over to whisper with Brooksfield.

"The second element, that at least some of the publicity is inaccurate and inflammatory, is also met, as I'm sure you can tell from Ms. Caldas's exhibits."

"Counsel, no need to make defense's argument for her." Judge Horton gave a low chuckle.

"I appreciate the concern, Your Honor." Euclid smiled. "However, the third element is where Ms. Caldas fails to meet her burden of proof. Ms. Caldas must thirdly prove that the pretrial publicity has caused widespread belief of the defendant's guilt within the potential jury pool in Eagle County. This element has certainly not been met. Quite the opposite, actually. The news stories surrounding the Brooksfield case are overwhelmingly in her favor. Furthermore, as defense counsel proved with the *National Enquirer* exhibit, the news stories being read by potential jurors are so widespread that a change of venue would not resolve the alleged prejudice that Ms. Caldas claims her client will suffer. Lastly, it is believed that Javi Castillo's murder occurred in Eagle County. The witnesses are located here, and so is the evidence."

Judge Horton nodded. "Thank you, Counsel." He turned to Caldas, and Euclid held her breath in anticipation. "While I appreciate your arguments, I do not feel as if a change of venue would properly address any prejudice felt by the defense—"

Sudden commotion from behind Euclid caught Judge Horton's eye, and he stopped. Euclid whipped around. Paul Brooksfield was standing, red in the face, fists trembling. The bailiff had jumped over the bar and was holding him by his shoulders.

Paul roared, wrenching from the bailiff's grip as if he were tearing through paper, and launched himself over the bar and pointed to his wife. "She's innocent! We can't even leave our house!" he yelled. "How could you do this to her?"

The bailiff grabbed at him as he continued to shout, gesturing to Adewale, who had stood and was calmly watching with crossed arms from the back of the courtroom. "You make this right, Ms. District Attorney. You make this right!"

A flood of blue invaded the room as four officers swarmed in. A tussle ensued: Paul took advantage of his size, throwing officers this way and that as they struggled to secure his wrists with handcuffs.

"Stop it, Paul!" Margie Brooksfield's voice suddenly rang out above the commotion.

Paul ceased his struggling and allowed the officers to cuff him. As he was led away, he met Euclid's horrified gaze with red-ringed eyes and mouthed something to her.

Euclid could just make out what he was saying. *Help her*, he mouthed. *Help her.*

38

Cash clambered onto a tall barstool at a table tucked away in the corner of the Third Street Tavern. "How's the wine?" she asked Standish, who had arrived early and was sipping from a glass, his nose wrinkled. It was a quiet Wednesday, and aside from a grizzled man who looked like he had been there so long he was melting into the bar, they were the only ones in the joint. The place smelled like cigarettes, and the table was sticky.

"Drinkable," Standish responded with a grimace. He looked jumpy, eyes shifting this way and that across the empty bar—as if he was expecting someone.

"So—you wanted to see me?"

"Yeah . . ." Standish leaned forward over the wineglass. "I found him. Krikor Khachatryan. Have a picture of him and everything."

"That's great news, but this could have been a phone call."

"No, it couldn't." Standish shook his head. His usual arrogant demeanor was gone, replaced by a nervousness Cash didn't understand. He leaned forward, eyes glittering. "The guy's a ghost. No digital footprint. Do you know how hard that is to achieve these days?"

"I'll take your word for it."

"I got really lucky. I found a mention of him in a DEF CON forum—a photograph from two years ago was posted by someone with his name. Recent post. I got a screenshot and posted a response to get some more information. But he must've had a name alert out, because the post was deleted within minutes. Check it out."

Standish slid over a printed photograph. The subject of the photograph was a skinny boy—maybe early twenties—with long, stringy hair, sitting cross-legged in front of four computers. Several massive hard drives stood on racks in what looked like a crappy shack, walls covered with aluminum foil. Posters of busty anime girls were the only other decoration.

"He's just a kid!"

"He's twenty-seven, just looks immature. But don't be fooled. He's whip-smart. Look closely here." Standish tapped the photo with a long finger. "See that?"

Cash strained her eyes. A small carved rooster with a sweeping red comb was stacked on one of the bookshelves. It was decorated with hearts and white dots.

"Yeah. What is it?"

"A Barcelos Rooster figurine. Traditional clay and handcrafted roosters famous in Portugal folklore and culture. Story behind it is a legend where a mystical rooster helps prove the innocence of a wrongly accused man. The Portuguese collect them, keep them around their houses for good luck."

"So what . . . you think he's in Portugal? He could have bought that and brought it with him anywhere."

"Yeah, I thought so too. But I did a little research on some of the items in his home. There's not much. But check out that throw blanket."

He pointed to a blanket thrown over the back of the guy's chair, comprised of eye-popping lime-green, mauve, and orange hues.

"That particular blanket is sold by the Burel Factory located in Manteigas, Portugal. The factory uses traditional techniques to make burel, the woolen fabric that blanket is made of. The colors, patterns, and fabric are unique; it's not sold anywhere else. The factory has stores in Lisbon and Porto as well. In fact, all if not most of his furniture matches furniture on their website."

"So that narrows it down to Manteigas, Lisbon, or Porto."

"Maybe. That's what I thought, but figured he might have imported the furniture. But I was able to narrow it down further—look at what he's eating."

Off to the side of the photo on his desk—half cut off—was what looked like a slice of cheese with some crackers scattered about a plate.

Cash strained her eyes. The cheese was unlabeled. The picture was grainy; she could hardly make it out. "Don't tell me you were able to figure out something from a bad photo of a slice of cheese."

"Well . . . yes. When you ask me to do a job, I do it well. I looked up all the different kinds of cheeses in Portugal and compared them all to this picture, just to see if I was right. I'm *pretty* sure that's called Queijo Serra da Estrela. Hard orange crust, gooey inside. It looks pretty good, actually. Cheese made in the mountainous region of Serra da Estrela in Portugal, which is a hike away from Manteigas—"

"Wait, hang on a second." Cash had heard that name before. "Serra da Estrela. That's the same place where Javi Castillo lost his leg."

"Jesus. Really? How? Bear attack?"

"Sepsis, a bad infection gone untreated too long. The person who told me claimed Castillo had gotten it while visiting a UAP crash site. Instead, I *bet* he was visiting Krikor Khachatryan when he got injured. While this was two years ago, there's a chance that he's still holed up in the Serra da Estrela mountain range somewhere. Look that up."

Standish typed on his phone and then showed Cash.

Cash looked at the screen. "Serra da Estrela? That's a vast area. How will we find him?"

"You're not gonna believe this, Cash." Standish gripped the edge of the table. "After I figured this out, *he* contacted *me*. Tracked me down based on my post on the DEF CON forum. That itself is impressive, since I was using a VPN and a newly invented handle."

"He contacted you?"

"Yeah. He overnighted me a throwaway phone with some encrypted chat app to speak with him. He knew all about this case. He didn't want to talk to me. He wanted to talk to *you*. That's why we're here."

Cash was astounded, suddenly understanding why the young agent looked so damn nervous.

Standish reached out and gripped her wrist. "He was adamant this was the only way he would communicate with us, and *only* with you. Didn't want you in the office. He picked this bar. I know it's outside of protocol, but it's not like we can subpoena his testimony—we'd never find him anyway."

Standish slid a phone from his pocket—some off-brand device with Cyrillic writing on it.

She hesitated and then took it. "Right now?"

"Yes. Now. Look, this guy is good. I think he might have hacked into my laptop."

"How do you know?" Cash asked.

"Battery drained faster than usual, altered code. I think he got spooked when I got close to finding out where he was." Standish must have realized he was gripping her wrist, and he let her go. He leaned back in his chair, cool again.

Cash nodded, feeling uneasy, and opened the phone. There was a single application on the screen—an app icon of a bird mid-flight. She clicked it, and a black screen with a messaging bar popped up. She typed into it.

Guest: This is Agent Cash

A couple of seconds later, and there was an answer.

Host: hello frankie. i see ur following my instructions.

Before Cash could even reply, a screenshot from a security camera in the bar popped onto the screen. It showed Standish and Cash, sitting across from each other—taken a couple of seconds ago. Cash turned the screen so Standish could see.

"How in the fuck . . . ?" Standish murmured.

Guest: Let's talk on the phone.
Host: fuck no. don't ask again.
Guest: You went to a lot of trouble to reach me. So tell me what you want.
Host: javi castillo was murdered and dismembered. who did it?
Guest: We don't know.
Host: theyre stalking and killing us cash. they killed castillo. they disappeared my partner. everyone in our organization is vulnerable. you're leading the investigation. what the actual fuck are you doing about this besides sending your script kiddie to insert his nose into my ass

"Script kiddie?" Standish said over her shoulder, annoyed.

Guest: Who's "they"? And who's this partner?
Host: we've had run-ins with these people before. look into a group called devotio. thats all ill say. my partner silva helped castillo steal the relic.

Devotio, Cash thought. Now she was getting somewhere.

Guest: What's your connection to Castillo?
Host: he's the front man of our organization paradox
Guest: What is Paradox really?
Host: we collect data on uaps
Guest: Why all the shell companies? The secrecy?
Host: we dont like people knowing what we're doing, what's wrong with that
Guest: Why was Margie Brooksfield sending Paradox money?
Host: its exactly like she said. they were donations from willy grooms. grooms saw a uap crash and castillo was putting together a group to go into the mountains to investigate. grooms was funding it. it was only forwarded through brooksfield's account because grooms was paranoid as shit.
Guest: Why did Castillo steal the relic?

The messages had been coming in one right after another, but after this one, Cash noticed a pause. Khachatryan—or whoever was sending these messages—seemed to be thinking before answering this one. Finally, a message came through.

Host: do you have it

Cash wondered if she should tell the truth, and decided she should.

Guest: Yes

This was followed by another long silence. Then:

Host: what are you going to do with it
Guest: Return it.

She waited, but there was no response.

Guest: If you want us to find who killed Castillo, now's the time
to tell us what you know. I think you know a lot more than you're
telling me.

Another pause:

Host: before you give it back, sequence the dna
Guest: What for?
Host: just do it. everything i mean *everything* depends on
sequencing that dna

Suddenly, the text from their conversation disappeared and the phone
went blank. Cash swore, trying to type something else, but it had turned
into a useless hunk of plastic and metal.

"Remotely wiped, looks like. Guess he was done chatting," Standish
said, staring at the dead phone. "Who the hell are these people—Devotio?"

Cash narrowed her eyes. They had a name now. "No idea, but we're
gonna find out."

39

The door to the small Cherry Creek bungalow opened and Nick Wu, Bart Romanski's husband, stood in it.

"Oh no," he said, staring at Cash.

"That's a nice greeting," she said.

"Sorry," said Wu, flustered. "It's just . . . well, it's nine o'clock at night."

Cash waited on the threshold. She could hear Romanski's voice from inside. "Who the hell is at the door?"

Wu stepped aside. "It's your boss."

Cash heard a groan and took the opportunity to step into the house. Romanski came around the corner into the entryway, dressed in a rich satin robe, carrying a martini. He halted in consternation.

"Oh no," Romanski said. "Not another stiff, is it?"

"No, nothing like that. There's something we need to discuss. Confidentially."

"All right."

Cash followed as Romanski shuffled into a small sitting room. Wu followed. Romanski seated himself and invited her to sit. He said, somewhat reluctantly, "Can I offer you something? Water? Coffee? A drink?"

"I want one of those," said Cash, eyeing the martini.

Romanski stared. "I see." He turned to Wu. "Babe, will you make her one and another for me?"

"Dirty. Three olives," said Cash.

At this, Romanski's eyebrows rose farther. "You heard the boss."

Wu got up and disappeared into the kitchen.

"I'm getting the feeling this is not a typical work meeting," said Romanski.

"It isn't. I've a favor to ask you. A big one. And it's to be kept secret."

"I'm intrigued."

Cash could hear Wu shaking the drinks in the kitchen. She would need a stiff one to get through this. "You know that we recovered the relic of Saint John the Baptist at Castillo's apartment in San Francisco."

"Of course. Holmes has it stored in my trusty evidence freezer in the lab."

"I want to do a DNA analysis of it."

A silence. "And you've come to me at this hour to ask me to do this, instead of submitting the request through channels?"

"I tried regular channels. Holmes turned me down flat. Her priority is getting the relic back to the Catholic Church—intact."

"I see."

Wu came back with a tray carrying three dirty green martinis, with three huge olives speared on a toothpick, chips of ice floating on the surface. He passed another to his husband and sat down, lifting his own new martini.

"Um, would it be okay to have some privacy?" Cash asked.

"No," said Romanski. "He's my life partner—Nick and I share everything. I rely on his sound judgment."

"Since he doesn't have any of his own," said Wu.

Romanski gave him a playful punch.

Cash decided not to press the issue.

Wu raised his glass. "Cheers." He took a deep sip.

She did the same, feeling icy liquid burn down the back of her throat.

"Why'd Holmes say no?" Romanski asked.

"Because it's a holy of holies, can't be touched, might cause a scandal, and there's a priest sent here by the pope himself to collect it."

"Ah. The plot thickens. But . . . Cash, tell me why *you* want to sequence the DNA. How could that possibly help the investigation?"

"I don't know. What I do know is that Grooms was sending large sums of money through Margie Brooksfield, and then through Castillo, to a nonprofit called Paradox. But then the money flowed through a bunch of offshore accounts and ended up controlled by a man named Khachatryan. We think he's somewhere in Portugal, but can't say for sure."

"Money laundering?"

"It would certainly seem so. Fraud as well, because the transfer of money from a 501(c)(3) to benefit a private party is fraud."

"Go on."

"Khachatryan contacted me. He was cagey but insistent: *Sequence the DNA*, he said."

"Did he say why?"

"No. But he said that members of an organization called Devotio were killing them. I think this DNA has something to do with why."

A silence. "So you want me to do it on the sly."

"Yes."

"Look, Cash, can you just *think* about this for a moment? First, that's a big ask. I could lose my job. Second, if word got out, CBI could be crucified by the press. Oops. Not a good metaphor. Anyway, we've already got a priest railing against us. Third, I'm going to have to bring Reno in on this. I don't have the skill set to do it alone."

"I realize that. But I'm pretty sure Reno will be onboard."

"I know he will, but that's not the point. The point is, it's a risk for him too."

"I wouldn't be asking if I didn't believe this could be something big."

"How could a DNA test possibly reveal information relevant to the case? What does it matter if the relic is real, fake, from an animal, or made out of plaster? None of that can have anything to do with the Castillo homicide—right?"

"Castillo risked his life to steal that thing to sequence its DNA. Khachatryan was adamant as well. There *must* be something to it."

"Like what?"

"I don't know. I just . . . have a *feeling.*"

"A feeling . . ." He shook his head.

There was a long silence, and then Cash said, "I know I'm being unfair pulling you guys into this. You're the best, and we've been through a lot together, including the Neander case. You saved my life. I owe you."

"And you saved mine."

"I did, thank you. Can you please trust me on this? I just *know* this is crucial. I can't tell you why. The relic's in your lab. You and Reno could pop it out of the safe, take a tiny sample, pop it back in. Five minutes. The amount you need for the test would be microscopic. No one would be the wiser."

Romanski gazed at her a long time and then turned to his husband. "Nick?"

Wu looked surprised. "What, you want *my* advice? How remarkable."

"Yes, because of your alleged *good judgment*," said Romanski with a laugh.

"Well," said Wu, "in that case, I think you should do it."

"What? Why?" Romanski sounded surprised.

Wu shrugged. "I'm curious as hell about what that DNA sequencing might turn up."

40

"You didn't clock in, I hope," said Romanski as Reno eased into the shadowy laboratory, closing the door with care so as not to make noise.

"Hell no," said Reno, slipping off his pack and setting it down. He snagged a lab coat off a hook and threw it on over his T-shirt, covering up his tattooed arms. He pulled on a pair of nitrile gloves and face mask. No hairnet, Romanski noted—Reno had no hair so he didn't need one, he supposed, but it still was against protocol. Fuck protocol; Reno was doing him a solid.

Fully gowned now, he came over. "So where are we?"

"Still waiting for the alignment program to finish," Romanski said.

It was three o'clock in the morning, and Romanski had been working off the clock since eleven, sequencing the DNA of the little brown square that now sat in a sealed vial back in the lab safe. That chip was supposed to be nothing less than a fragment of bone from the head of Saint John the Baptist.

Romanski had run the PCR amplification process earlier that evening, then through the genome assembler, and he was now waiting for the computer to finish analyzing the results. He'd asked Reno in because he was a savant when it came to reading genome sequences.

"I guess I'm Catholic," said Reno. "Even if I can't work up the nerve to go to confession. But this worship of the body parts of dead saints feels primitive to me. Someone once said there are enough bones of Saint Peter in all his so-called reliquaries to reassemble three cows."

"If this one's also from a cow, we'll find out in a moment."

"The things we do for Frankie Cash," said Reno. "I mean, what exactly are we supposed to be looking for?"

"Cash was kind of vague about that."

"And why off the clock?"

"It's like this," Romanski said. "You know our victim, Castillo, went to Rome, broke into a church, and stole a piece of bone from a reliquary supposedly containing the head of Saint John the Baptist?"

"Yeah. That's some crazy shit."

"Cash said he did it to analyze its DNA. Cash asked Holmes for authorization, but Holmes nixed it. There's some priest here from the Vatican who wants the sacred head bone back, and Holmes was worried there'd be a scandal if we messed with it. So Cash asked me to sequence the DNA on the Q.T."

"So what kind of analysis did you do?"

"Since it's supposed to be human and male, I figured I'd run an analysis on a bunch of well-known SNPs on the Y chromosome. Of course, if it's a bone from a female cow, we'll get some wild results."

The computer program halted with a *ding*!

"Avon calling!" said Romanski.

"Oh boy," said Reno, sitting down at the workstation and rubbing his hands together, then waggling his fingers. "Let's have a look." He began to type.

Romanski watched him work. This part of the process was recent, an innovation since he had graduated from CU forensics, and it was one he'd never mastered. Reno, on the other hand, had devoured the four-hundred-page digital use manual to the GeneMapp software like it was a Dan Brown novel. The PCR machine had amplified the DNA a millionfold, then the strands had been fed through a nanopore reader and the sequences recorded. That was fed into the computer to be aligned and compared against a known human genome sequence. The program then spit out the differences, or variants—a far more accurate mapping than gel electrophoresis. It was now Reno's job to examine the variants and figure out what they meant.

As Reno paged through the screens, one at a time, he issued little grunts and whistles. Romanski listened to this for a while and began to get a little irritated.

"So—is it human or cow?" he asked sarcastically.

Reno didn't answer immediately. He paged through a few more sets of numbers and graphs, ran a few quick programs, and then he sat back in his chair, looked at Romanski, and issued a loud sigh.

"That doesn't sound good," said Romanski.

"It ain't cow," said Reno. "It's partly a human male and a whole lot something else."

"Like what?"

"It's hard to say without running it through a bunch of DNA databases looking for matches, which would take days. Which is a waste, because I already know what the problem is."

"What?" Romanski asked.

"We—or rather *you*—fucked up. The sample was contaminated."

"I did not fuck up!"

"How did you extract DNA from the sample?" Reno asked.

"In the clean lab, I used a microdrill to come into the side of the sample, so there wouldn't be a hole in it. I found a closed cell in the cancellous bone, opened it, took out a microscopic bit of tissue—all by the book in a totally sterile environment."

"Well, it's contaminated."

"Son of a bitch. I was *so* careful."

"You gotta realize, Romanski, if this really is a piece of Saint John's skull, or even if it's just some random dude, it's been handled by the grubby fingers of God knows how many priests and worshipers for centuries. You also gotta consider that after someone dies, their remains are invaded by bacteria and other organisms, all of which leave their own DNA. Problem here is that over the centuries, the DNA in this sample has been totally swamped. It's a hell of a job to tease it back out. It's not really your fault—what you need is an aDNA lab."

"A-DNA?"

"Ancient DNA. There are labs that specialize in exactly this: sequencing ancient DNA that's been heavily contaminated over the centuries."

"Which ones?"

"Well, CU School of Medicine has an aDNA lab. They've been working with Harvard on the paleo-DNA mapping project."

"So if we brought this sample over to CU, they'd be able to do it?"

"Sure." Reno grinned. "And the guy who runs the lab's a good buddy of mine, Greg Strickland. If I called him and asked a favor, I bet he'd do it for free."

"On the Q.T.? Right away?"

"Sure." He rubbed his cheek. "I'll take it to Strickland tomorrow. You're gonna owe me, boss."

"Reno, I owe you so many favors, I might as well sign you over the deed to my soul."

Reno winked and shut down the program and got up from the workstation. "I'll close up. You go home."

"Okay, pard." Romanski gave him a fist bump, shucked the lab gear, slung his backpack over his shoulder, and left.

Whistling cheerfully, Reno went through the process of shutting down the lab. He took a moment to text Dr. Strickland about the DNA sequencing in between tasks. Twenty minutes later, he was done. He went over to the refrigerated safe, punched in his code, and took out the sample. He eyed it in its sealed tube, not much larger than a big pill. Incredible to think it might really be from Saint John the Baptist.

He wondered again why Castillo would go to so much trouble and risk to steal it, just to sequence its genome. A carbon-14 test made more sense: That would have returned the age of the bone and possibly proven it a fraud. But why DNA? What could that prove?

He slid the vial into his pocket. Tomorrow, he'd bring it over to CU School of Medicine and put it in Strickland's hands.

He let himself out of the building and walked across the parking lot toward his car. At four o'clock in the morning, it was the only one there—the rest of the lot was an empty space dotted with pools of sodium light.

As he pressed the unlock key, his car beeped at him, and the lights flashed. Funny, he thought. In his rush, he must've forgotten to lock the car when he arrived at eleven—and no wonder, because he was nervous about what they were doing.

He got in the car and started it. As he moved the transmission into drive, he felt something cold press against the point at the base of his skull. A low, calm voice said, "CBI has something we want, and you are going to get it for us."

41

Colcord pulled up to the old mill, a dilapidated building sitting on the edge of the Montenegro Reservoir. A thriving mining community had once been there, but when the gold ran out in the 1890s, the ghost town had been purchased and flooded to make the reservoir. When he saw the car parked next to the ruins, at first, he was confused. It was Reno's Audi Q3—the red one he was so proud of—with the bumper sticker that read PLEASE BE PATIENT: I'M ACTUALLY THREE DOGS IN A TRENCH COAT. But how the hell had Reno gotten there before he had—an hour from Arvada all the way up some dusty back road behind Uneva Peak?

A horrible feeling wormed its way into Colcord's gut. Even before he could process it, Cash was pulling up, with Huizinga in the passenger seat. He stepped in front of the Audi with his hands raised. If this was what he thought it was, it was best if he went in first.

"Cash . . ." he began.

Cash opened the door—all business per usual. "So, what's the story?" she said.

"Anonymous caller," said Colcord. "Some kid probably out here smoking pot." They had gotten minimal details on the phone. Years ago, access to Montenegro Mill had been closed off and chain-link fence put up, but some teens had cut a hole and now used the place to smoke weed, drink, and do whatever else kids get up to. It was secluded and quiet.

Colcord said, "But listen, Cash—"

Cash stopped, staring at the Audi. Colcord could see her brain working fast as understanding dawned on her—eyes wide, mouth compressed, pale. He had never seen that look on her face before, and it scared him.

"Cash, hang on and let me go in the mill first—" Colcord stepped in front of her.

"Get the *fuck* out of my way!" Cash dodged his arm, ducked through the fence, and half sprinted toward the millhouse. He followed at a jog.

She stormed through the front door of the mill, Colcord close on her heels. They passed a receiving hopper and an old millstone. Parts of the ceiling were hanging down, looking like they were about to collapse. The place smelled of mold.

"Reno!" Cash yelled, stomping around, her feet crunching on broken glass. "Hey, Reno, where the fuck are you?" She ran into the next room, and Colcord followed, ducking through a low entryway. The walls were covered in graffiti, and beer bottles and cans littered the floor.

Cash stopped suddenly. At the far side of the room, next to a broken waterwheel, Colcord could see a figure lying on a bench, dressed in white. As he got closer, his heart dropped.

With a strangled cry, Cash rushed over to the body. Reno was wearing the same white linen gown as Willy Grooms. His eyes—like Grooms's—were covered in coins. His hands had been arranged crossed over his chest. His left foot was mangled and bloody. He was pale, with a slight discoloration of reddish purple in his lower extremities—livor mortis had begun to set in. There was a hole in his neck accompanied by the sour smell of embalming fluid.

Colcord felt as if the wind had been knocked out of him.

"Reno. Hey, *Reno*." Cash felt around his neck. "There's no pulse. He needs CPR. Colcord!" she yelled, turning to him. "Jesus Christ, don't just stand there! Help me!"

Before he could find a way to respond, she ceased her fumbling and slumped down on her knees, withdrew her hands, and slowly placed her closed fists on her thighs. Colcord laid a hand on her shoulder. Reno had been dead for a couple of hours at least—but Cash knew that.

It was the first time he had ever seen Cash cry. He said nothing, could say nothing.

"Reno is gone," Dr. Huizinga said in a shaking voice from the doorway, but nevertheless came over, knelt, and checked his vitals.

After a moment, Cash rose to her feet. She turned her face to Colcord, no longer crying, her gaze suddenly ice-cold. "These motherfuckers will pay for this."

42

Nova Euclid and Officer Wiley followed Belen Caldas down the hallway of the Eagle County Jail and Detention Facility, where Margie Brooksfield was being held. The guard accompanying them buzzed them through various grimy doors, his gut swinging ponderously. He trailed his riot baton across the bars as he walked, the *klung-klung-klung* setting Euclid's teeth on edge. The place smelled like a bathhouse: a mixture of sweat and cleaning solution. The murmuring of female voices—heard but never seen—echoed all around her, as she imagined the inmates were congregating somewhere in the mess hall for lunch.

It had taken a monumental effort to persuade Caldas to allow her to talk to her client, and only after assurances and strict conditions that Caldas had laid down. The lawyer had to be present, obviously. All questions had to be fielded through Caldas or prewritten and given to her. No recording. Finally, Caldas could end the interview at any time.

"Adewale know you're here?" Caldas asked casually.

Euclid didn't answer. Adewale did not, in fact, know she was here. A prosecutor visiting the defendant was highly unusual—it brought up serious impartiality concerns and safety issues. Adewale would never have agreed. But this was Euclid's case, and in light of the new evidence and her own growing unease, she felt it was necessary. The investigation had tracked the money from Grooms's account to a Portuguese national. Other than the amount that went to her daughter's medical bills, she'd kept none of it. Plus, there had been another murder. One of CBI's own, a technician named Reno. Euclid had to stop this before more people died. She had to get Brooksfield to tell her what she knew about Khacha-tryan and his shadowy operation, even if it meant some sort of plea deal.

They halted before a dark jail cell in a sunless part of the building, the guard crossing his arms and standing a distance away. Officer Wiley stepped forward, brushing his blond hair out of his eyes. Euclid had asked him along as a witness—she couldn't very well call herself to the stand and become a witness to her own case. He smiled at her as he caught her gaze.

Euclid's eyes strained as she peered inside the jail cell. She beheld a sight of misery as her eyes adjusted. A tin toilet squatted in one corner next to a sink with a broken handle and cracked porcelain. Brooksfield was curled on her side on a threadbare mattress. As she sat up, Euclid noted she had lost weight—her orange prison-issued uniform hanging loosely about her frame.

"No interview room?" asked Euclid.

"This will be a short visit," Caldas said coldly.

Euclid supposed this was the best she was going to get. She approached the bars of the cell, Brooksfield's wary eyes taking in her measure.

"Good morning, Margie. My name is Nova Euclid. I am the prose-cutor assigned to your case. I imagine Ms. Caldas told you I would be visiting today?"

"I am aware."

"Let's get right into it, then. Where did you transfer Willy Grooms's money after it left your account?"

Brooksfield's eyes flicked to Caldas, who gave her a slight duck of her chin.

"An account of a nonprofit named Paradox."

"Who runs Paradox?"

"I was never told."

"Did you know where the money went after you transferred it into the Paradox account?"

"No."

"You didn't know a certain Javier Castillo was the custodian of the Paradox bank account?"

"No. His name wasn't on the account. Just Paradox." Brooksfield's fingers played over hanging braids.

"Why did you lie the other day about not knowing Javi Castillo? We have proof that he visited your ranch the day before his murder."

Brooksfield looked up at Euclid defiantly. "*That* was Javi Castillo?" She seemed surprised. "I had no idea who that crazy man was. He never told me his name."

Euclid stepped back in frustration and directed the next statement to Caldas. "I won't be able to help if your client refuses to answer questions and lies."

Caldas gave her a simpering smile. "Maybe you should be better at asking questions." She tapped an invisible watch on her wrist.

"What happened when Castillo came to your ranch the morning before he was murdered?"

Margie Brooksfield stood and approached the bars and gripped them, her voice shaky. "I-I didn't know that man was Castillo. I swear, he never told me his name. It was early in the morning and he was a stranger on our land, so I was nervous. Thought he might have been one of those protesters. Plus, he sounded nuts."

"What did he say?"

"First, he claimed he was Willy's friend. Said he was in Burns to help with the investigation. He began to interrogate me about Willy's death, as if I had something to do with it. I told him just what I told the police—I had no idea."

"What else did he say?" Euclid encouraged gently.

"He then asked me about the missing money from the Paradox transfers. He said he owned Paradox, that I'd stolen from him. I told him about Lolly and her Turner syndrome. He said I could pay him back in installments. . . . I didn't believe him. I suddenly thought he must be a scam artist who read some stories about the case and was trying to defraud me or something. Like one of those pig-butchering scams where they steal your life savings."

"Is that why Paul ended up chasing him off your land with a shotgun?" Euclid asked.

"That's an exaggeration. Paul *encouraged* him off our land with a shotgun. There was no chasing involved."

"Why threaten him like that?"

"I'm not comfortable saying it out loud. But Castillo said something terrible. I didn't want him around my family."

"What did he say?"

"It was about Willy Grooms. That he'd been sending the money through me to fund a project that goes against everything I believe. But I knew Willy Grooms; he was a *good* Christian. . . . He never would have done anything like what that man claims. It was all lies."

Euclid could tell Brooksfield was getting upset again.

"So what did he say Willy Grooms was doing?"

Brooksfield looked at Officer Wiley, who was standing behind Euclid. "I'm not going to tell you. I'm sure it will sound silly to you, and I don't want it used against me at the trial."

"If you just whisper it to me," Euclid said, "Officer Wiley can't testify to it. I can't be a witness to my own case. But I want to know."

"Hang on," Caldas said. "Whisper it to me first. I want to make sure this is okay to tell them."

Brooksfield pressed against the bars, whispering something in Caldas's ear. Caldas, with a practiced mask of neutrality, nodded.

"You may proceed," Caldas said. There was an odd look in her eyes.

"Okay." Brooksfield stood on shaky legs, pulling her uniform around her frame.

Euclid held her ear close, cold bars pressing into her cheek. Brooksfield whispered to her then, repeating to her what she had whispered to Caldas.

Euclid took a step back, feeling dumbfounded, and quickly tried to cover up her reaction. "Okay . . . Thank you for telling me." She composed herself. "I have a couple more questions, if you don't mind."

"Hurry it up," Caldas said, irritation playing across her face.

"What is Devotio?"

Brooksfield gave her a blank stare. "I don't know."

"Who is Krikor Khachatryan?"

Brooksfield gave a noticeable jolt. "How do you know that name?"

"Answer the question, Mrs. Brooksfield. Isn't he the true owner of Paradox, and he's been laundering charitable donations through offshore shell companies?"

Caldas stepped forward, and Euclid could tell by her puzzled expression she had never heard Khachatryan's name before. Despite every-thing, Brooksfield was still keeping secrets.

"Hang on." Caldas held out a hand in front of Euclid. "Are you look-ing for this Khachatryan fellow?"

"We are."

"If we can give you information on this man, I want assurances that all charges will be dropped against my client."

Suddenly, it seemed, they were on the same side: Caldas wanted to get her client off with this potential new defendant. Euclid wanted to get information about Khachatryan. And she had very serious doubts about Brooksfield's guilt. Yes, she diverted money to pay medical bills, but Euclid was now pretty sure she knew nothing of the murders. She paused to collect her thoughts. Reluctantly, she replied, "I can't promise anything like that. It's not in my power to assure such an outcome. Ade-wale has final say on dropping charges. I *can* promise you that I will have our investigators follow any lead that you give me. I'll do my best with Adewale to support a plea deal—but only in proportion to how helpful this information is."

"What if Adewale says no to her release? What will you do then?"

Euclid shrugged. "If your client can provide us with crucial informa-tion, I'll do my best with Adewale. Right now, your best bet at reducing these embezzlement charges is to cooperate fully."

Euclid could feel Caldas's eyes studying her. Finally, she relented. "Okay. I'm deciding to trust you. Margie, tell her about Khachatryan."

"But I promised Willy—"

"Grooms is *dead*, Margie. As your attorney, I am advising you to talk to Euclid here."

Brooksfield shook her head, lip trembling.

"Margie." Euclid leaned toward her. "Margie, look at me. There's been another murder."

Brooksfield looked at her, a haunted expression on her face.

"The murders will continue if you don't help us out. This was one of our own. A forensic tech named Reno. He was well loved at CBI. Tell me about Khachatryan," Euclid said again, "before more people die."

Margie's chin sank to her chest, braids falling around her face. When she spoke, it was quiet.

"Willy told me Paradox was run by a great man named Krikor Khacha-tryan. I overheard some phone conversations too. It sounded like Khacha-tryan was looking for the site of the UFO crash somewhere in the Flat Tops. And wanted something of Willy's, something he found up there. He made me swear on the Bible that I wouldn't tell anyone. He said Khacha-tryan would be killed if I revealed his name to *anyone*. Until just now, I wasn't even sure how much of what Willy told me about the man was just in his head."

"Where can we find this guy?"

"I don't know."

"Margie," Caldas said in warning.

"I really don't."

"Time's up," Caldas said. "Margie's cooperated. I certainly hope what she was able to tell you will weigh in her favor in a plea bargain."

"I'll do my best," Euclid said. She wondered if this could all be an act. It was so crazy . . . but could this information actually be useful? She stepped back from the bars, her thoughts whirling. One thing was certain: Whoever was after Khachatryan and the other Paradox mem-bers, they were bad people. They were cop killers. Nobody on the case was safe.

43

Director Blaisdell Holmes, gowned up, stood in the far corner of the morgue, notebook in hand, as Dr. Huizinga and his assistant performed the autopsy on Reno. Romanski stood next to her, pale and silent as a ghost. They had worked with plenty of homicides before—but never one of their own. It was important to maintain detachment. Emotions created an environment for mistakes. And Blaisdell Holmes would not be making any mistakes, not with this homicide.

A cold spear of anger was slowly working its way through her as she watched Huizinga cutting away at the cadaver, as she listened to his monotonal description of each cut, each observation, for the video record. He would occasionally pause and murmur a comment to his technician, Ellen Zubriski. Holmes could hear a tremor in Huizinga's voice, the occasional hoarseness brought on by emotion, which she could see he was keeping rigidly under control. She had told Huizinga that he didn't have to do this—they could bring in another forensic pathologist. But he had insisted. Huizinga paused to take a deep breath, closing his eyes briefly. Holmes wanted to ask if he was all right, but suppressed the question, knowing it was both unnecessary and possibly offensive.

The killing of Castillo and that viral video had caused the case to blow up and go national, but now, with the additional murder of a law enforcement officer, it had ratcheted up even further. CBI was expending more resources on this case than any other since Erebus, and it was by far their most critical. Everything was riding on the case—including the safety of her staff, the reputation of CBI, possibly even her position.

Huizinga paused in his description again, his voice actually choking up. But he collected himself and kept going, reading out his actions in that same dead voice.

Holmes jotted notes as Huizinga worked. The homicide displayed the same bizarre MO as Grooms's: Reno had been tortured and his left foot crushed using the Spanish boot. She wondered what they would find when they opened his stomach. More wafers?

Now they had detached and lifted out the organ set, placing it on a separate tray. It was all Holmes could do not to avert her eyes. She'd seen plenty of autopsies before, many with the cadaver in far worse condition than this, but never had one been as tough.

Huizinga and Zubriski shifted their work to the heap of innards, cutting and separating out the various organs, weighing them, taking samples, and sealing them in containers. She could see the stomach being separated and isolated. Finally, after the heart, liver, kidneys, pancreas, and spleen had been removed, they started on the stomach. First, they cut away the esophagus, diaphragm, and duodenum. Then, with one slow, smooth stroke of a scalpel, Huizinga opened the stomach and placed retractors in the incision. He peered inside with tweezers as Zubriski angled a spotlight to illuminate the interior.

Holmes realized she was holding her breath.

Huizinga began speaking again. "In opening the stomach," he said, "I note the presence of what appear to be Communion wafers, and furthermore note the odor of alcohol, probably wine."

Holmes let out her breath. They'd done it to him too. She steadied shaking hands against her pant legs. This was harder than she'd expected. One of the hardest days of her life. She glanced at Romanski, but he was as still and unmoving as a statue.

Huizinga began taking samples, drawing out crumbs and bits of wafer and placing them in sample containers being held out by Zubriski, who labeled and racked them. And then Huizinga seemed to freeze for a moment. He bent down closer, peering into the incision.

"I note a foreign object in here," he said. "It appears to be made of plastic."

Again with the tweezers, he reached inside, grasped something, and drew it out. There was a glint from it as he held it to the light, turning it around, examining it.

Holmes narrowed her eyes, trying to see, but she was too far away.

As Huizinga turned it around in the light, a look of puzzlement on his face, Holmes finally had to ask, "What is it?"

Huizinga glanced at her. "I'm not sure. It's a tiny, cylindrical vial, with something inside."

"May I have a closer look?" Holmes asked.

He nodded and she came over and stared at it—but she couldn't see inside, as it was smeared with gunk.

"Let me clean it up," Huizinga said. He carried it over to a basin of water and gently swirled it around, rinsing off the gluey stomach residue, and held it up again.

Holmes recognized it with a start. "That's the relic that Cash brought back from California!"

Huizinga asked, "Relic?"

"A piece of bone. Castillo stole it from a reliquary in Rome. I told Cash to turn it over to the priest who came here looking for it. It was supposed to be locked up in the evidence freezer."

At this, Huizinga's eyebrows shot up. "I know nothing about this."

"No, you wouldn't—I decided it wasn't evidence in the case, and I was trying to keep it under wraps on account of the Catholic Church being involved. I wanted to return the relic as soon as possible."

"What in the world was it doing in Reno's stomach?"

Holmes stared at it, her mind churning. She knew that Reno had been carjacked after he left the CBI parking lot last night. The relic was locked in the freezer in his lab, which means he must have taken it out and been carrying it with him. Then he swallowed it. Why? She realized both Huizinga and Zubriski were looking at her, waiting for an answer.

She had no answer.

Romanski broke the silence, speaking in a flat voice. "He swallowed it. Because that's what the killers wanted. They wanted that relic."

Holmes turned and stared at Romanski. "And what do you know about this?"

He continued in a dead voice. "He was taking it to have the DNA sequenced in another lab. The killers probably figured it was locked in the lab—that's the only place where CBI forensics would store it. And they knew he had access. I assume what happened was they demanded he go back into the lab and get it, and he wouldn't. He had it on his person. You know Reno—he doesn't like to be pushed around, and he didn't comply. He must've swallowed it without them seeing him do it. So when he wouldn't give it to them, or said he didn't have it, they took him to the mill and tortured him to make him tell them where it was."

"Why in the world was he taking it to another lab?" asked Holmes, although even as she asked the question, she knew the answer.

Romanski went on as if he hadn't heard. "But the horror is that after swallowing it, Reno *couldn't* tell them where it was, because it was now inside him. That admission would have been his death warrant: They would have killed and cut him open on the spot."

"*Cash*," Holmes said. "Cash wanted to test its DNA. I said no. But it looks like she went ahead anyway and enlisted you and Reno to help her. Am I right, Romanski?"

"Yes," he said after a moment.

44

That same morning, Cash entered the side conference room of the Eagle County Sheriff's Office. Colcord was there, and she could see he was exhausted. His Stetson was on the table, the top two buttons of his shirt were unfastened, and his cowboy boots were kicked into a corner. He was working on a giant corkboard display affixed along one wall with a bunch of pictures pinned to it, threads running every which way. A half-eaten pizza sat next to a jug of coffee and a conglomerate of cups from the crowd that had been in earlier.

He'd obviously been up all night—like she had. She'd spent the night in the Eagle Valley Library, working through a stack of books and articles on torture devices, Communion rituals, UAPs, and the Spanish Inquisition. It was mostly useless information, but it was a welcome distraction. Whenever she shut her eyes, Reno's dead pallid face materialized behind her eyelids. She couldn't believe he was gone. She didn't want to remember him like that.

She took a seat and watched what Colcord was doing, placing Margie Brooksfield's photo underneath Paradox. This was something she needed to clear up with Colcord if she was to get any real help from him.

"I don't think Paradox is behind the Shrouder murders," Cash said. Her voice was hoarse from lack of sleep and her mind was still numb with unprocessed grief. "And I don't think Margie Brooksfield killed Willy Grooms. In fact, I bet she didn't have anything to do with the case at all."

Colcord turned to Cash, a quizzical look on his face. "Why do you say that?"

Cash sighed heavily, taking a swig of black coffee. "Standish put me in touch with Krikor Khachatryan, the guy who controls Paradox. Khachatryan said that the money from Willy Grooms was to finance an expedition into the wilderness to find the site of a UFO crash as well as other expeditions across the globe—and that members of the organization were being targeted and killed." She hesitated and decided not to say anything about the DNA test just yet.

"Targeted? By whom?"

"A radical Catholic society called Devotio."

"Why?"

"He didn't say. Or wouldn't say."

"When did this conversation happen?"

"Two days ago."

"And you didn't tell me?" Colcord looked at Cash incredulously.

"I was just waiting for something more solid."

"And you believe this guy Khachatryan? That killer priests are out to get them?"

Cash hesitated. She still wasn't sure he was legit. She had tried to find out something about Devotio but had come up cold. Maybe she was being played. She shook her head. "I really think there might be something to it. He seemed scared, Colcord."

Colcord's shoulders tensed. When he spoke, he chose his words with care. "How am I supposed to run my end of the investigation without full cooperation?"

Cash felt a flash of resentment. "You've been pushing back on me from the beginning about this UFO connection, making fun of it, belittling my efforts. I'd be sharing more if you weren't so dismissive."

"Just tell me next time," Colcord said, moderating his tone. He looked away and changed the subject. "Did Romanski say anything about what he was doing that night at CBI?"

Cash thought about the piece of the head of Saint John the Baptist and the DNA testing. Romanski said Reno was en route to CU School of Medicine with the relic when it happened. All night, she'd been thinking it was her fault. It sure looked that way.

"The piece of the head of Saint John the Baptist is missing from the lab," Cash said. "Reno had it. I think he . . . might have been killed for it."

Colcord eyed her. "Something here isn't making sense."

Cash didn't answer. The same organization that Khachatryan was afraid of, Devotio, had probably killed Grooms. And Castillo. And Reno. She squeezed her eyes shut, overwhelmed with guilt. She realized she was near a breaking point.

"Anything else you've forgotten to tell me?"

"Just . . . be quiet for a minute," she said, covering her face with her hands.

A silence, and then she heard Colcord say in a gentler tone of voice, "I'm sorry. I know you're really hurting. I didn't mean to challenge you like that. I'm just . . . really frustrated."

She nodded wordlessly. Then she took a deep breath and tried to refocus on the case. "There's something else you need to know."

"What?"

"You know we've had a researcher looking into historical connections to some of the details in Grooms's homicide. He found something that might be significant."

"Okay." Colcord raised his eyebrows.

"A book called *Judgment of the Inquisitions* goes into the mass arrest and torture of over fifteen thousand Knights Templar in France, the persecution of heretic conversos, and the trial of Galileo in 1633 during the Roman Inquisition."

"Pretty heavy reading," Colcord said.

"In the book, he found a reproduction of an 1839 painting entitled *Communion of Dying* by Alexey Venetsianov. It depicts a woman in her deathbed wearing white linens, with a priest in red cloth standing by her bedside. The linens were just like how Grooms and Reno were dressed."

"Anything else?"

"A lot more. Viaticum, also known as the Eucharist or Holy Communion, is administered as part of the last rites—the ministrations given to Catholics shortly before death. It roughly translates to 'food for the journey' and is said to be a source of strength on their journey to eternal life. Apparently, it was *also* given to baptized Catholics being tortured or executed during the Inquisition—to ensure that even apostates be given a final chance to go to heaven. It was considered a kindness to them—even as they were being killed. Grooms and Reno were given Communion wafers and sacramental wine shortly before they died. Grooms is Catholic—remember how he was baptized in Solitary Lake? Reno was also Catholic, and they were both dressed in white linens, their bodies treated with respect, if you could call it that. Embalming is another sign of respect—the idea is that it preserves the body for the Last Judgment and resurrection of the dead."

"What about Castillo? He wasn't given Communion and dressed in linens."

"Because he wasn't Catholic. Since he wasn't a baptized Catholic, he didn't get viaticum. And his body was treated like trash—dismembered and thrown into a lake instead of embalmed, posed, and dressed in linen."

She showed Colcord a photo of the *Communion of the Dying* painting on her cell.

"Jesus Christ," Colcord said.

"Do you see what this means?"

"Not completely." Colcord steepled his fingers and leaned back in his chair.

"*Devotio* means 'devotion' in Latin. I believe it might be an extreme Catholic cult or something. It explains a lot. Why would four people go to the trouble and take the risk to clean, pose, and give viaticum to murder victims otherwise? And even embalm them?" Cash paused. "The killers believed they were *saving* the souls of Grooms and Reno by force-feeding them the Eucharist before they murdered them and preparing their bodies for resurrection."

"So why would a secret society of Catholics be targeting and killing a group of UFO researchers?"

"That, Colcord, is the very question I was just asking myself."

45

"Brother Armagh," said Father Moore, coming from behind the altar and walking briskly down the aisle with his hand extended, black robes flowing behind him. "Welcome to Saint Mary's!"

Armagh took Father Moore's hand and was surprised at the strength of his grip. "Very pleased to meet you, Father Moore," he said, wincing as his hand was vigorously shaken.

"It isn't often that we get a visitor from the Holy See. Come with me into the sacristy—we have much to talk about," said Moore. "I understand you dropped in a few days ago and met a dear friend of mine—Brother Gregory."

"We had a most enjoyable chat. The skiing monk. Very impressive."

"Oh yes. He's quite a figure," said Moore. "I'm sorry I wasn't here to greet you myself, but I'm glad you made his acquaintance."

"I am too." Armagh followed Moore through a low door into the sacristy.

"I'm so pleased you called," said Moore as they seated themselves. "I'm quite isolated here, and your visit is an event for me and my modest little parish."

"It's always a pleasure to meet a fellow religious," Armagh said, "especially while traveling in foreign lands."

"I understand you're here on vacation, visiting family." His voice was unexpectedly resonant, with a curious penetrating effect. "And please, let us be informal. Call me Timothy."

"And I'm Niall," said Armagh, adjusting himself in the hard wooden seat. He felt uncomfortable lying, especially to a fellow religious, but those were his orders. "The beauty of God's creation is certainly on display here."

"We are a little corner of heaven here in Burns," said Moore, "a refuge of sorts from the depravity of the world. Although even here, we see the moral decay creeping in, where anything goes. Same-sex marriage, gender flipping, mass contraception, abortion on demand."

"To be sure," said Armagh vaguely. Even though Brother Gregory had warned him, he was a little put off by Moore's sudden detour into vehemence. During Armagh's prison ministry in Chicago, his views on sin, damnation, and judgment had moderated considerably. "We are all sinners," he murmured.

"Indeed," said Moore. "For the wages of sin is death!"

"Right," said Armagh, looking for a way to lead the conversation out of the moral briar patch. "I must say, it's lovely for me to get out of Rome and fill my lungs with some fresh mountain air. What brought you out here, Timothy?"

"The desire to bring the discipline of faith to a lost place. Even though Burns is mostly Catholic, there was no parish priest here for over a decade."

"You have done good service here, then."

"Oh yes," said Moore, "but there is much more to do. *Much* more. There's no discipline of faith anymore; it's all relative. We've lost the country, and we need to bring it back."

Armagh's unease swelled into annoyance at this insistent refrain, and he said, flippantly and with sarcasm, "Yes, let us bring back the Holy Brotherhood!"

"Absolutely!" said Moore, with a disturbing note of conviction in his resonant voice.

Armagh realized his Irish sense of irony about the medieval Spanish religious police had gone over the head of this tiny priest, but before he could continue, Moore rushed on.

"The Inquisition provided the discipline that a sinful society needed to stay in line. As you surely know, the Inquisition is a much misunderstood phenomenon. It was motivated not by harshness but by kindness. Something the Holy Brotherhood understood at the time."

"Kindness," murmured Armagh, on edge.

Moore was unstoppable. "Not that I approve of their methods, of course. Not at all. But to save a soul from the eternal fires of hell, one must agree, is the ultimate act of kindness—and that's what the Inquisition was all about."

Armagh recalled what Brother Gregory had said about Father Moore being a bit "old-fashioned" in his views. He had no intention of getting into doctrinal disputes with this priest and tried to steer the course of the conversation in another direction. "Yes, of course," he said, nodding and smiling. "Quite right. Now—"

"*Inquisitionis*—it means 'inquiry.' Asking questions. Making sure people aren't misunderstanding the doctrine. In service of ensuring their entry into eternal life." Moore leaned forward and touched Armagh's knee with his finger, his minty confidential breath washing over him. In a lowered voice, he said, "Niall, I have a little collection I'd like to show you. I don't normally share this with others. But you of all people will appreciate this, and it isn't often I get a visitor from the Holy See. It's so refreshing to have a man of God like you to converse with about the Faith. Come with me."

Armagh felt a twinge of despair as he followed the insistent little priest out of the sacristy, down the nave to a locked door, down a set of stairs to the basement, through another locked door, down yet again into the catacombs, through a third locked door, and finally into a window-less stone room. Moore hit the lights.

Armagh was surprised to see a rather extraordinary collection of ec-clesiastical treasures arrayed along the stone walls—framed documents, antique vestments, chalices, reliquaries, and other Catholic items. This must be the "odd collection" Brother Gregory mentioned.

"Welcome to my little museum," Moore said, his voice effervescent with pride. "Documenting the Inquisition—the *real* Inquisition, not the caricature of it you see in the popular imagination. The real Inquisition was established by the Pope Sixtus V as the Suprema Congregatio Sanc-tae Romanae et Universalis Inquisitionis. How's your Latin, Niall?"

"Fair enough," said Armagh.

"Then you know that translates as *the Supreme Sacred Congregation of the Roman and Universal Inquisition*. In 1908, it was renamed the

Supreme Sacred Congregation of the Holy Office, then it was retitled the Congregation for the Doctrine of the Faith. Finally, only a few years ago, it was renamed the Dicastery for the Doctrine of the Faith. But of course, you know all this."

"Yes, of course," said Armagh. He had met many tiresome religious like this country priest in his life, but he couldn't help but find himself genuinely intrigued by the collection. It wasn't odd at all—it was in fact quite splendid. As he looked around, he realized there were some truly spectacular things in here and was amazed to find them in such a backwater—including antique crucifixes, a medieval chalice, some lovely old surplices, silver thuribles, a gem-encrusted aspergillum, and a magnificent ciborium decorated with gold thread. Incongruously, in a far dark corner were stacked some antique contraptions and devices made of iron and wood.

Moore went on relentlessly, "We're working to reestablish the Tridentine Mass, and we have other projects as well." Moore paused, eyeing Armagh. "My friends and I are *always* looking for more support, now that we have a new pope, especially from those of our conviction."

"Very nice," Armagh said. He was not a fan of the Tridentine Mass, the traditional Latin mass that had been retired decades ago. Father Moore was mistaken about his convictions. However, he didn't see any use in correcting the priest.

"There are some high points in the collection," said Moore. "Here, for example"—he indicated a framed document with heavy wax seals and ribbons—"is the first printed *Index Librorum Prohibitorum*, the index of banned books, issued in 1582. And this"—he pointed to another document—"is a heretical manifesto by a miller named Domenico Scandella, who wrote in here that God was created from chaos. He was investigated by the Inquisition."

"What happened to him?"

"He was burned at the stake by Pope Clement in 1599. But he recanted just before the fire was lit. So you see, Niall, while we certainly can't approve of the cruelty of it, the important thing is that he's now in the kingdom of heaven. This is what I mean about the *kindness* of the Inquisition. It may sound strange, and even contradictory, but the truth is this: If Domenico hadn't been disciplined by the Inquisition, he would have persisted in his heresy, and right now, he'd be suffering eternal damnation."

"I see." Armagh had a very different view but did not care to express it. This priest had gone from annoying to creepy.

"That," said Moore as Armagh's gaze fell on a gem-encrusted, miniature gold spire with a glass window, "is a reliquary from France that once held a foot bone from Saint Lidwina—the skating saint."

The skating saint. "Quite lovely," said Armagh. "But I'm afraid—"

"And *this*," said Moore, "is my most valuable item: a letter from Giordano Bruno in which he denies the divinity of the Virgin. You know who he was, of course."

Armagh did know: Bruno was an infamous heretic burned at the stake. But Armagh had had enough. "Thank you so very much, Timothy, for this thought-provoking tour of your museum. But I fear I must be getting back to my hotel."

"Of course, of course. Such a pleasure to show my little museum to someone who can appreciate it."

Armagh hurried outside. Back on the main street of Burns, Armagh took a deep breath of the summer air. He was relieved to get out of the stuffy little room and away from the voluble priest and his hobbyhorse. As soon as he could get the relic from the police, he was going to take his leave. While the mountains were beautiful, he was beginning to long for the cool, silent, stone-scented corridors of the basilica, the candles flickering in the chapels, and above all, his morning prayers to the holy relic of Saint John the Baptist, Forerunner of Christ, restored to its former state.

46

Blaisdell Holmes was seated at her desk, her mouth set in a grim line, when Cash rapped on her open office door. Holmes was having a difficult time maintaining an unruffled demeanor. She had a persistent and ugly idea that Reno would still be alive if not for her senior agent. In a male-dominated field such as theirs, where women had to work twice as hard to make it to the top, as she had, it angered her to see another woman screw up so badly and put them both at risk. What made it worse was that Holmes liked Agent Cash. But now she knew that Cash had been dishonest with her, even betrayed her.

Holmes beckoned for Cash to come in. She looked like she'd been run through the dryer. Her hair was a mess, eyes red, clothes unkempt. Holmes guessed she'd slept at CBI the night before.

Cash didn't sit, and Holmes made no effort to invite her to.

"Agent Cash, we need to have a rather difficult conversation," Holmes said, remaining seated behind her desk.

Cash did not reply. If she was self-conscious about her appearance, she didn't show it. She stood across from Holmes, her hands clasped behind her back, a wreck. Holmes felt a sliver of pity that she quickly quashed.

"First off," Holmes said, trying to keep her voice even, "I'd like to remind you that we have a psychologist on staff who can help with grief counseling and other issues related to the death of our colleague. I know you were close."

"I'm prepared to tender my resignation."

Holmes gave Cash a long, steady look. "Excuse me, Agent Cash, but I'm not going to let you fuck things up and then run away. Understood?"

Cash gave a curt nod.

"Back to what I was saying. Grief counseling isn't a suggestion. Schedule an appointment."

"Yes, ma'am."

Holmes kept her voice carefully neutral. "You contravened my direct orders and enlisted Romanski and Reno in an effort to perform DNA testing on the relic."

Cash stiffened. "Yes, ma'am."

"While I'm not blaming you for Reno's death, I must point out that it wouldn't have happened if you hadn't gone behind my back."

"Yes, ma'am. I blame myself." Her voice choked up.

Holmes went on, "I have made my decision. I am taking you off the Shrouder investigation, effective immediately. There have been too many missteps. Furthermore, while it isn't necessarily your fault, the press has revived your Maine incident. As I'm sure you're aware, this Shrouder case has gone national. *48 Hours* is literally camped outside as we speak. There have been questions about why you were hired here despite your history." Holmes paused, feeling the anger rising again. "Going behind my back is unacceptable. I have been very clear with you that there isn't—there *can't* be—the slightest evidentiary value in sequencing the DNA of this relic. And it means defying the Catholic Church and the priest sent here by the pope himself. We have enough trouble with Father Moore without adding the pope to our list of critics. And on top of that, as you already know, it appears there's a leak at CBI." She allowed a silence to fall while she looked pointedly at Cash. She didn't believe it was Cash, but you never knew for sure with these things. After letting an uncomfortable beat pass, Holmes took a deep breath. "Do you understand?"

"I understand, ma'am."

Cash looked almost . . . resigned. Holmes was grateful for her silence. Maybe she was finally learning to keep her mouth shut.

"Reno's effort to save the relic was not in vain. We will be turning it over to the priest to be taken back to Rome, where it belongs, as soon as we've finished the paperwork. And as I'm sure you know by now, we've given Romanski a leave of absence. Reno's death hit him hard."

She could see Cash's face burning with emotion.

"Any questions?"

Cash smoothed the front of her pants, as if in an effort to pull herself together. "Ma'am, who is taking over the Shrouder investigation?"

"I am. Standish will be my deputy. You'll brief him tomorrow. Then I want you to make that appointment with the psychologist, go home, and get some rest. Take a few days off."

"Yes, ma'am."

47

It was early morning, the air crisp and cold. Tendrils of the rising sun were just striking the treetops as Cash swiped her access card and entered the lobby of the forensics building. A few moments later, she had reached the lab, dark and quiet. The piece of the skull of Saint John the Baptist had been locked up in the secure evidence freezer. But she knew the code . . . Romanski's code for everything was his favorite number repeated: 474747. It was terribly insecure, and she had criticized him for it on several occasions. But now his heedlessness was to her advantage.

She dialed in the number, opened the freezer, and took out the tiny vial that contained the piece of skull, which was itself sealed inside an evidence tube. She replaced it with an identical evidence tube containing a vial with a tiny chip of brown tree bark inside it. Then she slipped the real vial into the pocket of her sweatpants. The paperwork to release the relic to the priest, she knew, would take longer than the twenty-four hours the DNA expert, Strickland, said he needed. Holmes wouldn't notice it was gone. The only one who would was Romanski, but he was on leave.

She exited the building and got into the front seat of the gray Nissan she had rented for the day—in cash. A hoodie was pulled tight around her face. The killers wanted the relic enough to kill Reno, and Cash was going to be extra careful. The parking lot showed no signs of activity, but as she pulled out into the street, she saw a dark blue Ford Ranger idling in a parking space, a person inside. She slowed down as she went past and got a good read on the license plate, memorizing it, but she couldn't quite make out the face—it was blocked by windshield glare.

She took a right turn and then slowed down, waiting to see if the car would follow. And it did: When she was halfway down the block, she saw the Ranger come creeping around the corner. She sped up, and it matched her pace—keeping just far enough away to make it difficult to see who it was. Cash halted in the middle of the road, and the Ranger did as well. She waited, silently, her throat tight, and then, in a surge of anger, pulled her Baby Glock from its holster and got out of the vehicle, pointing it at the truck. With a screeching roar, it pulled a U-turn and sped away. Cash watched it go, her heart fluttering, then re-holstered her weapon. That was a crazy thing to do, and she'd be in a lot of trouble if it got reported—but she knew those bastards wouldn't. She would run the plate later, but she was certain it wouldn't yield anything useful.

Cash debated whether to continue, but the Ranger did not return. She drove a roundabout route, eyes glued to her rearview mirror. There were two occasions she feared she was being followed, and she did the four-consecutive-right-turns test. Both proved to be false alarms, but it did alleviate her sense of unease.

Finally, she reached her destination—the Anschutz health sciences building of the University of Colorado—and stopped. She waited in the parking lot for a few minutes, looking around, but it seemed the coast was clear.

Cash felt jumpy, the vial burning a hole through her pocket, as she stepped through the doors. The health sciences building served as a welcome to the CU School of Medicine campus. The seven floors of the building enclosed a central atrium, and she was greeted by a modern, open-concept floor plan dotted with giant ferns and palms in wooden planters. A handful of tables and couches were occupied with medical students and staff chatting and laughing over coffee.

Having looked up his image on the university website, Cash spotted Dr. Strickland's bushy head in between two ferns, and strode over.

"Agent Cash," the man rose to his feet. He was completely different from how she'd imagined, with long unkempt hair, a big beard, wearing a T-shirt stretched to the max by a large belly. Peeking from the sleeve was a tattoo of the famous double-helix molecule. He did not, Cash had to admit, look like a prominent and accomplished professor.

"Dr. Strickland, it's a pleasure." Cash gave his hand a gentle pump.

Dr. Strickland shook his head. "I'm so shocked and horrified to hear about Michael Reno's murder. I'm just devastated by the news. . . . I imagine you were close to him. Any leads on who did it?"

"No," said Cash. "But we're all over it. We loved Reno." She felt her eyes welling with tears, and turned her head to the side and coughed, waiting for the emotion to pass. She pinched her arm to calm herself.

"Have a seat." Dr. Strickland gestured at the chair across from him. "Reno texted me you have a bone you want tested. It must have been one of the last messages he sent before he was killed."

"Yes." Cash fished in her pocket. She quickly palmed it over to Strickland, who took it and held the vial up to the light. Cash glanced around nervously, but nobody seemed to be paying them any attention. "Reno told me you needed an aDNA workup on it but didn't go into detail. What's it from?"

"It's . . . a bone fragment from a first-century AD burial."

Dr. Strickland's eyes widened. "Interesting. Why the need for an aDNA test?"

Cash had prepared herself for this line of questioning. "A friend of mine inherited it in a box with some fossils, with a note saying it was human. She asked if I could help her confirm that and also test how old it might be."

"Weird," said Strickland, but he seemed to be buying the story.

"She wants to keep it strictly confidential, if you don't mind. And please, if the test could be done without any visible damage to the bone, that would be ideal."

"I'm happy to do a solid for my friend Reno—poor guy. What a horror. I'll do it and let you know if it's human or not."

As the vial disappeared somewhere into the depths of his cargo pants pockets, Cash felt more than a twinge of concern. She was pretty sure they hadn't followed her to the campus, but she couldn't be certain. She was at least reassured that Strickland didn't look like an easy target.

He must have seen the troubled look on her face, because he said, "No sweat, Agent Cash. Your vial is safe with me. I'll have it back to you by tomorrow morning, intact, with no sign it's been monkeyed with."

48

"That's heavy. Let me help you with that," Standish said as Cash lugged the enormous box of files into the conference room.

Ignoring him, she brushed past and set it down with a thump. She fixed a baleful eye on him. "Don't patronize me."

Standish was thrown into confusion. "Just offering to help; no offense intended—"

"There's no doubt in my mind," Cash said, "that in an arm-wrestling contest, I could lay you down flat in five seconds."

Standish gave an awkward laugh, his face red, as Cash set herself down and began pulling out files. "Most of this stuff's been digitized," she went on, "but there are some things in here you'll need in hard copy."

She laid out the files, one at a time, and briefed Standish on the contents of each, showing him the important things, and then loading them back in the box. She tried to maintain a professional demeanor, but it was hard. She was exhausted, grieving, and angry: at Holmes, at Reno's murder, and especially at herself.

Going behind Holmes's back with that DNA testing had been a terrible idea. And here she was, doing it all over again. At the same time, she needed the relic to be important—Khachatryan had been so insistent—and Reno was gone because of it. She couldn't accept that Holmes was just going to let the bone go without a test, placing it beyond reach forever. That would mean Reno had died for nothing.

Now the case was essentially Standish's. . . . She tried to tell herself she was lucky to be rid of it. The press was hysterical, she and Colcord were in increasing conflict, and they'd lost one of their own. On top of that, there was a leak somewhere—and Holmes had the nerve to suspect her.

As they went through the files, Standish asked some rather incisive questions, which surprised and encouraged her to think the case wasn't going into altogether poor hands. When she was finally done and the files were repacked, she turned to Standish with a sigh. "And there it is, Standish. All yours."

"Thanks, Cash," he said. "Look, I'm really sorry how this turned out."

She shook her head. "My own damn fault. I really screwed the pooch with this one. But I'll tell you what really frosts me is that Holmes seems to think *I* might be the leak."

Standish colored, busying himself with the files and avoiding eye contact. "I'm sorry to hear that."

"Going forward," Cash said, "would it be too much to ask for you to keep me informed on the Shrouder case?"

"Of course."

"Thanks. So, can I ask—you got any info on Devotio?"

"None. Whatever it is, it has no digital or financial profile whatsoever."

"And Paradox? Anything more on that?"

Standish shook his head. "*On the surface*, they seem to be a harmless nonprofit that collects and analyzes UFO sightings, abductions, encounters, and whatnot. But there're quite a few UFO organizations and researchers out there, and nobody's trying to kill them. There has to be more to it. Something that threatens Devotio and maybe even the church."

"That's good work," said Cash. "Let me know what you find out."

"I will."

"I'll leave you to it. The case seems to be in good hands." Cash planned to go home and sleep for twenty-four hours—if only she could stop seeing Reno in that dressing gown every time she closed her eyes.

"Um, Cash?" Standish said as she got up.

"Yes?" He was red in the face and looked upset.

"I think I may have, ah, messed up too."

"What do you mean?"

"I think . . . I might be the leak."

Cash stared. "You *think* you might be the leak? What's that mean?"

"I borrowed some files to take home overnight, just to read up on the case. I . . . Well, I stopped for a burger at Murray's. I forgot my briefcase under the table when I left, then halfway home remembered and came back. As soon as I walked in, the bartender said he had kept it safe for me and pulled it out from behind the bar. But that reporter, Twen, was there."

"You think they opened it?"

Standish was sweating. "I went back later when Twen was gone and questioned the bartender. He swore up and down he'd kept the brief-case safe, that nobody had touched it—but he was really nervous, and I found out later that they're dating. So . . . I can't be sure."

"Jesus, Standish. Taking files out of the office? That's, like, a fireable offense. And it wasn't even your case!"

"I know, but . . ."

"But you're an ambitious guy."

"Yeah. I . . ." He swallowed. "I can't have Holmes thinking it's you. I have to go tell her."

Cash stared at him, mind racing. She couldn't let Standish take the fall for this, even if it was his fault. He was a capable guy, and the Shrouder case was in good hands. And plus, he was definitely going to keep her in the loop now. "Hell no."

"What do you mean?"

"You'll be cashiered."

He stared at her, thunderstruck. "And let her think it's you? You'd . . . do this for me?"

"Not for you. For the *case*."

He was really flushed now. "I can't allow you to take the fall."

"I'm not taking any fucking fall. Holmes doesn't know *for sure* it's me, and she'll never find the evidence, because it doesn't exist. As for you, Twen will never tell. You don't even know that Twen looked at your files. The leak might be in the sheriff's office or somewhere else. So . . . let it go. Do nothing. And never take files home again."

He hung his head. "I'm sorry, Cash. I'm so stupid."

"We're both stupid."

"Thank you. I won't forget this."

Cash got up. "Hey, Standish. If you want to do me a favor, find Reno's killer. Oh, and one last thing."

Standish looked at her expectantly.

"The baby oil. Lose the baby oil. It's not doing you any favors."

49

Colcord hurried to the front office, spying the dark outline of Brother Armagh through the cloudy glass, evidently waiting for him. He sighed. He really didn't have time for this right now. With Cash off the case and Standish not yet up to speed, a lot more work had been thrown at him.

He could hear Brother Armagh's protesting voice talking to their ornery receptionist, Maggie. "Yes, I understand that," he was saying, "but I've been waiting nearly forty minutes—" He caught Colcord's eye as the sheriff arrived, adjusted his clerical collar, and strode forward to shake Colcord's hand. "Ah, finally."

"I hope Maggie wasn't being too rough on you," Colcord said, trying to remain affable, winking at her. She was cantankerous with everyone—even those with legitimate police business. But she made an excellent gatekeeper. On cue, Maggie rolled her eyes and resumed filing her nails while glowering at something on the computer screen.

Colcord led the priest into his office. "Please have a seat, Brother Armagh."

Armagh seated himself with a flourish. "Sheriff Colcord, I might have been remiss in not impressing upon you the importance of returning the holy relic to our chapel." He was less genial today, his freckled brow creased with concern. "I have been waiting now just about *two weeks* since our initial conversation and I am, to be honest, getting a wee bit impatient."

"Right, I understand," Colcord said distractedly. He moved a mountain of Shrouder files off his desk. This pesky skull piece was really giving him a headache. "CBI is in possession of the relic, not us. The delay is because there was a homicide connected to it."

"What? *Another* murder?"

Apparently, Brother Armagh hadn't been reading the papers or watching television. "Yes. The relic was, ah, found at the scene of the crime. The victim is one of our own—a detective. Unfortunately, this has delayed our plans to return it." He added, irritated, "CBI should have been in contact with you about that."

Brother Armagh frowned. "I imagine that's why I had to push through a horde of press on my way in here."

"Yes. That and the controversy involving a local priest."

"Father Moore?"

"Yes." Colcord raised his eyebrows in query. "You know him?"

"I called upon him as a courtesy."

"Of course."

"What was the controversy?" asked Brother Armagh, innocently enough, although Colcord could see an unusual level of curiosity in Armagh's eyes about his fellow priest, and he wondered why.

"Just a misunderstanding."

"I ask because . . ." Here, Armagh hesitated. "Well, Father Moore has some unusual ideas, and I wondered if that might have caused any issues in his parish."

Colcord was brought up a little short. He could read Brother Armagh's face like an open book, and what he saw there was a surprising disapproval of Moore. "Unusual ideas? Like what?"

Brother Armagh faltered, and his gaze flicked away. "He's rather old-fashioned in his beliefs."

Armagh's skeptical tone made Colcord want to know more. "Can you be more specific?"

"Well." Brother Armagh cleared his throat. "For one thing, Father Moore wants to bring back the Tridentine Mass."

"What's that?"

"The traditional Latin Mass."

Colcord relaxed. This was no more than a doctrinal disagreement. "Well, I wouldn't know anything about that."

"And," Armagh went on, "he has some peculiar ideas about the Inquisition."

Colcord heard the penny drop as soon as the words came out of Armagh's mouth. *The Inquisition?* He quickly covered up his reaction. "How so?" he asked as casually as possible.

"Nothing I haven't heard before, just the usual prattle of how the Inquisition was a misunderstood phenomenon. Along with some rather conservative opinions on cultural matters. I just wondered if that had caused any . . . problems in the parish."

"I wouldn't know. But getting back to the Inquisition—what did he say about that?"

"That it was a *kindness* to apostates, which is certainly not my personal view. And that collection of Inquisition memorabilia in that little museum of his is rather eccentric, don't you think?"

Brother Armagh now had his full attention. "Never heard of this collection. What kind of memorabilia?"

"Mostly framed documents and letters, heretical manifestos, some antique crucifixes and old surplices."

"Anything like . . . a Spanish boot?"

"I'm sorry, I don't know what that is."

"An iron device shaped like a boot, used by the Spanish Inquisition to torture heretics."

"Oh goodness! Well . . ." He hesitated. "I can't say that for sure, because now that I think about it, there were some odd-looking contraptions in a corner."

"Such as?"

"He didn't show me those, but I seem to recall a chair and some other things. . . . I suppose an iron boot could have been among the assortment. I just can't say. It was rather dim."

Colcord could hardly believe what he was hearing. "Anything else that stood out?"

"Nothing particular beyond the Latin Mass and so forth, but these are rather commonplace ideas, Sheriff. Many in the church hold conservative views—especially here in America. In Rome, we're perhaps a little less doctrinaire."

Colcord could tell Brother Armagh was downplaying Moore's ideas. Regardless, he had heard enough, and now he needed to get a warrant to take a look at those "odd-looking contraptions."

"Thank you, Brother Armagh." Colcord rose. "I'll speak to CBI and see what I can do about getting the relic back into your hands as soon as possible. In the meantime, I can assure you it's under lock and key and being handled with the greatest respect and care." He began to usher him out the door.

Brother Armagh smiled and nodded, his large frame taking up the entire doorway. "*Grazie mille,*" he said, holding out a big hand.

Colcord shook it and snagged a deputy to accompany Brother Armagh out.

The search warrant took thirty minutes to write and send off via email. Fifteen minutes later, Colcord's cell phone rang, and he saw it was Judge Greenberg.

If the judge was calling instead of signing the warrant, it couldn't be good.

"Sheriff Colcord!" Judge Greenberg said in greeting.

"Good afternoon, Your Honor. I imagine you're calling about the warrant."

"Yes. I have some concerns," he said.

"What about?"

"You want to search the catacombs below Father Moore's parish church, looking for antique torture implements used by the Inquisition? Have I got that right?" His voice, loaded with skepticism, trailed off.

Colcord gritted his teeth. Of course Judge Greenberg would be concerned about the optics, but this was a problem they didn't have the time for right now. Father Moore could be getting rid of the evidence in that very moment. "Your Honor, I know it sounds a little crazy, but the explanation is all there in the warrant. It's of critical importance to the investigation that we search the church before Father Moore disposes of the evidence."

"I understand that. However, my name will be attached to this warrant once it's approved. I want to make sure we've got all our ducks in a row, so to speak. This warrant will be scrutinized by half the news networks in the country."

"Yes, of course, Your Honor. Just tell me what I need to do to get this approved."

"Simply put, I need more evidence. *Real* evidence. I can't sign a warrant to search a church on hearsay. Your affidavit needs more details on probable cause. So—what else can you tell me?"

Sheriff Colcord ran his fingers through what was left of his hair in frustration. His affidavit was five pages long, and he had included all of the details he could think of. But Judge Greenberg was both cautious and political. Colcord glanced at the clock on the wall of his office. Would Brother Armagh mention to Father Moore he had been to the sheriff's office? Had Brother Armagh been followed by Father Moore or seen by one of his people? If either was true, the evidence—if any— could already be gone. He *had* to get this warrant.

"You Honor—with all due respect, I believe there to be more than enough probable cause, and it's all there in the affidavit. The victims were tortured with a Spanish boot used by the Inquisition. Father Moore proclaimed to a credible witness that the Inquisition needed to be brought back in modern times. Antiques that appear to resemble our torture devices relevant to our case were seen in the basement of the church. Furthermore, the two Catholic victims were given the viaticum before they died. All the evidence points to the murders having a religious component. He has a church basement full of Inquisition memorabilia. Even his fellow priest, Brother Armagh, was suspicious of him! What more do you need?"

Colcord brought himself up short, realizing he was getting loud and might have gone a little too far.

There was a long silence on the other end of the line. "Sheriff," Greenberg said, his voice dropping into an icier register, "you're asking me to authorize a raid on a church—a place of worship. You're asking me to approve a warrant investigating a much-beloved priest. All you have is the hearsay of another priest who might or might not have a hidden agenda. If you want me to write this warrant, I need a smoking gun, and you don't have it. Come back when you do. Am I clear?"

Colcord heard the click of a phone line going dead.

50

Robin Twen watched as the waiter set the steaming lobster dinner in front of Ruby Barsconi. Barsconi, her face flushed, blond hair cascading around her oval face, was already three glasses of Merlot deep. In addition to ordering the lobster dinner and clam chowder, she had a dozen oysters on the half shell on the way. All on Twen's tab.

Twen turned to their own fried clams. They had skipped beer and an entree—the bill was wildly over the KBFR expense allowance. Even in Maine, lobster cost a fortune—and the station had already complained about the expense of flying them to Maine to begin with, to dig deeper into the Cash incident.

"Thanks for taking me out to lunch," Barsconi said, cracking off one of the claws and sucking out the meat with remarkable expertise, juice dribbling from her chin.

For a woman this pretty, Twen thought, her table manners were sorely lacking. They gave a strained smile. "No problem. You're doing me a favor by agreeing to meet with me."

"Oh, sure. I'm not surprised Cash is causing problems in Colorado. She was always quite aggressive here."

"How so?" Twen asked. Their eyes wandered down to the tape recorder they had placed on the table, to make sure it was still running. It was a big, clunky, reliable old thing—but Twen liked old things. Their house was full of antiques and knickknacks they had found at yard sales and junk stores over the years.

"Bossy. Imposing her opinions on everyone else. Walking around like she owned the place. The guys had a nickname for her." Barsconi leaned forward, and the scent of expensive perfume wafting over. "Shrek!" She giggled and leaned back again. "They used to put little plastic Shrek dolls on her desk."

"Hmm," said Twen, quickly smoothing a disapproving frown from their face.

Barsconi flapped a hand at the waitress and ordered another Merlot, then turned her dazzling green eyes back to Twen again. "Won't you have one? You a teetotaler?"

"I'm working," said Twen.

"I hope you don't mind if I do. It's not every day I get wined and dined by such an attractive journalist. You're quite pretty—or should I say handsome? Slim pickings in Portland."

"Let's get back to what you were saying." Twen consulted their notes. "You were about to describe the incident that led to Cash's termination from the Portland Criminal Investigations Division?"

"Oh yes." Barsconi worked a French-tipped nail into a lobster claw to draw the meat out. "Cash responded to a report of a vagrant on Sherman Street. She and her partner at the time, Monty Rex, responded. She ended up tasing the guy and he died."

"I'm a little confused about the accusation of racism. The person was white, wasn't he?"

"French Canadian. They've always had it tough in Maine, discrimination-wise."

"But French Canadians are generally white, right?" Twen asked again.

The waitress arrived with twelve glistening oysters. There was a moment of silence as Barsconi sucked one down with enthusiasm. Twen glanced out the window across Casco Bay, the wind whipping up whitecaps on the water. Maine was one of the few places they'd been that was as pretty as Colorado.

"Yeah, they are. But there's history here—centuries of bad blood between descendants of the French and British colonists. They get called a lot of nasty names, like frozen frogs, Canucks, or beaver-beaters. There's discrimination for sure. So when the homeless guy died, the Franco American community got upset. Justifiably so."

"But the man was threatening people, and the autopsy said he was high on meth. Wouldn't that make tasing justified?"

"Not as we saw it."

"Who's 'we'?"

"The chief and me." She then hastily added, "And the department, of course."

"It's my understanding that you did an interview with a newspaper about the incident, before Cash was terminated—is that right?"

"Oh yes. I felt people had to know. The chief and I felt it was the right thing to do."

"Of course, of course. What was Cash's position at the time?"

"She was a detective sergeant assigned to the East City Area."

"Did you work in the same unit with her?"

"Oh no. I didn't. I was working in street crimes conducting bail checks."

Twen took a moment to munch on a fried clam. It was delicious. "You were then promoted to detective sergeant yourself in the investigative section—the East City Area—after Cash's departure, right? You essentially got her job."

"Yes." Barsconi paused in her work shimmying the lobster tail from its shell, now eyeing Twen a little warily. "I was promoted because of my hard work. I *earned* that promotion."

"Of course. Quite a leap for you up the law enforcement ladder."

"There was a hiring freeze at the time."

"Right. The chief at the time was . . ." Twen pretended to consult their notes again. "Luke Mezey, correct? How well did you know him?"

"Not well."

"But weren't you close?"

Barsconi kept her eyes focused on the lobster tail, and her shoulders tensed up. "Just saw him at work."

Twen decided it was time to drop the bomb—and maybe even get the nine oysters that were left. "Detective Barsconi, I don't think you're being particularly honest with me about any of this. I spoke with Monty Rex. He was disciplined after the incident. He said you and the chief were *quite* close. In fact, he had a little photograph that I persuaded him to share with me. He said he'd never done anything with it—not wanting, he said, to wreck his career . . . but he kept it."

Twen slid a photograph over to Barsconi, who had completely stopped eating now. The picture was of Barsconi and Mezey with their tongues down each other's throats in the Portland Harbor Hotel lobby. "That was taken around the time you were promoted. Chief Mezey had been married sixteen years, three kids, wife pregnant—right?"

Barsconi's lips began to tremble. "Fake. Fake photo."

"Oh no. *Not* fake. This photo is ten years old." Twen wanted to get her to admit the affair on the record, and that would be tough. "It's also my understanding that he's eighteen years your senior. You seem like such a *good* person," Twen lied, and leaned forward, "I can't imagine you doing something like this without being coerced. Especially with the power imbalance. You know how men are. Mezey manipulated you into a relationship back when Cash worked for CID, didn't he?"

Barsconi's eyes lit up at the out Twen was giving her. But still she said nothing.

Twen turned off the tape recorder. "Not going to record this."

Of course, the conversation would still be on the record, although Barsconi was probably not going to understand that. Still, she had clammed up.

"I'm running the article and the photo," said Twen. "Now's your one and only chance to tell your side of the story. To defend yourself. Because it looks bad—really bad."

After a long silence, she said, "He took advantage of me."

Bingo. She had admitted to the relationship. "Of course he did. It wasn't your fault."

"It wasn't. He manipulated me back then and ever since."

Ever since? Twen had to fake an expression of sympathy and concern. Barsconi certainly had been manipulated, through expensive vacations and luxury handbags that Chief Mezey had been buying her over the years. That was also going in the story. And from what she'd just said, it seemed the relationship was still ongoing. Not to mention the promotions.

"So this was a scheme to get Cash out, vacate the position, and put you in. Right? All those pressers where he didn't defend Cash, left her to twist in the wind. All those things he said giving credence to the racism narrative? Usually, the police protect their own, but he did just the opposite."

Barsconi frowned. "No, no, it wasn't like that at all. You've got it all wrong."

Of course she wouldn't be admitting to that, Twen supposed—but when the facts were laid out, the viewers would put two and two together. The story would be a sensation: Cash, one of the first women detectives in the Portland CID, was forced out and replaced with someone the chief was sleeping with. The Shrek dolls thing was the icing on the cake. Not to mention they had also unfairly disciplined her partner.

Twen continued, "You see, Monty Rex told me what actually happened: The French Canadian guy was high on meth and threatening people in the street—but here's the thing: He was *holding a knife*. He refused to put it down. But the knife wasn't mentioned in your interview with the press, was it? And Mezey failed to mention the knife either. Somehow that crucial bit of information got buried or lost and the narrative was all about police escalation and overreaction. And then," they said, "the knife and the log of it disappeared from the evidence room."

Barsconi stood sharply and snatched up the picture.

"I have more copies, Detective Barsconi," Twen said.

Barsconi frantically looked around, seeming to weigh her options. "What are you going to do?"

"Since this Maine incident has become a big deal, I'm going to air the *true* story of what actually happened to Frankie Cash. With that photo. On how unfairly she was treated."

Barsconi grabbed her black-flap Chanel purse from the table. "You'll regret this," she seethed, and stomped away.

Twen was glad to see that those nine oysters were still sitting on their bed of crushed ice, undisturbed, along with the lobster tail. They began to dig in, smiling to themselves through mouthfuls of seafood, thinking of their story and not regretting anything at all.

51

As Cash walked down the path lined with electric tiki torches, the sonorous croaks of the American bullfrog filled her ears and fireflies flitted around the marsh that surrounded Strickland's isolated house. It was around ten p.m. when Cash rapped on his door.

The scientist answered wearing a Grateful Dead T-shirt. Cash noticed he had more tattoos than she had realized, all of which looked like chemical structures.

"Didn't know you were a Deadhead," Cash said. She stepped around a brown kitten that had scurried up to her ankles, mewing fiercely.

"I'm fostering the little bugger. Local shelter's a little overrun," he explained.

"Good on you. Noisy little fellow."

Strickland chuckled. "No kidding. But sometimes a little ruckus is nice when I'm all the way out here by myself. To avoid the quiet, I used to stay late in the lab. Any more news of Reno's death . . . ?"

He trailed off, and Cash noticed with surprise there were tears in his eyes. For such a tough-looking guy, Strickland was really quite open with his emotions.

"I'm sorry, no. But we're gonna find the bastards, I promise you."

They settled into Strickland's living room, which was awash with brown fabric and leather décor. Wild 3D art hung on the walls. Sitting in a manila file on the driftwood coffee table was the DNA analysis. Next to it was the vial with the piece of the skull of Saint John the Baptist.

"That's all yours," said Strickland, stroking his massive beard thoughtfully. She noticed he had a funny expression on his face.

She picked it up, and she thrust it into her pocket. She would secretly return it to the lab tomorrow. "You want to summarize it for me?" she said. "In layman's terms."

"Sure," Strickland said in an odd tone of voice, his face unreadable. He hinged open his laptop while Cash flipped through the report, trying to make sense of the graphs and numbers.

"I'm going to get right into it," Strickland said. "In the first round of testing, I received some strange results. I figured the sample must have been contaminated somehow. All it takes is some stray DNA from somewhere to screw everything up. I ran the tests a couple of more times and received the same results. Endlessly frustrating."

"How many more times?"

"Six runs. It's extremely rare when I have to do that, but of course, this sample has been handled by countless people over thousands of years, subjected to greasy fingers and God knows what else. Most of the aDNA we work with comes from burials, so it hasn't had the kind of continuous contamination that this one has."

"What were the results?" Cash said.

Dr. Strickland hesitated. "I'm afraid all the DNA runs proved to be thoroughly contaminated. I couldn't make sense of it."

"You didn't find anything? Anything at all?" Cash squinted in frustration. What a waste of time—at such huge risk.

"Well, I did get consistent results. . . . There were a lot of inexplicable sequences. Nothing that made a lick of sense."

"Tell me. Even if it doesn't make sense."

"Well, a fair amount of the DNA in the sample was similar to synthetic DNA, with new combinations that I've never seen either in nature or in the lab—"

"Synthetic DNA?" Cash asked.

"Yes. Scientists sometimes assemble artificial genes, strands of DNA that are not found in nature, to use in various applications, such as gene therapy, GMO crop improvement, and synthetic biology. Synthetic biology, for example, was used to create the mRNA COVID-19 vaccines. It was also used to integrate spider DNA into silkworms to produce lighter, more durable silk. Synthetic biology helped fabricate the protein SLH to make Impossible burgers—you know, the vegan kind that taste like real meat. It's pretty good, bleeds and everything."

"Right, right," said Cash impatiently. "So what does it mean?"

"Well—look, the bottom line is your sample is hopelessly contaminated. It's just not possible with our current technology to synthesize huge sections of the human genome, which is what this looks like, but obviously can't be. Scientists can synthesize DNA in a lab, but only in short strands. The largest-scale synthesis project that I know of is the 1,005-base oligonucleotide sequence created just a few years ago. But that project is not even *close* to what I found here. That was only a thousand base pairs. The human genome is approximately 3.2 *billion*. Scientists have never been able to synthesize the human genome due to numerous challenges: error rates in long sequences, ensuring proper folding and organization of the DNA, and, frankly, serious ethical considerations. There's no way this is possible with our current technology. . . . No way. What we have here must be contamination resulting in impossible results. It's the only explanation I can think of . . ." He trailed off.

"But wait. Are you saying it looks like synthetic DNA? And that's why you think it's contaminated? I'm not really understanding you."

"Look, these sequences are totally bizarre. Patterns, chemical modifications, and methylations that have never been seen before. Contamination is the only explanation."

"I see. And the age?"

He took a deep breath.

"Four carbon-14 runs show this sample is two thousand years old. It's obviously been contaminated over the centuries."

"So that's it? The DNA is too contaminated to be sequenced? There's no way to get around that?"

"Look, Agent Cash, aDNA sequencing often fails. Maybe not as bad as this, but DNA degrades over time, and sometimes you just can't pull good data from it. Sorry I couldn't do better. I mean, it is *sort* of human—that's what you can tell your friends. It's certainly not from an animal."

Cash thanked him, took up the report and sample, and bid the bearded scientist goodbye. *Sort of human?* What did that mean? Why had Khachatryan wanted her to sequence the DNA? She felt an almost unbearable frustration. Reno's murder, the risks she'd taken, the trouble she'd gotten Romanski into—all for nothing.

52

Not for the first time, Cash, breathing hard at ten thousand feet, wondered if she was losing it. This wasn't only a stupid little outing, it was downright dangerous. She could see Edge Lake below her and to the south, a glinting turquoise jewel set among dark evergreens. Above rose the slopes of Dome Peak, getting steeper as they emerged from the tree line at a large snowfield in the shadow of the peak itself. She paused to take a rest on a log, drink some water. According to her navigation app, she had just reached the slope below the tree line where Robert Drewe claimed to have seen the wandering lights. Those four lights might have been the four killers of Grooms—the timeline matched up—and she wondered what they were doing up there. Had they been looking for the alleged site of the UFO crash? It seemed plausible, even if absurd, and it was very possible they'd left evidence. To reach this godforsaken slope, she'd hiked off the Edge Lake Trail two miles back, bushwhacking through a dense forest of Douglas firs on rocky ground, their root fists gripping barren rocks and ledges. It was exactly the kind of place where nobody should ever hike alone.

And here she was, doing exactly that.

She put away the phone and pulled out the USGS 1:24,000 topo map that Drewe had drawn on. She scrutinized the map and then looked up at the slopes of the mountain in front of her, her eyes roving over the area she planned to search. If she climbed above the search area, she would have a better view looking down, because she couldn't see anything in this forest.

Folding up the map for the umpteenth time—it was starting to fall apart along the creases—she tucked it into her shirt pocket, hefted on her daypack, and continued along the slope, picking her way over fallen tree trunks, rocks, and brush. It was a gorgeous day so far, but the weather report had mentioned an approaching front, and Cash could see in the far west, beyond endless snowy mountains, a ledge of creeping dark.

Every ten or twenty steps, she had to pause and catch her breath, and it gave her a chance to look around. This was a hell of a place for people to stumble around in at night, as Drewe insisted he had seen. And Sassy too. Two witnesses had seen the lights up here. That had to mean something.

She continued upward another quarter mile to the top of the search area. The snowfield, evidently the remains of a winter cornice, was about five hundred yards above her. Great place for an avalanche. She turned and hiked along the contour line, crossing several freshets of melting water. It was treacherous going, with mud, grit, and loose stones to watch out for. Finally, she reached a vantage point in a small opening in the trees, where she had a broad view looking downward on the forest. The early-afternoon sun was just right, etching everything with clear mountain light. She paused at a dead tree, took a seat, and pulled out her binocs. She began sweeping the area Drewe had circled on the map, moving her view systematically, stopping and scrutinizing each fresh frame. It was frustrating, not knowing what she was looking for beyond vague indications of their movements, maybe a search for a crash site. Not that there was a crash—she reminded herself. If there had been, surely it would have left signs—old debris, perhaps, a crater or disturbance in the ground, signs of a fire. It had supposedly happened ten years ago, and at this altitude, with the exposed mountainside swept by storms, dumped with snow, struck by lightning, raked by avalanches and rockfalls, there might not be anything left. It might have knocked down some trees, but there was fallen timber everywhere. But she could see no evidence of that—of course not. The idea was ridiculous. She reminded herself *again* that she was looking for evidence or clues left by the searchers, not the alleged UFO. And hell's bells, she told herself again, she didn't *believe* in UFOs. What was she doing up here? Stupid. Stupid. Stupid. She vowed never to tell anyone of this little jaunt of hers.

Yet she kept looking.

She stopped. About a thousand yards down from her vantage point, she could see an overgrown oval clearing. The fallen timber in and around it seemed to be splayed in a similar direction. The timber was unusually splintered and fractured. She focused on the area, scanning it closely. Maybe it was just her imagination—there were literally thousands of dead and fallen trees everywhere. Close inspection showed the ground around them displayed no signs of a crash, disturbance, or debris.

It was worth checking out.

Packing the binocs away, she descended with care, afraid of slipping. In about fifteen minutes, she'd arrived at the clearing. It was overgrown with prickly currant bushes and ferns among dead fallen tree trunks. She wandered around, looking for anything that might be unusual, kicking over stones and thinking that she should have brought a metal detector. She could find nothing—no debris, trash, broken stones, disturbed soil, nothing. The trees were prostrate in a sort of parallel way, but anything could have done it—lightning, an avalanche, the domino effect of a blowdown.

She stopped again. There, in a muddy hole, was the blurry, but distinct, impression of a boot—and it was big, like the prints they'd found crossing the Brooksfield Ranch. She paused to take a photo and then looked in the direction it was pointing and saw more prints in the marshy sucking ground. She followed it downhill, into the clearing.

The trail ended in an area of loose boulders with no trees, in the center of which was a flat exposure of slickrock granite.

As she walked over the granite face, she saw something unusual: a straight, even groove, about three feet long, half an inch wide, and an inch deep at its deepest, thinning out at both ends—just like something moving at high speed had struck and gouged it, glancing off.

She stared at it. Even though it wasn't fresh and had patches of lichen on it, it also didn't look all that old. Running her finger along the groove, she felt it was smooth, the stone surface unweathered. She bent down, took some close-up photos with her cell phone. This was the bedrock of the mountain itself, and in it, she could see old glacial striations, common in the high Rockies. This groove went across those striations—so it could not have been caused by glaciers. Or gouged out by a falling rock, for that matter, since it went sideways to the slope.

She brought herself up short. The fact was, she had no expertise in geology. This could have been the result of some natural process that she knew nothing about. It just seemed absurd that this could be evidence of a UFO crash. She took more photos from every conceivable angle and dropped a pin on her cell phone GPS of the location.

She spent another hour scouring the area without finding any other evidence or footprints. At least she'd confirmed there were people up here, the lights were real, and one of the footprints seemed to match the shoe size of one of the killers. And then there was that groove in the rock. . . . Could it actually have been the site of a crash? If something had indeed gone down here, the site had been cleaned up pretty thoroughly. Or was this just her own overactive imagination at work, seeing things that weren't there?

It was getting on toward the late afternoon, and she could see that the dark edge of a storm in the west was now advancing. Time to head down the mountain.

53

Colcord cast his fly rod and watched the line unfurl over Brush Creek, the dry fly setting itself down perfectly in the slow eddy behind a rock. It was Saturday, and he was waiting for Cash, who had demanded to meet him somewhere secluded. That morning, when he had stepped outside and seen the gorgeous sun filtering through the elm outside of his house, his thoughts had immediately turned to Brush Creek Pavilion. It was a good feeder stream, with plenty of brown trout. Plus there was nothing like some fly-fishing to get his mind off the crazy mess the Shrouder investigation had now become. He shivered. . . . The Shrouder. He hated the nickname the press had given the killer—it didn't even make sense, since all evidence pointed to a group of four—but somehow they'd all begun using it. It reminded him of Reno, pallid and ghostly and dressed in that creepy white nightgown. He breathed in the crisp air, letting the familiar gurgle of the stream wash over him and drown out his thoughts for a second.

And it was a perfect place to meet Cash, with no chance of anyone knowing.

"Really?" he heard Cash say from behind him.

The wind riffled the stream. He smiled without turning around and started reeling in the line.

"Really what?"

"No fish yet? I thought you were good at this." She sidled up to his left and watched him for a beat in silence.

"Catch and release," he said. She looked haggard—hair unwashed, dark circles under her eyes.

"Colcord, I did something that you're not gonna be too happy about."

Colcord wasn't surprised. He already figured Cash would have continued investigating on her own. It just wasn't in her personality to quit something, even if Holmes had ordered her to. Plus, she had been close to Reno, and it was clear to Colcord she was on a crusade of sorts, maybe even headed over the cliff. He wondered what kind of boundaries she'd crossed this time.

"What did you do?"

"I had the relic's DNA sequenced."

Colcord swore and finished reeling the line in and leaned the rod against a tree. He should have guessed that.

"Damn it, Cash. You're gonna get yourself fired."

"Not unless you tell Holmes."

"Of course I won't, but Jesus." He crossed his arms. "Well, what did you find out?"

"Dr. Strickland said the results don't make sense—probably contamination."

"Okay. No surprise there. So you risked your job for nothin'."

"But he also said some of the DNA looks artificial. He said it resembled synthetic DNA, apparently impossible, even with today's technology. He also confirmed it's two thousand years old. That's what made him think it was contaminated."

"But you think differently?"

"Well, what if it isn't contaminated? What if it *really* is artificial?"

"I'm not sure I see where you're going."

"What if the reason Devotio is after Paradox is to keep something hidden? Maybe something to do with a man living two thousand years ago with artificial DNA and everything that entails."

Colcord looked at her. This was absurd. She looked exhausted and sounded crazy. "So what's your answer? That John the Baptist was a clone or something?"

"I don't know. But listen to this. I went up on Dome Peak. Where they saw the lights? To see if the killers might have left anything behind. I found some footprints—the big one—and also a groove in the rock and some trees that looked like they'd been knocked down and broken. Like something maybe did crash there."

"Something? *Please* tell me you don't think it was a UFO."

"It's *UAP*—fuck, now I'm talking like them. Look, I don't know what to think. I just want you to keep an open mind."

"I'm listening, but you're not making sense." Colcord felt frustration tensing his shoulders and tried to relax. He had to nip this in the bud. Cash *had* to stop this crazy talk before she destroyed what was left of her career.

"I think there may be something to this artifact. What if Grooms really did find something up in the mountains? Maybe alien, maybe not. The important thing is, *they think* it's alien. Everybody wants it—Castillo, Paradox, and Devotio. Something that threatens the foundation of the church. Those lights in the mountains were people searching for the crash site. They killed Reno to get the relic, to suppress the DNA evidence. They all believe the alien artifact is real, Devotio and Paradox, and they both want it. Devotio to suppress it and Paradox to reveal it to the world."

Colcord felt heartsick seeing this breakdown. She really was going off the deep end. "Cash, you're not making sense. I think you need to go home, get a good night's sleep, and revisit this in the morning. Okay? I'm saying this to you as a friend." He laid a palm on her shoulder to ease the tension.

She pulled away from him. "Whatever Grooms found—whether it's real or fake—is the key to this whole mystery. I'm pretty sure it's still up there hidden around Solitary Lake, and I'm going to find it."

Colcord frowned. "Cash, please, I'm really worried—"

"If you won't come with me, I'll go alone."

Colcord frowned, shaking his head. Losing Reno had really hit her hard. "Aliens aren't real. There's nothing at the cabin. Grooms imagined it—like the rest of his fantasies. This UFO idea is ridiculous. For God's sake, you need to get home and sleep."

"Okay, okay, I know the alien stuff sounds ridiculous. I hardly believe it myself. But these killings are real, and the only motive tying them together involves rumors of an alien artifact and a saint's DNA. Whatever it is, I'm going up there tomorrow and find it," Cash repeated, that characteristic stubborn look on her face. "Come with me. Even if you think I'm full of shit. Please."

"Holmes'll find out, and you'll be fired. I ain't helping you pound the last nail into the coffin of your career, Cash. Drop it, please. Just let it go."

Cash scoffed. "No. I won't. Thanks for nothing."

She gave him one last fuming glare before storming off toward the parking lot. Colcord watched her go, sick with worry and concern over her mental state. Her career was about to crash and burn, and Colcord hoped to God she would see sense before it was too late.

54

Nova Euclid stood with her arms crossed next to Belen Caldas in the near-empty parking lot. It was a sunny day, but not unpleasantly so—wind carried much of the cloying heat away and left them with a warm breeze. The buzz of a lawn mower operated by a hunched groundskeeper accompanied the sweet smell of freshly cut grass. A handful of deputies were leaning against their vehicles across the parking lot, chatting and sipping coffee. A box of assorted pastries from the Ore House—Sheriff Colcord's café—sat on the hood of the sheriff's cruiser. They said he often stocked his office with pastries, gratis. No wonder his deputies loved him.

Officer Wiley must have seen her, because he approached her with half a pecan bun and a bear claw sandwiched in a napkin. She opted for the pecan bun. Caldas snagged the bear claw.

"Hey, Officer," Euclid said to Wiley, grinning. "Thanks."

He was looking especially trim today, and she bumped his shoulder with her own in greeting. He gave her a dorky waggle of his eyebrows back. "Watsup, Counselor. Didn't think I'd find you here. This is taking an awfully long time."

Colcord ambled over and now joined them.

"Good thing the sheriff brought provisions," Euclid said. "I wanted to make sure this went smoothly." She took a bite. This was damned good. She wiped the corners of her mouth, crumbs cascading. "Say, Colcord, do prosecutors *also* get free pastries from the Ore House?"

Colcord adjusted his Stetson against the sun. "Sure do, once in a while." His eyes slid to Caldas. "And defense counsel too. And judges. Any court staff. Gotta be impartial, after all."

"I can't think of anything worse than being stuck in a room surrounded by Five-Os and charge stackers," Caldas said, but as she took a bite of the bear claw, her eyes widened. She said with her mouth half-full, "But today I'll make an exception."

Colcord chuckled.

The officers were there for crowd control in case anyone got wind of Margie Brooksfield's release. Luckily, it was apparent they hadn't: The press were nowhere to be seen, and the only other individual in the lot other than cops and deputies was Paul Brooksfield, seated in shadow in his truck. He hadn't gotten out of the car to greet anyone. Euclid didn't blame him, given the circumstances.

Caldas left them to go speak with Brooksfield.

"So how'd you convince Adewale to let Margie go?" Colcord asked.

"I made it clear that the evidence strongly suggests that Margie Brooksfield wasn't involved in the Shrouder killings and that Margie had valuable information on the illegal money transfers that Paradox made to Khachatryan. There's a major charitable fraud case here, breach of fiduciary duty, not to mention wire fraud. I pitched it to my boss as an opportunity to score credit even while turning the case over to the feds. It was enough to work out a plea deal. Adewale knew from the case files that Margie did it to pay for her daughter's heart surgery for Turner syndrome after the insurance companies gave her the runaround. It turns out"—she lowered her voice—"that Adewale's husband died from osteosarcoma and they also, it seems, got screwed over by a health insurance company. As part of the deal, Margie agreed to 'disgorgement'—she agreed to surrender the ill-gotten gains—which she can do out of the Grooms inheritance she'll be getting."

"But she witnessed the will herself—doesn't that invalidate it?"

At this, Euclid smiled. "Not under Colorado Revised Statues Section 15. I had to look it up myself. *The signing of a will by an interested witness does not invalidate the will or any provision of it.* Grooms's will is legally valid and—more importantly—uncontested."

Euclid didn't say that she had also showed Adewale some of the bad press she'd been getting over Brooksfield's arrest. Rumors had it that Adewale was considering running for governor—bad press was the last thing she needed. That had worked like a charm.

"So your PI was wrong about the fight she had with Castillo at the ranch?"

Euclid had made quick work on the pecan bun and began to lick sugar off her fingertips.

"Oh, they *did* fight. But it wasn't entirely about the fraud and inheritance. Margie didn't know him, thought he was crazy, and he never identified himself. He said some wild stuff to her, and they argued."

"About what?" Colcord bent forward inquisitively.

"Brooksfield whispered it to me when she was in jail. It's pretty absurd—" Euclid was about to tell them when a clang of metal interrupted them. Margie Brooksfield stepped out from behind the retreating prison gate, blinking, two guards on either side. There was the sound of a car door opening, and Paul Brooksfield ran up to her with a shout. What ensued was like a cheesy Hallmark movie—all blubbering and hugs and talk, too far away for Euclid to hear. She watched them in silent contemplation for a second. They looked so much in love. She wondered if she'd find that kind of love someday.

"So?" Wiley asked. "What did they argue about?"

"It was silly, really. A clash of conspiracy theories. You're both gonna laugh."

"Try me." Colcord turned a surprisingly blue gaze to Euclid.

"During their argument, Javi Castillo told Margie what Paradox's secret purpose was. She was *very* upset about it. They got into a shouting match, and she practically threw him off the ranch."

The Brooksfield truck revved to life and backed out of the lot.

"And?" asked Wiley. "What was Paradox's secret purpose?"

"Well . . ." Euclid smiled at the outlandishness of it. "She was aware that Willy's donations went to funding UAP research, but it was his money, so she didn't think much of it. Then Castillo told her that Paradox's true purpose was to prove that the earth had been visited by aliens for thousands of years, and more importantly"—she hesitated with a mischievous grin—"that among those alien wayfarers were—get this—Jesus and his closest followers."

They all broke into laughter. All, Euclid noticed, except Colcord . . . who seemed strangely disturbed.

55

The wind whistled through the treetops, and Cash heard, somewhere off in the woods, a branch cracking and falling. The storm that had been predicted in the mountains that day was arriving, but she hadn't expected the wind would be so strong. As she approached the cabin, Willy Grooms's sculptures, darkening in the rain, loomed around her. She could see Solitary Lake beyond the cabin, a roiling mess, surface churned into whitecaps, waves slapping the shore. The crime scene had finally been released, and the place was no longer being watched over by deputies.

She was alone.

She tried to put herself inside the mind of Grooms. Where would he hide something? The rain lashed down and the ground was muddy and slippery in spots. Cash worked methodically, dividing the search area into sections and taking each one in turn—overturning every rock, peering inside hollow logs, and searching each sculpture for something—*anything* that might be the artifact she was now certain Devotio had killed Grooms for. Next, she went down to the shore, turning over stones, and checking out two shabby canoes and a rowboat, pulled up amid some reeds at the edge of the lake and turned upside down. Nothing there. She poked around an old chair and a broken rod next to the spot that Grooms apparently used for fishing. Again nothing. By the time she'd finished, she was soaked and cranky.

She turned her attention to the cabin. It had been thoroughly searched, multiple times even, but there was always a chance something had been missed. Thankful to get out of the rain, she went inside and rechecked every board for looseness, tapping the walls, and moved every item. If only she had an idea, *any* idea, of what she was looking for—the size, shape, or material. Maybe some errant book pulled from a shelf would open a secret tunnel, or a trapdoor under a rug would lead to a basement full of wonders. The clichés made her laugh at herself as she continued to search.

But once again, she found nothing.

Discouraged and frustrated, she went out on the porch and plopped herself down in a rickety old rocking chair that looked out over the lake. The churning surface had temporarily settled; there was a lull in the storm, and the rain had turned into a light drizzle. The water was the color of slate, the mountains beyond wrapped in gloomy clouds.

For the thousandth time, she pondered where Grooms might have hidden it. What if he'd buried it deep in the forest somewhere? If so, Cash imagined it might never be found. The woods were *vast*. But no, Grooms seemed like the type of person to keep his treasures close. It was too important to have been hidden far away, where it could be stolen without him knowing. She felt sure it had to be somewhere nearby, somewhere accessible—*somewhere in view.*

She watched the lake lap at the edge of the shore, and her eyes wandered again to the canoes and the chair with a dilapidated fishing pole. It must have been an enormous pain to lug those boats up the trail . . . and why would he need all three of them, especially if he fished from the shore? One would suffice, she thought, for boating, fishing, or . . . hunting for gold?

She decided to give them a closer look.

Getting out of the chair, Cash walked down to the lakeside. The canoe paddles were inside each boat, stored upside down. She tilted one over to see if anything was in it, but it was empty. She turned her attention to the second canoe. There were paddles in this one, but it had no seats. It was pretty dinged and scratched up, and in the bottom, there was a lot of grit, sand, and pebbles, like it had been carrying rocks or something. Ore, perhaps? The rowboat was in bad shape, the oars battered, the blades cracked.

As she left the beach to return to the cabin, she caught a glimpse of a person in camo suddenly appearing where the trail came out of the trees—and then another. She froze for a split second too long, her heart suddenly pounding in her throat. They saw her and scattered, drawing weapons. She sprinted back down the beach and dropped down into the reeds, landing on her chest. Almost simultaneously, an explosion of mud rocketed into the sky where she had just been standing, to the muted snap of gunfire.

Holy crap, they were shooting at her. But the gun was oddly quiet—maybe from a silencer.

Panting, her heart hammering, Cash crawled through the tall reeds, trying not to cause them to move and give away her location, hoping to God they were hiding her from view. She heard a second shot and a gout of water went up in the reeds to her right. Quelling her panic, she instinctively felt for the Baby Glock at her hip for reassurance. But to return fire would only give away her position, and the sidearm had a short range. She had glimpsed at least two people and there were probably more, perhaps all armed. Almost certainly the same people who had killed Grooms, Castillo, and Reno. They must have followed her.

Cash was alone. Nobody knew she was here—except Colcord. She checked her phone, just to be sure. No service.

She heaved a breath and bear-crawled deeper into the reeds. Another bullet zinged ten feet in front of her, kicking up mud. Cash ducked her head lower, wiggling deeper into the shallow water, trying not to knock the reeds about, which fortunately were already being thrashed about by the wind. The gunfire seemed to be coming from the trees near the cabin, about a hundred feet away. They were shooting somewhat randomly into the reeds, which meant they probably couldn't see her. Cash looked down at her bright yellow raincoat. Son of a bitch, it was like a Day-Glo target. She wrestled it off and shoved it into the reeds.

Rolling on her back, she peered through the stalks, trying to get eyes on the shooters. She could see at least three dark shapes using the trees as cover. One of the individuals—a short one—leaned out from behind the tree and fired, the bullet smacking the water behind her. They ducked behind the tree again before she could make anything out.

Fishing out her binoculars, she leaned back and tried to get eyes on them. One leaned out and took careful aim with a handgun, and she thought she recognized the distinct outline of a Brügger & Thomet Veterinary Pistol. A gun meant to dispatch dying animals. It was one of the quietest 9mm pistols on the market—but it had an effective range of only about five meters.

Now she could see a huge man in what looked like a cape or robes opening a case and taking out sections of a long-range precision rifle and tripod. Working swiftly, he began assembling it. He was exposed, out in the open, but certainly out of range of her Glock. The wind and rain were hindering him, but she needed to get far away from that bastard before he assembled that rifle.

Cash looked around. The two canoes were behind her, out in the open. The rope that was attached to the stern of the first one was trailing in the mud and tangled near her feet among the reeds. The reeds were tall and covered the lakeside, spreading at least thirty feet out into the water. If she pulled the canoe toward her, and quickly launched it into the lake, she might just be able to put in some distance before they set up the rifle.

Another bullet zinged about eight feet behind her feet. She grasped the slippery rope in two hands, gritted her teeth, and heaved. It was difficult from the lying-down position she was in, but she managed it, biceps bulging. The canoe slid toward her—aided by slick mud and Cash's rushing adrenaline. It eased into the shallow water, and the bow nudged against her feet. Silently, she thanked her trainer, Max, again. If she made it out of here, he would be elated that his sessions had saved her life . . . what a terrific Yelp review that would make.

A round punched through the gunwale of the boat, sending splinters in all directions.

She maneuvered the bow with her foot so it was pointing toward the lake. If she ducked and ran with her hands on the gunwales, pushing it forward, she might be able to gather enough momentum to glide it out into the water and from there get out of range of the VP 9. It would be risky, but it was her only chance. She rolled onto her back next to the canoe, watching as two silhouettes ducked from behind pines directly next to the right side of the cabin. She waited. Two consecutive shots rang out—one round smacking the water next to her head, the other to her left. They were closer this time and zeroing in. Thank God the VP 9 was so inaccurate.

It was time to act. Keeping low, she ran through the shallow water, with her right hand guiding the canoe. The boat slid over the water with ease, and she launched her body over the side and landed heavily in the bottom. It rocked violently and almost tipped over before settling down, but continued to glide away, greatly assisted by the wind. She heard a trio of quick shots. Another bullet hit the water even farther from the canoe.

She sat up on the seat and began paddling furiously. She was certainly in range of that sniper rifle, which probably could cover most of the lake, but the farther she could get, the better. She aimed toward the far shore. Thank God, the rising wind was at her back, pushing her along through the chop and adding greatly to her speed.

Reaching the center of the lake, she spied something bobbing in the chop. A stick. A fairly large stick—but it was moving strangely in the water. Disappearing under a wave before reappearing, as if something was dragging it down. The canoe was heading straight for it, and Cash gave the stern a little rudder to avoid it—and then saw it was attached to something with a heavy fishing line wrapped around its center. Another shot rang out. It was louder and sharper—and she realized with a moment of terror that they must have set up the rifle.

A realization broke through the fear: Was *this* Willy's hiding place? Where there was a line attached to a stick, like a buoy. Where nobody would find it.

She reached down and seized the stick as it slid past the canoe, causing the boat to stop and turn sharply—and thank God it did, as the next shot struck the water where she would have been. It wasn't a stick at all, she discovered, but a cleverly carved and painted piece of plastic. Heaving it up and in, she ducked down and began pulling like mad, hauling in the line. Another shot tore through the top of the gunwale, showering her with splinters.

Suddenly, the shooting stopped. That was immediately followed by a fusillade of muffled shots that sounded farther away, coming from a different weapon. Cash peered over the top of the gunwale and saw that the silhouettes of the shooters had moved away from the shoreline and they were running to take cover farther back in the trees. She could see un-mistakable muzzle flashes from someone returning fire at the shooters, a man in a cowboy hat crouching behind a large stone by the lakeside.

Colcord, firing on her attackers.

Cash resumed pulling on the rope, and whatever she had been in the process of hauling up thumped up against the bottom of the boat and then came up from the water. She heaved it over the side. It landed on the floor of the canoe, a small yellow rubber dry bag. She didn't have time to look to see what it was. She seized the paddle and sat up, digging it into the water and shooting forward, expecting another shot at any instant. But Colcord still seemed to be fully distracting them, allowing her to get away across the lake.

Cash looked back from where she'd come. She needed to reverse course and get back on shore to help Colcord. As she turned the canoe to head back toward a landing spot farther down the shore, she saw from her vantage point in the middle of the lake something on the east-ern shore that wasn't visible from the cabin—a small waterfall. And she could just make out the shadow of a cave behind the falling water. Waves of rain and mist were now sweeping across the lake, partly obscuring her view of the shore, which she hoped would cover her approach.

She kept paddling frantically, weaving the canoe, expecting the shot that never seemed to come. Thank God she had grown up in Maine and knew how to handle a canoe. She saw a commotion on the shore and heard several more shots fired from a handgun—Colcord was suddenly swarmed by several people in camo. He seemed to have hit one, but then she heard him cry out, his Stetson flying off into the water. She stifled a shout as they dragged him back toward the cabin. His Stetson, splattered with blood, floating on the lake, was propelled by the wind through the water.

56

Colcord opened his eyes and saw patches of gray sky above lashing tree-tops, wondering where he was and what was going on. His head pounded, and his body felt heavy and wet. He saw faces and heard voices, and he felt himself being lifted and carried inside, the sky replaced by wooden beams and boards. He struggled mightily to stay conscious, his mind a swirl of confusion.

His vision swam in and out as he tried to remember how he had gotten here. Jumbled recollections came trickling back and his vision sharpened. He had been worried about Cash—he had followed her out to Willy Grooms's cabin—she was being shot at—he fired at her attackers—and then nothing.

Now his carriers dropped him down hard against a cold surface, and the pressure in his ligaments eased. He groaned and tried to sit up, but he was shoved back down and he felt his hands being tied. The sluggishness of semiconsciousness made him weak.

He felt warm wetness trickling down his forehead and into his left eye, and realized it was blood. His head—he'd been shot. Winged, maybe. Adrenaline pumped through him. With a cry, he tried to sit up, but ropes securing his wrists held him back down—painfully. He tried to move his legs and discovered they were tied down as well, so tightly he could barely move from his spread-eagle position.

Clarity crawled back, and with it, a realization that he'd been taken prisoner. He strained to look around. He was inside the Grooms cabin. There were four of them. One was huge, with long hair, a monster dressed in a camo rain jacket over black robes. His face was craggy and rough. A monk, apparently. He was standing next to a thin dry man with glittering black eyes, whose priest's collar peeked above a down jacket. Colcord couldn't understand what they were saying and realized, as his head cleared further, that they were speaking Italian. The priest was angry and seemed to be calling the shots—commanding the others in a powerful voice and making sharp gestures as he spoke. There was blood dripping from his arm—this was the man he'd hit. The injury looked like it was to his forearm and, unfortunately, not serious.

Straining against his bonds, Colcord tried to speak, but his mouth wasn't working, and only a mumble came out. The rough rope dug into his wrists. He could see the storm had returned in force, sheets of water battering the windows of the cabin, and he realized he was tied down on the same table Willy Grooms had died on. He wondered if Cash had made it out. He hoped like hell she had. Maybe she would come back with reinforcements. Of course, by then, it would be too late for him.

He focused on the others, trying to calm his racing mind. One was a bald man with thick eyebrows on a shelf of a forehead. He was pacing from window to window, looking out into the storm. The other was a tall, lean woman with a scar that ran across her throat—as if it someone had once tried to kill her, unsuccessfully. She stood back, watching him with steady dark eyes. Both had the quick, practiced look of those with military training and were lean and athletic in different ways.

The woman said something in Italian to the priest. He clasped his hands behind his back and approached Colcord. "Where is it?"

Colcord stared. "Where is . . . what?" he said, managing to get the words out.

At this, the priest turned to the woman with the scar. "I'm telling you, he doesn't know." He turned back to Colcord. "I'm leaving you with my two compatriots while my monk friend and I track down Agent Cash. It would be in your best interest to answer their questions. You know better than anyone what happens to those who refuse."

The priest turned and opened the door into the storm, the giant monk stooping to follow him, temporarily letting in the roar and tumult of the wind and trees.

The door slammed, and the scarred woman walked over to Colcord and stood over him, staring down.

He was alone with only two of them now. His mind began to race, his past military training kicking in as he weighed his options. If he hurled his weight to one side, he might be able to topple the table over. But that was hopeless; he'd still be tied to it. His sidearm had been taken, and he could see the two killers were both armed, guns in their waistbands. He would be shot before he could do anything. He had to stall them, somehow . . . if anything, to give Cash time to get away.

The woman smiled, and it was not pleasant. "One more time. The artifact," she said in a slightly accented voice. "Do you have it?"

He shook his head.

The lean woman shook her head, straightening. "Does the big woman have it?" Her eyes gleaming in the twilight like those of some creature of the night.

Colcord knew that no matter what he said, they would kill him in the end. His only hope was delay. "I don't know what you're talking about," he said, his eyes glancing to the cabin windows. He wriggled his wrists again. There was no chance there: The ropes were tight and cut into his skin. He was finished; that was clear enough. He tried not to think about it. Cash might just escape them and survive.

The bald man stepped forward, fury playing across his features. "I'm telling you, he doesn't know anything, and this is a waste of time." He pulled out a gun and pressed it into Colcord's ear.

Colcord had always wondered how he'd react in a situation like this. Now he knew. He was scared shitless. He wouldn't give them the satisfaction of showing it, though. He took a deep breath to ease his quickening pulse, trying to clear his mind. He had to stall.

"Wait. Hold on. Are you asking about the *alien* artifact?"

"What do you know?" said the bald man. "Where is it?"

Colcord tried to think. Now the muzzle dug so hard he could feel it cutting his skin.

"Wait," said the woman. "Not yet. There's another question we need to ask." She leaned over Colcord. "Where is Krikor Khachatryan?"

Jesus, Colcord's head swam. Was that the guy behind Paradox, that

Cash mentioned? Was there a reason not to answer, a reason to protect the man? He couldn't think of one. "Portugal."

"Portugal? Where?"

Shit, where was it? "The mountains."

"The mountains? What mountains?"

The gun dug in.

"Give me a moment," said Colcord. Where was it Cash had told him? He couldn't recall. "I'm trying to remember."

The bald man swore. "He's wasting our time."

"No," said the woman sharply. "He knows where Khachatryan is. I could see it in his eyes: He *knows*. We'll make him remember. Get out the boot."

Colcord stared as the bald man retrieved an ancient wooden box from one of the packs, laying it on the kitchen counter. With practiced movements, he opened the lid and began to lay its contents on the tile: a pair of plyers, a set of tweezers, a bone saw, some things he wasn't sure what they were, and what he was pretty sure was an eyeball scoop—still covered in what looked like dried blood. Lastly, she reverently lifted out something Colcord recognized: an iron contraption, crude but all polished up and gleaming. She opened it, exposing wicked rusted spikes on the inside. The infamous Spanish boot.

"My deputies are on their way up here now." Colcord tried to project his voice with strength. "If any harm comes to me, the FBI will be on you like a ton of bricks. You won't get away with this."

"You're lying," the woman responded. "We followed Agent Cash up here. She came alone. You followed. Alone." She added, "We know more about you than you think."

Colcord could feel the bald man removing his hiking boot and sock. He tried to jerk his leg away, but the rope had no slack and chafed painfully on his ankle. He felt the cold grip of iron as well as tiny pinpricks that tickled the bottom of his foot. He could feel the leather straps tightening around his calf.

"Where is Khachatryan?" the woman asked pleasantly. "You said Portugal. Where?"

Even if he did remember, Colcord had no intention of telling them. They were going to kill him anyway, and he was done talking. He was a sheriff, entrusted with protecting people. He'd been trained for this. Even if decades had passed, it stayed with you.

"I can't remember."

The woman nodded at the man, and Colcord heard the squeak of an iron screw and felt a sudden pressure mounting around his shin. Another squeak, and suddenly the feeling of dozens of cold needles boring into the sole of his foot radiated throughout his body. He stiffened and suppressed a scream, focusing on a whorl in the wood above his head. The pain eased to a hot throb. Colcord felt wetness on the sole of his foot.

"Where is he?" the woman said.

"Fuck. You," Colcord said, and successfully kept his voice from shaking.

The bald man's brow furrowed.

"Give it another turn," said the woman.

That hideous rusty squeak sounded again, and the pressure on Colcord's shin mounted to an unbearable level, the sole of his foot on fire with an insane amount of pain. Colcord gritted his teeth against an involuntary, guttural scream, but couldn't hold it in, and he heard himself roar.

The woman smiled and held out a palm to the man. The mounting pressure stopped, but the agonizing pain continued. The coppery smell of blood filled the air.

"This can stop, if you tell us where Khachatryan is," the woman said.

"I don't know," Colcord gasped. He wondered what his foot looked like. Hopefully not a mangled mess like the others'. Nothing felt like it had broken yet, at least. He supposed it didn't matter—all things considered.

The bald man said, "We're wasting time. He doesn't know. Maybe we'll get what we need from the other one."

"Fine," said the woman. "Do it."

The bald man brought out his gun again.

"I'm Catholic," Colcord managed to gasp.

She laughed. "Oh, please. Don't make this harder than it needs to be."

"*I'm Catholic.* You can't just kill me like this. You're not going to give me last rites like the others?"

The bald paused from checking his gun, head cocked. "You're full of shit." He raised it.

Colcord wracked his brains for something Catholic to say, something, anything.

"*Hail Mary, full of grace . . .*" he gasped. How did it go?

The bald man exchanged a glance with the woman.

"Keep going," the woman said.

"*Holy Mary, mother of God, pray for us now and at the hour of our death.*"

"That's not right," said the bald man.

"I've forgotten it," said Colcord. He tried to calm his breathing. He was surprised at how afraid he was of death. A vision of Cash, nose red, cranky, and bundled up against the cold, flared across his mind's eye. He had to delay. He had to make sure she had gotten away. "I was *baptized* Catholic. And I believe . . ." He choked up, unable to finish.

There was a sudden silence. Then the man swore. "We don't have time for this."

"Are you really willing to take that risk?" Colcord said. "It would be a mortal sin *on you* to deny me last rites. God sees and knows all."

The woman scowled, the scar on her throat twisting and enflamed. "Ready the viaticum to assist him on his journey. Hurry up."

The man swore again but did as she said, retrieving a packet of wafers with the Baby Jesus on them and a chalice, which she poured wine into.

The woman placed the host on his tongue, and Colcord took it.

He then felt the cold press of a chalice rim against his lips, the sweet Communion wine spilling into his mouth. He swallowed, playing along with the charade.

The woman made the sign of the cross and began to pray in Latin. Colcord listened to the pattering of the rain outside, desperate for the sound of footsteps. Maybe Cash had escaped and was bringing the cavalry. But no, it was only the fervent wish of a condemned man. There hadn't been nearly enough time for that.

She took some oil on her thumb and anointed his forehead, saying more prayers in Latin. The seconds dragged on, Colcord straining his ears for any sign of Cash. After two minutes, the woman finished her prayers.

Colcord could see concern play across the man's face.

"Brother Gregory's been gone a long time," said the man, staring out the window. "Hurry up. Get the embalming kit ready. *Quickly.*"

Brother Gregory—at least Colcord had finally identified one of the killers. A lot of good that would do him.

The bald man paced from window to window as the woman opened a black case and began to take out various tools and lay them out. Colcord tried to keep from panicking. They were going to embalm him alive. He knew from the investigation that the next step in the process would be the one that killed him.

The chemical smell of embalming fluid filled his nose as he heard the clinking of bottles she was arranging next to him, laying out rubber hoses and instruments. The woman then retrieved a scalpel from the black case. It glinted wickedly in her hand. Her beady eyes gleamed in the light from the window, the angry pink scar across her neck looking like a writhing snake in the shifting shadows. She leaned over him.

Colcord felt the pressure of her fingertips, and the tip of the blade bit into his neck. He squeezed his eyes shut and waited for the end.

57

Back on the lake, Cash had just seen Colcord carried into the cabin, and she redoubled her efforts to get the canoe to shore, paddling hard against the wind. She drove it up onto a sandy beach. Leaping out, she grabbed the bowline and dragged the canoe into a thicket, where it was well hidden. Scurrying through the bushes, staying low, she entered the forest. The storm had intensified and the sky had become dark, furious rain lashing down to the bluster of wind in the treetops—providing her with good cover as she dodged through the trees in the direction of the cabin.

In the storm, with her heart pounding like a sledgehammer, every minute seemed like an eternity. She tried not to think of what might be happening in there, but she knew that time was of the essence.

The outline of the cabin loomed ahead, visible between the tree trunks and sheets of rain, the windows glowing a dull yellow. She paused behind a bush, next to one of Grooms's junk sculptures, trying to think of a plan. She could see the outline of people moving past the glow in the window of the kitchen, busy with something. Every fiber of her soul was telling her to run in there, guns blazing. *Save Colcord*, her mind shouted at her. It took a monumental effort to calm herself. She had to be calculated about this. Think through it. Otherwise, they would both be killed.

Without her raincoat, she was drenched and shivering. She squeezed her eyes shut for a brief moment to think.

Lashed by rain, she worked her way toward the cabin. Suddenly, the door opened, and she flattened herself on the ground as a beam of light illuminated the porch. Her heart felt like it would beat straight out of her chest. Two men came out—it was a priest and a huge monk, dressed in camo over their robes—the priest with a handgun and the monk with the long rifle. Somehow, they didn't see her. They separated, the monk heading down to the shore, the priest running toward the trail. They were probably looking for her. Fortunately, it hadn't occurred to them that she would return to the cabin.

The priest disappeared, and she could see the monk now moving along the shore, scanning the lake with his binoculars, sniper rifle slung over his shoulder. *Good luck with that.*

That left two in the cabin with Colcord. She could hear raised voices, and Colcord's low one in response, but couldn't make out what they were saying.

The storm had picked up again, the wind roaring through the canopy, trees swaying and creaking as rain came down in sheets. Staying low, she sprinted to the back of the log cabin. It was too risky to look in the broken window. Instead, she grabbed a loose piece of cement caulk from between two logs, working it back and forth until it pulled free. A sliver of orange light appeared, and she knelt and looked inside.

The vantage point offered a narrow view of the kitchen, but it was enough to seize her with horror. Colcord was strapped on the kitchen table. At first, he looked dead, his head and face covered with blood. But no—he was conscious. Two people were in the room with him, a woman and a man. Several kerosene lanterns were hung on hooks around the table, casting a bright yellow light. The man was holding a gun to Colcord's head, pressing it into his ear, while the woman seemed to be asking him questions. She couldn't hear what they were saying over the sound of the storm. Colcord was responding, shaking his head, and he could see the woman was angry.

Colcord was still alive, thank God. For now.

The man with the gun stepped out of view. He returned a moment later with a box and began taking out various things—tubes and steel needles. Her blood froze when she saw one of them was a metal device—the Spanish boot.

Now with the woman apparently giving orders, the man stripped Colcord of a hiking boot and sock. She watched as he unscrewed and opened up the torture device, exposing a cluster of rusty points. Col-cord's foot was strapped to the table by his ankle, and the man fitted the device over the foot, while Colcord strained and jerked on the straps. He enclosed it around the foot and bolted it shut. The thing had a sort of screw on one end with a geared wheel, like a pinion. Those psychopaths were going to torture Colcord. Cash felt a torrent of cold fury wash over her, remembering what they had done to Reno. She couldn't allow it to happen to Colcord too.

Cash eased out her Baby Glock, just to feel the reassurance of it in her hand. She still had a full magazine of ten, plus one racked in the cham-ber. Both the people inside were armed, and they were not amateurs. In a surprise assault through the door, she could probably take down one, but not both, and Colcord would likely be killed.

Better to separate them, take them down one at a time—but how? She could lure one out of the cabin. . . . Glancing around, she could see no sign of the priest or monk. She hoped their search for her was taking them far and wide.

The storm continued to rage, and suddenly, she had an idea. She scur-ried down to the lakeshore, to where she'd ditched the raincoat in the reeds, and grabbed it. In the junk sculpture area, she remembered seeing a set of wind chimes. They were all tangled up and silent, but they could easily be set right, and in this wind, they would make a mighty noise.

Carrying the raincoat and moving swiftly, she found the chimes. They were made from rusty old dip cans and big metal washers hung on wires around pieces of steel pipe. Scoping out the lay of the land—the door to the cabin, the open area in front, and the location of the chimes— she picked out a tree on which to hang the yellow raincoat in such a way that only a bit of it would be visible, peeking from behind the trunk, as if she was hiding there. It was a fairly lame decoy, but in the lashing wind, it would be moving.

Tying it to the tree, she went back to the wind chimes and untangled the metallic mess, hugging them close to keep them from drawing at-tention prematurely. Then she eased her arm off; the wind instantly set them swinging, while she quickly moved to a spot she had preselected behind a fallen log, which offered an open field of fire taking in the cabin door, the yard, and the forest in the direction of the yellow raincoat.

The dip cans and washers swung madly, clattering into each other and also striking the hanging pipe. The noise was impressive, a loud jangling punctuated with surprisingly clear high notes—a ruckus that, she hoped, would serve its purpose.

And it did. The door to the cabin flung open, and the bald man came out, gun drawn. He scanned the forest and spotted the sliver of yellow raincoat. He quickly dropped to a crouch and began advancing toward it.

Cash felt a cold, calculated anger take control. Rising up, she braced the muzzle of her Glock against the trunk, carefully took aim, eased out her breath, emptied her mind. With a slow even movement, she squeezed the trigger.

The gun fired with a loud report and the shot struck the man square in the back. He went down like a sack of potatoes. *Piece of shit*, she thought, feeling not a drop of empathy for him. They had killed Reno. They were torturing Colcord. They would all rot in hell if she had her way.

The gunfire brought the woman to the door. But she became a lot more cautious when she saw the man's body sprawled on the ground fifty yards from the cabin. She'd heard the shot, of course, but by the way she moved, Cash could see she wasn't sure which direction it had come from. Crouching low, the woman advanced. Keeping to cover from every possible direction, she crept alongside the cabin, gun in hand, scanning the woods. Cash couldn't get a clear shot, and she was sure the others had heard the report and were on their way back.

But then the woman apparently glimpsed that bit of fatal yellow peeking from behind the distant tree trunk. She moved like lightning to get in cover from that direction, and with the same caution began working her way around to where she would have a better shot. *God bless that raincoat*, Cash thought. If the woman continued on, her approach would put her right where Cash wanted her. Cash waited as the woman circled around toward the decoy, closer and closer, disappearing into a thicket of brush. When she emerged on the other side, she would be exposed and offer Cash a perfect shot.

But she didn't appear. She seemed to be moving slowly through the brush. Too slowly. The priest and the monk were surely coming.

Still Cash waited, both hands on the grips, her sights trained on where she expected the woman to appear.

There was a temporary lull in the wind, and in that lull Cash heard the crack of a twig behind her. She threw herself sideways just as the blast of a gun sounded and a shower of bark blew off the log where she'd just been.

Cash rolled as the second shot came and, lying on her back, squeezed off a round at the woman, now charging her—and missed.

The woman fired, the round punching the ground so close to Cash's head that she was sprayed with wet dirt and moss, blinding her. Cash sprang up, firing several rounds into the blurry confusion of her vision. A moment later, she was struck hard and knocked down by the woman, who shrieked like a wild animal. Cash landed on her back with the woman on top of her, clawing and grappling for the Baby Glock even as she tried to jam her own handgun into Cash. They were locked together, struggling as each tried to bring their gun around to bear on the other. Cash was strong, but the woman was younger and more powerful than she looked, and Cash realized she was about to lose the contest. She released the woman's arm and let go of her own gun at the same time as she whipped both arms around the woman's neck and jerked her down with all her might, smashing her face into Cash's head with a great crackle of cartilage. The woman shrieked again as blood gushed from her crushed nose, her gun firing out of an involuntary contraction of her hand, the bullet going off into nowhere.

Taking advantage of her size and the woman's shock, Cash rolled, flipping the woman over and under her, pinning the gun arm. She could feel her twisting and squirming like a giant eel, but from her superior position, Cash slammed her forehead down again into the woman's crushed nose, hearing a second crunch, with more blood spurting. Cash slammed her forehead into the woman's nose a third time and watched as her eyes rolled up into her head. Cash got off the unconscious woman and yanked the gun out of her limp hand. For a brief moment, she regarded the woman's brutalized face, and then finished her with a shot between the eyes. She shoved the woman's gun into the back of her waistband.

Too much time had passed already. Throwing all caution to the wind, she picked herself up and ran to the cabin. Had they already killed him? Was she too late?

Colcord was tied to the table beside several jars that stank of mortuary chemicals. What had to be the Spanish boot was secured to his leg. Her heart leapt as he moved, and she let out a breath she hadn't realized she had been holding. He was alive.

"Frankie," he groaned. "My God, Frankie."

"Why'd you follow me out here, you big idiot?" Cash said, breath hitching. She realized she was full-on crying now, more with relief than anything else. With shaking hands, she grabbed a scalpel lying on the table next to him and sliced off the bindings from his wrists. Then she grabbed the boot, unshackled the tie bolts holding the pieces together. She yanked it open and tossed it aside—staring at the bloody mess that was Colcord's foot. Even if they made it out of here, he might be permanently injured. She tried not to think about it as a few quick cuts freed the ropes around his ankles.

Colcord said, "Is it bad?"

"Just a flesh wound," Cash lied. She grabbed him and raised him up into a sitting position. "Can you walk?"

"Got to. Gimme my boot," he said, adding, "better stop cryin' or I might start to think you actually like me."

Cash dragged a sleeve across her face, grabbed his boot off the floor, and handed it to him. With a grunt, he used his sock to bind his foot as tightly as possible, then shoved his bloody foot into the boot and tied it up tight. Cash winced, feeling sick.

He rose, staggering as she steadied him, and said, "Let's get the hell out of here."

"The canoe," said Cash. It was their only option: With Colcord hardly able to walk, they'd never get away down the trail.

Grasping his arm, she helped support him as he stumbled and limped down to the lake, moving as fast as possible, making no effort to hide. As they ran, she spotted the huge monk emerge from the far trees, his black robes flapping from below his jacket like a bat out of hell, rifle in hand. He saw them, dropped to his knee, and fired. The shot went wide, but not by much.

Cash returned fire with her Baby Glock, which at least sent him scrambling for cover. But where was the priest?

They approached the shore where the canoe had been stashed, crashing through the prickly bushes. Cash felt the dead woman's gun slip from her waistband.

"Shit!" she said, but kept running, as rounds clipped through the vegetation around her.

More gunfire now sounded to their far right, Cash firing back with her own weapon.

They reached the canoe, and Cash grabbed the painter and heaved it, hauling the boat out and down, Colcord pushing the stern from behind. The canoe slid into the water, and they leapt in, Cash at the bow, Colcord at the stern. They both paddled, and the canoe shot out into the roiling lake, whitecaps combing past them with the strong wind at their stern.

More shots came from the shore, spouts of water rising up around them.

"You saved my life," said Colcord, gasping as he paddled.

"Pretty sure you saved mine first," said Cash. "What's your condition? Is that blood on your head yours?"

"I think I was winged."

More shots from the shore. They were still within range of the rifle, but the roaring wind and rain seemed to be affecting the man's aim.

"We've got a problem," said Colcord, nodding toward shore.

Cash turned and looked back across the gunwale. The monk and the priest were climbing into the second canoe, shoving it into the choppy lake. They began paddling after them, coming along fast, the same wind also at their backs. The monk was at the bow. He laid down his paddle, picked up the rifle, and aimed.

"Watch out!" yelled Cash. She fired several rounds, which, while they missed, slowed the monk down and put him off his aim.

Colcord threw himself over Cash, and she was shoved against the bow of the boat.

A shot sounded and a round smacked the water to one side. A second shot struck on the other, and a third finally found home, striking the stern where Cash had just been. Water began to pour in, filling the bottom. They were sinking.

A fourth shot rang out. Cash jerked, feeling a sudden force punching her back against the boat once more, hot agony radiating from her right arm.

She'd been hit.

58

"Son of a bitch," said Colcord as the water gushed in around his feet. He scrabbled over to Cash, who was panting and lying against the gunwale of the boat. Blood swirled in the water around her. "Frankie?"

Cash winced and sat up, the fingers clutching her upper arm and coming away with red.

"I got you, I got you," Colcord said. He made a quick inspection. "Went clean through. Didn't break the bone." He ripped one of his sleeves off and secured it tightly around her upper bicep.

The boat was filling with water. Cash would hardly be able to swim, not with her arm like this. Colcord desperately looked around, but there was nothing to plug the leak beyond an old rubber dry bag swilling around in the bottom of the boat. He grabbed it and stuffed it in. It seemed to stem the flow, for now. More shots from their pursuers sent up columns of water near them. Colcord grabbed her Glock and returned fire, causing their pursuers to drop down in the boat.

"Son of a bitch," Colcord said as the Glock's slide locked back. The magazine had been emptied.

"Can you bail with your good arm while I paddle?" he asked Cash.

Cash gritted her teeth. "Yes."

She began scooping up the water with a cupped hand. Another shot rang out and struck the water behind him.

"Christ!" he exclaimed. He shifted his position forward, paddling on his knees from amidships like the voyageurs of old. The shift in weight steadied the canoe, keeping it on an even keel and lessening the water coming in the stern.

"Cash, move forward; let's get the stern more out of the water."

Cash slid forward gingerly.

Behind them, the monk fired again, and the bullet skipped through the waves to their right. The shooter was having trouble taking aim in the brutal slap and chop of the lake's surface.

"Go to the waterfall," Cash called out to Colcord. "There's a cave or something behind it. Maybe we can lose them in there."

Colcord paddled furiously. He was an experienced canoeist, and in glancing back, he could see that even with everything slowing them down, they were holding their own against the pursuers. Every once in a while, they heard a shot and smack where it would hit the water, but the roiling lake was their friend, making aiming the long rifle in a tippy canoe nearly impossible.

As they approached the waterfall, the dark opening behind it loomed up. It would, Colcord hoped, lead to an escape route.

The canoe shot into the waterfall, suddenly dousing them in an icy blast of water. A moment later, they were through it, gliding into a flooded tunnel.

It wasn't a cave; it was a mine shaft.

The water calmed, and the sound of the storm behind them was drowned out by the steady noise of the waterfall. Cash fumbled out a penlight with her good arm and flicked it on. She shone it ahead, and it revealed a curving waterway that led into the mountain. As they came around the bend, they saw the water ended at a sandy cove. Driving the canoe forward, they grounded it, and Colcord jumped out along with Cash. He stumbled slightly, swearing, as his leg hit the ground and hot fire shot through the sole of his foot.

Cash's brows drew together in concern, and she held out her good arm to steady him.

"I'm all right," he said. He gritted his teeth and tried to keep his expression from showing the pain.

On a shelf of rock nearby, new mining equipment had been neatly laid out.

Cash quickly shone her light over it. Colcord could see there was a canvas pack, a respiratory mask, a bottle of oxygen with a hose and harness, and a handheld device with a screen. He suddenly recalled the hand-drawn map that they had found in Grooms's cabin, among the golden nuggets. That blue symbol at the mine entrance—the sideways *J*—maybe was a symbol for the waterfall at the entrance. A darker thought crossed his mind. CO_2 and CH_4 had also been written underneath. This mine—if he was correct—was deadly.

"What's that?" Cash asked, shining the light on the electronic device.

Colcord snatched it up. "A gas monitor. Looks like there's an air problem in here."

"Let's go," said Cash. She paused. "Think we'll be okay?"

"Maybe. Not a lot of options here." He switched on the device. "Still charged," he said. "If it goes off, we'll start sharing the mask."

Cash nodded, brow furrowed.

He squeezed her good arm reassuringly. "We'll be all right."

They continued deeper into the mine, the weak penlight barely penetrating the murk. Colcord's sliced-up foot hurt like hell, and he could feel the blood accumulating in his boot, squelching with each step. He watched with concern as blood dribbled down Cash's arm, dripping off her fingers and leaving a trail of ruby droplets in the sand. She was bleeding despite the makeshift bandage. He stopped to tear the other sleeve off his shirt, securing it around her gunshot wound. They hurried on.

The tunnel walls were moist, and there were many old footprints in the sandy bottom—all, Colcord figured, from Willy Grooms, who it seemed had entered the mine often.

The tunnel, about fifteen feet wide, went straight in, not branching, not going down or up. Colcord felt himself running out of breath, the air strangely unrefreshing, feeling heavy and cold.

A shrill tone sounded from the gas monitor, confirming his fears.

Raising the device, he glanced at it and swore under his breath. "Methane," he said. "*And* carbon dioxide. Use the mask."

Cash turned on the oxygen bottle and held it to her face, taking a few deep breaths. She handed it over to Colcord, and he breathed likewise, feeling his head quickly clear. When he breathed in without the mask, however, he could feel a wave of dizziness take hold. He started holding his breath in between, taking extra deep breaths when he had the chance. That seemed to work better.

Moving as fast as Colcord was able, they eventually came to a bend, and another. This was not good: It seemed to be a single tunnel with no branches. The faint light from the entrance vanished quickly, the darkness pressing in on them. After another turn, the tunnel ended abruptly at a blank stone wall. Colcord's heart sank.

"Fuck," said Cash, staring, the beam of her penlight playing over the rock face. Her voice held a tinge of despair Colcord had never heard before.

The wall was almost entirely of white quartz, but as the light moved over it, Colcord could see a crooked seam running diagonally across it, gleaming in the feeble light. This was obviously where Grooms had discovered his gold. It was too bad they were trapped in a dead end—with no way out.

The alarm was beeping insistently. Colcord checked the screen. "Thirteen percent methane, five percent CO_2."

"We're gonna have to turn around and fight our way back out." Cash glanced at the Glock in his waistband. "Oh shit."

"Yeah. Empty." A fresh trickle of blood started down her arm.

"We're really fucked now," said Cash, her voice quavering.

Colcord realized this was the second time he had ever seen her truly scared. The first was when they were in the mines with the Neanders. He shone the light around, thinking furiously. They were trapped with an empty gun, no route of escape. Cash was injured and losing blood, and he could barely walk. Meanwhile, their armed pursuers were closing in. As if on cue, he saw two wavering lights appear in the darkness of the tunnel fifty feet away—the priest and the monk coming after them.

They were in a truly desperate situation. But they did have one advantage—the oxygen mask. "Maybe they'll suffocate before they get here," he said.

That proved not to be the case as the priest stepped into the glow of his flashlight, his gun aimed in their direction. The monk approached from the other side, his rifle also leveled. They were wheezing, but very much conscious.

"Drop your weapon, *now*," the priest commanded.

Colcord hesitated, then let it fall to the ground.

Keeping his weapon aimed, the priest staggered toward Cash, gasping in the bad air, and snatched the mask and bottle from her. He took several deep breaths before passing it to the monk. They then backed off, passing the mask back and forth, gulping in air.

Breathing heavily in a rising panic, Colcord could feel the dizziness coming on. How poisonous was methane? He had no idea. The air was thick and toxic, and he could feel the hunger for oxygen building in his lungs. Another wave of dizziness passed over him. Unarmed, bad air, trapped like rats in a cul-de-sac—they were absolutely screwed.

He heard Cash cough and gasp.

"Where is it?" said the monk, raising his gun and aiming at Cash.

Cash coughed again. "What?"

"You *know* what," the monk raised his voice, waving the gun.

"I really don't . . ." Cash gasped.

"The alien artifact!" he shouted. "*Where is it?*"

"Artifact?" Cash tried to speak; now she could only seem to gasp.

Colcord's throat felt like raw meat, his lungs burning. Another wave of lightheadedness passed over him, and he stumbled.

"Forget it," said the monk angrily. "They don't know anything." He took a deep breath from the mask and passed it back. "Let's go. Leave them to die in the dark."

"Right," the priest said.

They began backing up, guns trained on Cash and Colcord.

Colcord sucked in the bad air, his head spinning. Everything seemed to be getting far away. He looked over at Cash and saw the whites of her eyes. This was happening too fast. The cave was rotating. He needed to do something, anything, to rush at them, but found his legs weren't working, his sense of balance nonexistent. Colcord gasped for air and fell to his knees. Bright stars popped into his vision.

Cash staggered and collapsed herself.

Colcord watched the flashlights of the monk and priest back down the tunnel, guns still raised. Even on his knees, he felt himself swaying, the last remaining strength draining from his body. He grimaced, trying to say something, but all that came out was a groan. He toppled to his side, paralyzed, unable to move. The two men were thirty yards away and would soon disappear around the curve of the tunnel.

And then, from the dim recesses of his wavering mind, a desperate idea appeared. The empty gun lay in the sand nearby. He reached out and grabbed it, and then with a menacing shout, pointed it at the monk.

"Watch out!" the priest cried as the monk raised his rifle and fired.

There was a blinding flash and explosion, and then blackness.

59

Agony surged through Cash as she swam back into consciousness. Opening her eyes, she was blinded by swirling dust and sand and closed them again. Her ears were ringing. She inhaled a mouthful of choking dust. The air smelled burnt. All around her, there was a pattering sound, a hard rain of gravel and debris. What the hell had happened? The events of the past few moments returned in force—the suffocation, the shot, the explosion.

Her eyes felt gritty and were watering like crazy. She tried to raise her head and was felled by a blinding headache. She lay there, trying to gather her thoughts. And now she felt a cool eddy of air drifting over her, clearing the dust. She breathed deeply, hungrily. Her vision began to clear. She raised her head again. The air was clearing, and she saw a dim glow of light, faint, hovering in the distance above.

Cash breathed again, and again, her mind finally sharpening. "Colcord?" she was able to whisper hoarsely. Then louder: "Colcord?" She could hardly hear herself, with the ringing in her ears.

She thought she heard a pained groan coming from her right.

She reached out in the direction of the sound and encountered the fabric of his uniform. She grasped at it with shaking fingers. "Colcord!" She jerked on the fabric.

He mumbled something again.

"What . . . happened?" she asked.

His voice brought a wave of relief to her. "I got the monk"—he gasped—"to fire his rifle. It . . . lit up that methane like a bomb . . . blew them to kingdom come."

"It blew us up too."

"We're alive, aren't we?"

Cash tried to sit up, her head swimming with the effort and forcing her to lie down again. Her arm was useless, and she'd lost a lot of blood. She could still hear gravel and rocks falling around them. They were not out of trouble. Her flashlight, now dead, lay half buried in the sand some distance away.

Strangely, however, there was a fresh, steady river of cool air carrying the scent of the forest flowing past her. A dim gray light now filled the tunnel. Where the monk and priest had been, the ceiling had caved in, creating a gaping hole, which was where the light was now coming from. Colcord looked a fright—lying on his side, entirely covered with dust, pale as a ghost, only his blinking bloodshot eyes gleaming from the powdery coat. Some of it was mixed with blood from his head. The wound had opened up again.

"You look like shit," she said. "Are you able to walk?"

"Gee, thanks." He tried to stand up, winced as he struggled to get to his knees, and sank back. "Give me a moment," he said, breathing hard while lying on his back.

The falling of debris from the ceiling continued, and she wondered if they even had a moment. She peered into the murk, trying to see what had happened to their two pursuers. To her horror, through the dust and falling pebbles, a figure began to emerge, holding a light. Colcord saw it too. It was too small to be the monk. Had the priest survived? Cash felt a wrenching twist in her gut—the priest had somehow survived and was coming to finish them off. She struggled to rise, but again, her head went to spinning so much she couldn't get up.

"Bastard," said Colcord to the figure as it loomed over them.

"Good heavens," the man said in a sonorous voice. "Sheriff Colcord, Agent Cash! Thank God you're alive!"

Cash stared in disbelief: It was Father Moore. Was he also a member of Devotio?

The priest rushed over and knelt beside her, gently lifting her into a sitting position.

"Don't touch me," she managed to gasp.

"I'm so terribly sorry this has happened. I had no idea what Brother Gregory was up to." He looked into her face, his eyes full of concern, "I'm here to help. We need to get out of here—the tunnel could collapse at any moment."

"Are you with them?" Colcord asked.

"Heavens, no!" said Moore. "Hurry, we need to get moving. I'll be happy to answer all your questions as soon as you're both safe."

Cash's head began to clear somewhat, and Moore helped her to her feet, supporting her as she swayed.

As if on cue, a large rock detached from the gaping hole in the roof and fell with a crash and shudder, along with a shower of cobbles. The grinding sound of shifting rock was almost continuous.

Colcord staggered to his feet, breathing hard, before groaning and sinking back down on one knee.

"You need to help him," said Cash. "His foot is crushed."

Moore rushed over and raised Colcord to his feet.

"Both of you, lean on me and we'll make it out of here together."

Clinging to Father Moore, who, although short, was as sturdy as a fireplug, they staggered down the tunnel, only to be blocked by an unstable heap of fallen rocks. As Moore shone his light ahead of them, it illuminated a gruesome sight—the monk's dismembered arm, still enrobed in tattered black cloth, plastered against the tunnel wall, bony fingers splayed out like a white spider. Farther on, the light glinted off a shoe sticking out from under a heap of boulders.

Moore looked on the remains without comment, then turned and played his light over the heap of rocks. "We're going to have to climb over that. All together now. Hang on to me."

Slowly and painfully, they worked their way up the unstable surface, the rocks shifting and grinding against one another as they climbed. At times, the priest hauled them along. As they reached the top, Cash heard a sudden cracking noise from above. But Father Moore remained calm.

"One step at a time," he said.

He helped her down the shifting rock pile, leaving her at the bottom and going back for Colcord. A few minutes later, he reappeared, bracing Colcord, even as a frightening sequence of cracks, like gunshots, came from above. A huge rock fell with a shuddering crash—and then another and another—barely missing them. What remained of the ceiling began to crumble and rain down upon them.

"Run, my friends!" Moore cried. The priest practically dragged them along with fierce energy as rocks peeled from the roof and crashed down around them. A rock fell in front of Cash and she tumbled over it, Moore hauling her back up, and they loped and staggered to keep ahead of the collapse.

Eventually, they reached the canoes, as well as the rowboat that had evidently delivered Moore to their rescue. One canoe was now half sunk, but the other was good. Cash grabbed the dirty yellow dry bag that had been stuffed into the hole in the bottom of the sunken canoe and tossed it in the other, then scrambled in herself. Moore followed and helped Colcord in. They could hear continuous cave-ins behind, the thunder drowning out the sound of the waterfall. Huge clouds of choking dust billowed past them.

"Paddle!" cried Moore, sitting cross-legged in the center of the canoe. He had grabbed a paddle from the other canoe and now started flailing uselessly at the water. Cash and Colcord began paddling in unison, Cash almost fainting from the pain of using both arms, but adrenaline kept her going. They propelled the canoe forward and around the bend in the tunnel. The waterfall came into view and they shot through it, once again drenching them in freezing water.

They emerged out into the lake to find that the storm had subsided and the rain and wind had ceased. They glided across the still water and were well away from the mine entrance when a thunderous final roar came from the tunnel, along with a dirty cloud billowing out of the side of the hill from the hole left by the cave-in.

The canoe glided along. Cash breathed deeply, again and again, sucking in the good air. The cold shower from the waterfall had done wonders, jolting her mind and washing off the dust. She could feel her strength returning, despite the throbbing pain in her arm. It was a miracle they had made it out. The priest, who didn't seem quite so spiteful anymore, sat in the middle of the canoe, swiping at the water with a paddle, having no idea what he was doing, but trying nonetheless.

"Hey, look over there," said Cash, pointing to Colcord's Stetson floating in the water, waterlogged and half sunk.

"I want it," Colcord said.

They paddled toward the center of the lake where he could snag it. He shook it out and secured it on his head once more. He looked a fright.

"That's a sad sight," said Cash.

Colcord tried to smile. "It ain't just felt and leather—it's my badge."

As they continued paddling, Colcord asked, "What's this?" nudging the dry sack with his foot.

Cash hesitated. "Willy's artifact."

A silence. "The *alien* artifact?" he asked.

"You said it, not me."

Just then, the cabin, its windows still aglow, came into view in the distance.

"Let's have a look at it," Colcord said. He laid down his paddle and pulled the dry bag toward him.

"What are you doing?" asked Moore. "We really should try to keep going. You both need to get to the hospital."

"Give me a moment," said Colcord as he hefted the bag, unlatched the fasteners, and unrolled the top. Then he tipped the bag over, and an object fell out, landing in the water in the bottom of the canoe. Colcord stared at it and then began to laugh. "Old Willy," he said. "Crazy old bastard to the end. There's Willy's alien artifact for you."

Cash and Moore stared at the thing wallowing about in the bottom of the canoe: a cue ball. A ridiculous dirty white cue ball.

Colcord laughed. "Like I said right from the beginning, total madness. That's just something Old Willy found in some junkyard with the rest of his stuff." He picked up his paddle and dug it into the water, the canoe skimming forward.

Cash stared at the ball now rolling about in the dirty water in the bottom of the canoe. It wasn't quite round, like a real cue ball, but ever so slightly egg-shaped. And it had the faintest purplish sheen to it. She suddenly realized she'd seen something like it before: the illustration from the medieval manuscript in Castillo's apartment, of a scholar in a trance holding that strange egg aloft. She reached down and picked it up. Heat suddenly emanated from the center. It didn't hurt, but she wasn't expecting the sensation, and it surprised her. "Whoa!" she cried, dropping it.

"What?"

"It . . . started to heat up."

"Real funny, Cash." Colcord laid down the paddle, reached into the bottom of the canoe, and picked it up himself. Then he gave a cry and dropped it. "What the hell?"

They both stared at the thing lying by their feet. Cash reached out and picked it up again.

"Cash, damn it, be careful with that thing," Colcord said.

The ovoid object rested in the palm of her hand. It rapidly became lukewarm and then toasty, but never hot. This time, she didn't drop it but instead closed her fingers around it. A pleasing, even delicious tingling sensation began in her fingers, traveled through the palm of her hand, and worked its way up her arm. It felt nice.

"You all right?" Colcord asked. He sounded a little panicked.

Colcord's voice sounded like it was far away, as if Cash were floating up above the lake. She knew she should probably let go of the artifact—whatever was happening to her, it wasn't normal. But she did not *want* to let it go. It made her feel amazing, like a drug. The feeling rapidly climbed to her shoulder, her neck, and then into her head. Suddenly, a rush of images, and understanding—all packed together—erupted into her mind like a computer ZIP file being extracted at high speed. A burst of extraordinary knowledge was being downloaded into her brain. She saw things happening—imprinted in her memory as if she had actually experienced them. Wonderful things. Otherworldly places beyond her comprehension. The artifact was like a massive hard drive of information.

A moment later, or an age—Cash had lost all sense of time—the artifact went cold again. Her outer vision returned. The pleasant sensation in her limbs was now being replaced by the chill from her wet clothes, the throbbing pain in her shoulder, and the hard edge of the boat against her spine. She was back with Colcord and Moore, who were both staring at her, their faces full of alarm. The sphere dropped from her hand, but the revelations remained.

"How . . . how long has it been?" Cash asked, dumbfounded. It felt like part of a lifetime had passed.

"What the hell happened to you?" Colcord snapped. "You lost consciousness and you started shaking like you were having a fit!"

But she hardly heard him, her mind still grappling with what she had experienced. It was crazy, so utterly bizarre and disturbing. It challenged everything she had known.

"Cash? Wake up. Are you there? Hey!" Colcord snapped his fingers in front of her face.

She stared at Colcord, but her mind was still in turmoil. She didn't . . . *couldn't* explain what had just happened.

"Are you okay? What the hell is with you?" Colcord asked.

"I . . . don't know how to explain it," said Cash.

"What do you mean? Did something happen?"

"There's absolutely . . . no way . . . to describe it. You've got to see for yourself."

"I don't mean to interrupt," said Father Moore, "but we should really get moving. I don't think you realize how severely injured you both are."

Colcord waved the priest off and turned back to Cash. "Okay. I will." His hesitation from before seemingly gone, Colcord seized the artifact from where it had fallen, and held it in both hands. A moment later, his entire body shuddered and his eyes rolled up in his head—and then, after no more than a minute, it slipped from his fingers.

Colcord stared at Cash, wide-eyed and speechless. She wondered if he had had the same experience as she had, learned the same things. Had he . . . understood the message?

"My Lord," said Moore, breaking his silence. "What is going on here?" He reached out and, before Cash could warn him, picked up the object himself. Again, just like with Colcord, his whole body began to shake and his eyes rolled up, and then after a long moment, he let it go. When he came back to reality, he looked dumfounded, if not horrified.

Colcord, still recovering himself, shook his head as if trying to clear it. "*What . . . the . . . hell.*"

"Did you get . . . *it*?" Cash asked.

A long silence. Colcord nodded silently.

"What do we do?" Cash asked.

Colcord's dirty face was screwed up with perplexity. "I . . . don't . . . know."

Moore remained thunderstruck, paralytic.

Cash struggled to find the words. "Are we . . . just going to . . . bring this thing back with us? Into the world?"

Colcord shook his head wordlessly. The canoe drifted on the silent lake. Nobody spoke for a long time—until Father Moore finally seemed to shake off his shock.

"No," he said.

Cash looked at him.

"No," he said again. "We *can't*."

"But—the knowledge—" said Cash.

"Exactly," said Moore. "The *knowledge*." Moore's voice was strangely calm and collected. "Think for a moment what this revelation would do." He paused. "It would upend every religion. . . . Think about it, my friends. There would be wars fought over this beyond any the world has ever experienced."

Cash stared at Moore. The narrow little priest seemed to be in the grips of a profound sorrow.

"This knowledge was never meant for us," Moore went on quietly. "It will . . . take from humanity that which is most precious . . . as it has just robbed me." His voice dropped a notch.

He reached down and picked up the artifact. Cash watched him, unable to formulate her thoughts. She sensed, on a profound level, that he was right. She glanced at Colcord and saw the same immobility, the same uncertainty, in his own face.

The priest, holding the artifact, slowly extended his arm out over the gunwale of the canoe and held it above the surface of the lake.

"Yes?" he asked.

Cash and Colcord stared. Finally, Cash said. "Do it."

Moore let go, the artifact falling into the water with a soft splash. The strange purple-white roundness of it was visible for a beat as it sank before it disappeared into the depths of Solitary Lake.

60

"He will see you now," said Maggie, the receptionist, with a frosty smile directed at Brother Armagh, hardly pausing in the filing of her nails.

He smiled back, stood, and made his way into the inner office. He stopped short at seeing Sheriff Colcord. The man's head and face were bandaged, and his foot was elevated, resting in a cradle on a wheeled device.

"I see you've had quite the week," said Brother Armagh. "I hope you're on the mend."

"It's nothing," said the sheriff, waving his hand. "Just chasing some bad guys. All in a day's work. Please sit down, Brother Armagh."

Armagh arranged his garments and settled in a seat opposite the desk. "I'm told you've got good news for me?"

The sheriff nodded. "I certainly do." He swiveled around, unclipped a key chain from his belt, and wheeled-walked himself over to a small safe tucked into the wall behind him.

"Allow me to help," offered Armagh.

The sheriff waved his hand. "No, no. I need to get used to this contraption, at least for the next four weeks."

The sheriff used a key to unlock a keypad—then he punched in a code and opened the door. Reaching inside, he retrieved a sealed glass test tube, inside of which was another sealed container, and inside of that a tiny brown chip.

He wheeled back over and laid it gently on the desk before leaning back and returning his leg to an elevated position.

Armagh reached out. "May I?"

"Of course."

He picked it up and peered inside. There it was, a half-centimeter square of human skull, dark brown and waxy. He felt a shiver, the electricity of faith, as he contemplated the tiny thing that had caused so much trouble. For a moment, he couldn't speak, so great was the feeling of emotion that swept over him.

"I'm infinitely grateful to you, Sheriff," he finally said in a quavering whisper. "More than I can possibly express."

"I can't take all the credit," said the sheriff. "Many others contributed to its recovery. We're grateful ourselves to be able to return this holy relic to the church, intact."

"May you be blessed."

"Thank you. I need it." The sheriff smiled ruefully at his injured leg. Opening a drawer, he reached in for a piece of paper and slid it toward Brother Armagh. "You'll need to sign this affidavit, which says you've received the relic in good condition and absolve us of any further responsibility. If it's agreeable to you, I'll have Maggie come in to witness and notarize it."

Armagh found the document to be both simple and in good order.

It only took a few minutes to get everything signed and processed.

Colcord turned to Maggie. "Please make a copy for Brother Armagh and give it to him on his way out."

She left with it, closing the door.

"Well, that's that," said the sheriff. "Is there anything else I can do for you?"

Armagh hesitated, but curiosity always got the better of him. "Did you, ah, ever solve the mystery of why that man stole it in the first place and why he was murdered?"

The sheriff gave him a broad smile. "I had a feeling you'd ask me that question. The answer is no. Our investigation is ongoing—and that, I'm afraid, is all I can share with you."

"Very well," said Armagh, only a little disappointed. "I know I speak for the Holy Father when I say that he is eternally grateful to you and everyone else involved in recovering this sacred relic."

Armagh slipped the tube into an inner pocket of his robe, patted it, and extended his hand. They shook, and he rose. "Please don't get up," he said. "I can see my way out."

"Safe travels," said the sheriff. "And"—he hesitated—"may God be with you."

"And with you too," Armagh said, and turned to open the door.

61

Dr. Greg Strickland hung up from one of the strangest calls he'd ever received. He pursed his lips, musing about the odd request. The whole thing was inexplicable. First, he'd been asked to sequence the DNA of an ancient bone fragment. The results were incomprehensible. Ever since, he'd been racking his brain, trying to come up with some sort of rational explanation, a hypothesis that was even a tiny bit plausible—and had failed. He had told Cash it was contamination, but in reviewing the results of the many test runs, he realized they were too consistent, too clean, to be contamination. And yet they were. . . . impossible.

And now she was telling him to destroy all evidence of having performed the analysis, including the data files, lab report, notes, and any emails he may have exchanged with Reno before the man's death—everything. She'd been somewhat vague on the *why*, but it was clear she was very serious about it. It was also clear that whatever the true reason was, she was keeping it to herself.

The thing is, it wasn't a simple thing, getting rid of everything. First, it was difficult, if not impossible, to completely erase data from a distributed computer network. Second, even if he managed to do so, he was pretty sure there would be a record of the erasure, and that, itself, went against CU School of Medicine policy. If a crime was involved—and it probably was, given that Cash was law enforcement, and the story behind the bone fragment was clearly phony—it might be considered suppression—or even destruction—of evidence. But most importantly, Strickland did not want to erase the data. He couldn't stop thinking about the mystery of what he'd discovered. He had lied to Cash on the call, agreeing to do what she asked with no intention of following through. Especially since she was so adamant on getting rid of it. There was a mystery there worth looking into, and he intended to probe it.

In fact, that's what he was currently doing. He had laid out the files across his desk, going over the data yet another time. It still made no sense. If the DNA wasn't actually contaminated, this meant that well before humans knew what DNA *was*, someone—or something—had sequenced the entire human genome and then synthesized it, rebuilding it into something better and cleaner. Sophisticated technology that far surpassed present-day technology. Two thousand years ago.

There was no way he would be erasing his files. On the other hand, it *did* make sense to encrypt it. That could always be justified on the basis of security. Because someday, somehow, he was going to get to the bottom of that mystery.

62

Warrant in hand, Cash waited while Father Moore unlocked the final door to the basement room at Saint Mary's Church and turned on the lights. He held it open for them. It had taken a lot of suppressed cursing to get Colcord down the stairs with his wheeled leg contraption, and only with Father Moore's assistance. The priest was stronger than he looked. But they had finally made it, sweaty and panting. Colcord was the grumpy one for a change, which delighted Cash.

"All right, Thomas the Tank Engine, you first." She gestured him forward.

Colcord squeaked ahead, grumbling under his breath.

Inside the door, they both stopped and peered around.

"Here is my little collection," said Father Moore. "With my sincere apologies for my role in this tragedy. I'm not a worldly man. I was greatly deceived by Brother Gregory and his lies. To think that I gave those killers room and board during their visits! And then borrowing items from my collection—they had said they needed them for an exhibit as they closed down their monastery, why, I had no idea—"

"No need to go into it again," said Cash, cutting off the voluble father. Moore had saved their lives at great risk to his own. He was still a doctrinaire, narrow-minded, and sexist person, but he had good in him as well, courage, and even a kind of wisdom.

The priest hadn't a clue what Devotio was or why it existed. Based on the papers they had found in Brother Gregory's belongings, the society was supposedly an offshoot of the Dicastery for the Doctrine of the Faith, the church office descended from the original Inquisition. They had been operating independent of church leadership for over a century, since the first members had come together over the revelations involving the origin of Jesus and several of his followers, pledging their lives to keeping such knowledge buried. Paradox, run by Khachatryan and Castillo, had been equally determined to find the proof they needed to reveal the truth. The struggle, she knew, would continue. The artifact at the bottom of Solitary Lake, she'd learned, was one of several. From what she'd heard, Khachatryan had disappeared, but Cash was sure that Paradox and its mission lived on.

Father Moore had explained that he'd become suspicious of Brother Gregory when it was first reported that Grooms had been tortured with a Spanish boot. Moore recognized it immediately as one of the devices Gregory had asked to borrow for the exhibit he was organizing at the Aspen monastery, which was in the process of being shut down. Moore had thought it rather surprising that Aspen would want to display such devices for the general public. Most people didn't share his interests in such things. His suspicions had grown when he found a gun among the monk's things, while he was looking for other missing relics from his collection. And finally, when he'd overheard Brother Gregory speaking with one of his odd friends staying in the rectory, Father Moore's suspicions had crystallized, and he had pursued Gregory, following him up to Grooms's cabin, where he'd heard the explosion.

"If you don't mind," said Cash, speaking to the priest, "protocol requires that we work in private."

"Of course," he said, bowing and retreating, closing the door behind him.

Cash looked around. It was a curious little room, this museum of the Inquisition that Father Moore had set up. Framed manuscripts, letters, and various church garments hung from the walls, along with several illuminated glass cases displaying the priest's treasures.

And in a dark corner, Cash could see the collection of old iron contraptions that Armagh had mentioned—stuff that Brother Gregory had asked Moore to store for him.

Now that they were alone, Cash asked, "How's the foot coming along, Inspector Gadget?"

Colcord scowled. "Hilarious. It's a pain, but I can wheel myself around pretty good."

"At least you can't fit your foot in your mouth anymore," Cash said.

"Ha. Ha. I thought you were the expert in that department. Stitches coming out tomorrow. Another turn of the screw," he said, more seriously, "and it would have been a lot worse. You saved my foot and my life."

"Let's not go into that again," said Cash, embarrassed. "You saved mine too. We were just doing our jobs."

They turned their attention to the collection of torture devices, Colcord crutching and wheeling himself over.

They contemplated the iron equipment, cleaned, restored, and oiled. The Spanish boot, the chair, and three of the other contraptions were noticeably missing, locked up in the evidence room.

Cash started taking photos and drawing up an inventory.

"This gives me the creeps," said Colcord. "If you think about it long enough, you can kind of figure how each one works."

"Yeah, and I wish I could un-figure it. I can't believe people did this to each other."

"They're still doing it. All over the world. They always find excuses to torture. The Inquisition believed they were saving people's souls by torturing them. Unbelievable that they thought God would approve."

At the mention of the word *God*, a long silence ensued. Cash felt uneasy. They had not had a conversation yet about the alien device and what it had communicated to them.

After a moment, Colcord said, "You know, Cash, we need to talk this thing out."

Cash shook her head. "Why? What's done is done. The artifact's at the bottom of Solitary Lake."

"Because we need to. *I* need to."

There was a long silence, and then Colcord went on, "When I was a kid, the Jehovah's Witnesses used to come around. Two sweet, middle-aged ladies with their brochures and pamphlets. My mother, God bless her, invited them in for tea because they looked so discouraged and tired from rejection after rejection."

"We had the same thing in our neighborhood in Maine, but my mother always sent them packing."

"Knowing you, I'm not surprised."

"That's another wisecrack of yours I'm going to overlook, Colcord."

Colcord went on, "Ever since we held that thing, I've been wondering if we got the same, ah, *revelation*."

Cash shook her head. "A lot of it was just so . . . utterly strange and incomprehensible."

"But the gist of it? The *plan*?"

"I got that, all right—clear as day," she said.

"Me too."

"No wonder the church felt threatened. . . . I mean, holy crap!"

"Did we do the right thing?" Colcord asked.

"Hell yes," said Cash.

They fell into a pensive silence. Then Colcord roused himself. "Well, Cash, we got a lot of work to do. We better get to it. And . . ." He hesitated. "Let's never talk about this again. We're going to let the world go on believing what they believe. Agreed?"

"Agreed."

63

Colcord wheeled himself over behind the counter, watching as Nova Euclid pushed through the front screen door of the Ore House, arm in arm with Officer Wiley. Since the Shrouder investigation had come to a close, those two had been openly going out. . . . Was it still called *dating? Friends with benefits?* Colcord had no idea what kids were calling it these days.

It was late Sunday morning, and the place was, as usual, full. He watched as his barista, Melody, fixed them their usual. They looked happy—Euclid all rosy-cheeked and giddy compared to her usual reserved demeanor; Wiley, with his arm possessively cupped around her shoulder. The Ore House being the nearest eatery to the courthouse, a handful of officers, clerks, and even Judge Greenberg himself were seated around several of the low tables. The murmur of conversation filtered through the air to waft with the sweet smell of warm pecan buns.

"Busy day?"

Colcord started as the familiar voice interrupted his people-watching. He pivoted to regard Cash standing before him, a round box under her arm. Her other arm was still in a sling, but she looked good. More color to her face, a healthy dash of freckles across her cheeks. Her auburn hair was down today and fell about her face prettily. Not a lick of makeup, as usual. But she looked . . . different, somehow.

"Looks like that sunburn finally turned into a tan," said Colcord.

"It takes us Irish awhile to brown up," she said.

"And what's this? Are you actually wearing a dress?"

Indeed she was, a comfortable-looking yellow sundress that flowed down to her knees, paired with sandals.

"Let's not make a big deal out of it," Cash said, sitting down on a stool next to him and placing the box on the bar.

"Nah, you look . . . good. Not that you usually *don't* look good. It's different—nice," Colcord stammered.

"You, on the other hand, don't look so good without your hat."

"It's too messed up to wear in public. I gotta do something about it."

With a grin, Cash pushed the box over.

Colcord opened it, looked inside, and smiled broadly.

"I had it all fixed up—cleaned, re-blocked, relined."

Colcord took it out. The battered, bloody old thing had been hanging in his office that very morning. *How had she . . . when did she . . . ?*

"I had help from a certain ornery receptionist," said Cash. "She's efficient—when she wants to be. And the hatter in town's a big fan of yours too."

Colcord fitted it to his head. "Thank you, Cash," he said, quite moved.

"And on another note," she went on, "that reporter called to let me know about a noon broadcast today. Can we turn the volume up on the TV? Channel eight."

"Sure thing."

Colcord snagged her a cinnamon roll from the warming case and placed it on one of the china plates he had inherited from his grandmother. Cash dug in earnestly.

"You got Bustelo by chance?" she said through a mouthful of cinnamon and frosting.

"Sure do." Customers never ordered the stuff, but he kept a jar special for Cash. He fixed her up a cup, placing it steaming in front of her.

Robin Twen popped on-screen at twelve p.m. sharp, flaunting their familiar spiky hairstyle and a pastel-purple bow tie.

"Breaking news today," they said. "In an update to our previous reporting on the Shrouder investigation, KBFR Investigative Beat has uncovered additional information surrounding CBI Agent Frankie Cash and her termination from the Criminal Investigations Division in Portland, Maine."

Colcord exchanged a glance with Cash, who had her mouth set in a firm line. He wondered what this was all about.

Twen continued, "I recently spoke with Cash's former CID partner, Monty Rex, who had this to say about what occurred at Portland CID." The image changed, and Twen was now seated next to a man in a living room, holding a microphone up to his face. He was close-shaven, with a strong jaw and a distinctive cleaved chin. He looked a little bit like a grizzled Superman, Colcord thought.

"How was Agent Cash's performance during her time at the Portland CID?"

"Cash was a terrific police officer." Rex's face morphed into a mask of anger. "There was an ongoing campaign of discrimination and harassment against Cash from the moment she joined the squad. The worst of the harassment was spearheaded by Ruby Barsconi, an officer in the street crimes unit. Barsconi was having an affair with Portland Chief of Police Luke Mezey."

A picture of a pretty blond woman—Ruby Barsconi—and an older man exchanging a very passionate kiss in a hotel lobby flashed up onto the screen. The entirety of the Ore House was silent now, enraptured.

On the screen, Rex continued the story of how Cash tased a man high on meth, who'd been threatening people with a knife—and how the police chief had used the incident to fire Cash during a hiring freeze and promote his girlfriend.

"Mr. Rex, why didn't you bring this up at the time?" asked Twen.

He lowered his head. "I was afraid. I'm ashamed to say it. I couldn't lose my job; I had a family to support." He stared straight into the camera then. "All I can say is Cash was the best partner I ever had. And Chief Mezey is a corrupt—"

The interview bleeped out the last word. Finally, the camera returned to Twen. "It is clear that Agent Cash's history is quite different from previously reported, by myself and others. And now, after her courageous actions on the Shrouder case, many are calling her a local hero. Robin Twen, reporting for KBFR Investigative Beat."

The report ended. There was a brief silence, interrupted by Euclid, who stood and began to clap. Pretty soon, the Ore House devolved into raucous cheering and applause. Cash colored, and Colcord clapped her good shoulder with an open palm.

"Saved my life too," Colcord said loudly, grinning and tipping his cowboy hat to her. "Local hero indeed."

Cash rolled her eyes, but a smile stretched across her face.

AFTERWORD

Paradox, the novel, is built on two central ideas, neither of which we invented. The first is the Fermi paradox, and the second is the idea held by some that the great spiritual leaders in human history, such as Jesus and the Buddha, were in fact alien visitors to Earth, bringing truth and enlightenment.

The Fermi paradox dates back to an amusing conversation that took place in 1950. In that year, someone began stealing public trash cans from the streets of New York City, causing a minor scandal. On May 8, 1950, *The New Yorker* ran a cartoon that showed aliens from a fleet of flying saucers unloading New York City trash cans on their home planet. A week or two later, in the then-secret city of Los Alamos, New Mexico, four physicists involved in designing the H-bomb were walking to lunch—Enrico Fermi, Emil Konopinski, Herbert York, and Edward Teller. Konopinski brought up the funny *New Yorker* cartoon, and the conversation turned to flying saucers and aliens. The conversation then drifted on to other subjects. Halfway through lunch, Fermi suddenly burst out, saying, "Where is everybody?"

There was general laughter at this. Teller recalled years later: "In spite of Fermi's question coming from the clear blue, everybody around the table seemed to understand at once that he was talking about extra-terrestrial life." Fermi then scribbled a series of equations on the proba-bility of technological civilizations arising in the galaxy. He concluded that "we ought to have been visited long ago and many times over." And yet nothing: There is no reliable evidence that we have ever been visited or contacted by extraterrestrials. This became known as the Fermi paradox.

In the 1960s, the astronomer Frank Drake worked out a more formal equation similar to Fermi's, called the Drake equation, which calculated the probability of a technological civilization arising somewhere in the galaxy. It goes roughly like this (we've simplified it somewhat): You start with the number of rocky planets there are in the galaxy that orbit in the habitable zone of their stars. From there, you calculate what proportion of these *could* develop life, what fraction *did* develop simple life, what fraction went on to develop *multicellular* life, what fraction became *intelligent* life, what fraction became *technological civilizations* capable of interstellar communication, and finally, how *long* did those technological civilizations last before they died out or destroyed themselves?

Unfortunately, we don't yet have actual numbers to plug into the terms in the equation, so it can't be solved. We do know, however, that the galaxy has something like ten billion rocky planets orbiting in the habitable zone of their stars, and that possibly as many as half a billion of these have oceans, land masses, and atmospheres capable of sustaining life as we know it. That is a staggering number, much higher than anyone had assumed even twenty years ago. To add to the puzzle, scientists have calculated that a single technological civilization capable of space travel at only a fraction of the speed of light, and making only short hops to their closest star systems, could colonize the entire Milky Way galaxy in less than three million years. When you consider the galaxy is ten billion years old, why isn't it teeming with technological civilizations?

The most widely accepted solution to the Fermi paradox is called the Great Filter. This is the idea that somewhere in the Drake equation, in the long journey from nonlife to a star-traveling species, there is a filter—an extremely difficult barrier to overcome. This barrier might be the jump from nonlife to early life. It might be the jump from single-celled life to multicellular life, or maybe from multicellular life to intelligent life.

Looking at our own planet, we know that simple life began almost immediately after Earth had cooled. No obvious filter there. It took several billion years for multicellular life to develop from single-celled organisms. That could be a possible filter. Following that, it took five hundred million years for highly intelligent life to develop—early hominins—and then a few million more for hominins to create a civilization capable of interstellar communication. That looks like a difficult but not impossible leap, since we did it. We may have already passed through the Great Filter and are now the unique technological civilization in our galaxy. Over the next three million years, we might spread out and colonize a beautifully empty galaxy and live happily ever after.

There is a much darker and likelier possibility for the Great Filter, which is that advanced technological civilizations like ours quickly destroy themselves. We don't see any advanced civilizations in our galaxy because as soon as they achieve the technology of mass destruction, or the capability of destroying the ecology of their home planet, they snuff themselves out. We might be headed that way in the near future ourselves.

But what if there's another answer to the Fermi paradox that doesn't involve a Great Filter? Many hypotheses have been proposed:

The Dark Forest Hypothesis—The galaxy is like a forest at night, full of dangerous predators looking for resources to gobble up, and as a result, technological civilizations are hiding in silence, trying to remain undetected.

The Zoo Hypothesis—We are in a protected area of the galaxy, like a nature preserve, where advanced aliens are not allowed to go for fear of disrupting our civilization. Or we are in a sort of zoo, where adventurous alien tourists can visit on the sly to observe us in our natural habitat.

The Grabby Alien Hypothesis—Grabby aliens nip developing technological civilizations in the bud by destroying them as soon as they are detected. We are living in a bubble of our expanding electromagnetic broadcasts that is now about one hundred light-years in radius. When our bubble passes into a grabby alien realm and they detect it, they will come and destroy us.

The Incomprehensible Aliens Hypothesis—Aliens might be so different from us that we cannot recognize them, or they us. Or intelligent aliens might find the concepts of communication and space exploration so strange that they haven't even thought of them, or they lack curiosity to such an extent that they simply aren't interested.

The Virtual Reality Hypothesis—The astronomer Avi Loeb at Harvard has suggested that sufficiently advanced extraterrestrials might retreat into delightful virtual reality worlds of their own making, much preferring that to looking for real worlds to contact, explore, and colonize. They might even dispose of their bodies entirely and upload their minds into virtual worlds, abandoning the physical universe.

The second core idea in *Paradox*, that Jesus and other spiritual leaders of the past were aliens, is a concept that has been widespread now since the 1950s. There are groups and societies who believe that not only Christianity but many of the world's major religions were founded by extraterrestrial beings. Adherents believe that intelligent aliens with highly advanced technology have visited us throughout the millennia, disguised as spiritual leaders to help guide humanity and save us from disaster.

One of the most prominent of these groups is called the Aetherius Society. It is a quasi-religious organization "dedicated to spreading, and acting upon, the teachings of advanced extraterrestrial intelligences." The Aetherius Society was founded in 1955 by a British mystic named George King. Born in England in 1919 to an eccentric Quaker family, King was a pacifist and conscientious objector during World War II. He was fascinated by certain esoteric religious movements of his time, including Theosophy and Spiritualism, and was an early Western practitioner of yoga. In 1954, King claimed a voice spoke to him from the beyond, saying, "Prepare yourself! You are to become the voice of Interplanetary Parliament." He claimed to be able to communicate with "Cosmic Masters" (including the aforenamed Aetherius). These advanced beings living on other planets telepathically communicated with him through what he called "Transmissions." King was born to the role of self-proclaimed prophet—a tall, striking man with dark slashing eyebrows, piercing blue eyes, and silvery hair, who dressed in exquisitely tailored Savile Row suits. His voice carried the calm, intelligent tone of a reasonable man, delivered in a fine Yorkshire accent. The Aetherius Society, which is still going strong, explains its mission on its website.

Earth has been visited by advanced extraterrestrial intelligences for millennia. Identified as angels, prophets, avatars, divine incarnations, and even as gods—these beings were in fact not from the

*realm of the supernatural—but from other planets—with technology
so advanced as to be indistinguishable from magic.*

*The Master Jesus, the Lord Buddha, Sri Krishna, St. Peter, Confucius, Lao Zi, and Sri Patanjali are among those who have graced
our world with their enlightened alien presence.*

*Sometimes born among us in terrestrial bodies just like ours,
sometimes making more fleeting visits in spacecraft, the good news
is that their intentions are friendly—in fact more than friendly—they
have actually saved us from destruction on several occasions.*

King died in Santa Barbara in 1997, but the Aetherius Society lives
on, with thousands of followers in the UK and US. In 2019, *The Catholic
Herald* named King the "heretic of the week," showing that even today
his ideas might be considered a threat to the church.

The idea that extraterrestrials have been involved with humanity and
interested in our welfare are loosely gathered under the rubric of "UFO
religions," of which the Aetherius Society was just one. Others include
the I AM Temple, Scientology, and the Raëlism Church. This latter organization claims that an extraterrestrial species created humanity using
highly advanced biology and that Jesus and other religious figures were
alien-human hybrids whose mission was to enlighten humanity. The
Raëlian movement believes that humans can gain immortality through
cloning. In 2002, a company founded by the movement claimed to have
cloned a human baby, a girl named (of course) Eve, who is still allegedly
alive today. The movement has tens of thousands of members around
the globe.

There are serious scholarly efforts to explore how Christianity's belief
system intersects with the idea of outer space and the possible existence of
"extraterrestrial" life. Dr. Catherine Hezser, a prominent religious scholar
at the University of London, posits that while ancient Christians did not
have an understanding of outer space, they still distinguished between
this world and a second, higher sphere. She writes that this outer sphere
was understood by Christians to rule over the lower sphere. Other scholars, such as the prominent Christian skeptic Dr. Richard Carrier, liken
early Christianity's depictions of "heaven" to "outer space." Carrier points

out evidence that the earliest Christians themselves believed Jesus was an extraterrestrial of sorts, a being from above who put on a "bodysuit of flesh" to visit humanity before dying and returning to "outer space."

As Hamlet said to Horatio, "There are more things in heaven and earth, Horatio, / Than are dreamt of in your philosophy." We hope you have enjoyed our fictional exploration of a few of these things in *Paradox*.

ACKNOWLEDGMENTS

Aletheia Preston: I would like to sincerely thank Robert Davis, Linda Quinton, and the excellent team at Tor for their great support and help in making *Paradox* the book it is. I'm very grateful to our agent, Eric Simonoff, for his extraordinary representation. I thank my friends and family for their love and support. I'm especially grateful to Mom and Dad—Doug and Christine—for telling me stories, teaching me to read, and showering me with books when I was growing up, which gave me the inspiration I needed to become a writer. A special thanks also to Susan Medina and AIC Gregg Slater of the Colorado Bureau of Investigation for their invaluable advice.

Douglas Preston: One of the best writing lessons I ever had was when Aletheia was three years old and I was telling her a story. Long before she could read, she was a voracious consumer of scary stories. I was telling her a story about a girl who tripped into a hole in the Maine woods and fell out of the sky into another world, landing in the sea. She was rescued by a sea captain driving a tugboat full of peppers. As I was describing the sea captain—his big red whiskers, his corncob pipe, his funny hat, and big nose—I could see Aletheia getting restless and a little frustrated. Thinking the story wasn't good enough, I redoubled my efforts at describing the captain and his ship, until finally Aletheia blurted out, "But where are the dangers? *I want the dangers!!*" It was the best lesson I ever had in how to plot a good thriller, and whenever I'm stalled in writing I think: "But where are the dangers?" I've learned so much writing *Paradox* with Aletheia, and I am looking forward to working with her on the next one in the Extinction series, entitled *Resurrection*. It will, we promise, have plenty of dangers. . . .

Read on for a sneak peek of

RESURRECTION

by Douglas Preston and Aletheia Preston,

the explosive next novel in the Cash & Colcord series

1

Elsa Finn reached the top of Pinkney's Hill before her dad, Owen Finn, did. She turned around and watched him come huffing up after her.

He joined her at the top with a grin and a thumbs-up, and they spent a moment enjoying the view. It was a breathtaking look across the valley to Eagle's Nest at the top of Vail, the summer ski slopes like green ribbons winding down the mountainsides, shining under a cloudless sky, and mountains beyond.

Her father checked his watch. "Seventeen minutes," he said. "A record."

Elsa could have gone even faster, but she didn't want to embarrass her father, who was slowing down a touch as the years progressed.

"We've earned lunch," he said.

They turned and started down the trail, heading back to Tugupaya, the name her father had given to the family's house—the Ute Indian word for *sky*. It was a log-and-glass mansion with green copper roofs that sprawled along an adjacent ridge, with its own private ski slope that connected to the Vail system—an embarrassing display of wealth that had earned Elsa the "rich kid" nickname at her school.

They hiked in silence—her father did not approve of yakking while hiking, and that was fine with her. At the bottom of the hill, they passed the entrance to the old Laceyman Mine, with the weathered skeleton of the mine's former headframe and hoist standing next to it. The trail threaded by the mine entrance, now draped in vines and weeds, from which flowed a small stream.

Her father slowed and then stopped. "Footprints," he said.

Elsa looked. Along the muddy verge of the stream, she could see a pair of boot prints.

"Damn trespassers," he said. "With all these millions of acres of public land, why do they always seem to come here?"

This was a pet peeve of her father's. Elsa didn't care. They had six hundred and forty acres—a square mile—which was more than enough to share. Vail backcountry skiers were frequent, accidental visitors to their land as well. But her dad, annoyed, had taken out his phone and was checking his security app, which he did often. He messed around with it for a moment and gave a low curse. "Down again," he said, putting the phone away.

They hiked on, crossing the stream over a stone bridge. From there, the trail switchbacked up the ridge to Tugupaya, its massive adzed timbers looming above them. As they entered the foyer, Elsa could smell something cooking.

"Let see what Mom's got going," Owen said.

She shed her hiking boots and shuffled after him, thick socks on smooth walnut. Her mother, Jenny, was fussing over a simmering pot on the Aga stove.

"Whatcha cooking?" asked her father, slithering his arm around Jenny's waist and pulling her in for a kiss.

"Boiled tripe," she said. "Your favorite."

"Sure, right." He laughed and bent to kiss her neck again before releasing her to her work.

"Lunch in ten."

Elsa, bored, wandered into the living room and sank into the leather sofa, curling up in the nook where the couch cushions met the arm, idly flicking away at her phone, scrolling through the latest reels. She loved her parents, but they were smothering her, and she couldn't wait to go off to Stanford in the fall and get out of Vail, which felt smaller and ever-more obnoxiously wealthy as she got older. She pulled up a new track by one of her favorite dark house DJs. Inspired, she told herself that after lunch, she'd spend the afternoon on her Mac improving the synth chord layer to the track she was currently working on. The album she had distributed through DistroKid now had over one hundred thousand Spotify streams, and it was getting a ton of attention on Tidal and even some sales on Bandcamp. It amazed her that she was actually making money.

She heard a loud thump from upstairs and paused the track, listening. Sounded like May, their housekeeper, might have fallen. But as she waited, May hustled in from a side room, head cocked.

"What was that?" Elsa asked.

"I was wondering the same thing," she said.

As if on cue, another low thump sounded—as if someone had stamped on the floor.

"Who's upstairs?" Elsa asked.

"Nobody," said May.

Owen came in the room, a glass of juice cradled in his fist, glancing up. "It might be a golden eagle landing on the roof. That happened once."

Another thud sounded, and with it, the muffled sound of stifled laughter.

"What the hell?" Her father set the glass down, suddenly alert. They all listened intently.

"Was that someone laughing?" Elsa asked. Suddenly, she felt nervous. Her dad was a celebrity of sorts, and her parents had long been concerned about stalkers.

He held up his hand to signify silence. A heavy footfall echoed into the silence, and another, and another, as regular as a processional.

"There's someone up there," Elsa said.

Owen slid his phone from his back pocket and punched in a number, stared, and cursed under his breath. "Internet's down and no bars."

Another giggle sounded, high and raw. Elsa felt frozen with fear. There were definitely people up there. Drunken teenagers, maybe. But how did they get in? The place was supposed to be safe.

Another thump. It sounded deliberate, like someone had stamped on the floor just to spook them. At this, without a word, her father went to the oriental carved cabinet Jenny had gotten on a family trip to Zhejiang, pulled his keys out of his pocket, unlocked it, and took out a 9mm handgun.

"Dad!" Elsa's eyes widened in shock.

"There's someone upstairs," he murmured as he ejected the magazine, checked it, and pushed it back in. Then he racked in a round. "Just a precaution."

"It's probably just some dumbass kids," she said, "streaming themselves breaking into a billionaire's house."

"Could be," he said mildly, "but that's the best-case scenario."

Despite his collected demeanor, Elsa felt a shudder of fear. She could tell he was staying calm so as not to scare her. This had never happened before. Her dad was rich; maybe they were kidnappers. The family had a plan in case of a home invasion. They had rehearsed it. But the safe room was on the second floor, in the master bedroom. Whoever was in the house was already upstairs. How had they gotten there without anyone seeing it?

"You both go into the kitchen, quietly. Get your mom and lock yourselves in the side bedroom. Then call 911," he said in a low tone.

"Dad—"

"Do as I say."

He turned and strode across the living room, toward the stairs leading to the second floor.

Elsa hurried into the kitchen, May following. Jenny was standing with her hands on her hips, listening intently. She'd heard the sound too.

"Dad wants us in the side bedroom. There's someone in the house."

Jenny nodded firmly, but when she guided Elsa with a hand on the small of her back, Elsa could feel it trembling. Her parents were scared, but they were trying to hide it from her.

Jenny quietly closed the door to the bedroom, tugging the big chest they used for storing blankets in front of it. Elsa pulled up Wi-Fi calling to see if she could reach 911, while her mother drew the curtains over the windows and the sliding glass doors, and checked to make sure they were locked. But the call didn't go through—the Wi-Fi was down, and where they were in the mountains, they had no ordinary cell reception.

"Where's the sat phone?" Elsa asked.

"Upstairs in the bedroom."

There was a moment of quiet as the ramifications of this sank in.

Her mother, saying nothing, noiselessly went and slid open a side table drawer, and another, searching. Finally, she took out a penknife.

Elsa swallowed. She couldn't believe this was happening.

A shadow suddenly fell across the drapes covering the sliding glass doors. Elsa stared, hardly able to breathe. Her mother whispered, "Get in the bathroom and lock the door."

"You come with us," Elsa whispered.

"No." Her mother opened the knife and gripped it with white knuckles. The shadow had stopped, and Elsa could hear the sound of someone trying to open the sliding door.

"*In the bathroom,*" her mother whispered, holding the knife out to one side, tense.

May did as they were told, gesturing for Elsa to follow, but Elsa couldn't leave her mother. She looked around for a weapon, picked up a lamp, and ripped the cord from the wall. The curved edges of the metal design created a reassuring heavy weight in her hand.

The shadow didn't move.

All of a sudden, there was the muffled *boom!* of a gun from above followed by a cry. At the same moment, the sliding doors shattered as the shadow leapt in. With a guttural scream, her mother lunged forward, slashing the knife at the intruder. The intruder took a step forward, smacked the knife from her hand, and seized her by the throat. Elsa screamed and heaved the lamp back to hurl it at the figure, but he spun around and jerked it from her, dealing her a stunning blow to the side of the head.

All went black.

Elsa came to, swimming back into reality from a strange jumble of hallucinations. The room spun, and it took a moment to realize she was tied in a chair, in the living room, at the game table. She jerked her wrists, which were held behind her back, and tried to move her legs. Zip-tied. A belt, pulled tight, encircled her waist and went around the back of the chair.

As awareness returned, she realized a blurry group of people standing around in a circle behind her. She squinted, trying to clear her vision to see who they were.

She froze. Neanders.

She'd seen the pictures. Like everyone in the country, she'd followed the story with horror and fascination: the murders, the beheadings, the cannibalism, the attacks, the fires, the explosions. But all that had happened in the Erebus Valley, and then they had disappeared into the Flat Tops. Those were mountains north of I-40, far from Vail. And everyone said they'd gone north to Canada. Why had they come here? What could they possibly want with her family?

As the brain fog finally cleared, she realized her father was sitting opposite her, also tied to a chair, blood on his forehead. Her mother and May were seated on either side, all of them bound and arranged around the game table.

"Dad!" she cried.

"Elsa," he said. "Elsa, listen. We're going to do what they say—"

One of the Neanders stepped forward. He had her father's gun in his hand. He gestured at her dad with it and spoke in a high, nasal voice. "Open the safe."

"Safe?"

The Neander slashed the barrel of the gun across his face. Her father's head knocked back. He began to bleed profusely from a gash across his cheek.

"Stop it!" Elsa cried, and she was then struck on the side of the head so hard she briefly lost consciousness, her eyes full of stars, ears ringing. The whirling slowed and stopped again. Her head pounded. She didn't know who had hit her, but there was someone behind her.

"The safe."

Her father, face dripping blood, said, "If you promise not to hurt my family, I'll open it for you."

"The safe," the Neander repeated.

Now Elsa, getting her terror somewhat under control, began to take in the full tableau. There were four Neanders in the room. They looked like Vikings, with long reddish or blond hair, but with heads that seemed too big for their bodies, big noses, beetling brows, long, wide mouths, and no chins. Pinkish-pale, almost translucent skin. The Neander doing the talking was over six feet tall with a monstrous physique, pale blue eyes, and a long, wispy blond beard that had been woven into two braids.

They looked young, maybe even teenagers, although it was hard to tell. They were dressed in preppy L.L.Bean outfits, with checked shirts, khaki pants, and leather gloves, and carried Osprey day packs. They could have been in an advertisement for outdoor gear, except that they were filthy and smelled bad, and the clothes didn't fit their bodies well.

"I'll take you to it," her father said. "Untie me."

"Where is it?"

"You'll need me to show you. And to open it."

Without a word, the Neander reached down and cut the zip ties around her father's legs and arms, then stepped back, gun still held on him. Owen got up, taking a moment to put his hand on the edge of the table, steadying himself. He locked eyes with Elsa. "We're going to be all right," he said quietly. "We're going to do what they say."

The Neander ignored this, simply gesturing with the barrel of the gun. "Safe."

Owen walked unsteadily over to the closet at the entryway to the living room and opened the door. He turned on the closet light, and Elsa could see him shove aside a row of old coats that nobody ever used, to expose the back wall of the closet.

What *was* this? Elsa wondered.

But then he fiddled with something, and the back part of the wall slid open, exposing the dull gleam of a steel door with a crank and keypad.

Elsa stared. She had not known about that safe.

"Open," the Neander said.

He punched in a code on the keypad, then pressed his finger on a screen. A light turned green, and he opened the safe.

The Neander handed the gun to a companion and said, "Cover him." He turned to Owen. "Step back."

Her father stepped back, and the Neander pushed in past him. She couldn't see what he was doing beyond taking some things from the safe and stuffing them into his pockets. He then stepped out, took the gun back from his companion, and pointed it at Owen.

"Sit down."

"I gave you what you wanted. Please don't hurt my family."

"Sit down," the Neander repeated in a patient tone that gave Elsa a flash of hope. They got what they wanted, whatever it was. Maybe now they would let them go. But even as she said it, she knew it wasn't true.

Her father sat down, and a Neander zip-tied his feet to the legs of the chair and drew the belt back around him, cinching it tight. He nodded, and a moment later, another Neander arrived, carrying a box. A Monopoly box. He set it down on the table, opened it, and began setting up the game.

Elsa watched in confusion as the Neander arranged the board in the middle of the table, set out the Chance and Community Chest cards, then counted out the money, tucking it under the board—money for each of them, it seemed, to play with.

The Neander with the gun stood back while another went around the table, cutting the zip ties that bound their hands.

Elsa brought her hands around and rubbed her wrists, getting the blood flowing again.

"Play," said the Neander.

"We want to cooperate," said Owen. "But I need assurances you're not going to hurt my family."

Now her mother spoke. "If you hurt my child, I'll kill you." She said it in a low, menacing voice that Elsa had never heard before, and it frightened her.

The Neanders ignored her.

"I hope you heard me," she said.

Again, no response. May, for her part, was silent and terrified to the point of paralysis.

"Play. Now." The Neander put the dice on the board.

Elsa could hardly remember how to play, it had been so long.

"We'll cooperate," said her father. It amazed Elsa how calm he was. He picked up a die and rolled it. Five. He passed it to May, who stared at it in incomprehension.

"Take it and roll," said her father quietly. "The high roll goes first."

She still stared, lips trembling, hands squeezed together hard.

"Play," said the Neander to May.

All she could do was croak a nonsensical response.

"You won't play?" the Neander asked. He reached behind and removed a big knife that had been tucked into his belt.

May shook her head.

With a swift flash of movement, he cut her throat. A spray of blood showered the table, and May, nearly decapitated, slumped in her chair, head falling back as if on a hinge.

Elsa screamed, holding her head, shaking it and wiping and wiping, trying to get the blood off her.

"Elsa . . . Elsa . . . *Elsa*."

The insistent voice finally broke through her terror.

"We must do what they say." It was her father, speaking in a calm and strange voice. "Roll the die."

Her hands shaking, she tried to pick up the die, fumbled it, picked it up again, rolled. Six. She could feel tears of horror streaming down her face.

She passed the die to her mother. Her mother's face was collected and frighteningly dark. She rolled the die. Two.

"You roll," said the father to Elsa. "Then we go counterclockwise. We do exactly what they say. Our lives depend on it."

The Neanders stood back, arms crossed, watching intently.

Four pieces stood on the GO square. Elsa tried to concentrate, to blink away the water and blood from her eyes, to stop herself from shaking and hyperventilating. She rolled both dice now. Two and four: six. She reached out with a shaking hand, picked a piece—the old shoe—and moved it six spaces ahead. Oriental Avenue. She stared, unable to think what to do. May was slumped in the chair to her right, head tilted back halfway off. Elsa could hear the steady dripping of her blood on the floor.

"Will you buy it?" asked her father, his voice rigidly calm.

She tried to focus, nodded.

"Then buy it," he said.

The voice steadied her. The price was one hundred dollars. She removed a hundred-dollar bill, splattered with blood, and held it out. Her father took it, put it in the bank, and sorted through the property cards, pulling out Oriental Avenue and giving it to her.

"Pass the dice to your mother."

She did as she was told. Her mind was now numb.

Jenny took the dice. She didn't roll. Instead, she asked, "Why are we doing this?"

The Neander said, "Because we want to watch. It's fun to watch you play your little games. We want to see who's going to win. Winner takes all."

Elsa tried to stay focused. One step at a time. The game was all that mattered.

"Roll the dice," said the father.

She rolled the dice. Seven.

"Move your piece."

She picked up the top hat and moved it seven, landing on Chance. Without further prompts, she picked a card and read out loud, "Pay poor tax of fifteen dollars."

At this, the head Neander began to laugh, a high-pitched, whistling laugh that the others joined in, until the raucous sound of it echoed in the large room.

When the laughter finally died down, the braided-beard Neander said, "Keep going."

They played. Jenny and Owen played badly, exchanging pointed glances before each turn. An hour passed. Before long Elsa was ahead by a mile, with the most properties out of the three of them. Elsa had never played Monopoly to the end, but now it looked like that was where they were headed. The game went on and on, and the stakes got higher and higher.

By the time Elsa realized what was really happening, it was too late. She already had hotels on some of the properties she owned and houses on the rest. Her parents didn't stand a chance. When her father landed on Boardwalk, owned by Elsa with four houses on it, and went bankrupt, they cut his throat. Elsa screamed, finally realizing why her parents had been exchanging those stares of silent communication. They had known. *Winner takes all.* They had known what that meant.

Jenny was next.

When her mother landed on Marvin Gardens, owned by Elsa with a hotel on it, and went bankrupt, they cut her throat.

And then they took Elsa, the winner, away with them.

ABOUT THE AUTHORS

Deborah Feingold   Deborah Feingold

DOUGLAS PRESTON has published forty books of both nonfiction and fiction, of which thirty-one have been *New York Times* bestsellers, a half dozen reaching the #1 position. He is the coauthor, with Lincoln Child, of the Pendergast series of thrillers. He also writes nonfiction pieces for *The New Yorker*. He worked as an editor at the American Museum of Natural History in New York and taught nonfiction writing at Princeton University. He is president emeritus of the Authors Guild and serves on the Advisory Board of the School for Advanced Research in Santa Fe.

prestonchild.com
facebook.com/PrestonandChild

ALETHEIA PRESTON is a reformed lawyer originally from Santa Fe, New Mexico. After working as a prosecutor in San Francisco, she moved into private practice as a trial attorney before embarking on a journey as a writer. She is a lover of thriller and science fiction novels and has been an avid reader and writer in both genres since she was a little girl.

An admitted adrenaline junkie, Aletheia spends much of her free time outdoors finding ways to risk her life, from skiing and mountaineering to paragliding and winter camping. She is also a PADI-certified deep-water and wreck scuba diver. Fluent in Italian and Spanish, she spent much of her childhood in Florence, Italy. She and her cat, Mochi, live in Bozeman, Montana.

https://aletheiapreston.com
instagram.com/aletheiapreston